I0831145

Our Galaxy, The Wolf Trail

Our Galaxy, The Wolf Trail

Written by Theo Cecil DeCelles

Revised First Edition

Published by White Clay Moon Press
Missoula, Montana

ISBN # 978-0-578-07718-5

Prologue

During the last days of nomadic existence of the old country, a woman sees the harsh realities of two very distinct heritages resulting in a clash of cultures. Dawn Red Sky is accused of being a woman of ill morals by her own people from the Pikuni Nation. She must attempt to escape the ultimate persecution in order to save her dignity. While on a long journey alone in the wilderness, she learns about being a lone wolf, a woman of fierce independence under the stars, finding strength in ways she never could have imagined.

She is captured by an enemy nation and sold as a bargain to a frontier bachelor with a shady past. He changes her name to 'Victoria' trying to make her look 'white' to blend in with the gold mining town of Helena and the other rowdy new communities in the Territory of Montana. Victoria Redsky finds dirty challenges that has herself questioning her submissive circumstances and playing second fiddle to the white women in town. An evangelical tent revival wants to reform Hell's Gate, Montana to God hoping to shut down the bawdy houses where Victoria scrapes on by, known as the badlands full of whiskey whores, cross-dressers, and women's husbands on the prowl.

Victoria longs to return to her people adrift in America's official first drug epidemic. She is caught between saints and sinners, women against women, trying not to get attached to men who are fly-by-nights. If she returns to the Indian reservation, will she be able to handle the truth about the devastating changes wrought there?

The true west that the politically correct history books are afraid to show your kids, a cosmopolitan and exotic Old West of contrasts between the influence of Victorian society and the rebellious lawlessness of America is portrayed in an extraordinary unorthodox way in this unique and peculiar tale of female pioneering spirit. Written by Blackfeet and Gros Ventre Native American author Theo Cecil DeCelles (Ninastako).

Our Galaxy, The Wolf Trail

To my mother Peggy DeCelles or Kills at Night, my father Teddy DeCelles Sr. or Storyteller (Bullshit Artist).

Thank you Ryan Davis for inspiring this book with your love of intellectual matters and preliminary historical research, which gave me a deep and loving motivation for my own historical research. I thank the Bear Secret Society for their medicine. Bawdy Poem Lil the Whore is a dirty folk poem, a variation that was featured in an underground novel called Immortalia long ago by A Gentleman About Town. I thank my ancestors; front cover photograph is of author's great, great grandmother Mary Noechief and is not Dawn Red Sky. I want to thank the Lakota, all four nations of the Blackfoot Confederacy, and the other sovereign republics of the Gros Ventre, Salish, Kootenai, Assiniboine, Nez Pearce, and Crow nations for continuing their unique Canadian and American independent spirit. Thumbs up to Charles Flowers of Lambda Literary Foundation for giving me hope one summer when I needed it most. I want to thank Kate Shanley and David Moore, Katie Kane, Casey Charles, Mladen Kozul, Charles Exley, Gregory Campbell, George Dennison (Fast Buffalo) and many others at the University of Montana for helping me open my mind during undergraduate studies to a cosmopolitan worldview. Thanks to my sister Donna DeCelles (Blanket Woman) and my astrologer Mooncat for their support. Go native! *Nitawahsi has risen.*

Our Galaxy, The Wolf Trail

Contents

Preface

The older Blackfeet woman looked back at her life. She had graying hair parted in two braids and was quite chubby. The government commodity food fed her well. She was penniless, but managed to find cheap daily entertainment in newspaper headlines. She stared at the frost covered window with a crack that was never fixed. Drafts often caused her to shiver. Browning, Montana was just like any American town, but somewhat desolate from poverty stricken changes. If she gave away secrets of relatives, or told too much, there might be surprises to those still living on the reservation. Hell forget it! Everybody knew everybody's business anyway.

She spoke excellent English in a tribal accent similar to a Canadian backwoods accent. She held on to memories in her mind that she wrote down. She showed excerpts from her handwritten diaries to nobody. Neat handwriting with sentences straight in line. She told an old friend about her time with the white people as they sipped tea together beside an old potbelly stove to keep warm in such a cold and barren town. That was when the gritty details were revealed. When she had the time to sit and really ponder her memories, certain elements, certain faces, smells, and names were quickly fading like her language. It was all too long ago anyway, literally a different century. She often had trouble explaining some words and concepts of her prior world to her grandchildren who were raised in boarding schools. She kept memories immortalized on paper locked in a chest in her niece's attic. Along with eagle feathers, a pipe, the only surviving photo of her parents, and an old newspaper clipping of a teepee. The mud of years gone by. Secrets of a woman with a different name.

Chapter 1-Life in Camp

How two worlds clash, when a scorching day submits to a cool evening as Thunder hits his drum. His drum alerts us to the storms. I have seen the good and bad of two worlds. Stuck in the middle is a storm of a different kind. Children see *everything*. Sometimes they see things for what they truly are, even better than adults. They don't hug deep emotional scars like adults yet. Often like the rocks, we never forget and keep the molds that are sculpted forever. I was playing with dolls and my world was beginning to take shape. My auntie Moon Pond at Night made the doll's bodies out of dried blue corncob. The doll's heads were small bison buckskin pouches. The pouches were sewed into balls stuffed with grass. Their faces painted with black paint.

My auntie explained to me that she stored corn in her belongings. "This corn made a long journey traded from the Pawnee tribe, then to the Lakota, then to the Apsaalooke. When the corn got here, we divided it up among the three bands of our people. We are the Kainai, the Siksika, and the Pikuni nations of the Blackfoot people. Although we have bountiful meat, there are other tribes blessed with other goods. We Pikuni don't grow corn, but get it from somewhere else. Now I have bagged corn in my teepee."

I was careful with my three dolls intricately beaded buckskin dresses. My dolls were climbing up the side of a teepee. They were huffing and puffing as the teepee represented a distant mountain. An arrow pierced the head of Little Willow who was my favorite doll. Little Willow's head fell to the ground. I turned around and standing proud with a glare stood Summer Fire who I despised since birth.

I began to wail as my auntie came running from making the delicious moki-maani, our Blackfeet pemmican. She had bison grease on her hands as she grabbed my doll. She comforted "Don't cry. I'll make you a new doll." My auntie glared at Summer Fire. "I'm going to tell your father that you're ruining little girls' dolls."

"You do so. While you're at it say that I was a good shot," Summer Fire said as he stood beside his laughing brother Beaver Teeth and the rest of the boys.

"Go away," My auntie waved them away.

Summer Fire's father was named Swift as Lightning. His stupid father didn't care about his ill-behaving sons. Their daddy was so busy trying to up his influence in the tribe. He was always telling pointless jokes to others or giving away food, not out of generosity, but just to look good. When my auntie complained, he just laughed and said to his sons, "Shoot gophers instead of dolls. You might become a better warrior and hunter than your dad."

"Aren't you going to punish your sons for destroying Dawn Red Sky's dolls? It takes me a long time to make them," My auntie asked Swift as Lightning.

"Nah! It doesn't matter. My sons are useless little fuckers," then he added, "They'll never be a better warrior and hunter than me."

His sons glared at their father. My auntie walked away from that braggart shaking her head with disgust.

I started playing with my doll's head. Her head was rolling around the dirt as a trickster spirit chasing after my other two dolls. The head was screaming. A nice boy named Scruffy Hunter came over and asked, "Why are you playing with just a head?" I pointed at the boys who were throwing elk bones at each other. I began crying again.

Scruffy Hunter must have thought that it was his boyish duties to protect a little girl. I saw him walking toward the other boys with his arms lifted out to his sides ready to fight. He suddenly kicked Summer Fire in the face. They rolled around the ground like two fighting badgers when a sick brave who stayed home from hunting broke up the fight. He grabbed Scruffy Hunter and Summer Fire by the arms and led them into a teepee. I caught Scruffy Hunter's eyes as he was getting a lecture about the importance of good behavior. At that moment, I felt warmth in my heart. A warmth like when Natosi our sun warms up the day with his heat rays. I wondered if Scruffy Hunter felt it also.

Auntie asked me to help her finish making the moki-maani. I stirred soft bullberries in a copper pot. Auntie added shredded dried meat that she crushed with a stone mallet. The mixture was stirred with a willow stick. She slowly poured in heated fat to give it a soft stickiness. When the mixture got thick and greasy, she put her two tan hands in the pot and began massaging it. She gave me a piece out of her hand and I felt better. She put more sage into the fire pit. The enticing aroma of the berry-sweetened meat was attracting flies. Flies and bees hated sage smoke, but loved fatty meat mixed with bullberries.

We ate what remained of the last hunt. Natosi slowly set his majestic orange and mauve rays over golden rolling foothills before jagged mountains. We heard Thunder who banged the world like a divine drum. Dark storm clouds rolled in from the mountains. Cool wind and the fresh smell of mountain-wetted pine blew into our camp. We hoped the distant storm reached us so that the thirsty prairie grass was quenched. "Dear rainstorm, please rain on us. We don't want any more grass fires this year," Moon Pond at Night loudly prayed. The dry yellow glass blew violently, but the storm missed us heading north.

We felt peace as the hot day drifted into a pleasant dusk. Every child liked dusk, the time the stories started. A grandma sat in front of the central campfire to tell us a tale about Napi. That grandma greatly enjoyed telling us stories about the old man who created the entire world. How he did goofy things like mistake his reflection in the mirror for a real person. Napi was really an idiot! How an idiot caused so much goofy happenings in this world explains everything.

We were relieved when a short thunderstorm arrived later that night. The sweet smell of prairie-wetted grass mixed with smoky scents of campfires. The horses whinnied over barking dogs at the edge of camp. I heard thunder rumble and echo in distant mountains. Mosquitoes always liked to come out after the rain. The miniature buzzing of mosquitoes irritated me. The earthy smoky odor was imprinted deep into the buckskin of our teepee all year. The scent made me so relaxed that I drifted in a daze.

My family heard the crickets making music right next to our teepee near the Marias River. I was scratching a mosquito bite when we heard the clomping of many horses. We knew the war party sent out days before received some prestige, because none of them were dead. I was supposed to be sleeping. I secretly peeked outside my teepee through the circular entranceway. I peered into the dark trying to make out the shapes of the braves and horses. One of them was my uncle Blood on Robe.

The next morning I smelled burning tobacco coming from the ceremonial lodge. The elders were always the first ones up speaking in their raspy voices. I quickly threw off my blankets and went out into a crisp breeze.

I stood beside the ceremonial lodge with my ear to the buckskin wall. Uncle Blood on Robe was bragging about two horses he had stolen from an Assinoboine warrior. On the way back, a few braves from the Shoshone tribe shot at them with rifles. A warrior by the name of Rattlesnake Venom and my uncle described how they tricked the Shoshone by doing a cowardly retreat. From out the darkness both our warriors snuck slowly and gracefully like starving bobcats. They pounced quietly on the two Shoshone braves killing them. I wasn't supposed to be spying on them. The ceremonial lodge was supposed to be only the domain of prestigious men.

I peeked through a small hole. I saw my uncle dangle enemy scalps from his hands as proof of victory. When Blood on Robe left the ceremonial lodge, his wife ran up to him giving him a hug. "Dawn Red Sky, help me cook your uncle some food. He hasn't eaten for two days," she said. She saw me standing beside the lodge spying on the men. She smiled and gave me a knowing wink. We prepared a soup of herbs and fresh venison, which was the last of the remaining food. Some people were hording their food. Generosity suddenly disappeared when everybody got hungry. We tried to remain patient for the hunters' arrival from hunting buffalo.

A day later, there was no more meat in camp at all. It was a time when the bison herds were becoming sparse. We loved the texture, the taste, and the scent of buffalo meat. We called buffalo meat "real food." Anything else was called "not real food," including deer, elk, and whitehorns. Life that day continued as typical, but quieter than usual. Hungry people do not talk much.

There was a fear that maybe the hunters might not return at all. "I hope the American savages didn't slaughter them," auntie Moon Pond at Night said. The men left behind at home were a few wounded braves, a medicine man, and Swift as Lightning. He caught a sickness a week before the hunt. He was unhappily resting in his teepee wounded with too much pride.

Woman and girls continued to make rattles, sew hides and cloth, and all the other womanly duties. At midday, we took an extra long bath in the soothing cool of the Marias River. We could not completely relax as we rested on the riverbank. We knew that the adults were worried. They discussed that the hunters had to travel farther more often. It was because other tribes were trespassing on our Blackfoot territory, which were mainly Cree, Apsaalooke, and White Men. There was a chance our men might not come home at all.

We were so hungry. Some of the younger children complained that their "tummy hurts." The older children knew better not to complain. I was probably six winters old. Ihtsi-pai-tapi-yopa always provided for us before. Maybe not when we always wanted the Great Spirit to provide, like the rains, but we knew the Great Spirit wouldn't fail us. It would guide the men to real food.

Crazy Grandpa Bear, the one who told us many tales about the follies of Napi. Some of his stories made some sense to us kids. Other stories didn't make much sense. Whispers were that he was getting so old and crazy that he forgot some parts of the tales. He tried to make up parts of stories on the spot. We always gave each other strange looks when the stories didn't make any sense to us. Crazy Grandpa Bear just laughed and laughed at our confused faces. Well that scrawny 'ol Grandpa Bear was complaining that he was so hungry, he was going to eat his mutt dog.

"No grandpa, we aren't like the Assinoboine, they eat puppies," a little girl said.

"Hee hee hee! Come here you old mutt," Grandpa started chasing the mutt around with a stick. All of us started to laugh at such a wacky old man who was limping after his dog. His toothless smile was overly exaggerated between thick white braids. The poor starving mutt hurried away from him with a tail between its legs. That dog was skin and bones, which would have never of provided a decent meal at all. Crazy Grandpa Bear said to his favorite dog, "Hey now you mutt, you know I'm just joking and I'm not going to eat you. You are just as hungry as grandpa. So I want you to find me a rabbit. If you can't find a rabbit, then get me a gopher. I'll even eat a damn gopher!" We all knew that animals understood humans, and people understood animals. The dog disappeared after some time.

I followed an older woman named Rattling Butterfly. She always made the impossible possible with her powerful medicine. I saw her make a brew out of white and black dried roots. I followed her into a teepee. There was Swift as Lightning sweating like a frog. Dim light reflected off his eyebrows, like sun rays shimmering on the surface of a stream.

"Drink one cup of this right now," she said. He barely lifted his head to sip the pungent smelling drink. "Later two more cups." He made a sour face. His sons were not allowed to sleep in their father's teepee, or even see their father in sickness. Summer Fire and Beaver Teeth sat outside with a concerned look on their faces. The day before those two boys asked Rattling Butterfly why I was allowed to go inside their father's teepee and not them.

She answered, "I'm teaching Dawn Red Sky how to make medicine so she can heal like me." When she said that to the boys, they began to act more aggressively toward me than ever before. I was told by one of the grandpas that Swift as Lightning's sons were jealous of me. Rattling Butterfly asked me to leave the teepee so she could speak privately with their father. His sons were usually the loud ones, but they were really quiet worrying about their father's ill health. We all enjoyed hearing the sacred prayer she was singing over sage smoke and pine needles burning in seashells.

Suddenly off in the distance we heard laughter. Rattles rattled. Drums banged excitedly. "Haiya! Haiya! The men have returned with the nitapi-waksin, the real food!"

The men proudly and silently came back, thirty men in all. A dozen bison were piled on top of the dragging travois. That old mutt was trailing behind the men with a bloody gopher in his mouth wagging his tale. "See you kids, I told you my dog would hunt for me," Crazy Grandpa Bear said to the laughter of us all.

The women with the help of us girls quickly went to work preparing a feast of boiled bison stew cooked with wild onions and herbs. We roasted bison steaks on sticks. Some people were waiting impatiently to eat the raw bison kidneys. We began the preparations for blood sausages and blood soup that took more time. Rattlesnake Venom threw a choice piece of meat into the fire thanking the buffalo for sacrificing their physical bodies to let others live. We kept in mind that Grandmother Earth one day will devour us too so others could live. The initial feast was always celebratory. We were mighty hungry. Moderation was kept for later days. Somewhere down the line might be more days of hunger.

We dried the meat on poles. When the meat was dry, we stored the jerky with wild mint in rawhide containers called sootski-man. We boiled the bones skinning the fat off the top of the brew. The fat was added for even more delicious moki-maani. We had plenty of dried berries to mix in. Nothing ever was wasted, to waste something was considered a crime against Grandmother Earth, and what our hunters couldn't carry back to camp, fed the wolves, the eagles, and the bugs.

Weeks later our friends the Atsina tribe arrived to our lodges in peace. They came with goods that they traded with some of their allies. They brought mainly tobacco and seashells that they received from more easterly tribes. Our men were excited that they brought guns to trade. They got bear skins and we got premium rifles to shoot the white men like rabbits. They all went into the ceremonial lodge that had the cross painted red and black above the entrance. The cross represented the butterfly to us. As butterflies are givers of good fortune. "It's nice to take something made by the white man, and then turn it back around and use their weapons against them, well at least the bad ones," Blood on Robe said.

"A double crossing white man with bullet holes is a holy white man," Swift as Lightning said.

Our tribe felt a brotherhood and kinship with the Atsina tribe. Atsina was our Blackfeet language word for our friends, but they called themselves A'aninin. Their word sounds more pretty. They signed a treaty inside and smoked from a sacred pipe of peace. The Atsina did not stay for very long.

Sometimes other traders insisted on staying all night drinking firewater with us. They were called the good white men. I was told our leaders balked at allowing the white fur traders to stay all night at first awhile back. Our leaders used to order any unwed women and newly fertile girls to stay inside our teepees when they used to come. Then one day our men started trading us women to the white men.

The white men always had, if not the most useful, then the most unusual goods. They had gunpowder, coffee, sugar, metal decorations, metal utensils, and the interesting crucifix. I stared at the skinny dead man who was hanging from the metal cross. I often played with the crucifix as my dolls danced around it. My grandma looked at me crossly when she noticed that I was playing with it. "The cross means spiritual blessings for the stupid white soldiers. Don't play with it like a toy. Throw it away. I don't like it," she said.

"She's just scared of it. She thinks somebody put a curse on it. It's holy, don't worry about it," Moon Pond at Night whispered into my ear. How beautiful I thought as I stared at the cross as I held it in my hands up to the sky, the sun was shining on it as puffy white clouds passed behind it in the sky. I was young but what I felt was a reverence for creation.

Chapter 2-The Man with Autumn Leaf Hair

Visitors on horses were coming toward our camp. They looked like they might be white men. Initially a ruckus occurred because some *Napikowann* were hostile and others were more peaceful. We called all white men Napikowann which means an "old man person." Old man is translated as *Napi* in Blackfeet. Napi was very powerful and acted goofy when he made the world. To us the white man acted like they were gods yet they were always making mistakes just like Napi did. Such a term is both an honor and an insult.

We would have sent our warriors out if they were Canadians. We called their warriors Redcoats. We had to look out for Redcoats in the north. We were truly alert in the south because Americans were especially warlike. The year before they killed over a hundred people from the Heavy Runner band. They were mostly women, children and babies who were stricken with smallpox. There were a couple of older Heavy Runner girls who met a few boys in my camp at the all tribal gathering. They were in love with them. Those boys took the bad news especially hard. We felt relief that the visitors were only four Frenchmen, one had an Assinoboine wife.

I was eleven winters old in the year 1871. We knew about the five tribes of Napikowann: French, Canadians, Americans, and English. My grandparents laughed while they retold the tale about how our explorers had stolen horses from the fifth Napikowann tribe. It was a long time ago when our men used to travel out really far, they went as far south to a settlement called Sante Fe. They were called the Spanish tribe. Area natives said that they had the reputation of being the most feared of all Europeans. We got word that they weren't so ferocious after all because the Mexicans beat them.

I knew just a little about the trappers from what the elders said. They said the four men spoke the most beautiful language out of all Napikowann languages. The Frenchmen spoke seriously with Thorn in Moccasin who was our tribe's interpreter. He learned not only French but also English. He also knew the language of the Atsina. He probably knew all the regional languages!

Thorn in Moccasin seemed magical to us children when he spoke to us in the exotic foreign languages. Those Frenchmen were only interested in trading and living in freedom on our lands in peace. They were nomads too. They had no interest in living within the villages that do not pack up and go elsewhere. They wanted to trade their pathetic donkey for a big sack of jerky. They were especially interested in our women and beaver skins that we had. They were much unlike the Americans who were interested in gold. We didn't understand why a shiny and too heavy rock meant so much to them. If it was of any usefulness like horses, then our war parties would had snuck into their settlements to steal gold instead of horses.

The traders did not have guns to trade, but they had firewater. Thorn in Moccasin translated, "whiskey for women and beaver." They insisted on staying all night instead of leaving right after the trading ceremony. The chiefs allowed them to camp out, and to stay with a couple of women to keep them company for the night, that happened in a very discreet manner, but as I said at the beginning, children see *everything*. Our people were attempting to learn a new concept called hospitality anyway.

The vivid smell of tobacco wafted from the ceremonial lodge. I sat entranced listening to the flowery tongue of French being spoken softly by them. The women and older girls tended to their duties deep into the night. The adults were nice enough to let us children play later than usual. We normally would have been ordered inside when the last hint of light was in the evening sky. Though we ran around the night campfires haphazardly like wild bank robbers that we had heard descriptions about, the elders watched us even more closely, everybody was cautious when firewater was in the lodges.

The laughter! We Blackfeet love to laugh especially during the evenings. Our storytellers who told the funniest tales were the most popular with many invitations to dinner. The people drunk on whiskey laughed like a bunch of crazy old coyotes. Those drunkards left the lodges more often to pee in the bushes. When they came outside to dance, drum, and sing, oh that was when we watched them. We knew it never lasted all night like most of the nightly dances. Drunkards passed out by the campfires, or stumbled back to their teepees. They usually got too tired to dance all night.

Raven of Prey tried to teach one of the white men how to dance Blackfeet style. The white man wiggled and stomped during his dance lesson. He was very goofy like Napi. He reminded me of a toddler who was being taught to dance. He tried to fancy dance but he stumbled over. "Just another drunken paleface!" a grumpy grandmother said who obviously did not like Napikowann. The white man lost his balance as he tried to mimic the movements of Raven of Prey clumsily stepping backward into the campfire. She watched him more closely after that so he wouldn't become burnt Napikowann meat.

Swift as Lightning was responsible for the foolish joke. He asked his wife to take pity on the funny man by teaching him a female style of dancing. She grabbed his shoulders and led him to a safe spot to dance “like a wife.” Women's style of dancing was easier to do than the fancy dances of the men.

He showed her how to dance like a Napikowann. They stood facing each other, eye to eye. They did what Thorn in Moccasin described as a slow waltz. I found the dance to be quite intimate. It made me warm inside knowing that such a dance allowed an unmarried man and woman to be so close. They were pressed against each other as they slowly moved to the beat of the drum. Raven of Prey seemed to be in a dream as she stared at the Frenchman in the eyes. The warm hue of her dark brown eyes met his inviting sky blue eyes. The entire tribe watched with silent smiles except for a few of our elders. I looked over at her husband who was frowning uncomfortably. A grandpa of the tribe shook his head in anger walking away.

Early the next morning, I heard clomps of hooves passing my family's teepee. I looked outside seeing a couple of white men on horses leaving our camp. Two of them stayed longer. Aye! They were the two men who had the two hospitable women sitting beside them. The elders were always the first ones up praying in gratitude to the morning star. They didn't say goodbye to the Frenchmen who left, or nodded in friendliness to the two who stayed for a longer visit. The rest of the tribe woke up just a bit later. Most of us viewed the remaining stars in the sky fading as Natosi was rising in the east.

Most spring days revealed the same pink, orange, mauve and purple hues reflecting off the clouds high above. Nobody could've ever hoped to touch such smooth clouds except silly Napi. Some of the younger adults added a newer tradition to the mornings by drinking black soup, which was coffee traded from the white man. Some elders sneered at the metal utensils and tin plates and continued eating food in old-fashioned wood carved bowls. I watched them eat on buffalo shoulder blade plates with bone carved spoons and knives.

Moccasin quillwork was strictly women's activity. It was very competitive as women competed to make the most beautiful moccasins for children and husbands. Although I was still a girl, but like the purely white chokecherries blossoming across the fields, I just turned twelve winters old, closer. I was growing ripening into young womanhood. I was becoming very talented at quillwork that might impress a potential mate. I spent many weeks, sometimes up to three months at a time decorating the painted quills onto rawhide. I found myself having much difficulty concentrating at my preferred line of work. I took a break once or twice from decorating moccasins with the valuable porcupine quills. I visualized the beauty of men of my Pikuni nation and the Napikowann.

I stayed in the teepee during my break thinking about the Frenchman that danced the prior night. I thought about his red hair and the stubble on his face. He was younger than the other three Frenchmen were. He did not grow hair on his face as long as the hair on top of heads. We children thought that the older Frenchmen became, the longer the hair grew on their faces. I adored the red stubble on his face. The color of his stubble became lighter as Natosi's rays reflected off them, like flames of a fire, the color of reddish golden dawn. I went outside to do more moccasin quillwork hoping to see him again. He was wandering about the tribe staring at people. He noticed me decorating the moccasins. My face grew warm. I had sweat on my brow. I got shivers from him being so near. I never felt that way before.

Others told me in the tribe that I was going to be a woman soon. The way the younger Frenchman looked at me. He looked at me in a way that made me feel confused. He came over to me smiling and said "Bonjour" with a beautiful smile. I smiled and said my greeting to him, "Oki." We stared at each other for a while. I quickly looked away because I felt guilty. He was about ten winters older than I was. I knew that I was too young to be traded. Our nation didn't hardly ever trade women anyway. I was once warned by an auntie that, "White men like our women."

A chief added, "The older they get the more they like our women."

"Why?" I asked.

"That is a mystery. They probably want a wife to grow old beside them. Who wants to die alone?"

"You must be careful around Napikowann when they come to trade with us," my auntie said.

"They're like mad bulls during mating season when they drink their whiskey. They find our women to be more pleasant than their own wives. I should know, they have told me discreetly in English and French several times," Thorn in Moccasin indiscreetly said.

From a distance, the adults of my tribe stared at me doing quillwork as the young 'redhair' stood over me watching. I looked at my hands, which were shaking as I decorated moccasins. I felt uneasy with everyone's attention directed at me. I lowered my head pretending not to see anyone as I did quillwork. The 'redhair' walked away to speak French with his partner. The adults motioned for me to sit beside them.

"Dawn Red Sky is going to be the right age for marriage in a year or two," Thorn in Moccasin said.

"One or two more years if she finds love in camp, three more years if she finds a Kainai or Siksika man from a distant camp. Love takes longer with a boy from a distance. Perhaps her parents have somebody who they hope she might marry and have not said anything to us yet," Rattling Butterfly said.

My mother Fawn in Rain and my father Bearsnarl were passing by while holding hands. They heard what Rattling Butterfly said about me.

"She's surely to marry somebody outside of this camp. There aren't many of us left after the sickness," my mother said.

"Only a few eligible young men are here that aren't relatives of the Early Finished Eating band. Two she obviously doesn't like too much. Sure to have less men here as death takes them in battle or in hunt. I bet she'll marry somebody from the Flatbows or Skunks," my father said as he looked at me with pride. I blushed as he said that.

The conversation quickly stirred to the topic of the sickness. I felt the air thicken around me. I felt an elusive coldness deep within as they spoke sadly about the sickness. When I was very little sickness was all around me. I must have been about five or six winters old. Our camp was a larger population. We usually had split up to hunt during the summer in bands of around thirty people. Then bands camped back together during the winter. So there was much to discuss during the summer separations. There must have been one-hundred teepees that winter. That winter there was hardly any conversations but more coughing. We heard everybody coughing all over camp like many frogs croaking and it never stopped!

We asked a medicine man, "What is this sickness?" He went into the solitude of the wilderness. One day later, he came back and said, "Those whose lives are being sacrificed today, the seventh generation in the future will prosper in bounty and knowledge. Those who die today will be our great, great grandchildren's spiritual ancestors. It is a great honor that the flesh of today will become a spirit elder of those tomorrow. With the rampant changes that are to come, many more spirits will be needed to guide more than ever for those in the future who will suffer at the hands of injustice. Those who are presently sick are meant to die."

That spiritual message did not sit well with some people in our band. The ones whose close relatives were wheezing were mad at him.

"Stop the sickness," some said.

"I can only attempt to help. Some will live, but most will die. Physical death is never pretty," the medicine man said. I looked into the eyes of the medicine man. I could tell he wanted to cry. His eyes were getting moist and his face grew stiffer. I could see his hands were shaking. We thought that our medicine people before the sickness were all powerful. We thought they had the powers to make it rain when the land was thirsty. Some people thought that the medicine people clapped their hands and made lightning in storms. They could touch a tree and make it bear fruit faster than normal. This medicine man could not stop the sickness. Some realized that only the Great Spirit was the only one all powerful. The medicine women and men were just the Great Spirit's helpers and messengers. Some people lost faith and trust in the ways of our medicine men as their loved ones died.

I was told by Thorn in Moccasin that the sickness was the name whooping cough and many white people suffered from it too. He explained that they were already familiar with the sickness, so they knew what to do better than our tribe knew how. Thorn in Moccasin said that the white people suffered with many sicknesses almost as greatly as much as us Blackfeet. He told me that white people were not dirty or inferior to us because of their many sicknesses. He said that they explained to him that they left their homelands across the waters because their homelands were too crowded, and they had a sickness once worst then smallpox called 'the black death.' The medicine people had said such sicknesses were a result from too many people and animals crowded together. Pressed neatly together in the villages that do not pack and move elsewhere.

I went by myself to sit on a large boulder in nature to breathe in the surroundings. The beauty of solitude within nature always made me feel better. I knew that I wasn't supposed to leave camp all by myself because it was too dangerous. Sometimes I sat in silence. Other times I sang sacred songs, my odes to nature. A cottonwood tree caught my eye. Peaceful the slight breeze whispered between rattling leaves. Cotton blew from the tree floating like tiny clouds in the wind up to the sky.

I began to relax, but the memories of such coughing of my early childhood felt heavy on my heart. I began to speak to the cottonwood tree. "I still do not know why the aunties and uncles, the grandmothers and grandfathers had to sacrifice their bodies to Grandmother Earth. Why is death accompanied with such misery? Why is life not arranged differently? Can't life be gentler on the bodies of man and beast? Bodies should perish as gently as your leafs dry up brittle and brown. Every year your leaves fall from your tree branches. People should die as gracefully as a wildflower in a meadow. Petals that wrinkle and sway gently to the dirt are beautiful deaths. Everything that is beautiful is also deadly. Humans are beautiful, but cause each other to die from sickness just from touching each other. Mountains are beautiful, but they are impossible to navigate if a person is alone. Rainbows are beautiful, but they sometimes are harbingers of deadly rainstorms. The sun, even though he is our creator, kills with too much heat at times. What beauty is vomit, paleness, and physical pain? There is no beauty in a mother crying over the death of a newborn. Does a tree ever witness a newborn child never knowing a mother's milk, but only suffering until death?" I complained to the tree. My bitter prayer.

I didn't know if the tree understood me. I knew the medicine people spoke in trances to the elements. A voice answered my sad pleas. The tree started speaking to me almost as though its words were my own thoughts. "There is both beauty and treachery in the world. Does a tree feel beauty in a forest fire? Does a clover feel pain when being chomped in a horse's mouth? All life feels pain in death."

That wasn't enough to answer my questioning heartache. I closed my eyes and a woman appeared in my mind. She might have been a Blackfeet woman, but she felt and looked more ancient than that. She was dressed in gray cloth. She had some of the features of women in my tribe. Her hair wasn't in braids but flowing and free. I felt a surge of energy go through my body. Shivers went up and down my spine. I felt comfortable as Natosi warmed my face. She smiled saying, "Horses will become the currency of the past as gold is becoming the currency of the land. Love will always remain the true currency of the world and all the worlds." She walked into the bark of the tree and disappeared.

I went for shade later when Natosi was shining his brightest. The meadow I rested in was abundantly green from the rains of Motoyi season, which is my favorite time of year. The fragrant budding always dotted the greenery. I could tell by the little patches of yellowish brown that the moist land was beginning to dry. Hotter days were going to arrive for summer. Sacred butterflies flew above purple and yellow wildflowers. I smelled blossoms in greenery. The rustle of the Marias River was in the distance. I stared at the puffy clouds and the shape of it reminded me of a beautiful man.

I began thinking about the redheaded Frenchman shades of the orange autumn leafs. I began rubbing my body. I heard male laughter nearby. My heart was beating excitedly. I moved as quietly and gracefully as a mountain lioness. I heard twigs cracking under my feet, which made me stop moving. I glanced at tan skin between the breezy thick of trees. I moved slowly to spy on the men and boys bathing in the river.

I crept forward seeing Scruffy Hunter. After he splashed in the cold water, he rested nakedly in the rays of Natosi. I saw a penis for the first time. It looked exotic and delicate. Their penises looked like shriveled thick earthworms at first to me. What a peculiar sort of beauty that dangled. I felt feelings in my body that I could not name. I viewed Scruffy Hunter's father. He was very muscular, muscles everywhere, in his stomach, arms and chest. His penis was much larger than the boys were. Such an adult penis was surrounded by thick dark hair. I looked forward to the day Scruffy Hunter would become a man like his father. That day, I saw Scruffy Hunter like the stirrings of a rainstorm that would rage. I turned around because I heard some twigs breaking behind me. I was alarmed to see Thorn in Moccasin staring at me disapprovingly. I didn't know what to do. I felt like running away in shame, but I just stood frozen in fear like a fawn cornered by a salivating wolf.

"Dawn Red Sky. It isn't appropriate to spy on men bathing themselves," he said with a stern frown.

I didn't know how to answer him, so I just gazed at my moccasins. I glanced up, as his disapproving look became one of compassion mixed with anger. I recognized that it was the look my mother often gave me when I spoke badly about others in our band.

"I didn't know that they were so close to where I was napping," I said.

"Don't be a liar. You went out of camp alone again without the other girls. There's an English word that describes what you're doing. It's called lust. Lust can make us do actions that we regret later."

I was very ashamed of being caught doing something wrong. I didn't mutter anything else. I knew he was going to lecture me, because he wasn't just my mentor, he was my elder. He had authority to discipline me. He often went on and on. Sometimes his point got lost in his long-winded attempts at correcting us.

"Your cheeks are red. Your eyes are like a hunting wolf. You sweat as you rapidly breathe. Such lust might make this happen: A highly respected woman lusts after a man. They go to be alone far way from camp. Later she has a baby she doesn't want. She marries the man she felt lust for, but there's a man who she really loves. She prefers that he should be the father of her child instead of the one she lusted after. She spends all her winters for the rest of her life wishing to be with the man she really loves. She never experiences true love, because she's married to somebody who she doesn't love at all. Such are the actions and results of lust."

"I now understand."

"Now come with me back to camp and I will teach you more foreign words."

Lust wasn't the first English word that I had learned. I was becoming quite good at speaking English. My particular talents besides quillwork were remembering the medicines put in a brew, and learning different languages. The first English saying I said all the time was "damn it!" Thorn in Moccasin used to say it when he got frustrated or excited.

Almost every person in my band was good at doing a particular task. Some became good storytellers. Some became excellent dancers. Others were good at painting or became healers. Even the child born of Raven of Prey, although she only lived fourteen winters stricken with the shaking sickness. The poor child was good at cooking but had to be watched closely by us. I was told that I could speak phrases of English at age three. When I was five, I spoke phrases of French, Atsina, and some Salish words here and there.

I loved my mentors Thorn in Moccasin and Rattling Butterfly. They were almost like my second set of parents. Thorn in Moccasin had the gift of being able to travel to many places. He spent time in the Bitterroot Valley with the Salish, even though the Salish disliked us Pikuni. They accepted Thorn in Moccasin in their presence because a popular Christian missionary requested him as a guide. Our tribe highly respected Thorn in Moccasin because he was a favorite of holy Blackrobe. He was a missionary Priest who wanted Thorn in Moccasin to return home teaching the holy word to us.

Thorn in Moccasin was a half-breed. He traveled with French fur trappers to Canada and back. He told us that the white men's teepees were square dwellings. I tried to picture square teepees. The cone shape seemed best. The snow gently fell off teepees during winters. He told me about buildings in the center of white men's camps that were so high that they resembled the cliffs above the Two-Medicine River valley. "A hunter could probably run Bison off the side of the buildings. Those manmade cliffs are as high as a buffalo jump."

"How very different these newcomers are," I said.

I felt giddy all day after viewing the bathing men. I wanted to tell the girls at camp what I saw on the banks of the Marias River, but I kept my mouth shut. I went about cleaning my parent's teepee. I helped my mom cut up plants for soup. I was sewing with a smile on my face.

"Why are you smiling so much today?" my mother asked.

I said nothing. Later I took a break from working sitting near two aunties. One was Raven of Prey, and the other was Moon Pond at Night. We sat at the edge of camp while resting in Natosi staring at the puffy white clouds floating aimlessly in the sky.

"Look at Dawn Red Sky. She's been smiling all day like she's in love," Moon Pond at Night said.

"She looks like you. You've been smiling all day too," Moon Pond at Night said to her. Both women shrugged their shoulders in giddy laughter as they enjoyed the well-earned laziness. They rested on their colorful patterned blankets dyed red and yellow. Their hair was unbraided and messy in a relaxed manner. Red ochre paint decorated their faces protecting skin from bright Natosi.

"Quit joking!" Raven of Prey said. She was giggling. Her face was red with embarrassment, not just from paint.

"I bet the redheaded white man will have dreams about dancing with you," Moon Pond at Night continued.

"Haiya! My husband has been so mean like a bear that didn't hibernate all winter. He was only pretending to laugh when he saw me do the Napikowann dance. He asked me, 'Did the man feel hot to the touch? Did you like being so close to him? Did you want to hug him?' No, No, No," she said with a devious coyote's smirk.

"Yes, Yes, Yes. He was very handsome. Our men think the white men want to steal all of the plains people's women. White men think all the plains people's warriors want to steal all their white women. We aren't horses to be stolen. I like our handsome warrior men anyway," Moon Pond at Night said.

"I do too," I declared.

Both of the aunties gasped and quickly turned around staring at me with surprise.

"Oh you are such a silly little girl. I bet you can't wait until the all tribal gathering, so you can meet some boys from the other bands," Raven of Prey said.

"No," I said with a demure look on my face. I shrugged my shoulders while blushing. I was curious to see what the new boys of the Siksika and Kainai nations looked like. All of them would have been one year older. I truly didn't want to meet them to find a possible suitor. I already met a boy that I felt warmth for.

I watched Raven of Prey braid Moon Pond at Night's hair as golden Natosi was setting. A red dusk reflected off her hair being combed and put in braids. Red sky made her naturally dark auburn hair glow a deep red tint.

Chapter 3-An Apple Tree without Blossoms

I remember the ako-katssinn very well, which is the all tribal gathering, seeing many splendid boys there. Several girls my age giggled and laughed about marriage with some of them. We were getting to be almost the right age to begin courtship, but I still felt like a young girl. Life was happening too fast. It was frowned upon by elder tribal members for any girls to marry their first lovers. We were told not to give in to our emotions right away. That we must give much consideration of any possible marriage proper time to blossom.

We often played with boys the game of husband and wife. I pretended to cook and clean the teepee. A boy usually brought in a rabbit pelt pretending he killed some meat for dinner. Parents were always around us making sure that boys and girls weren't subscribing to hasty love.

"Courtship is a process. The summer rays don't thaw the icy streams right away. Look at how Napi in the stories wants things to happen right away. Nature must take its course in a full circle. If the summer heat melted the snowy peaks in the middle of winter, does anybody know what would happen?" She looked around the teepee at us. Rattling Butterfly seemed powerful and full of dignity, as her face was radiant from the evening campfire. We younger girls didn't know the answer to the question. She decided to answer it for us. "If winter snow melts too fast then a flood happens and we drown. Virtue is the pure white snow of early winter. The hot heat of summer is passion. Don't drown in sorrow caused from moving too quickly to marriage. Boys are sly foxes and have a way with words."

Our mentor asked us to leave the teepee to think about what she just said over the next few days. We knew that we needed to remember what she said word for word, and that she would test us. If we didn't remember the exact details of what she taught us about the ways of the world, then she often corrected us until we knew everything by heart.

I envied the girls a couple of years older than me. They arrived at the age of marriage. I saw how eyes sparkled in courtship while dancing the owl dance or the snake dance. How they had stolen glances at each other from a distance. How happy they appeared while holding hands.

I asked my mother, "Do you think a boy will ever ask to marry me?"

She giggled at what I said. "Oh my young doll wants to get married one day and leave her parent's teepee? Don't be in such a rush. Once you're married, you'll have to stop playing with the boys. You'll be around just the girls for the rest of your life. Surrounded by girls, you'll all grow into women working very hard together every day." She gave me a compassionate smile. Growing up and becoming an adult didn't sound like too much fun. I attempted to find more pleasure while playing the last days of my childhood.

Over the next couple of years, I saw girls my age going through courtship while I felt pain and emptiness. Boys played their flutes to show interest in their potential mates. Girls served meals three times a day if she loved a suitor until they moved into a teepee together. I often silently cried in my bed many nights. A girl who is fourteen winters old should already have one potential suitor at least. Nobody ever played the flute for me.

"Mother am I homely?" I asked my mother while we were cooking dinner.

She frowned and gave me a funny look like I just said something dumb. "My name is Fawn in Rain and we named you Dawn Red Sky, we're both as pretty as our names and don't you forget it." She said with absolute finality.

"Summer Fire calls me ugly. He says that I have buffalo eyes."

"I tell you that those boys aren't being raised right by their father for treating girls in such a disrespectful way. I'll talk with their father," she said. She was cutting up a wild onion and bitterroots with a bone knife. She looked angry.

"If I'm so pretty, then why am I the only girl left who isn't being courted by a boy? I have nobody my age to play with anymore. I feel as useless as an apple tree that never blossoms. I have nothing to give anybody." I couldn't hold it in much longer and my tears flowed.

My mother stopped cutting the vegetables and looked at me with alarm. "My girl, don't worry. You're still young. When you become age seventeen without a husband, then we should worry. No go play," she ordered.

I wanted to ask her whom I should play with, but walked slowly away instead. I stared at a few younger girls playing with dolls. I wanted to play with them, but knew I would feel ridiculous if anybody saw me acting immaturely. You're still playing with dolls like a little girl! Summer Fire might taunt.

I concentrated on solo activities sewing quilts and making dolls for the younger girls. Doll making allowed me to practice beadwork instead of decorating with porcupine quills. My dolls weren't elaborately made with blue corn traded from back east. They were made out of buckskin filled with grass and buffalo wool. We made dolls from anything we could find, even rocks.

Another winter came and went, and yet I was still all alone. I defied my parent's orders and went out into nature all by myself again. It was in the spring just after my band migrated from Bad-water Lake to the Cypress Hills. I was sitting alone on a hillside in the flowers, when a spirit visited me. This spirit was invisible at first.

I felt a warm sensation that was more subtle than Natosi's bright rays. It whispered to me as if her thoughts were mine saying, "Dawn Red Sky, you're not like the others. There will be many more storms that you will be forced to endure than the average person." Natosi's rays were shining into my eyes so brightly, in the glare I saw her, a spirit with a headband of exquisite beadwork. Long thick braids were down to her ankles. She glowed a golden light pleasantly, like squinting eyes seeing through tears in a sunny glare.

"Will I ever find a husband?" I asked her.

Before the spirit answered me, I heard a loud scream from behind me. I jumped up and immediately yelled in terror. Since I was all alone, I thought that I was possibly prey for a wild cat. It was stupid Summer Fire who was laughing hard at me pointing his finger. Several other boys were standing around him laughing too.

"Who do you think you are, some wise medicine woman? No you're just a crazy imitaa (dog) barking at the rocks," he mockingly said.

I was so angered by him. Summer Fire and Beaver Teeth all my life called me names. They continued even after the elders punished them for ridiculing me, by taking away their privileges from racing horses and playing hand games.

"She's so homely that she dreamt up an invisible boy to court her, that's who she was speaking to," Beaver Teeth said in a stupid chuckle.

"Who would want to marry an imitaa?" Summer Fire added.

Action often leads back to the same action again. Earlier on, my hatred for Summer Fire made full-circle back to even more hatred for him. As a storm, that hatred grew stronger. Years before I got into a physical fight with him. He cried like a little girl in front of everyone. After that, the boys teased him; in return, he haunted me forever after, encouraging his brother to do so too.

I walked over to him with a sweet smile on my face. He didn't know what to do. I busted him hard in the face. I noticed that my fist landed on his eye. He didn't cry. He jumped on top of me kicking and punching.

"You jerk! A boy never hits a girl!" several boys yelled at him while pulling him off me. I stood back up and dusted myself off. I refused to cry. I looked at him in the eyes and said, "I curse you with that spirit that I was just speaking with." His eyes got really big.

Word got around about me speaking to spirits. My father Bearsnarl came up to me after I just got back from riding a ponokaomitai-ksi (horse) all by myself. He looked really mean with his face in a snarl.

"My daughter, how many times do I have to tell you that it's too dangerous for anybody to go horseback riding alone, especially a young woman like you. If some Cree warriors saw you alone, watch out! You might be killed if you're lucky, but more likely you'd have to marry one of their men. I don't know which might be worse for you." He was quite furious. "You know how much your mother has been worrying about you!?" I should've felt remorse while my father berated me for my foolishness, but I stared at the gorgeous clouds and rolling hills in the distance instead. "Are you even listening to me? Oh, you must be hearing one of your spirits."

That night we were sitting around the dinner fire. An elderly couple visited my parents for dinner. We sat around the campfire eating roasted rabbit. The elderly woman named Fox Killer said, "Last night I had a dream about your daughter. She was a gray haired and plump elder in a strange place. She was ordering spirits around. She was telling many people about wise things. I heard nobody wants to marry her. Perhaps she's special, that is why she must remain single."

My parents stopped eating and stared at me. My father always wanted to know why I acted so manly-hearted. I sometimes heard the adults speaking about the manly-hearted women who married other women but not men. They dressed like men, and one named Running Eagle even became a chief.

"Father you've always asked me why I act like a boy. Now is the time to tell you. I'll never wear male clothing or take a wife, but I do like riding horses like the boys always get to do. I long to learn how to shoot a rifle. I know that men don't want to marry a woman who acts like that."

Everybody was quiet for a while. They began speaking about other things. Like how it is difficult to trade with the half-French/half-native Metis people, because they were often arrogant and insulting to us. Later my father decided that he was going to teach me some male activities anyway. From spring all the way to autumn, I learned how to shoot my father's heavy sawed-off rifle at small game. He taught me some complex equestrian skills. I was riding across a flat basin of a valley when I saw a gopher in the distance. I quickly loaded the rifle and shot it. I brought the gopher home to my father who was very proud that I shot well.

The next day other young women my age pointed in fascination when I rode my father's mustang in circles around camp. My father decided that my steady hand was good enough to protect the tribe. That day he began teaching me how to shoot arrows at a buckskin effigy of a Cree warrior. "It's best if you shoot arrows in surprise ambushes in the night. Guns are so loud that they always warn the enemy that you arrived in their territory," he cautioned.

The first snow of autumn fell while I stormed off by myself into the distance. A white sky and a foot of snow surrounded me. My hoarse whinnied while I stared up into the sky and prayed to Ihtsi-pai-tapi-yopa. "By next year please, have a man come to me and ask me to marry him."

One year later, I was sixteen winters old and still nothing. I subdued my heartache by asking my father to continue teaching me manly skills. My father comforted my mother when

I rode off into the countryside alone again. "If Dawn Red Sky was a man traveling out there alone, then I wouldn't worry so much. She thinks she is so tough. I am proud that she is fearless, but her body is tiny like mine." My mother's wrinkles creased more when she worried. I was riding on my horse when women were never allowed to own horses. Manly-hearted women were not considered women or men, but something entirely different. They owned horses. I was still very girlish but I still owned my horse, which confused the men wondering what I desired. I was breaking some lesser taboo, which caused a stir with some men. My father told my mother that I had learned to shoot his rifle and a bow and arrow so expertly, he trusted me going out alone. She never believed him. I was riding in a gully when I suddenly noticed that Summer Fire and his brother Beaver Teeth were riding horses on both sides of me.

"Oki," Summer Fire greeted. Dawn Red Sky, I see your father is teaching you how to be a man. Do you think you'll be like Chief Running Eagle going on the warpath while topless? Great chiefs are usually men. When a rare woman does become a chief, her horseback riding skills are better than a man's skills."

I tried to ignore both of them by pretending that they were sick coyotes in the distance, but I turned around and challenged them.

"I bet you both can't beat me back to camp," then I took off. I turned around seeing the boys galloping quickly behind me. I kicked the sides of my mustang to go full trot. I screamed in excitement scared at going over the foothills too quickly. My father told me that I was good enough at riding horses to hunt but not to race. I almost fell off my horse as it whinnied avoiding some large rocks. I held onto the reigns for dear life when we ran up a steep hillside. I saw the campfires twinkling through the silvery midday fog. I saw little children excitedly pointing at us. I was the girl who dared to horse race against two boys. I made it to camp slowing the horse down. I noticed that Summer Fire and his brother were far behind me. Some of the women smiled at me. A few of the braves stared at me in respectful disbelief. I glanced at handsome Scruffy Hunter, he was still single too. He gave me a look of warm admiration. He was the one that I truly wanted to impress.

I was very hungry after the race. I shared a meal with Scruffy Hunter's family at his father's request. His father also invited Summer Fire and Beaver Teeth who reluctantly joined us.

"You're a good racer. You're probably the best out of every young person in camp," Scruffy Hunter's father complimented me in front of everyone. Auntie Rattling Butterfly happened to be passing by hearing what he said. "Some of us women need to be stronger than men. After all Ihtsi-pai-tapi-yopa is in everything including both man and woman and those in between. Our wise elders say the creator created everything to be equal."

I saw Summer Fire roll his eyes glaring at the sky hearing her remark. It is true that even though men ruled by making choices for everyone, some medicine people claimed that the original creator is our Great Spirit mother. Others said it isn't man or woman but exists in everything. For some reason Ihtsi-pai-tapi-yopa became crazy old Napi who made everything in the seas and lands. He made First Woman from clay on this living sculpture Grandmother Earth. First Woman argued with Napi about things, even whether people should live or die forever. Some of us women had to show how strong we are once in awhile. Ki-yo! I guess it was me that time.

Chapter 4-A Young Woman

I saw seventeen winters pass me by while living on Grandmother Earth. The seventeenth winter was the worst winter of my life. We Blackfeet have winter in the blood. Many of my tribe loved the cold. There has always been a certain gentle hearted isolation with the long cold winters throughout Blackfeet territory. One dreadful day it was too cold to enjoy being outside. Those who foolishly went outside wore smeared bear grease on their skin under thick buffalo robes and deer leggings. I tied my long sleeves not forgetting my fur lined moccasins. The men wore badger fur hats with flaps covering ears. Scruffy Hunter stood beside me as I warmed myself near the campfire for a moment before working. I didn't want to talk to him like I wanted to when I was younger, our conversations never went anywhere. I walked away from him. I was strong by braving the cold, and not staying comfortably inside my parent's teepee all day. A woven blanket covered my head and shoulders. He stood by the fire watching me collect wood. My dog carried firewood from a nearby wooded area, but I was hesitant and slow at my daily chores. I looked up as he stared aimlessly into the fire. I noticed tears were coming out of his eyes. His face was almost as pale as the snow.

"My family is dying," he said.

I was stunned. Several people in camp died from a mysterious new illness. The people were coughing up blood. The elders said it was different from whooping cough since they didn't make a high pitch gasp between coughing. Every time a new illness came swiftly as a thief in the night, the entire tribe got fearful. We heard about the black plague that killed most of Europe that was said to have happened a long time ago. We plains people had our own black plague of smallpox. We knew that illnesses had wiped out entire tribes. It wasn't a leap of imagination to think our entire tribe could die from this terrible new sickness.

"I'm saddened to hear about your family. I hope we are all safe and survive this winter."

I placed my hand on top of his hand. I saw my touching him as a gesture of comfort and an act of blatant intimacy. I noticed that his eyes relaxed a little. His face warmed up just a bit. I shivered with both excitement and literal coldness. I turned to him and our breaths moved toward each other. The steam that our breathing produced warmed me just a bit. We held hands tighter. I touched boys with casual familiarity before, but it was the first time I held a man's hand for an extended time.

We stared at each other for a long time without words. He had a long hawk-like nose with lighter skin than many of the Blackfeet people. Of course, some of the shades of skin were lighter and darker than others. His eyes were like a coyotes, which were very intense, and always searching. His face was framed with chipmunk cheeks and slightly squinty eyes. High cheekbones gave his face some definition. He had a body of a man, but the face of a boy. I saw a reflection of myself in his dark eyes, pupils darker than the deepest night of a new moon. His eyes reminded me of when I first saw my reflection as a child in a gentle pond. That moment was so intense that I had to look away.

"My grandfather wants to talk to you, but don't get too close to him, he is wheezing." he gently said.

"Poor man, I'll follow you to him." My heart felt like a light feather blowing in a breeze with no will, just going the way of the wind. I made a vow once to drift to wherever I was needed, even jeopardizing my health by being in close proximity at catching possible sicknesses from the dying. I wasn't considered a medicine woman yet, but those close to the next world asked for me to speak with them. My father said that I was wise, and wisdom comforts.

We walked hand and hand not hiding our affection from others. Two of the elders who were drinking an herbal soup nodded at us as we passed them by. Two girls smiled and pointed at us as we walked together. I entered a shabby looking teepee with ragged skins. A hole was messily patched up with deerskin. His grandfather lay with his eyes open expecting me. His mother and father shivered under covers sweating and coughing as they slept holding each other. I almost gagged because the unpleasant sickly odor of the teepee. Such a stench wasn't subtle under faint remnants of sage smoke. The hideousness of sickness mixed with sweat, the smell of humans dying has a subtle distinctness.

"You have always been a very lovely young woman," his grandfather said very weakly. He coughed and gagged as he closed his eyes in pain. He was wheezing deeply. He motioned for Scruffy Hunter to leave the teepee. I turned around and saw fear in Scruffy Hunter's eyes as he left.

"You must keep this band going and have many children. You must remain a pure and virtuous woman. Even when times are difficult," he coughed, "Now is a difficult time. You remain as graceful as the Above Beings In The Sky. You will make a good wife to somebody." He motioned for a tin cup. I put it under his mouth. He spitted out some thick phlegm.

"Promise me one thing my Dawn Red Sky. Please be a good wife and make many children."

I felt tears running down my cheeks. I put my hands over my face.

"Grandpa, I will do anything for you."

I bent forward to caress his cheek. He looked of skin and bones. I saw one of my tears land on his cheek. He looked at me and smiled meekly. I knew he felt my teardrop on his cheek. Scruffy Hunter noticed my tears as I left his family's teepee. He called my name but I waved him away as I hurried to my teepee. I stayed under the covers crying all day. The Great Spirit only produces tears I thought. Several times the wind screamed a lonely howl as an icy draft came from under my family's teepee. The howl of wind reminded me of the lonely howls of the coyotes at night. I peeked outside the teepee seeing various shades of gray. I felt even grayer inside my spirit.

His grandfather died the next morning. He came over to me as he did the day before, "My grandfather has passed. My grandmother's heart is broken as she lies near death too. Her grief will only make her sicker. My mother wasn't eating much before but now she doesn't eat anymore. My father has not eaten for two days now." He looked down at his feet in a hopeless stare. The blasting cold wind blew his braids from behind his back to the front of his shoulders. It was one of those winter gusts that threatened to bring down the teepees but never did.

My parents looked at him with compassion. "My heart feels sadness for you," my father said. My mother went over and gave him a hug. She held him for some time warming him. She motioned for my father to leave with her into the teepee. Being in the presence of Scruffy Hunter kept me warm enough, even on the coldest days. We were too grief stricken to speak. We just sat staring blankly at the campfire. We were the only two outside that day.

The next couple of days we took walks together when it wasn't too cold. Our winter camp was on the Milk River just north of the Bears Paw Mountains. We walked among the trees mostly in silence.

A dismal morning Scruffy Hunter came to me and said, "My father is dead." I held him in my arms inside my teepee. My parents were resting trying to keep warm right next to us. They overheard the bad news. They stared on in silence as I felt his tears on my neck.

We walked later that morning holding hands near the river. I looked up at the hills above the curving white landscape. I felt comfortable in the presence of Scruffy Hunter, but I also felt trapped. I yearned to run away from him up to the hilltops away from my father and mother, and away from anybody that I ever knew. I felt like running past the rolling hills into a blizzard to disappear forever. I wanted to be as free as an eagle. I wanted to fly into the sky for eternity.

"I feel trapped inside my own body," I quietly said.

He stopped walking. He stared at me with his intense coyote-like eyes. "This horrible sickness has got everybody shook up. The Kainai named it. It is called isttsikssaa-isskinaan. Some American medicine men call it tuberculosis. It is like a savage fox which kills all in its path in sneaky ways."

We sat on a hollow log on the riverbank hugging each other. I felt like holding him forever. I stared at the ice-covered Milk River wondering if the winter would last forever.

That night was star-filled after two back-to-back blizzards. I finally went to bed after staying awake for a long time. I heard nearly silent footprints in the snow outside my teepee. I went outside into the night. Scruffy Hunter did not have to say a word as he stood outside. I could tell from his tragic eyes that his mother died.

"My heart feels like a rock that has sank to the bottom of the river," I said to him. I tried to hug him, but he backed away from me. He looked angry, but I could tell his anger wasn't toward me.

"I can't accept pity right now. All I have now is my grandmother. I need to concentrate on being a better man than I am now."

"You're a good man."

"No I'm not. When I get better at hunting. When I become a better warrior. If I get plenty of horses, then I will let you hug me again. I won't let you get involved in the misfortune of my family."

I tried to understand what he was saying. He was a good enough man for me, yet I realized that he was feeling inadequate as a man. He was going to attempt the impossible for himself, because the entire tribe knew that he was very nearsighted. Many of the prestigious tasks required the eyesight of an eagle. He looked up at the black sky and hurried back to his teepee. I silently cursed the stars. I did not sleep for three nights after that night. My lover's passion grew as icy as the frigid winds that blew southward from winterland up north.

We talked casually a few times, but neither of us initiated any kind of physical contact. Not touching him made my heart ache. I dreamt a vivid dream that I was laying naked in the hot rays of Natosi. I was on a sandbar on the banks of the Missouri River. Scruffy Hunter came up to me. He whispered into my ear, "Physical beauty isn't the way to my heart, only intelligence." I awoke with my heart beating fast.

Our newfound cold acquaintance became even more distant on my terms. I became angry at not getting his attention, so I ignored him. I refused to feel his presence. When he called my name a couple of times, I acted as if he was a silent spirit. More than a few people probably were confused when our closeness became suddenly distant. I was especially confused.

Normally winter is a spiritual time, when people have more time to sit still and ponder all of creation. At night, our newly white unpainted teepees glowed orange-yellow from the fires lit within. Above the blue-silver tinted snow shined Kikomi-kisomm, which made the land feel magical. Magic died that winter. That winter felt like all people were punished by coldness. The Great Spirit remained frozen in ice unable to hear our crying.

Chapter 5-Thunder in the Sky

When spring season finally came, the last of the snow patches gave a playground for all the groundhogs. Nineteen souls passed that winter shrinking our tribe to twenty-two. A chief said that it wasn't safe for our tribe to remain traveling alone in isolation. We wouldn't be able to grow adequately, even if all the women of childbearing age gave plenty of births. We were going the way of the Mandan nation and the buffalo. They both were becoming extinct. We often traded seashells from the Cree who traded with the Mandans. I treasured such seashells. I often wondered if the Mandans disappeared for good, where would our shells come from? We were decorating the old shells recycled onto new buckskin.

The elders and chiefs emerged from the ceremonial lodge. They motioned for the entire camp to surround them. We sat on the ground before them. My uncle Blood on Robe began his speech that riveted all of us that day: "The days of the buffalo are ending. They're becoming too few and too far away to chase. Not worth looking for buffalo that we can't find anymore. Our enemies are great. If our tiny band came across any Apsaalooke, Assinoboine, Cree, or Americans, we will be no more. We will go north to where the Redcoats of Canada are attempting to invade our territories. We will help our northern brothers and sisters. I have received a vision. We shall prosper as a new larger band. We will join a smaller band of Kainai who have been reduced by sickness just like us. Together we will be able to protect ourselves from the 'Napikowann' American soldiers."

Many felt excitement and reluctance. The Kainai nation was inside the Blackfoot confederacy. They did everything the same way as us of the Pikuni nation. They shared the same sort of sacred medicine as our people, but they hunted and camped in different places. I wondered if I would be able to see my beloved Missouri River and Judith Gap ever again.

The next day our dogs were wagging their tails, barking and yelping in excitement as they saw us take the teepees down. We folded the buffalo hides and put the lodge poles on the horse travois called manistsi-staan. We loaded the travois on the backs of the horses. The five mothers of our camp strapped babies on their backs. Other chiefs from other camps of the Pikuni nation were supposed to meet us near the Two-Medicine River. We set off avoiding a traditional trail that we knew existed for many generations. We did not want to be ambushed by our enemies. If they were searching for us, they were following our trails.

We walked through the golden rolling hills of the plains avoiding the perils of rattlesnakes and cactus. Days later, we saw the majestic mountains and the sacred home of Thunder. Thunder is a spirit who lives on Ninastako, or the-mountain-that-stands-apart. Thorn in Moccasin told me Ninastako Mountain was called Chief Mountain by the Americans. We did not stop long enough for our men to take part in any sweat lodges or vision quests on sacred Ninastako. Our security was still at risk even though we were deep in our own territory. The journey was becoming more treacherous due to the foothills. It seemed as though each hill was larger than the prior was as we moved northward parallel to the Teepee Liner Mountains. We never entered the Teepee Liner Mountains because too many malicious spirits were in them. Buffalo never went up there to the mountains at all. Where buffalo didn't go, we didn't go.

One particular hill was so high; I turned around and saw Swift as Lightning's wife collapse. I ran toward Raven of Prey thinking she had heatstroke. Perhaps she was just too exhausted. We knew from her hollow coughing that she was stricken with tuberculosis. We loaded her limp sick body on top of a travois. She was writhing in pain as we traveled to our new home. Then she was dead. Swift as Lightning took her limp corpse to have a funeral ceremony in the distance.

We reached the banks of Lakes-Inside. Our chiefs made the last minute decision to keep the summer camp there. There were plenty of elk and venison, berries, and roots to keep us satisfied, but not content. They said that when the season of shorter days happened, our chiefs would join the Kainai chiefs for a celebration. We couldn't wait until the sun dance so we could officially join the Kainai and make new friends. There were arguments that most other Pikuni camps never wanted to go north to combine nations. There was some indecision and much disagreement between or leaders, our chiefs. They told us that the decision wasn't final, but we were merging into a new bigger nation. We prepared for making home for good anyway with our distant Blackfoot relatives. The Kainai camp we were going to join was merely fifty-one people. We prayed that the Great Spirit would bless us. Singers sang with the drum over and over, "May we have healthy births. Everyone will survive the harsh snows." The adults hoped that there might be possibly one hundred eight people in our combined camps within the year. Whether or not the rest of camps inside the Pikuni nation joined us was up to them.

The cool wind blew from the glaciers above us. The forested pine covered lands beside the mountains were so amazingly precious to us. Children begged the elders to always camp there at the Lakes-Inside area every summer. Life went beautifully from spring into deep summer. One big change happened to me personally.

One day I was beading decorations for several garments when my mother came to me with a gentle smile. "Swift as Lightning would like you to visit his family for dinner right now," she announced. She led me by the hand to Swift as Lightning and his two vile sons Beaver Teeth and Summer Fire. His family sat in a circle around a cooking fire. His sons were on both sides of him. They had the most food I had ever seen: elk stew, dried venison jerky, broiled duck eggs, roasted duck and sage grouse. All food placed on top of a blanket.

"Please beautiful woman join us for dinner," Swift as Lightning motioned for me to sit right next to him. My mother smiled and walked back to her teepee. As soon as my mother turned her back on us, Swift as Lightning put his greasy hand on my knee rubbing it. Apparently, he was living up to his name. Beaver Teeth laughed a goofy laugh while Summer Fire glared at me while making a condescending groan.

"Here is some whiskey," Beaver Teeth's wife Little Shell Woman said. She poured a small amount of firewater into a tin cup. I took just a little sip at first. It tasted just horrible. I must have made a sour face as I guzzled it, because everyone went "oooooohhhhhh!" I drank it fast hoping that I couldn't taste it. Just get it over and done with. It was the most disgusting liquid I ever drank. Perhaps some herbal remedies Rattling Butterfly made tasted worse. Everyone laughed that whiskey laugh as I put the cup down on the ground.

"Mix some water and put some sugar in her drink," Beaver Teeth suggested to his wife.

"Your family always has the most food," I said to Swift as Lightning.

"That is because we are the most successful family. If we join the Kainai, we will still be the most successful family. Our lineage is strongest," he bragged as usual.

He motioned for me to take a sip of the sweetened and watered down whiskey. I took a sip and it tasted so sweet. I was so thirsty that I drank the whiskey like water, unaware of the poisonous qualities of such a potion.

"Thirsty? Have some more. Drink fast! This firewater is good medicine," Beaver Teeth said.

"Yes, this is your only summer for whiskey. The Redcoats made it illegal for our people to drink up north," Little Shell Woman said.

I began laughing for no reason as I finished the full cup. The drink made me feel warm inside. I looked around and the world seemed more colorful, clearer.

"This whiskey makes me feel more comfortable," I said.

The men bragged about their hunts. They were slurring how more challenging and elusive deer and elk were than bison. How they saw a few spirits dance above the water of Lakes-Inside. We all laughed at a couple of silly Napi tales spoken by our best tribal storyteller. He was named Wind Above Smoke who had partaken in the whiskey. “Oki everyone! I get really fancy with my words telling stories while drunk,” he hollered. I was over fascinated with everything as I became drunk for the first time. A memory made me feel glistening moisture within. I began thinking about how five years before, I saw Swift as Lightning naked. How he rubbed his body with cloth as he bathed in the Marias River. I saw images of his tan body over and over again. I looked at his muscular legs and stared. He noticed me staring at his legs. The evening was so hot that the men were dressed only in breechcloths. Women were always dressed modestly. I was shocked that the men were telling sexual jokes in front of women. I used to be too embarrassed to repeat the naughty tales, but I will admit this: I noticed the leather strip that connected Swift as Lightning’s loincloth flap to the flap that covered his butt. I moved my index finger down his leather strap.

"You! Look at you! All grown up to be a beautiful Pikuni woman," he said to me.

He moved closer to me. We sat hip to hip on the log in front of his well-maintained teepee. He took out a pipe and smoked some tobacco, but not like traditional smoking in the ceremonial lodge. He mentioned he liked to inhale the smoke, not just tasting it. I always did not particularly admire Swift as Lightning because I found him to be too boastful. The women in our tribe did not like him ever since he made inappropriate remarks to them sexually and even to his sons' wives. His wife, when she was alive, caught his infidelities at the circle camp gathering. Word got around, yet she refused to name the two women she caught with her husband. She did not want to have the women get their noses cut off with a knife. The night of my first good drunk, I found Swift as Lightning charming for the first time. That night was the first for more than one thing. I went into some bushes to pee. I turned around seeing a dizzy world. He was staring at me like a hungry wolf with a playful smirk.

"You're the most beautiful woman in the tribe. I have yearned for you. I'm very lonely now since the death of my wife. I know she has been dead only a couple of weeks, but it seems like a long time for somebody who is as virile as me," he said to me making a mock sad face.

I stood up from crouching. I walked slowly toward him. I moved forward and hugged him. He slowly pushed me back carefully watching my reaction. He began cautiously fondling my breasts. He patiently waited for any hint of yielding from me. I allowed him to slowly caress all of me. His hands moved up to my face as he caressed my cheeks with the back of his hand. He led me gently by hand to a large rock. I sat on the rock and he lifted my robe. He kneeled on the ground as he pried my legs apart. He didn't shave, because his face was tickling me down there. I moaned so loud that he looked up at me and said, "Holy smoke! Be quiet now my girl." He continued until it felt like the entire sky exploded with love and pleasure. When he dropped his breechcloth, what I wanted for five years was near to me. It was bigger than I remembered. I found it to be intimidating. He pushed himself into me and moved back and forth. I laughed as we did the "crazy dance." I arched my back as the world spun around in joy. He moaned with pleasure and collapsed on top of me while breathing fast. He lifted me up and carried me in his arms like a baby. I laughed and screamed and kicked silly-style as he carried me into his teepee. We crazy danced some more on his bed. Then we both fell sweetly asleep while holding each other underneath a bearskin. I petted the soft fur from time to time as I awoke periodically that night.

I awoke the next day with a gasp. I sat straight up looking around not knowing where I was for a moment. Inside his teepee did not look the same as mine. He had many more items than my parents ever had during our best days. I saw a feathered headdress, many cooking utensils and many containers. I looked to see who slept beside me. I realized what I did the night before. The cool morning blast of air made me feel awake and alert as I hurried to my parent's teepee. I got quickly under the blankets feeling shame in my parents' presence. I fell quickly asleep again. I slept rather later than normal. Natosi was half across the sky when I opened my eyes, and that was when I felt a horrible throbbing pain in my head. I hurried outside feeling a strange sort of panic. The day lit brightness made me feel shaky. I saw my mom who was boiling coffee.

"I think that I might have the sickness," I said to her.

My mother hurried over to me placing the back of her hand to my face. I hurried to the west side of the teepee to vomit but nothing came out. She followed me and said, "Dear ancestors, please do not let her have any dreaded sickness."

She went away and came back with some water. I was incredibly thirsty as I guzzled the water like I did the firewater the night before. She grabbed me by the hand and led me back into the teepee. She said, "Stay here and rest while I get somebody to help you."

I was sweating and breathing heavy. My body felt like a landslide of rocks landed on my stomach. Though terribly sick, I did not cough. I had no phlegm. I didn't even have diarrhea, but it still felt like I was almost dying. I thought back to when I was a child stricken with food poisoning from meat not being properly dried. That poisoning felt like a slight cold compared to what I felt that morning. I wondered if anybody kicked me in the head the night before and I forgot about it. Every moment felt like a day. I put my hand on my aching forehead. My mother finally returned after what seemed like forever. An older medicine woman named Yellowcloud came in. Yellowcloud was a mentor to my mentor Rattling Butterfly. I felt relief just being in a medicine woman's presence. I sat beside my bed with my head held low. She told me to stick out my tongue. Her eyes winced when she looked into my eyes. She put her ear to my chest. I felt invaded as she sniffed around me.

She waved my mother away, bent over on her knees, and said in a discreet low voice. "I know the cause of your sickness. I can smell the stink of the night before coming out of your skin. Stay away from Napikowann poison, firewater! Here this will make you feel better." She took out a couple of small buckskin pouches out of a larger rattlesnake skin leather bag.

She went outside and told my mother, "Your daughter will be fine. She just has a minor sickness. Go boil some water so I can make medicine." Yellowcloud waited patiently for the boiling water just outside the entrance of the teepee. My mother returned with a wooden bowl of steaming water. Yellowcloud put in dried flower petals, some dried leafs, a root, and dried mushroom bits into the steaming water.

"Sip this slowly," she said, then she whispered to me, "Go back to sleep and if you become sick like this again, save your mother from worrying. Don't ask anybody for help," she laughed an old woman cackle and hobbled out of the teepee.

My mother looked at me with some suspicion, but went out to do her womanly duties. I slept the rest of the day. When I woke that evening, I felt much better.

"Dawn Red Sky, I need to ask you a question. Do you admire Swift as Lightning?" My mother asked as I left the teepee that evening to take an evening walk of serenity.

I blinked my eyes at such an unexpected question directed at me. Did she somehow know what I did with him? I was still groggy fresh out of sleep. I stared at a stick that stuck out of a ground. It was tied with eagle feathers near the cooking fire. I thought about the night before as I stared in a daze. The way every movement he made seemed fascinating. The way he touched me made all of creation seem balanced.

"Maybe," I answered.

"Swift as Lightning has been mentioning you to everyone. He is saying how well you decorate moccasins. How well you tan buffalo. How intelligent you are."

I smiled at the thought that one of the most popular and wealthy men of the tribe spoke about me in such a way. I had some doubts about him though. He was so much older than I was, perhaps twenty winters more than I was. The hair on both sides of his head was black while on top white. He reminded me of a skunk-man. He was boastful, but he had much to boast about.

"Your father and I think it's time. Perhaps you need to share your life with somebody in another teepee."

I felt a combination of surprise and sadness. Perhaps there isn't a Pikuni word for such an emotion. It was of comfort and not comfort at the same time. Everything was happening too fast. Swift with Women was a more proper name for him.

"When a chief makes a good decision, then he should not change his mind. I am so proud that such a generous man has chosen my daughter to be his wife. He has assured us that you are to remain his only wife. He will never probably marry a second or third wife. Isn't that wonderful?" my father said as he returned from visiting a friend.

My mother added, "If he did take another wife, you would remain his main wife. You would be able to order his other wives around like younger sisters." She stared at me waiting for my reaction.

"He has no admiration for any other women?" I asked.

"He had hoped to marry another woman in another camp, but he assured us that if you marry him, he promises to only be with you. Of course, if he changed his mind, it will be his dutiful decision as a man of honor. We would just have to learn to accept it."

"I will need to walk by myself and think about what to do." I made a motion to leave but my father said, "He has agreed to give your parents seven horses, much needed cooking utensils, and some pretty beaded hair clips for your mother. He promised me a headband. His great grandfather used to own the headband and dance with the headband only at the sun dance."

He lifted his eyebrows with a smile as to tell me "well, tell us!" I still had to go outside. I walked across the camp and called for some company. I whistled for a dog to follow me.

"Dawn Red Sky," Beaver Teeth called out to me as I walked away from the camp, "My wife hunted for eggs yesterday. She collected in her basket dozens." He bent over a steaming pot while staring at eggs like a hunting wild cat. His wife Little Shell Woman sat by the edge of the fire. Her thick flowing hair was blowing in the wind. The distant Tipi-Liner Mountains framed her body with beauty. Beside her stood goofy buck toothed Beaver Teeth.

"I'm honored, but I need to take an evening walk. You always collect the most eggs," I complimented Little Shell Woman. She smiled coyly. She was a very demure wife who moved delicately, and she was prettier than I was. I often wondered how she landed in the proximity of her ugly husband. Comfort is just as valid as beauty I thought. The lineage of her husband was strong but not very handsome. I knew Little Shell Woman was always provided for well.

I walked a deer trail toward a small creek that led into the lake. The trickle of clear cascading water of a nearby spring was like the Great Spirit's music. Some bats flew haphazardly for their evening meal of mosquitoes. I concentrated on the distant hoot of an owl. I sat in meditation trying to sort out how I really felt about marriage. I noticed the reflection of a mountain in a small patch of still water. The Tipi-Liner Mountains loomed as haunting and gigantic shadows revealing craggily cliffs.

I thought about how mount Ninastako was the home of Thunder, and how he stole a Pikuni woman. How Raven fought with Thunder to return the wife back to her human husband. Whether human, animal, or elemental, love and passion runs very deeply when it comes to marriage. I threw a stick into the stream. The dog ran after it to fetch back to me. Dogs, they're so simple, if only humans could be as simple as dogs. The dog shook off the water splashing me in the face. I took out face paint from a small bag that I carried with me. I painted my face with paint made from a mixture of earthy red ochre, animal fat, and berries. I painted a butterfly cross on my forehead. I painted my chin the color red. I said prayers to the four sacred directions.

We are in the middle of the cross. The cross means balance of all life. I stared in satisfaction at my reflection in an inlet of still water of the lake. The final mauve of the setting sun reflected off the lake. I prayed in silence asking for messages from the spirits. I heard nothing at first as I pondered the significance of painting my face. My mother told me paint was used sometimes to symbolically enhance the meaning of prayer. Many also wore paint to protect skin from the dry wind and hot Natosi. The red circle on my chin represented Natosi. I planned to sleep with the butterfly cross on my forehead, doing so I was to receive good dreams and guidance, which might help me make the right decisions.

The spirits often spoke to me in visions, or to my emotions and desires. Sometimes they spoke in words, other times in gut feelings. Nature omens occurred when something just a little out of the ordinary happened. Perhaps a bird landed on a nearby rock with a twig dropping the twig in front of my feet. I stood at the lakeshore in silence hoping to communicate with a Spirit Helper who was an ancient ancestor. Sometimes I was guided in dreams. I was told this from Rattling Butterfly; Spirit Helpers lived as people once on land but died and went to the spirit world. Other spirits never lived on Grandmother Earth at all. All benevolent spirits were very wise and guided us always. I took an eagle feather out of my hair, waved it with some sage smoke, and closed my eyes. I walked along the rocks with a definitive answer without having to wait for the answer in my dreams. I quickly bathed and sang a short prayer of thanks to the spirit that answered me.

My personal possessions were already packed by my mother and arranged neatly when I arrived back at home. I carried my packs to Swift as Lightning's teepee. We never went through courtship of me cooking him three meals a day. He never played the flute to me. He was just so damn fast I just didn't know what to do. He smiled at me as he smoked a tobacco pipe just outside his teepee. Boiled eggs were placed on a rock in front of him. I noticed elk meat broiling in a pit inside a dried buffalo stomach. I smelled the savory aroma cooking through the dirt covered with hot stones. There was going to be a celebration feast that night. I smiled at him as I entered our fancy painted teepee.

Our teepee was painted with purple spots symbolizing Thunder. Eagle feathers hung everywhere inside. His pillows were decorated just fancy with red feather fringes. I rubbed my fingers across a pillow and it was the softest suede I ever felt. I went back to fetch the rest of my belongings, but he stopped me from exiting. "Please, don't work today after you fetch your belongings. We must rest well for tonight. Nap with me. You young ones tire me out. We will celebrate our new partnership by dancing all night."

I spent most of the evening inside our home quietly taking my time unpacking everything. I took a late evening nap while he held me, when I woke up, I was still sore from the night before. I went outside to eat some eggs when Summer Fire said, "Don't eat them all. You're already getting fat and you aren't even married yet." My future husband chuckled hearing the mean remarks of his son. I looked at his father and then back at his son, then back at his father again. I sighed and took the eggs inside saving them for later.

"You should've picked a better woman to marry. I've never liked Dawn Red Sky. I don't trust her. She'll cause you grief," Summer Fire indiscreetly advised his father. He knew I heard what he said from inside.

"It's natural that sons are jealous of their fathers, especially when their father is Swift as Lightning, who is stronger than his girly sons even when I am nearly forty winters old," I heard my charming future husband boast. Late that night I heard singing and drumming. When I went outside the entire band was arranged in a circle singing and dancing.

Between songs my husband said, “I have a gift for my new wife.”

Wild Rose Petal, Summer Fire's wife, came from behind me and put a finely stitched robe in front of me. Such a delight was decorated with cowry shells. The robe was elaborately painted red, with yellow jagged lines and black triangles. Horsehair tails hung from the collar area. About forty weasel tails lined the bottom of the long sleeves. Everybody gasped at such a beautiful gown. I went inside and eagerly put on the robe. I returned to hollers of praise. I gave my husband a long hug. The drumming began again. Summer Fire came by me and said, “You look like a second wife," but Beaver Teeth quickly defended me. "He says that because he would never get a first wife as beautiful and well-liked as you Dawn Red Sky." Summer Fire was stung by his brother's remark. He glared as he sat on the other side of the campfire. My husband put his arm around me while watching the singing and dancing. It felt like the people were performing only for us newlyweds. They took a few extra seconds longer to dance in front of us. A pink dawn drew near after dancing all night. We both collapsed in bed but somehow managed to get our second wind. My husband ravished my body and I had no complaints. "Like I said, you young ones tire me out with your eagerness, but it is well worth trying out how much I can take," he said as he rolled onto his back. It was one of the best mornings of my entire life.

Chapter 6-Justice and Pride

I was grateful that my parents moved their teepee farther from my husband and his kin. My parents went to sleep early every night, but my husband and his sons liked to stay up late smoking tobacco and drinking whiskey. Many people complained that they were loud. They went off not too far away and started a campfire on the other side of a hill. Drunk was when my husband became even more boastful. I was sure my parents heard him brag from a distance, but they never complained to anybody that I knew regarding his arrogance. A woman two years older than me was invited from a neighboring camp. She did not leave our camp ever after.

Swift as Lightning did not treat her with any romantic overtures at first. I thought that she was meant to be a second wife for one of his sons. Little Shell Woman finished the last touches of tanning buffalo hides. A new teepee went up next ours. A few days later, the woman's parents visited us. They drank whiskey and we were having a good evening. My husband went into our teepee and brought out two blankets and a bear hide rug. Beaver Teeth brought over a horse.

"I would like to present these gifts to you in honor of your daughter whose name matches her beauty. I would like to take Lavender Field at Dusk as my second wife," he gaily announced.

My eyes widened and my jaw dropped. I saw Summer Fire laughing at me. I felt like slapping my husband and his bratty son, but husband slapping never happened. A husband easily divorced a husband-slapper by sending her back to her family. I did not want a bad reputation. I wanted to be alone and hide away from everybody. I just sat there staring at the campfire in demure grace hearing my husband propose to another woman. I looked up and saw Summer Fire staring at me with a certain vague satisfaction. Lavender Field at Dusk had a blank look on her face. Her parents were smiling staring expectantly at her.

"I know she deserves to be a first wife, but a second wife to somebody who can provide a good life is lucky. I have plenty of horses." He pointed at himself, "I protected my people successfully several times and I am the best warrior of all. A second wife to a prestigious man like me is as good as being a first wife to an ordinary man. She will have high respect from our people if she decides to join my family."

"What's your answer?" her father asked.

"Yes," she said giving smiles to those all around.

"You'll get to stay in your own teepee right next to mine. I share my teepee most nights with my beautiful first wife," my husband explained to her. He put his arms around both of us and smirked as we sat on his left and right side. The men of the tribe looked at our husband with more envy and respect. I looked at Scruffy Hunter who stared at me with compassion in his eyes. I knew right then that I made the biggest mistake of my life by not marrying him instead. He was a man of less distinction. He wouldn't have been able to afford a second wife.

I was relieved that such a horrible evening was ending. I pretended to smile at those around me before entering the teepee. I heard men speaking quietly amongst themselves. They laughed occasionally as I was falling asleep. Later I heard my husband come into our teepee. He came over to me and lay gently on top of me. I felt his heavy palm petting the side of my hair. I closed my eyes really tight holding my breath. Everything in my body wanted him out of there. His breathing, the smell of whiskey on his breath, everything about him made me sick. I felt worse after he left because I knew he was spending the first night with his new wife. I said to myself that I just had to accept sharing my husband with a more beautiful woman than me. She was considered more talented than me in quillwork too. Her designs were not just admired by my people, but the entire Blackfoot Confederation knew her quillwork. My husband probably had the entire scenario planned for many moons. I firmly believed he married us not for love. We had esteemed standing and talents. Women like us were something for him to be boastful about. Boasting was his greatest talent. I heard the high-pitched moans of a woman in a teepee. I covered my ears blocking out all sounds as much as possible.

My husband's strong arms were wrapped around me early the next morning. I was unable to fall back asleep. I went outside and sipped black soup. Black soup was delightful coffee, a commodity that was brought back from trading with the Americans. Wild Rose Petal was cooking breakfast. The sky was a light mauve as I gave thanks to the Great Spirit for another day. The elders huddled in blankets for warmth. I saw my breath that frosty morning. I knew autumn was coming. The busiest time of year was quickly arriving and I didn't have my winter clothes mended yet. Preparing for winter always took a lot of energy. I hoped to be too busy to be sad about marrying the wrong man. The grass was covered with frost that slowly melted into dew as the morning progressed. Birds sang their morning prayers. No matter how difficult my path became. Even if the trail of life went through rocky terrain. I always had the morning. The clean scent of dewy grass and the sweet aroma of distant pine scented breezes soothed my ailing soul. Scruffy Hunter's lone surviving member his grandma was sipping black soup. I never had awakened so early since I was a little girl.

"Hello my girl, I give my blessings on the new addition to your family."

I took a deep sigh.

"I know my girl. It's very difficult to accept. I've never been one of two wives like you. Sometimes I think it's the first wife who is to blame for a man to take a second one. Our men haven't been so successful these days that they had the opportunity to marry a second wife. I sense a lot of ambition in your husband. He's the first to marry more than one wife in a very long time here. Don't consider being a first wife a humiliation but an honor. Just look at Lavender Field at Dusk because she's so happy by being a second wife. You're spoiled you know that?"

I knew she was mad at me for not marrying her grandson. "Some other Blackfoot men have more than one wife, but during the all tribal gathering I've never seen any men with three or more wives. There are always just two. Who has the riches to take more than two wives anymore? I often wondered why the men in our little camp never married more than one wife. I thought we were special. I thought we were different, but I was wrong," I said sighing in regret.

"Men who have plenty of horses, plenty of goods, and plenty of wives. See it as a symbol that our people are becoming more robust. Our poor men must have felt so inadequate during the sun dance. They saw men from the other camps owning so much," his grandma said.

"Oh poor men!" I rolled my eyes while sipping black soup in silence. Natosi was growing hot. The grandma took off her blanket and sat on it. She swapped at some very large horseflies. I respectfully got a nearby backrest for her.

"Ki yo! My grandson wasn't even good enough for you," she bluntly said as she leaned back to relax.

I was glad that she did not see the expression on my face because the old woman had it very wrong. It was so very confusing I suppose to everyone. One moment we were very much in love, the next morning we were barely speaking to each other.

"This inadequacy that you speak about that our men have felt. I think Scruffy Hunter felt it. I think he thought he was not good enough for me, but he was everything to me.

Everything a woman wants in a good man, kind and gentle. He knows how to give comfort to the sick and dying."

"He had much practice with his family," she said.

"Grandma, I was ready to be his wife, but he wanted to get plenty of horses, plenty of blankets. He wanted to give me cooking utensils. I had to wait too many moons. Now I'm *cursed* to be with my husband."

His grandma lit a pipe. Dried bearberry leaf mixed with tobacco smoke rose above her wrinkled face.

"Cursed?" she repeated.

I was surprised to see Scruffy Hunter walking our way. He normally avoided any side of camp where I was. His grandma looked up at him and smiled. He gave me a surprised look as he saw me sitting beside his grandma. He cocked his head to the side just a little.

"What a rare visitor we have to this side of camp, what brings you here?" I asked him.

"I was just looking for my grandma, that's all," he said in a flat tone.

My heart began beating faster. I felt the gentle buzzing of sweet energy in his presence that I first felt when I saw him bathing so long ago. I felt ashamed also, because I ignored him.

"Good black soup!" his grandma said.

His grandma decided to take a walk and visit the other elders who were sitting in the rays of Natosi. I knew she wandered the camp visiting others because her grandson had nothing to trade, so she went out and got it by visiting others. Scruffy Hunter turned to leave, but I asked him to stay. He impatiently stood in front of me with a pronounced frown. I had to tell him how I felt about him. My heart overflowed like boiling water spilling into a cooking fire. Words flowed as gently as a white waterfall.

"I have made a mistake by marrying somebody else not you."

Tears began rolling down my cheeks. I quickly wiped away my tears. I didn't want anybody seeing me crying while I talked to him. He gave me a look of intense concern. He lifted his large hand and stopped a tear from falling with his index finger.

"I'm sorry Dawn Red Sky. Men have been taught that they do not deserve a wife unless we meet certain expectations."

"I've never cared about you owning a lot of horses. I don't care about you having a particular talent to benefit the tribe. I just wanted to be with you. No matter what! I know you can't see very well to hunt or count coup. You have no goods to trade. I saw your empty teepee. Some men think they are better than you because of that. You are good at something, and that is being a good person."

"What's the benefit of being a good person when I can't see very well with each coming season? Did you know that I see worse now than I did last summer? Will I be only thirty winters old and be blind like a grandpa? It would be torture to see your beauty in a blur for the rest of my life. You say you don't care about having less than others. I've heard about it before. How resentment grows like a slow growing prairie cactus. Yes, we should be husband and wife. That can't happen now! You would be in danger if you ever left your husband. I was a young stupid man just a few moons ago. I had too little pride in my abilities. Then you married another. I was never so unhappy in my life. I debate with myself if I was more unhappy when most of my family died last winter--or losing you."

We thought only the elders were awake being so early in the morning, so he put his palm up to my face. I closed my eyes and inhaled deeply. His palm felt warm and comforting. I didn't feel true comfort since the day I last held his hand. Somebody was spying on us from behind a teepee. It was a sick coyote named Summer Fire. I went back home on the other side of camp. I looked up revolted at seeing my husband crawling out the other teepee. The other wife was following behind him.

Weeks went by as I gained little acquaintance with the new intruder. We spoke to each other only when necessary. I treated my husband with the same respect as before. He was just merely a man. Men always have more of an appetite for things. They ate more food. They yearned to acquire more items. They dressed their hair as fancy as possible. They revealed their bodies in breechcloths that made them showier. They required more esteem from others, especially from us women. Worst of all, they attempted to make babies more often than women wanted.

Our camp continued southward to traditional hunting grounds. We stopped for three nights to pick vegetables. The children needed a break from traveling. Women had a special place by a small lake that we remembered very well. The soil was known as a fertile area. We dug up wild turnips and camas roots.

We were heading toward a sacred bison jump called a pis-skaan. The hunting cliff was in well loved golden flatlands. I couldn't wait to get near the pis-skaan to meet the other Pikuni camps who always joined us to hunt together. I felt a peace in the area found nowhere else. The pis-skaan was sacred to all the area tribes. When I look at the sand colored stones of the area, Grandmother Earth feels as ancient as my people. The elders told us that long ago, all the peoples of the plains used the pis-skaan in peace. No war was to be at such a sacred site. Buffalo were easier to find back then. Somehow, the norm became that most buffalo were hunted with sawed-off rifles. The men in a frenzy traded buffalo skins with white men. It seemed as sudden as a blizzard hitting us in the darkest night--bison became scarce. We always hoped the Great Spirit would provide big herds of buffalo again. We longed for it to be just like old times so long ago. When I was a child, I remember some of the last hunts using the pis-skaan. Hope kept us coming back to the same spot year after year. The same disappointment happened every year; hunters killed only a few to take back to hungry mouths.

Women were packing up to go to the pis-skaan area. I was determined to set a good example for the second wife. I swiftly took down my teepee. I hurried packing my husband's possessions before Lavender Field at Dusk even got the lodge skins off the lodge poles. I knew the men were judging our wifely duties by the way they were staring at us. They spoke with each other while lounging under trees.

The men are resting, I angrily said to myself. They are not lazy, but probably tired. I sometimes found it difficult to convince myself that their duties were just as physically hard as women's duties, especially when I grunted while lifting a heavy teepee pole.

They spent the majority of their time hunting, which was amazingly physical. They also patrolled, traded, and were responsible for all the things women had to work with. They were sometimes gone for days when I sweated at home grunting from manual labor. I had to remind myself that somebody had to stay at home and make things. My back ached from working so hard. Men made weapons, pipes, and drums also. They held most of the ceremonies and governed. Behind all their power, they sought women's advice discreetly in teepees.

So many important tribal decisions were actually women's suggestions. No women received credit unless a medicine woman healed. Healing was the ultimate aspiration of many women revered equal to motherhood. Haiya! Sometimes when it was hot and dusty, I felt like maybe the men should've helped us take down and put up the teepees. They were good at admiring us women all right while we were working so hard. That bugged me.

I finished loading all our stuff onto a travois. I sat on the ground and relaxed in comforting Natosi. I refused to help a capable woman with her duties. Thorn in Moccasin left his friends and came over. We practiced speaking English with each other while the rest of camp finished preparing for the journey. At first, we were to move north to the Kainai, but chief Blood on Robe had a vision that we should remain safe for a few more winters south of a place called the forty-ninth parallel. He told everybody that a good hunt would come about if we left for the pis-skaan right there and then.

"Dawn Red Sky, how's the marriage situation going?" Thorn in Moccasin said in fluent English.

"I'm the better wife. So it go good," I said.

"No, say 'it goes good'" he said correcting me.

"That Lavender Field at Dusk, she's very pretty. Your husband is lucky."

"She's dumber than a river rock. She's lazy. I try to make good speak with her two times but she knows nothing. She's just a good cook and makes pretty clothes. Perhaps she's good at raising children. She can raise my children while I visit others."

"Everybody has a talent leading to the perfection of the people," he said.

"I agree," I hesitantly admitted.

I heard in the distance the laughter of men as they sat comfortably in the shade. They were teasing my husband.

"You think you know how to make love with both wives every night, but you don't know how," one man said.

"You shouldn't have to marry all of the women now that you got two wives," a bachelor said.

"Dawn Red Sky is better at packing than before. When many wives compete with each other the camp benefits. When one wife gets lazy, get another wife, then they both become superwives," Beaver Teeth said.

"They even get better at making babies. They want to be the better lover than the other wife," my husband said.

The men all went "Ho'innit!" in unison and laughed. My face turned red with embarrassment.

My husband came over and sat behind me. He gave me a porcupine quill comb decorated with male sage grouse feathers. "I made this comb for you." He began gently combing my hair. He tightly braided my hair as we both watched the lesser wife clumsily packing what little items she owned.

Our band moved slowly across the rolling foothills. The drying grass on the late summer hills was a creamy golden hue. Small ponds dotted the valleys as large swaths of visiting geese drank water. They migrated southward in the sky making V formations. Brisk eastbound breezes blew sometimes too swiftly from far off mountain peaks. Dusty gusts blew throughout the curving foothills stinging my eyes. Although there were no complaints from anybody, not even from the children as we moved through the rugged terrain. It was never a custom of plains people to complain about any hardship. We just told what was bothering us only if somebody asked.

We sometimes took a trail called Riplinger Road that was made by Napikowann. We purposely avoided that trail even though the travel would have been faster, because we wanted to avoid the Americans. We heard at the sun dance from the others that the American chiefs back east wanted to force us onto a little pieces of land called reservations. *How dare they* many said. We were told the land was north beside something stupid called the forty-ninth parallel. "Oh the mighty white man! He lives most of his life in concepts, but not in experiences," Chief Blood on Robe said. Even though we knew not of maps, we knew that the white man had invisible lines going from east to west. We were shown by traders where the forty-ninth parallel was. The north side the Canadian tribe claimed it as their own, and to the south, the American tribe claimed it as their own. They fool-heartedly did not see our Blackfeet land claim. It was a country called

Nitawahsi. They only decided to recognize a small part of land for us.

We were disgusted that the Americans had already forced some Blackfoot camps onto that land trying to break up the confederacy. We knew that it was the same fate northward even if we did intermix with the Kainai. The dirty Redcoats, pale warriors who called themselves Canadian Mounties oozed over the plains like diseased blood. All led by a female chief called Queen Victoria. The Metis half-breeds told our chiefs that she's a moralistically frigid, rigid, and power hungry chief. Chief queen who champions her warriors taking over the world.

Several days later, we camped beside the Missouri River. The camp was only a quick horse ride to the pis-skaan. The men went out to hunt right away. Our patrolmen also went out to see if our enemies were nearby. The rest of us went about our duties. Sometimes early fall can be a very unpredictable season. Sometimes the snows came early, other times it seems like the hot days lasted forever. It was such a day of lingering heat. I un-pegged the birch bark pegs. I sighed pleasantly as I lifted the lodge skins to let wind inside to cool off. I peeked inside the neighbor's teepee. The lesser wife's bed wasn't made as nicely as my bed. Her blankets were ruffled. I was satisfied that her home was very empty.

At least our husband's most cherished items, tobacco, medicine bundles, eagle feathers, headdress, woven baskets and copper jars were all in my teepee. I did quillwork as children played around me on stilts made out of small lodge poles. Young girls were playing kick ball made out of a buffalo stomach filled with grass. I planned to go out and pick turnips by the river. My stomach was growling for turnip and ground bone soup. I followed a deer trail to the river. I prayed some evening prayers while ankle deep in the river. I wanted to bless the turnips before picking them. I stopped singing when I heard twigs breaking in willows behind me. I instinctively thought that it was an animal.

I continued to sing letting the animal know about my whereabouts.

"I always loved your voice whether singing, talking, or in my head," Scruffy Hunter said as he made his way out of the shrubbery.

I turned around and smiled. He stood on a small boulder and faced me as I sang to him. He slowly walked over to me with a smirk. He leaned forward and hugged me. I stopped singing as he rubbed my back with his big hands. I pushed him gently backward. Sorrowful that I did that, I took a step forward and placed my palms over his cheeks. I felt that clean tingling feeling that I felt not long before when I was closer to him.

Of course, he didn't go on the hunt because of his bad eyesight. He lived up to his name. How he hated staying at home with the womanly men who liked working alongside us. Women's duties he didn't do well either. Men who stayed home were treated like women. The successful warriors mocked him for being like a woman. Their meanness made me feel protective of him. It wasn't his fault since childhood his eyesight was slowly fading like twilight to night. To me he was very forceful and striving like a chief. He was good at playing with the young children keeping the youngest ones busy. The women loved to order him around which irked me. He said he was cutting wild onions slowly, trying to be careful not to cut his hands with the bone knife. He accidently cut himself when he saw me leave toward the river. He said he had to follow me.

We knew the rest of the men were far away. Fortunately, my husband was far away with them. Out of sight, out of mind. We embraced and rested in the rays of Natosi. He was dressed only in his breechcloth typical for such a hot day. I ran my fingers over his smooth stomach and chest. He began rubbing my breasts with his palms.

"We can't do this," I said losing my breath.

"We can't but we're doing it anyway," he said after a moan.

"No," I said as I sat up, but then I moved back down. We basked in the sunrays of the Great Spirit witnessing our napping, our sun is named Natosi, he is our Great Spirit, and nothing can ever be hidden from our creator shining on us during the sunniest of days. Scruffy Hunter knew I would be in grave danger if I foolishly attempted to take on more than just my husband. He caressed my face for a while. I moved on top of him like a comfortable blanket. We put our cheeks together. After awhile he went back into camp while I picked turnips. I heard a child yelling in the distance, "Buffalo! Buffalo!"

Hunters rode back into camp with twelve carcasses of real food. It was always a joyous occasion whether the meat was few or many when they returned. They were gone not very long. Blood on Robe reported that the herd was too small. There should have been about one hundred and fifty buffalo but they said they counted only sixty.

Two days went by as we skinned and dried the fresh kill. My husband refused to talk to me. He spent both nights in his new wife's teepee. I was tanning hides when my mother came up to me with a very concerned look on her face. She gave me a hug and began crying.

"Mother, please tell me what's wrong?" I asked her.

She looked at me gently and said, "My daughter, the men are in the ceremonial lodge and are waiting to speak with you."

"Why?" I asked fearing the worst.

"I can't tell you. I'm forbidden to say anything just yet. The chiefs must tell you."

She sat on the ground and stooped over. I was distraught at seeing her so unhappy. Children were standing in a circle staring at her.

"Go on," she said and waved me on.

I hesitantly moved toward the ceremonial lodge. I felt like I had a hive of bees in my stomach. My hands were shaking in nervousness. I turned around seeing women staring at me in silence. Staring faces were scattered throughout standing next to teepees. My mother wiped her tears away and walked away from camp. I entered the ceremonial lodge feeling weary. Four of the elders sat inside with serious looks on their faces. Blood on Robe, Rattlesnake Venom, my father Bearsnarl, Running Fox, and my husband were the five chiefs present. Running Fox thought he was the main chief. They were dressed in ceremonial clothes with faces painted below headdresses. My husband's sons were present sitting adjacent to Scruffy Hunter. I stared at everyone in confusion. Running Fox began, "Dawn Red Sky, you have been seen as a woman of infidelity."

My eyes widened and my heart dropped. I felt like falling down because a married woman who cheats on her husband was a great crime. Perhaps killing a child was worse.

"We have a witness who saw you and Scruffy Hunter together," Running Fox said.

Scruffy Hunter gasped, then yelled, "Bring in the liar!" I noticed my husband's eyes were moving back and forth from me to Scruffy Hunter without much expression. He seemed almost bored in such a tense situation.

"Summer Fire, stand up and tell us what you have seen," Running Fox said.

My father remained still and stoic. His eyes glared at Summer Fire and Swift as Lightning. My father was a wise man. I knew he never believed his own daughter to be a loose woman. Summer Fire stood up, stared each elder chief in the eyes, and lied! "I was patrolling up and down the big river to see if any of our enemies were camped out. I heard some laughter. I got off my horse. Like a mountain lion, I spied in silence. That is when I saw Scruffy Hunter and Dawn Red Sky making love. I felt repulsion at seeing her defiantly ignoring her proper faithfulness of being a sits-beside-him wife. Whore!" He was such a fake. I saw Scruffy Hunter give Summer Fire the look of death. Summer Fire stood in front of the men with an arrogant stance. All eyes were on him, he must have enjoyed what little attention he could muster. He must have rehearsed the accusation in his mind for two days. He looked down at the ground and pretended to be sad. "It hurts me to see her hurting my father with such a weak man such is Scruffy Hunter."

"You're a liar. We were only talking to each other," Scruffy Hunter yelled.

"My dear chiefs and elders," I said, "Scruffy Hunter does not want to see me getting hurt. We did speak to each other. We talked, hugged, and took a nap in shining Natosi. I felt guilty, so we did not go any further than that. If there is ever to be a child in my womb, it will only be Swift as Lightning's blood." The men looked at each other in bewilderment.

"I have taught my daughter to be honest. She has human faults and she makes mistakes. Don't we all? That isn't grounds for punishment. She knows she was heading down the wrong path. She quickly turned around and chose the right path. When you accuse my daughter of being of ill morals, you accuse her father of the same crime. Everyone knows that her parents are honest simple people and we created an honest simple daughter," my father said with bold forcefulness.

Running Fox stared at my father and said, "We know what Dawn Red Sky has said isn't true. We might have difficulty believing Summer Fire's accusation. They have never liked each other, but can any reasonable adult doubt the words of a child?"

A child came inside the ceremonial lodge. He was about nine winters old. He looked scared as his eyes wandered around the ceremonial lodge at those who were staring seriously at him.

"What did you see when you were walking by the river two days ago?" my father asked the child.

"I saw Dawn Red Sky sitting on top of Scruffy Hunter," the child said.

I was stunned hearing dark words spoken from a child.

"What do you think they were doing?" my husband asked the boy.

"I thought she was tickling him at first because they were both laughing. Other kids told me that they were making babies, because she was hopping like a rabbit on top of him."

Everyone was too shocked to speak. An uncomfortable silence remained for a few very long seconds. I tried to understand why the child lied to all of us. I had my suspicions as to who told the child what to say. I looked at Summer Fire with a knowing glare.

"Summer Fire, everybody knows that we hate each other. Your hate has grown so cold and dark that you taught an innocent child to lie to make truth your lies? I hugged Scruffy Hunter. We held each other as we slumbered in the rays of Natosi. Nothing more happened than that. I only will have my husband's children."

"We don't believe you," my stupid husband said.

My father got up angrily and rushed over to the shrugging child. He grabbed the child roughly by the arms and snarled, "He taught you to lie, didn't he? Say it! Say it!" He shook the child violently. The child began bawling. The child's mother came in to retrieve her son. I continued my speech hoping reason would seep into the men's minds, but anger overcame me. "Summer Fire doesn't like strong women. Remember when we got into two physical fights a few summers ago. I beat him both times. He got a black eye the first time and a swollen lip the second time. Is he a real man? No. I don't think so. He has never forgiven me. He got the reputation as a woman beater. Yes, he is married all right. He is truly married to his arrogance," I said defiantly as my father ever could.

The men stared at me without any warmth or understanding. I felt like they were staring at a worm that was slithering out of dirt. They had no expressions on their faces showing no emotions, except my father and Scruffy Hunter who looked disgusted. Running Fox motioned with his hands for me to leave. I sat outside while all the children and women stared at me. I heard the men mumble amongst themselves inside. My father walked outside passing me by while walking very fast to his teepee. "Dawn, come in," Running Fox yelled.

I came back in with a brave face not showing any fear. I was too angry to feel fear.

"We've decided to give you a light punishment. I wanted to banish you, but we've decided on the typical punishment. You're sentenced to be a cut-nose." I could tell sadistic Running Fox enjoyed giving me the sentence. His eyes did not fool him. He probably wanted to be the one to do it. He had everyone in the tribe fooled.

"So it's with our justice that believes in lies," I said. Maybe they expected me to scream and cry. I refused to show any weakness. No women ever dared to criticize her own tribe as I did. I was in a world of men and their fear. Fear of never truly knowing if a child was of their own blood or not, whether the women cheated or not. We *never* cheated in our tribe. Nobody was that way. Okay perhaps one or two did, but they ran away with their lovers hopefully surviving if they were lucky. I thought about running away with Scruffy Hunter.

"Tonight in silence after dinner we will carry out your sentence. We have a new name to call you for the rest of your life, it's called Stolen Wife," Running Fox added. "Now go away," he said in anger, probably angry that I refused to cry upon hearing my sentence.

I walked back to my parents' teepee. My father was waiting for me. He quickly stood up to give me a hug.

"Father, you know I never did such a thing."

"My daughter, I believe you. I don't understand why they want to do that to you. They only make a cut-nose if a woman is a problem on a regular basis after repeated warnings. I'll try to reason with them, they're bluffing to use you as an example I think." I cried very hard knowing a decent man believed me. I cried for a long time in his arms as I thought about the elders' tales about seeing a woman from the Atsina nation who was a cut-nose. Her sliced off nose gave her a flat face. People remarked how she looked like a cat. The cut-nose was treated without much respect by her people. One time I saw a cut-nose at the all tribal gathering who rarely left her teepee out of shame. The next year we did not see her at the gathering because she jumped off a cliff. I was ready to jump into the river.

"I'm thinking of a plan to kill Summer Fire and make it look like an accident. I'm willing to challenge that cutthroat in the middle of camp. I would even challenge Running Fox. He's a cruel hothead. I saw him kill his enemies slowly while we were at war enjoying it by mocking their pain."

"No father, don't play into their game, to fight dark spirits in the flesh like them is their fun. You're an old man. You must accept your fate as a weaker fighter."

He continued to clean his rifle as I went to hide my face under the blankets. My mother returned already having my items packed. She whispered to me that when my father was to confront Summer Fire, I was to escape. She had my horse ready at the edge of camp. We knew that such a plan was risky. My father wasn't scared of a bullet. He was willing to die for my honor. My mother was prepared to let him die. "Dawn, you are caught in a storm not of your making," my father said while looking at my tear reddened eyes. "Your mother and I didn't like how your husband acted when he was drunk, and the way he was treating you. I told him that we were planning to take you back if he didn't mend his ways. He didn't, so I think he thinks this is the best way to get rid of you."

I visualized Scruffy Hunter's sad face if I drowned myself in the river. Perhaps losing a nose was a sacrifice worth taking if it meant that I have to be with him for the rest of my life. I knew he would love me even without a nose and if others in the tribe ignored us. Nobody was going to ignore us. My people were mostly compassionate. I was going to find a useful place among them even with facial scarring.

I dreaded the smell of food cooking as the evening came too quickly, because I knew what was to come after dinner. Surprised, I heard children running toward the camp yelling "Lakota people!"

Most of the men hurried onto their horses to find our enemy nation who were trespassing too close to us. My father put his war bonnet on his head. He hurried outside to the other warriors. I peeked out the entrance seeing him disappear into the darkness of the night. I wondered if he brought his sawed-off rifle to kill a Lakota warrior or somebody else who deserved it more. It was an easy plan to murder someone in the struggle of night and make it look like a Lakota did it. My mother went outside to see what was going on. A patrolman rode back and told everybody to put the fires out and lie silently in our teepees. He said that many Lakotas and Cheyenne were in small bands in the area.

He explained about two dozen circled our camp in bands of three to four. He quickly added that they were younger than the average warrior. They were about the ages of twelve or thirteen winters old who decided to prove that they were men. An action that was against the advice of their parents. Boys who were fighting against men made my heart beat in confusion. Such boys were foolishly endangering themselves by straying from their lands. The Americans killed Mountain Chief and much of the Heavy Runner band because they refused to stay within a small area. If the Americans caught those boys trying to steal our horses, they'd be dead as the babies that were massacred by those dirty American cutthroats.

Older boys always got permission to slip away from the camps to explore. Girls were watched closely all the time, but boys sometimes left in groups for days without their parents around. Perhaps their parents didn't even know that their sons were actually going out on a raid, instead they thought that their boys were just going out on an adventure. It wasn't proper counting coup. We knew that some rowdy gangs of young men sometimes traversed amongst the plains people undetected. We suspected that maybe some of our young banished hotheads were guilty of doing such stupidity too.

The sound of hooves disappeared into the distance. My mother turned to me and said, "Leave this place my baby girl. Do not fear to travel alone at night. You have the strongest medicine out of all the women in our tribe. You will be safe. Always let the stars guide you and walk the wolf trail." She grabbed my capote that she made for me. She gave me a quick hug then a slight push to leave. I fled in the dusk not knowing where I was supposed to go. I only knew to go far in one direction away from my people forever. Even though some men didn't treat me fairly in my tribe, I still loved my people because they were mostly good-hearted people. I would miss them dearly if I survived.

Chapter 7-A New Quest

I ran as fast as I could in the twilight. When twilight turned to evening, I rested for a few moments. I looked up at the stars in the east figuring out what direction I should go. East is the direction of new beginnings. The night isn't scary, I repeated, I'm like a wolf nothing can see me. There was too much quietness. I was so terrified I could hardly move. When I heard something in the distance, my heart jumped hoping it wasn't a vicious animal. Even worse than animals were the dreaded sta-au, who are the ghosts that haunt us. Some mean and cruel people became scary spirits after they died, but I heard nothing but my own breathing.

On such a new moon night, it was almost impossible to navigate. I stepped slowly almost tripping on large rocks trying to avoid any cactus. Every time my foot hit something, I bent over to caress it. Twice I bent over and felt small plains cactuses. My ankle got twisted in a badger hole. I was limping all night without any sleep. As the sky toward the east lit indigo nearing dawn, I heard the Lakota language being spoken somewhere in the distance. I hunched trembling in fear like a rabbit. I stayed still hoping to be a rocky shadow. I saw some Lakota boys in the dimly lit distance, six aspiring warriors going down the hill with several extra horses. They led stolen horses from my camp. With the boys was a man who was their leader. What a shame that he is using them, I thought. I recognized the black spotted mustang given to my parents from Swift as Lightning.

I continued southeast feeling like a powerful lone wolf. Any fears that I had transformed into brave determination. I usually used the falcon as my animal spirit. I decided that a falcon could transform into a lone wolf whenever it wanted to change shape.

I slept during the day in some bushes at the bottom of a hill. I reached the bushes and unpacked my belongings. Inside my pack were pouches. Curiosity had me seeking what else my mother packed. The first pouch was filled with powder to be made into red face paint. I saw a sage bundle, a porcupine quill comb, pemmican, dried roots and jerky, water in a dried buffalo bladder container. To my relief I saw a gutting knife beside my father's sawed-off rifle. No wonder it was so heavy. I opened a strange pouch that had two eagle feathers decorating it. It was beaded with the butterfly cross. Inside the pouch was some sacred tobacco. I closed my eyes attempting to have a Spirit Helper give me a message. Moments later, I smiled thanking the spirit for telling me that the tobacco was powerful medicine to be smoked before a vision quest.

I saw a sacred medicine pipe wrapped in a white cotton cloth at the bottom of the heavy pack. The spirit continued whispering into my ear. *Dawn Red Sky, I will tell you a secret. Once a medicine man who was a spirit like me appeared in your world. He fooled everybody. They didn't know he was a spirit. He visited your mother during the sun dance. Nobody who sat with your mother knew who that medicine man was. No thoughts that maybe he was a spirit ever crossed their minds. They didn't think it was out of the ordinary that a stranger visited them since hundreds of people go to the sun dance. He told your mother that her only daughter had very strong medicine. Your life journey will be unique. He gave her a tobacco bundle and pipe telling her to give it to you when you go on a long journey alone.*

I packed my bag after eating some jerky. I felt sleepy with some food in my stomach. In the dream world, a Spirit Elder appeared to me as a bear. The bear spoke to me as all animals do, in the mind. The bear said that if I ran into any enemies not to fear. I was protected. If I feared when I ran into the enemy, that fear would make me weak and I would be dead. I awoke very thirsty the next evening. I attempted to conserve my water, but I drank most of it. I began worrying that I wouldn't have enough water to survive. I continued eastward.

I was grateful for warm evenings during the last days of summer giving to the cooler days of fall; the season of crinkling brown leafs. I could never make the lone journey in blizzards or in blistering heat. I'd die of thirst in heat or frozen in the icy cold while journeying during the more extreme seasons. I turned around to see how far I traveled seeing the Teepee Liner Mountains were farther away. I felt sad like I was the last woman on Grandmother Earth forced to wander the plains forever. I saw no animals, very few insects, only a couple birds flying above the grasslands that I was heading.

As the evening darkened, I continued onward. I felt the temperature become cooler as wind swept through a tree-thickened gulch I was entering. I smelled welcoming water. I slowly made my way down to the stream and rested. Off in the distance a pack of wolves howled. I sat quietly like a rabbit. Slowly the wolf pack came closer. I'm like a wolf; they can't see me I whispered. I closed my eyes. It was so dark that when I blinked my eyes, I couldn't see the difference. I heard the wolves surrounding me. They howled trying to intimidate me. I knew they smelled fear. I sat near the creek as I called my animal totem. I imagined a wolf running toward me jumping into my body. I became like a wolf ready to fight. I felt around my pack locating my knife. The wolves were so near that I heard panting. I stood up but quickly crouched back down ready for the wolves to pounce on me. I wasn't scared and was ready to die fighting. I waited and waited. Moments later the wolves howled on the other side of me. My medicine was strong. I fell asleep knowing that I was protected by Ihtsi-pai-tapi-yopa.

I awoke the next day when a tongue licked my cheek. I grabbed my knife jumping up ready to kill. I only saw a favorite dog of mine from camp! The mutt dog barked several times while wagging his tail. Knowing dogs protected us barking at the shadows of the night, whether those shadows were animals or man enemies coming to steal horses. I happily realized that an animal guardian was with me. I called him Smoke Jumper. Sometimes he jumped over the campfires that blazed, flying through smoke after I whistled for him. Smoke Jumper became like a son to me. I often fed him and didn't feed any other dogs. He grew accustomed to sleeping outside my teepee when I lived with my parents. I was surprised he followed my scent so far away. He jumped up as if he could give me a hug. I patted his head. He ran into the stream and began lapping up water while wagging his tale. From then on, I went to sleep without much worry as my dog slept beside me. He woke me up with his barking a few times scaring animals away.

The Great Spirit kept me company lighting the sky every day. Natosi was low in the sky when I awoke late and ate pemmican. I took a bath in the stream. I threw a stick in the water and my dog took a bath too. I hiked out of the gully feeling I should move northeast. I knew the Atsina nation was in that direction. Although they were once allies with my people, they became enemies of my people. Fond memories of those friendly people from my childhood provoked me to seek them out. They might allow a lost Pikuni woman to live with them if my plan was successful. I hoped to become an adopted Atsina after proving my usefulness. How I wished my people didn't go to war with their people and the Apsaalooke nation just south of the Atsina. I remember hearing men bragging that they protected us against hundreds of Atsina and Apsaalooke warriors during a war when I was about eight winters old.

I filled my dried buffalo bladder container with water from the stream and put it in my pack for a long trip northeast. If any of the plains warriors captured me, I might survive…but…did I want to survive? At least I spoke some basic

Atsina phrases as I limped their way. My ankle that was twisted from the badger hole the night before slowed me down. I felt hopeless thinking would I ever get anywhere at all?

Two days passed and I ran out of food. I knew that my dog was hungry too. When he saw a jackrabbit, he ran after it with such a speed that I never saw him do before. The rabbit swiftly hopped up the hill but hunger made my dog move faster. I heard my dog growl ferociously as he sunk his canine teeth into the neck of the rabbit. The rabbit went limp. I was grateful that I didn't have to use the rifle just yet. The campfire was lit. I stared at the matches thinking how they were a lovely commodity that the white man brought; otherwise, it was sticks and flint. I skinned the rabbit and my dog and I feasted.

"Smoke Jumper, you help me find food," I spoke aloud to him. For some reason my people talked to dogs like people, but bears and other such animals we spoke to silently in our minds. Dogs lived side by side with us people and learned some of our words even though they only barked back to us. Wild animals never learned our words but there was a silent communication between all living beings. My dog licked his chops understanding my intentions for him. Whenever I saw a rabbit or prairie dog, I pointed and told him to go get it. He was mostly unsuccessful, so I used my sawed-off rifle. We feasted on sage grouse, ducks and geese. I felt drained of energy despite having foul easily hunted. It was the heavy pack full of items. My back was aching like never before. If only a travois was around. Then it dawned on me; dogs were used to carry our loads before horses. I needed to find two branches to carve and trim into a dog travois. We could travel faster if Smoke Jumper carried my pack.

We continued onward beyond the point of exhaustion. I looked around at the dusty grasslands without hearing a sound, no cries of birds, no chirps of prairie dogs, nothing at all. I heard my heartbeat that was all. For days, there were no animals to hunt. I was becoming quite desperate and weaker by the minute. I began hallucinating. I saw gigantic trees in the distance as tall as mountains, and after shaking my head, they weren't there anymore. "Ihtsi-pai-tapi-yopa (Great Spirit), if you can provide me with a vision, now is the time. I need guidance."

We found ourselves standing at the edge of a cliff midday. We rested on top of rocks near the edge. The view before us extended for miles. The panorama was breathtaking. Golden hills curved like a body, a knee, a breast, the curve of a cheek, or the round of a foot heal. Golden mounds like buttocks. Grandmother Earth was alive and well. I should have been wise enough to have known to stay away from the maze of boulders near the ledges. Where there is rocky terrain there are snakes. I wasn't surprised when I felt dry scales slithering past my ankle, and to my nightmare, a rattlesnake hissed!

My dog growled. I attempted not to move at all hoping the snake slithered on by. The snake felt my body heat. It jumped and aimlessly attacked, biting a rock near my ankle. I screamed and my dog began a showdown. He barked several times as I got away from it. The snake rattled. I got a large rock the size of a baby's head and I aimed for it. Ho'innit! That rattlesnake looked mighty angry. Its head got mashed under the rock as its body violently wiggled. It took a long time for the snake to stop moving. My dog sniffed the carcass. I pondered for a moment thinking I could have roasted snake, but I hurried away from the rocks. Where one rattlesnake existed, many more were between and underneath such rocks. I put on my heavy pack falling sideways over the cliff.

I fell landing on a giant boulder that jetted out of the cliff. I held my ankle that was already twisted from the badger hole. It felt broken. I cringed with my eyes tightly closed, but to my pleasant surprise, the pain was subdued with an inexplicable burst of anger.

I searched looking for a way back up. I looked sideways at mysterious cave that was inside the cliff. The cave was hidden when I was at the top. There were ceremonial markings around the entranceway. I wanted to get my dog but it wasn't possible. Smoke Jumper barked looking for a way down. I wanted to enter the cave; somebody was calling me inside. Grandmother Earth was calling my name. Snakes surely weren't in the cave. The cliff was too steep for them to slither down. My pack landed in front of the entrance, which was an omen to me.

The entrance wasn't too large. It was just enough for one human body to crawl into, more like a hole than a cave. Inside the hole appeared a cavern. I cautiously crawled inside with my head just past the jagged entrance. The shape was mostly flowing and uneven, but there was one side that was smooth. No signs of any animals inside, neither bats nor bird nests were in there. On the smooth wall were ancient paintings. I recognized the paintings as my ancestors. I crawled out to fetch my medicine pipe and matches on the boulder. I took tobacco and sage back inside. I put tobacco into the pipe and leaned back after smoking it. I smudged myself with the sage.

I sat there for some time feeling exhausted. A voice came from behind the paintings. I was unable to tell if the voice was man or woman. It said, *"People are not given the right to rule over and exploit their grandmother."* I closed my eyes and the vision that I had hoped to receive appeared behind my eyelids. I was a falcon who flew out of the cave. I flew westward recognizing the oncoming Teepee Liner Mountains. Below me were a couple dozen teepees. I flew lower seeing my mother sitting just outside the entrance of her teepee looking very sad. She was missing me dearly as I was crying as squawking. I sent her love. I could tell that she felt my loving presence as she blankly stared at the mountains. It probably was going to be the last time that I ever saw her in this world. She saw me flying away. I couldn't fly back to her, because I would remain flying around the camp in bird form never wanting to leave her again. Perhaps a medicine person would figure out the falcon was me. I only wanted my mother to know me in my human form.

I flew back into the cave and changed back into myself. I realized that my eyes were never closed during the vision. I reclined on the flat top of a rock farther back in the cave. Burnt markings were on the rock. Perhaps it was where a sacred fire was burned as blessings, it looked like an altar. Visions were flickering like the reflection of a moonlit pond on the ceiling. A great white puffy cloud in the sky turned grey. It solidified into a great boulder almost the size of a mountain floating in the sky. The floating mountain-boulder fell to the ground. The ground shook and rumbled as the mountain broke into smaller boulders when it hit. The boulders on the ground changed and morphed into a herd of bison. The bison looked like granite rock carvings but slowly turned brown and fur lined.

I saw a trout leap out of the water and grow horns. The fish leaped onto a riverbank flapping and gasping for air, but shrunk into a colorful butterfly that flew into fields. The butterfly landed onto a sleeping bear cub's nose.

Every part of creation changed and morphed into another part of creation like I did as a human into a falcon. I knew that all things were a part of each other and made from the sacred essence of Ihtsi-pai-tapi-yopa, the loving Great Spirit.

An elderly woman was calling my name. She was standing halfway in the rocky wall. She was beating a drum and singing. The song seemed ancient like a distant dream that one only remembered in bits and pieces, but still had such dreamy peace always remembered. I curled up in a ball like a baby in my mother's womb. When I opened my eyes, I was on top of a very green hill covered with short grass. I was led by several bears toward a green valley with an expansive meadow of purple and yellow wildflowers. All those who danced around the valley were forty generations of diverse people. Trillions, countless amounts of people, both white and redskin, some had purple skin. I couldn't tell if they were wearing face paint. People were wearing strange head coverings and wearing foreign clothing. They were dancing a circle dance. Thousands of circles within circles of dancing people. In the middle of all the dancing people stood a man as tall as a mountain.

White light was shooting from him in every direction. He was playing a drum and singing a sacred song in the first language. I didn't understand the first language produced by the ancient ones. I wanted to join in the biggest powwow I ever witnessed, but the bears behind me growled. They spoke to me in their strange growling language. I finally understood them. The bears told me that I had to return to the cave. I climbed up the green hill hearing my dog distantly bark. The old woman at the top of the hill was still singing sacred songs. Her soothing voice made me sleepy. I curled up like a baby again. I opened my eyes knowing that I was inside the cave again. I saw a wolf sitting beside me. I reached over to pet it like my own dog. The wolf said in her mind, *"You can't be a lone wolf forever. Makoiyi, who you know as the first wolf in the world, has taught your people how to live the wolf trail. The wolf trail is to live together in harmony and rely on each other for survival. Now you will know the two basic principles that will apply to all people no matter what nation: People weren't created to rule over nature, and you must live in cooperation as the wolf trail."*

The Great Spirit was still beating his drum very distantly in the valley of the powwow. The beat of his drum kept in sync with the beating of my heart. Deeper still I heard a third heartbeat. It was the heartbeat of Grandmother Earth that became in harmony with my heartbeat and the Great Spirit's heartbeat. Three hearts beating together in proper unison. All the beating hearts of every nation joined us. The beating hearts of every animal joined in. The beat was gentle and deep, although it reverberated throughout my body like thunder. I tried to speak to the wolf but the words that came out of my mouth were the ancient language that was all emotion but no meaning. I spoke like a baby before it learned words. I realized the cave was the womb of Grandmother Earth, and I was reborn as something greater. I had lied in the past and vowed to be more honest. The wolf squeezed through the cave entrance. The sound of her claws on the rocks was scratchy like bones knives on a flat cutting stone. Outside she stood on the rounded ledge of the boulder. The wolf's howl turned into a squawk changing into a hawk that flew away.

For what I experienced was intensely emotional. All that happened to me was as real as flesh and blood. My vision was as solid as the rocky walls. It doesn't have to be felt by the skin, heard by ears, nor smelled, seen, or tasted to be real. Starvation from eight days of unwilling fasting had me in touch with wisdom that only I interpreted.

The world looked brighter and sweeter as I left the cave. The blue sky looked a shade richer. The clouds had the shapes of beings resembling swans lounging lavishly on top of the rolling hills of the plains. I climbed up the cliff with my pack and looked for Smoke Jumper. I figured sadly that a snake had attacked him, because he never came after I yelled out. Suddenly a dog ran from behind a rock. I hugged him but he was more interested in sniffing the foul odors on me. We walked for some time looking for a not too steep passage to go down. I discovered a deer path leading downward.

A few perilous jumps over some gaps and we were down on the bottom. The cliff might have been an an excellent buffalo jump. Perhaps my ancient ancestors used the cliff for hunting when the buffalo roamed plenty.

Chapter 8-A Woman Warrior

I did not see the Teepee Liner Mountains for two weeks as the rolling grasslands went on forever. Dark storm clouds gathered westward. The pretty golden grass swayed as the wet smell of grassy rain blew from the west. There was no shelter for not many trees were around to take refuge under. A spooky looking thunderstorm was quickly coming our way. A sudden wind blew violently. I ran but fell into a stream camouflaged by the tall grass. There were several old cottonwood tree branches stuck in the dried streambed. The remnants of one lonesome tree with no other trees to keep it company for miles around. I laughed in glee because a few of the branches were the perfect size for a dog travois.

We rested in the stream as a downpour engulfed the surrounding land. Hail pelted my skin. Such beady ice stung my face and arms as I huddled with my dog. I looked up once or twice watching hail cover the arid land. Muddy puddles filled with dirty water within the nearly dried streambed. My mouth opened looking skyward. I felt cold droplets covering my face and tongue. I bent over to drink from a puddle.

A thirsty woman didn't look ridiculous bent over a muddy puddle sucking up water beside her thirsty dog lapping the same water. I took off my clothes and bathed relieved that the grime of days before was being washed away.

Three men jumped into the ditch to escape the downpour not seeing me. Smoke Jumper barked and acted like he was going to bite them after I screamed. I had no idea what people they were from. Perhaps they were Cree, but their facial features were not familiar to me. They were warriors. Their faces were covered with dripping paint. The feathers in their hair were sopping wet. One warrior covered my mouth. The other took his pistol and shot at my dog who yelped and ran away. Luckily, the damn cutthroat missed shooting him.

I bit the man who covered my mouth. My teeth went into the skin of his palm. I quickly kneed the other who had pulled down his breechcloth. He was completely naked ready to pounce on me. I was sure my knee hit his crotch with full force as he squirmed on the ground. He was covering his groin moaning in pain. The other grabbed me by the hair. The third warrior continued shooting at my dog. My wet hair slipped out of his hand.

I immediately jumped on the back of the warrior who had the pistol laughing at my dog. Luckily, his back was toward me. I bit into his neck. I imagined myself as a she-wolf protecting her pups. I tasted a bit of blood in my mouth. My hands covered his hands. My anger and will to survive made me stronger than him. I didn't fear for it would have made me weak. He couldn't move his arms. I clasped my arms around his torso with my hands tightly locked. His pinched soft flesh was clamped in my teeth. He finally yelled and let go of the pistol.

The one who grabbed me by the hair was punching my back and trying to pry me away from the one holding the pistol. I kicked my leg backward. My ankle hit the one behind me in the groin. I had two very strong warriors huddled over covering their privates in pain. The one who shot at my dog raced with me for the pistol on the ground. I got to it first while continuing to yelp like a wolf. He cautiously stood before me attempting to get the pistol from me. I held the pistol tightly. He lunged at me but I shot him in the chest. His face was stunned as he fell to his knees. He experienced the worst of insults of being killed by a woman.

Two warriors left to go I thought. The first one that I kneed in the groin was trying to escape from me because I had a pistol, but he slipped. I shot him from behind. He fell to the ground on his back. I tried to kick him in the head but missed kicking his nose instead. He covered his nose with his hands as blood oozed out.

The naked warrior who first approached me somehow managed to escape. I saw his brown ass running in the nearby distance. I aimed to shoot him but the pistol ran out of bullets.

Blood oozed from nostrils from the warrior lying in the mud. He quickly got up from the mud ready for more. He faced me for a hand-to-hand fight, but my dog attacked him from behind. He turned around to fight the dog. He fell down face first as my dog stood above him growling. I quickly located my hunting knife and stabbed him deeply in his back. He got up on his hands and knees but wasn't dead yet. He stood up while staggering toward me. The look in his eyes was one of absolute hatred. I screamed because he stared straight into my eyes with a creepy smirk on his face. I took my knife and stuck it down his throat. I moved the knife back and forth until blood oozed out of his mouth in spurts. My dog was biting his ankles drawing more blood. The warrior looked at the rain, slurred something in his language, and fell to the side. His body made a plopping sound. I checked to see if they both were dead and so they were. The one who escaped was bait for wolves since they love the smell of blood.

The Lakota have a motto, "Woman shall not walk in front of man," but in a kill or be killed world, I learned an important word from Thorn in Moccasin, don't fuck with a Pikuni woman. Then I thought, Ki Yo!!! None of the Pikuni women walked in front of their husbands either! I felt stronger than ever before. I didn't have anybody walking in front of me.

Chapter 9-A New Place

I must have been quite a sight after the fight in the storm. Hair not braided in a mess, blown every which way by the wind. I undressed myself from my sopping wet buckskin robe. I took out another robe from my pack. I put both robes in the swaying prairie grass. One robe was made out of white cotton and decorated with ribbon and beads, the other a simple undecorated buckskin dress. I also took off my wool capote that I had worn since I left. I felt empty knowing that they were the only clothing items that I owned. I left them to dry. I rested in the wet grass as Natosi warmed me. The fanning flutter of flies kept me alert. I heard the echoes of thunder in the distance rumbling farther and farther away. I remained in the tall prairie grass in exhaustion for two days not eating or drinking anything. My cotton robe quickly dried in the bone-dry breezes. My buckskin robe was almost ruined by the storm. I pulled it into shape every so often as it slowly dried throughout the days I recuperated. My capote was still damp but I wore it anyway. It was my favorite clothing item decorated red, yellow, and indigo stripes.

I used my knife to shape the tree branches into poles. I searched for the horses of my attackers. I located them just on the other side of a hill drinking around a mosquito-infested pond. The high pitch buzz of mosquitoes annoyed me. I searched through the two dead men's possessions. I found pemmican and rope. I led six horses tied to each other behind me. I used rope for a dog travois. I got on top of the lead mustang. I drank muddy water from my container and continued eastward toward the Atsina.

I rode on the acquired horse feeling as if I owned the world. I thought about a story that I was told when I was a child. The Pikuni didn't have horses a long time ago. Through trading, we got horses from the Nez Pearce, Kootenai, and Salish. That was long before I ended up in this world.

When I was younger, allied tribes came into our camp to trade horses. Unwed girls on the verge of womanhood were forced to go into teepees or be punished. The foreign men were a mystery as we heard their voices throughout the camp. One day a chief allowed his unwed daughters to keep a comfortable distance around strangers. He let them continue to do work outside. Thereafter we all got to see outsiders finally. Other tribes who didn't want their women to be shown to outsiders conducted trade just a few short horse gallops away from camp. Far enough away, so their women wouldn't be stolen or hurt--as badly as I almost got hurt.

I thought about many things while traveling alone. My thoughts were often interrupted by my heartache and sobbing. I cried for many nights for the warriors I killed. I wondered if all of our warriors cried silently at night when they thought nobody heard them. Despite their bragging rights of being brave, I saw my father's tears glisten in starlight one night after he took a scalp. Not in a many moons would they ever readily admit grieving for murdered enemies. Even the American savages silently cried after they killed my people's women, children and old people. That shocking massacre we can't mention because of the hurt. I traveled even more cautiously than before staying very alert to wild animals or men. My hearing was becoming keen.

Maybe I would wander the empty landscape forever. I was searching for allies eastbound for two full moons. I realized that I wasn't going northeast to Atsina territory. They shared a part of their tribal territory with ours. The land was looking dryer and flatter, it felt foreign. I ran into a large river that I never saw before. I was lost. On each side of the big river camped eighty Apsaalooke teepees. My heart jumped from fear. I gently moved away and took several footsteps backward. I'm like a wolf, nobody can see me. The Atsina were due north instead. I missed that area by a long shot. It was days upon days before reaching their territory. I walked briskly away when several Apsaalooke 'Wolves', who were their lookouts spotted me. The earthen thuds of galloping horses sounded loud after being surrounded by silence for so long. I couldn't find a way out as six of them surrounded my barking dog, the mustangs, and me. My dog stopped barking, but let out a happy yelp and was wagging his tail, probably mistaking the Apsaalooke Wolves as people from my tribe. The yummy smell of roasting buffalo made Smoke Jumper happy and my stomach growl. One of the men made sign language telling me to walk behind them toward their camp. My dog followed with the loaded travois trailing behind him. A brave laughed at the old-fashioned display of my dog dragging a load.

Many eyes stared at me as I entered the enemy camp. Children stopped playing and stared at me in silence. Women stopped working and spoke in Apsaalooke amongst themselves. Eyes watched me following the Wolves as I stared wearily at the ground. One of the Wolves jumped off his horse and motioned for me to sit down by a campfire. Two braves came with rope lying me down on my stomach. My hands and feet were bound with rope. My dog was fed roast meat as I was tied. So much for a protector as my dog sniffed around me after he finished gobbling up what was thrown. He growled when the children tried getting near us. Periodically through the day, women and elders stopped to stare as through I was a wounded hawk tied to a stick kept on display for curiosity seekers. The smell of buffalo was too enticing. A brave came up to me waving meat in front of my nose. He put the meat to my lips, and then moved it away. A hunk of meat landed on the dirt. The sloppy sounds of a dog eating meat normally disgusted me.

A few elders, several men and women surrounded me and spoke about me. I saw their hands motioning about. Finally, somebody pointed to himself and patted his chest, "Blood

Shield," he said. He pointed at me. I said, "Dawn Red Sky." Even though they were speaking a foreign language, I knew what they were saying. I pretended not to know. They were negotiating about who would feed and care for me as I worked for them. My tribe had done the same. We adopted women and children captured from enemy tribes. A smiling woman came up to me and cut the rope. She led me back to her area motioning for me toward a ragged and fraying teepee. Her voice cracked with age. I went inside the pitiful looking teepee. The only items inside were two beds and a grown woman who looked at me with surprise. She tried speaking with me in her language that I pretended not to know. Their language sounded complex and twisting. There was no way I could move my tongue as she could.

The pleasant older woman put food in front of the teepee entrance and motioned for me to eat it. She patted her chest and said her name, "Waterfall at Night." Her voice was soothing and soft as a sandbank. Broiled buffalo was steaming on top of a buffalo shoulder blade plate. The smiling old woman served water in a mountain sheep horn cup. I felt relieved as I drank the soothing water. A life for a captive was going to be all work and no play. I saw the woman who fed me outside laughing with her neighbors just outside the entrance of the teepee. Her graying braids were past her hips. Nobody close to her had died for a very long time. Perhaps their tribal women never cut their hair in mourning. Her husband was inspecting the items in my bag. He was heavy and looked mean. He was trading my belongings with others in the tribe. I truly had nothing then making escape impossible.

Chapter 10-Work

The Apsaalooke territory was freezing cold. I spent most days shivering in discomfort all winter going down to the big river fetching water. Nobody wanted to go down there to fetch water because it was always colder near there. Damn cold air always blasted up the rippling water. The hollow sound of frigid wind blasted my ears. I had earaches all winter long. I led the horses to the water even in the deepest snowdrifts.

My days were the same without variation that winter. To my surprise I had begun liking their territory as spring was about to turn into summer. It seemed a little warmer earlier than where my tribe hunted. The winds died down just a bit. I still longed for brisk chilly Tipi Liner mountainous breezes blowing into the foothills. One thing I learned was that those people were very similar to the Pikuni in many ways. I yearned to learn their language better. Their name is Apsaalooke, but my people couldn't pronounce it like they did and it always came out as Absaroke. Perhaps they had different customs, creation stories, and a belief system, but plains people are plains people. The longer I stayed with them, the more I didn't understand why they were enemy to the Pikuni.

I spent much time picking up dog poop around camp. I just didn't do work for my master. Various members of the camp asked my masters permission to use me. Of course, it just meant more work for me. I wasn't allowed to participate in any gathering, singing, and dancing. I was expected to sit in the teepee when not working until a new task was ordered for me to do.

I didn't know why that grown woman shared my teepee. At first, I thought that maybe she was a captive who learned the Apsaalooke language. Her name was Bear Woman. She was homely and her nose was almost double the size of the others. From certain angles, she had an exotic beauty. I eventually gathered that she was an equal to the other Apsaalooke women. She made excellent moccasins with excellent quillwork. I tried to show Bear Woman that I was capable of doing quillwork too, since I was accepted in the quillwork society back in my camp, but quillwork was considered a privilege. Captives were not allowed to express their creativity in decorating moccasins or anything. Every night I heard the clicking sounds of her quillwork in envy. She told me not to make any or she would tell my master. I didn't want to get on her bad side. She was taking time to teach me the language of her tribe more fluently.

There was one big surprise I was about to reveal to everyone that spring. I couldn't hide my pregnancy much longer. I was eight moons pregnant. Nobody got close enough to me to really know. I wore my capote all the time. My heart fluttered every time I heard a baby cry. They probably thought I was just getting fat. My master Blood Shield had noticed that I lost my breath as I led the horses to the river with him. I pondered if Bear Woman wondered if Pikuni women ever had a monthly moon cycle. We shared the same teepee, but we never mentioned moon time to each other. One day Bear Woman came into the teepee and she pointed at my stomach. I finally took off my heavy capote after wearing it like a second skin. I was beginning to look ridiculous wearing such a heavy blanket coat as it was getting hotter.

I learned pretty well how to speak proper Apsaalooke after being engaged with them after so many moons. Bear Woman was also taught Pikuni by me. We had the agreement that she spoke to me in Pikuni and I spoke to her in Apsaalooke. We sometimes lost patience teaching each other's languages. We continued on though knowing we needed more practice. I rubbed my stomach and said, "Yes." She said, "Ho now! Good woman."

She went away with a big smile on her face. She came back and told me that she already told my master Waterfall at Night about confirming their suspicions that I was pregnant.

She told me in broken Pikuni about the plight of Waterfall at Night, "She now too old and make no baby. She try and try. She made husband want new wife. Then my blood parents drowned in Big River and me an orphan. Me was sad for many moons but Waterfall at Night adopted me. Me like a blood daughter to her." I tried correcting her speech, but it wasn't much help. "Now she sad because I no husband. Many men die at the hands of enemy, so I wait. One day maybe I marry. Give adopted parents grandbaby. Now Pikuni woman will give birth to adopted grandbaby in time," she said gently as she clasped her hands together and rocked her arms back and forth as if a baby was in her arms.

"I no choice. I give baby for them," I said in stunted Apsaalooke.

"You lucky because baby will be born and healthy. You're no longer a captive woman. New baby is part of the family and Apsaalooke people. Newest mother will be part of nation." Her usually somber voice lulled gently when she was happy.

We continued speaking to each other while helping each other translate certain difficult words while speaking a very general sign language that many plains people understood. It was good for trade when our tribes weren't fighting each other.

"I no like my baby," I said.

Bear Woman's eyes got big as if I said something very offensive.

"Baby father a bad man. A very, very bad man," I explained.

She signed to me that she understood and then loudly pondered, "Did you run away from your people? You have being forced to marry bad man you no want any feelings for?"

“No, I fell into gulch. My people left me behind. I tell you story already. Why do ask my past again?” I said feeling anger rise.

“Some women have ran away alone rather than marry of somebody without good feeling. I was just wondering that is all. I’m not calling you big liar. I feel women run away is better than killing self. Two women here have committed suicide who no want to marry Scabby Face. He feels bad. No more shall I question you and pry into privacy about your history before here. Your baby will call Waterfall at Night ‘grandmother’ and Blood Shield ‘grandfather.’ Such child will never know that he never is not of blood, but he grows up thinking he’s a real Apsaalooke man, not Pikuni at all. Pikuni are a profound enemy and he would be ashamed."

"I’m in thanks my child be grandbaby of two good grandparents is amazing honor."

"You Apsaalooke woman now," she gently lulled.

I nodded in thanks. I never became accustomed to sitting in the sparsely decorated teepee, while waiting for any member of the tribe to tell me to do something. Just when I thought about leaving the teepee to take a walk in the surrounding hillsides, a man peeked his head inside and ordered, "Dawn Red Sky. You watch my three young children while my wife and I visit friends and eat supper."

"No, you stupid thing! She’s an Apsaalooke woman now, go away," Bear Woman said just ornery. Her soft lull became grating while shooing the man away with hand gestures.

"It is wise that you should speak the Apsaalooke language for all future days. When you finally speak Apsaalooke people’s language pretty, you will become a real member of tribe," she said.

“Yes I agree,” I said while nodded.

“Bear Woman, I have sad secret, but you must not tell anybody the secret.”

She nodded, I took out a pipe, and we smoked from it. The sharp scent of tobacco sealed her promise.

"I was accused of infidelity by bad husband and sentenced to become cut-nose. I escaped," I said as I began crying.

"You poor woman. I have heard of tribes who do that, and even slice ears onto ground. This tribe different. A few women have cheated on husbands and no punish them. Even we sometimes whisper and giggle about it. Sometimes we sad about it. People go *teepee creeping* from one teepee to a different teepee because they got bad marriages. You're safe now," she said while giving me a hug.

Bear Woman left me for a few moments and reentered with a nicely decorated cotton blanket. It was soft and was better than the ragged and stinking wool blanket with holes that was used by me. I covered my entire body with the blanket welcoming warmth, comfort, and acceptance of the good people, the strong survivors known as the great Apsaalooke. I found myself feeling emotionally attached to them, for they didn't treat me with too much disrespect. I did my duties well and I think they liked that I was such a hard worker. It would've been a different scenario if I were lazy.

I never could be completely accepted by them as a true Apsaalooke woman if I didn't marry one of their bachelors. Two Lakota women were former captives who married into the Apsaalooke. Some men joked that those women didn't want to go back to the Lakota, because the Apsaalooke men were better lovers than the Cheyenne and Lakota combined. The Lakota women seemed content there.

Chapter 11-Smothering Hope

Everyone no matter how talented or disabled contributed in a plains tribe. It's a wonderment knowing how each person has a specific talent, whether an important task or just a little task. It made me wonder about our creator Napi having such power that he gave gifts to all people on Grandmother Earth.

My task was to be a translator between the Pikuni and the Apsaalooke. How did enemies trade? It was very simple to us. If they were in war paint with rifles at their sides, then they were a war party. If they arrived very slowly with no war paint, they were traders. The many goods and packages on their travois gave it away too, especially if a woman traveled with them. Blood Shield told me that he was a good trader. Several Pikuni traders were camped a distance away. He told me the next morning I was to ride behind him and four other Apsaalooke traders. I was nervous about speaking for both nations. Trade was to be good and peaceful with my presence. The people who adopted me didn't know the truth about me.

His wife woke us up the next day. We were to go out after a breakfast of potato and bone soup. I was happy to know it as my first official meal as a real Apsaalooke woman. Blood Shield asked to speak to his wife alone. They went into their teepee and came back with smiles on their faces. Waterfall at Night said, "We have been given good baaxpee (spiritual power) from the creator, first-maker Akbaatatdia, The One Who Has Made Everything. We have been given a daughter who knows how to work hard, who can translate, and will give us a grandchild. We have a gift to give you." Bear Woman came out of their teepee with a robe. I recognized it as my buckskin robe that was initially sold. They decorated my once plain robe. It was transformed into one of the fanciest robes I ever saw. The Apsaalooke really knew how to decorate their clothes.

The entire robe was dyed black. Six stripes were made out of quillwork. Those stripes were made from white quills that crossed the chest. Tan glass beads highlighted both sides of the white stripes. Shells hung around the hip area. Small shells dangled from a sash. Black ribbons went down from the waist to the bottom hem of the robe. I was awestruck. I was unable to do anything but smile with my hands over my mouth while staring at such a thing. Blood Shield handed the gift to me. His typical grumpy voice sounded jovial. I couldn't try it on, I knew, because my pregnant stomach.

Blood Shield prepared the horses for the short journey north of the big river. It took two men to hoist me onto the horse. Three men plus Blood Shield and I went to trade with the Pikuni. We rode slowly because they knew I was very pregnant. I hoped the Pikuni men weren't anybody from my camp. My stomach felt like a small sack of river rocks as it bounced on the horse. Sweeping sounds of cascading water came nearer. We slowly crossed a shallow area of the big river, too slow, not because of me. Because a prior heavy snow led to much melting drawing a steep springtime river.

We continued onto the other side beginning to gallop at a faster pace. My stomach bounced. I felt the baby kicking hard. I told the men to slow down. We located five Pikuni men resting in a circle around a campfire with their horses near them. I immediately recognized them as men from my camp. Packages and goods were already set out on blankets when we arrived. The Blackfeet had dried bull berries, dried huckleberries, and vibrant flower based powders. Flowers that only grew in the foothills of the Tipi Liner Mountains. We Apsaalooke had tobacco, shells, blankets and guns. Thorns in Moccasin, Beaver Teeth, and to my greatest unhappiness, that cutthroat Summer Fire were there. I gave a petulant and arrogant smile at Summer Fire who was so surprised that I not only survived, but that I was thriving and pregnant. My people helped me off a horse. We all stood facing each other while giving each other signals of peace. I said to Summer Fire in our language, "Your dirty lies have not killed me. I have become stronger than ever before. If you try to destroy me and my medicine, you destroy yourself."

He glared and looked sheepishly away.

"You're just a silly woman who thinks she can be like a man," he said. His deep voice was full of tension.

"I'm a warrior and a woman. Three brutal men tried to rape me. I killed two of them. The other ran away from me scared, like you should. The Apsaalooke found me and adopted me into their tribe," I said. My voice had a mocking tone.

My Apsaalooke counterparts stared in silent confusion. Even though they did not understand the language, it was obvious we were not speaking friendly talk.

"You don't believe me," I said. My voice began quivering with anger. He was the cause of my problems. I always carried a hidden buckskin necklace with a medium size pouch filled with tiny miscellaneous items. The buckskin pouch necklace was made by my mother. I usually carried berries, flowers, or such in it, but I stuffed snippets of two scalps inside. I undid the pouch and showed all the men the snippets of skin and hair. I was sure by the look of surprise on their faces that they never saw a woman present scalps before.

"Yes, I'm like a man, but I'm a woman too, twice the medicine, twice stronger than you Summer Idiot," I said trying to keep the dam restrained.

I threw the snippets of scalps over my shoulder. I clasped my hands and gave a serious look at them. Men kept scalps reminding themselves of victory. I didn't need such a thing. My throwing the scalps on the ground caused a stir amongst them. I didn't want to push my luck too far and cause a fight.

"I killed two men from unknown tribe. They attacked me before your tribe gave nice gift of new home," I explained to my fellow Apsaalooke. I repeated what I said in my mother tongue. I knew all the men believed me, but Summer Fire whined, "A woman could never do such a thing, they're too soft."

"We need to trade," I said letting him know nothing he said could ever say to me affected me. Blood Shield brought out a peace pipe. The men sat on the ground smoking tobacco and passed it around passing on the left hand side. When they were finished, I was handed the pipe and took some puffs. Thorn in Moccasin surprised Blood Shield by translating because he knew both languages, but the men preferred to ask me questions instead. He finally sat down on the ground rejected and not useful. The men smoked some more out of the pipe. Thorn in Moccasin asked to speak with me in private. We walked a short distance from the others. "Is your child Swift as Lightning's child?"

I answered, "Yes."

He wanted to know how the Apsaalooke were treating me.

"Perhaps they will treat me better after I have my masters adopt the baby as a grandchild. I'm now an Apsaalooke woman.

Two men onto a horse hoisted me yet once again after trading. As we left, I turned to see Summer Fire staring at me differently. He no longer stared in anger, or glared like a mean child. He looked at me with a look of respect. The Blackfeet gave us dried powdered berries and crushed dried flowers for paint. We gave them only guns.

I spent the rest of my days in pregnancy making little moccasins for the baby, resting and waiting. The sounds of children playing in the distance grated on me. I knew that I wasn't ready to be a mother yet. I was treated without high regard just as I suspected, being a former captive permanently kept me from receiving full respect. I had hoped the longer I stayed with them; perhaps they might treat me as fairly as they did the two former Lakota captives. I had doubts about staying with my adopted tribe for the rest of my life. Thoughts led me to think about fleeing to the Lakota. I heard their men were dark and handsome. The Apsaalooke women seemed overprotective of their bachelors and especially their married men. The bachelors refused to speak to me. When they thought that nobody was noticing, they were all red-faced smirks, eyebrows lifted and flirtatious. The married women were vicious. I tried to talk to a couple of the married men and I was physically pushed away by their wives. A couple of other wives got in between their husbands and me and said, "Go away!" I couldn't figure out why they acted like that, and I was a pregnant woman! Unless the Apsaalooke men lusted for pregnant ones. Aye jokes! I heard of stranger things.

I knew it was the day that I was to give birth. I felt different and lighter. I felt uncontrollable peeing. Then I noticed after peeing accidentally twice while in the teepee that my water broke. My back ached with each contraction with intense dull aching. I went out on my own to let a new life emerge from me. I didn't want to give birth in an Apsaalooke maternity lodge. Apsaalooke women had to walk through hot burning rocks right before giving birth. I think it was a shock to the system that made the womb pop out the baby easier.

I went as far as I could and I crouched in a patch of flowers underneath a lone ponderosa pine tree. The spring breeze cooled me as my face grew hot covered with sweat. I felt like my entire body was being torn apart as I let out a high-pitched scream. I never heard myself shrieking like that ever before. My ears rang from my own screaming. I felt a bit of regret, that I should have had the baby in the maternity lodge blessed by Akbaatatdia. I continued to grunt and breathe heavily and until I heard the horrible grating cries of my newborn child. I felt exhausted and relieved. I held the bloody baby in my arms. He was a boy. When he cried my entire world directed love toward him. He stopped crying as he suckled my breast. I slowly came back to camp cradling him in my arms. I was suddenly feeling heavy sadness that such an important life was all my doing. That helpless life depended entirely on me. I looked into his eyes and cried. He looked just like his father, so handsome and strong. My adopted parents laughed in joy. Blood Shield cut the umbilical cord as Bear Woman wiped fat on my baby and sprinkled buffalo chip powder onto his skin. My new child was wrapped in soft suede. I recovered in the comfort of my teepee.

I thought that by being a mother that the Apsaalooke women might stop viewing me as a threat to their men, but they still treated me with low regard. It was two days after my son was born. I was hoping to begin some quillwork on new moccasins of mine when I figured that somehow the Lakota women found a way. I didn't know how to be accepted by the others. I figured that they hated Pikuni more than Lakota. I immediately gave up hope of ever finding a husband. I was half-insider and half-outsider. Just when I resigned myself to a life of being forever single, my parents called me into their teepee.

"Those men came back later that day after we traded. They told our Wolves that they knew of your bad character when you were a member. They said you cheated on your husband with four different bachelors then you ran away with one," Blood Shield said.

"How could you lie to us? You told us you fell into a gulch and that you couldn't get out for four days, and by then, your tribe moved far onward," Waterfall at Night said.

"We're very disappointed in you. Not just one, but two of the Blackfeet men told our Wolves about you. Now word has quickly gone around to everybody and you can't be trusted," Blood Shield said.

"We don't want a liar creating disharmony here," Waterfall at Night added.

I was so angry about the lies that were told about me. It was surely the dubious work of Summer Idiot. I did my best in their language to explain my ordeal.

"The man we trade with named Summer Fire. We've hated each other since all the time of babyhood. He doesn't like that I have man strength. He has been jealous that I shoot arrows farther than he ever do. We had two fights as children. I beat him two time. That gave him bad words in tribe from girls. Then his father married me, which made him furious. His jealousy of me creates much imbalance boils him, he tried, now trying to destroy me by lies."

"My daughter how I believe you. Such lies has made our lives difficult these last two days. We're grateful that you provided a child for us, but you must go away," Waterfall at Night sadly said. I wasn't surprised that she told that to me. I knew something was wrong by the way the women acted when I was around them. They never acted so mean before the day we traded with the Pikuni men; they were usually nice but distant before the rumors spread.

"We have a white man who visits and has traded with us for many years. We know he's a good man. You'll be treated well by him. We've traded you for fourteen rifles. He saw you for only a few moments when he glanced out of a teepee and decided you were worth so much. That's good! Most women are worth only four or five rifles or a horse or two," Blood Shield said trying to sound excited.

"I'll introduce him to you," Bear Woman sadly said. I was sad knowing I was going to leave my adopted sister. She was my only true friend in camp. She went into another teepee. She returned with the paleface who had the exotic red hair color like the Frenchman I saw years before. I didn't like the hair on his face. He was also stinky. A weird black cloth covered his left eye under a cowboy hat.

"My sister, meet your new master, his name is Jack," she said with little enthusiasm. My parents looked conflicted as they stared at me from a distance. I secretly planned to leave the Apsaalooke after giving birth, but I didn't plan leaving in such a way.

"Howdy little girl," Jack said in English.

"Hello," I said in a weak girlish voice.

"Wowee. You know English," he said as he took off his hat and scratched his messy hair. His voice was deep and had a goofy tone. He grabbed my hand and put his mouth to the back of my hand. His lips felt slimy and his facial hair tickled. I shot my hand back.

"Gee whiz. I hope you ain't one of those feisty ones. It don't matter. I own you now," Jack said to me with a wink.

There was a long awkward silence. The sounds of horses whinnying in the distance over many conversations of the camp was all that we heard.

"When's the funeral? Everybody is so quiet and serious here," he said with a laugh. I didn't understand what Jack meant by asking about a funeral.

"Well little girl, we're taking off in the morning. So you get some sleepy eye."

He whistled as he went over to brush his horse. I gave my family a questioning look. They made their decision. I couldn't imagine Jack on top of me. The thought made me nauseous, not that he was ugly. He was just too foreign. I turned around noticing Scabby Face, the elder bachelor of the tribe. He attempted to marry five women with two committing suicide. His lustful stare alerted me of his possible intentions. Scabby Face received his many facial scars from being stabbed by a bone knife nine times in war, yet he survived. He began playing a romantic tune on a flute as he stared at me from a distance. The melody was dark and evocative. Two women giggled as they noticed his yearning stare. His scars were below his eyes, across his cheeks, and a big crevice divided his nose that separated his nostrils. I hurried into my teepee feeling grateful that being traded to Jack was probably luck instead. I made several empty sighs that night as I fell asleep. I was hopelessly lucky.

Chapter 12-Big One Eyed Jack

The day was drearily raining when I awoke. Birds were chirping over a newlywed couple arguing in the distance. The sweet clean smell calmed my trepidation about the day just a little. I remember looking at Bear Woman who was silently watching me sleep. She looked very sad that her sister and friend was leaving for good. Waterfall at Night said that Jack traded with them for many years. She hoped to see me from time to time when he passed through again. I moved forward to give her a hug. Tears streamed from both of us. As I hugged her, I realized that I would miss her the most.

"I'm going to miss the good speak about everything in the world late at night," she said.

"Thank you for speaking to me about Apsaalooke stories," I said.

We put our foreheads together as we lingered not wanting to leave each other. Life is too fragile; we knew there was always a possibility we would never see each other again. Deadly accidents were not rare living on the plains.

"We should be one big tribe," she said.

"Maybe one day," I said as faint as a distant wind.

Bear Woman went over to her adopted parent's teepee next door. She came back with an eagle feather. She put it in my beaded headband.

"I'm honored," I said forcing a smile.

"This eagle feather will help to the protection," she said. I laughed at how she said things in Pikuni. I spoke her language better than she spoke mine, because of the early lessons that Thorn in Moccasin provided me. I spoke English better than any tribal language, because my mentor was formally trained in English in a Jesuit missionary school. Since the Americans were the biggest tribe, he insisted on English lessons more than any other language. He said that it would come in handy more than I could ever realize. *We sadly knew that no matter what we did things were going to be changing in a direction we refused to go.* "Dawn, be prepared. I had a dream that if you learn from the white people. Get what you can from them, then come back and use their assets against them," he told me. He must have known I was going to leave one day.

I went to see my son one last time. He was cooing and shaking his hands. Everything in that moment wanted me to take my baby with me. He smiled as I looked into his eyes and I sobbed loudly. Bear Woman came into the teepee and had to physically lift me to stand. "Be strong. He isn't your child anymore, but he love you as long as the stars shine," she gently said.

"I know but saying goodbye….." I couldn't finish what I wanted to say.

I left my child to finish packing. The only material possessions I owned was a plain cotton robe that was a hand-me-down, and the fancy buckskin dress that I vowed to wear on special occasions. I was a modest sight just wearing the plain cotton robe for the trip that had muddy stains on the hemline. I was surprised a man wanted to trade me for anything. I put my fancy buckskin robe in a pack. I left the teepee with hesitation. Waterfall at Night looked down at the weeds. She carried some items saved for my trip. She handed me a blanket and returned my folded capote all tied with rope. Since white man was the Apsaalooke's ally, they had many white man goods. She handed me a metal canteen full of water with a strap that I wore over my shoulder. I also was given an iron cooking pan and a leather strap with a metal buckle. I tightened the strap around my waste so my frumpy robe looked more womanly. My family gave me lots of pemmican in buckskin pouches, gifts that lessoned the pain of my leaving. Pemmican was loved that much, even more than frybread. I remember when my people had frybread for the first time when a white trader brought his Navajo wife with him into our camp. She taught my aunties how to fry the flour with lard. The men liked their women cooking that bread more than sex. I vowed to never make any for the man who purchased me.

Jack was waiting to leave. He nodded at me and tipped his cowboy hat. I silently giggled just a little despite my departure sadness because he looked so goofy wearing his big shiny belt buckle. Why he exchanged some goods for that gaudy buckskin jacket with tassels I don't know, each tassel ended with a big glass bead of the colors red, white and blue.

He loaded a gelding palomino with packages on each side of the gorgeous horse. The larger packages were placed on his donkeys. The donkeys made their ridiculous hee-haws. No proper Indian wanted any stubborn donkeys. Only Bear Woman was standing nearby to say farewell. Waterfall at Night and Blood Shield were nowhere in sight.

"Dawn Red Sky, how much English do you know?" Jack asked me.

"I spoke it for eighteen of my years on this land, the interpreter of my tribe spoke to me since I was a baby."

"You'll be a nice asset to me in more ways than one. How many languages do you speak?"

"Five, mostly plains tribal languages."

"Five? That'll be helpful for me when trading, and it might just save our butts from being slaughtered, by both sides. You know I risk my ass now 'cuz now the American soldiers don't even want white guys like me going onto reservations without papers."

I didn't know what the hell he was saying, so he probably thought that I was a stoic silent Indian maiden. He was very animated. He had the clumsy enthusiasm of a child. I realized looking at him that's why we call the white man the

Napikowann, because many white men act goofy like our creator Napi. Such a name is both an honor and an insult.

"What languages do you speak little girl?"

"Blackfeet, Atsina, Apsaalooke, Salish, and English. I know Atsina a little. Not so good Apsaalooke and hardly any Salish. English really good. My mentor Thorn in Moccasin is a Cherokee half-breed adopted by Pikuni when he was a little boy. Then he left to be taught by Jesuit missionaries. He left after three years with them, because he don't like too many rules they have. He says their god acts really weird."

"Gee whiz, I want to be adopted by the Pikuni like him," he said.

"No! You can't. They usually only adopt women and children, not adult white man. They felt sorry for Thorn in Moccasin because he was a child. His white papa was going to Oregon on the great trail that leads to the grand water. He went to pick berries with his sister. They got lost. His little sister died. He ran into my people who thought he was all Indian not just a half-breed," I explained sadly.

"He taught you relate complex incidents well too. I say you're a well-spoken lady. Jesus, you're some little girl!" he said favorably under a deep and weaker voice. He moved closer to me putting each of his large hands on my waist. I didn't move away. We Pikuni didn't touch each other very often. Body contact amongst strangers wasn't taboo, but it wasn't common. I thought his moving toward me in a peculiar manner with his eyelids lowered like a sleepy bear was a custom of Napikowann men. I got a closer look at his orange haired beard at close range. I could not believe a face produced so much hair, even more hair than animals. Animal hair is short on their faces. His hair was long above and below his mouth. He thought I was leering at his mouth. He moved his face very close to mine and opened his mouth a little. Such a strange custom! I thought he was going to bite me on the face so I backed away.

"Oh. I'm sorry, but you're one of the most beautiful women the Great Spirit has ever made. I'm never around pretty women for months when I'm out trading," he said acting embarrassed as his face matched hair.

I couldn't understand why he was calling me a little girl. Maybe I did look like a little girl to him. I was going to turn nineteen winters old during the end of summer. Maybe childhood lasted longer for Napikowann? I guessed that Jack was only ten years older than I was. I turned around hearing a familiar cough. My Apsaalooke father joined my sister and mother who came to say goodbye. I couldn't believe they were making me leave with such a strange man. Although deep inside, I yearned to see what would be around the hills for me to discover. I've heard so many of our men speak about how the Napikowann lived. What they described was so different. Waterfall at Night and Bear Woman both looked very guilty. Now the Apsaalooke can pick up their own dog poop in camp I thought as Jack helped me get on a donkey. The children laughed and pointed at me sitting on the donkey. Jack stopped to untie two more donkeys that were tied to a post. Next to the post was a wagon with eight barrels. He lined his two donkeys in front of the wagon and tied them with rope.

We headed out of the camp. The smell of horseshit and pine wood scented fires slowly faded. Jack was before me in the wagon. I trailed behind the wagon on a donkey. His horse was behind me tied to a rope connected to the donkey that I rode on. I heard the distant wails of my son become weaker in the distance. His cries disappeared as we traveled around the bend of a hill. I wept tears in silence.

We headed northwest. Jack explained that our destination would be a trading post called Fort Benton that I already heard the chiefs speaking fondly about. Fort Benton was a trading place that brought much wealth to my people. Our men traded bison skins for provisions for many years until bison were hard to find. We carefully passed the Yellowstone River in a known shallow section. Jack yelled back to me that he felt safer with an Indian woman, that wanderers named Lewis and Clark would have been massacred by hostile Indians without their wise guide and interpreter Sacajawea. We settled the night at a place called Big Lake.

"We'll have to sleep together. We don't got enough bedding," Jack told me. I didn't want to share the bed with him without us taking a bath.

"You must bathe in the lake first," I said.

"Of course I will. Anything for you! I got a nice big bar of pine soap!"

He kindled the fire and set up an iron kettle for black soup. He smoked tobacco rolled up in little squares of white cloth. I thought the paper was made out of cotton.

"You have no pipe?" I asked.

"No ma'am," he said. He took out a harmonica. I never heard a harmonica before. I felt entranced by the tune he was playing. The tone of the harmonica was just a bit shrill for me. Jack seemed to enjoy my attention and company. I felt relaxed in his presence as he played the tune. I looked around at the lake seeing an opportunity to be alone.

"I must bathe," I said.

I stood up to leave toward the lake when Jack asked, "Dawn Red Sky, aren't you going to use any soap?"

"I don't know how."

"Sheesh," he chuckled. "Just rub the bar slowly on your skin. Rub slow and hard back in forth in places that feel really good," he said almost breathlessly. I took the soap and turned to go down to the Big Lake far down the shoreline so he couldn't see me naked. When he looked far enough away, I got waist deep into the water. I looked around carefully looking out for water snakes and monstrous beings in the water who grab people called suyi-tupi. I was hoping not to be attacked and dragged underwater. I wished that I had grabbed Jack's tobacco to offer the lake so I wasn't in peril. I looked over at Jack. My eyesight was almost like an eagle's and I knew what he was doing from afar away! I saw Jack looking at me through binoculars fondling it. I knew that Napikowann used glass to see farther. They tried to trade binoculars but we had no use for such an item, except Scruffy Hunter who needed glasses. However, he crushed them with his feet when the children pointed and laughed at him. I washed my body noticing many tiny white bubbles covering my skin. The lather smelled very sweet like the pine trees in the Teepee Liner Mountains, making me miss home. I went back to camp and drank coffee with him.

"You know about Fort Benton? They have big steam powered canoes taking your buffalo skins back east to the white chiefs. The fort will be a safe place for you and me. A friendly feller by the name of James Willard Schultz. He's loved and respected by your people."

"You mean Apikuni, that's his Pikuni name. I've heard about him. I'd be pleased to meet him."

"Apikuni is his name now, well I'll be damned. I'd be honored if I were given an Indian nickname. What would I be named? Rolls in Mud, Beer Hopper, Horn Dog. How many white men are given real red injuns names. How the hell do you say his name again?"

I tried to teach him to say "Apikuni" and "Pikuni" correctly, but he mangled those words, so I resorted to just saying the white man's name for my people, which is called *Blackfeet*. I smiled thinking of a name for him. He was so tall. He had a black cloth over one eye. I couldn't think of a name in my mother tongue that described him, so I blurted out, "You're Big One Eyed Jack."

He had a funny laugh that was like the hee-haws of his donkeys. "I've already been called Big One Eyed Jack after I had the accident and had to wear this. You need to get more creative lady. Okay, I'll accept your name. Darling, it's official, my Indian name is Big One Eyed Jack. Maybe soon you'll find out that my Indian name does accurately describe me to a tee." He stared at me with a playful smirk. I blushed and had to look away from him.

"Sheesh it's hot. I'm going to take a bath," he said. I looked around. It was a cool evening, not hot at all. Gosh, he's crazy I thought. He took his soap and a pail and went to bathe, although he chose to bathe too close. I was forced to see all of his pale skin. I stared at him as he covered his body with white creamy bubbles of soap. He rinsed himself off with the pail of water. He turned around and smiled at me. It felt like I was younger when I first spied on the men bathing in the river. I noticed his penis was slightly pinker than the others were. He came back with no embarrassment and got dressed in some funny red clothing. Red cloth covered him from just below his neck to his ankles.

"Why are staring at me so strangely?" he asked.

"You look like a man berry," I said. He frowned in confusion for a moment then smiled. "Oh, my sleeping clothes. I'm wearing a union suit. I don't know why they're manufactured always red. Don't you have any nightclothes? Pajamas?"

"What is pajamas?" The word sounded strange to me, it didn't seem like an English word.

"Sleep clothes," he said.

I then realized white man had separate clothes to sleep in.

"Oh, I see. No."

"You sleep naked?" he eagerly asked.

"Yes, or we sleep in whatever clothes that we want. Why separate clothes? When we sleep, we're still awake, just in a different world. Why dress up strangely in red cloth to visit that world?"

"I can't answer your questions because you distract me in a nice way. You're a sweet dream," he said deeply and quietly as he leered at my face with his sleepy bear look again.

He ate pemmican as he watched me comb my hair. Then I watched him fetch his pail from the lakeshore. He filled it with water, placed a bizarre metal knife by the side of the pail. He took out a looking glass and stared at his reflection. He took out scissors and began to cut his beard and hair on top of his head to a shorter length. He put fluffy white cream on his face with a brush that had a wooden handle. The brush looked like it was made out of horsetail. He used the weird knife to skin his face, almost as if he was going to scalp his own face off. He dipped his knife smeared with cream into the water pail. He did this very carefully while staring into the looking glass. I realized that he was shaving his face. Our men used shells and fat to shave. He took out a jar and put what looked like sweetly fragrant grease and wiped the grease into his hair. He looked better with his hair slicked back. Soon after, he rinsed his face with water. I finally saw his face without hair. I remember thinking how handsome his face was.

"Big One Eyed Jack, your blue eye is pretty. Too bad you have the other one covered with that black cloth. You're handsome." His eye was blue like a clear sky. His face fur around his mouth distracted me from it before.

"Why thank you missy," he said genuinely touched. We ate pemmican as Natosi set. Geese were migrating northward. We played a game of counting geese to get us sleepy. They flew deep into the evening in V formations. Their honking above echoed against the clouds. The smell of fresh sage grass in the plains always reminded me how sacred the land is. The stars came out looking like the inside of a black cotton cloth bag with quill holes letting in tiny points of sun. Our galaxy The Wolf Trail looked like a faint but giant cloud of fog floating but it refused to move.

Chapter 13-Moose, Rivers and Mountains

Jack got tired of yelling back at me while I rode on the donkey while he rode on the wagon in front, so he had me sit beside him. He tied a rope to his horse and a rope to his donkey behind us. We passed places by day that I never saw before. I knew I was back on Blackfeet land, but even to us Blackfeet, there were many desolate places. We passed over the gentle swiftness of the Musselshell River. We avoided a few hunting parties of Cree that we saw far off in the distance in the Judith Gap area. Jack said that we were between the Little Belt Mountains and the Big Snowy Mountains.

I felt like crying when I saw the bluish purple mountain ranges again; they're like a family that I haven't seen in many moons. I was not with the Apsaalooke long enough to know if they ever traveled near mountains. We crossed the Judith River. I saw some familiar hills. A giant hill looked like a breast. "Titty hill!" Jack laughed. I knew we were getting back into the heart of Blackfeet territory when we saw the Highwood Mountains somewhere east of a waterfall called Great Falls. All English names given to such places explained by Jack.

"Why such a name as Great Falls? Do great men fall and drown there?" I asked.

"You're a funny Indian squaw," he said.

"I'm not a squaw. I'm a Blackfeet woman! Don't be rude." I couldn't understand why he thought I was making a joke about the big waterfall down the river from the cascading springs.

"Well, I'm sure some great men do fall over if they spend too much money on women and liquor in all the mining towns out west, and on gambling in the rowdy saloons too. Sheesh fall from grace."

I didn't know what fall from grace meant, but according to his tone, I could tell it wasn't a good thing. Firewater might hurt those who are great if they weren't careful. Maybe that's what was wrong with Summer Fire, he drank too much whiskey at one time. He got ill health in the head from it doing permanent damage.

"Does Firewater make you sick forever? I once drank whiskey and I was sick the next day. Am I permanently damaged?" I asked.

"No, just the next day you feel like hanging yourself if you drink too much. I got some gin packed with me. Do you want to make camp and drink some with me?" he asked.

"No," I firmly said. I made that mistake once and I vowed never to make the same dirty mistake twice.

We camped at Arrow Creek. There were a bunch of willows where I decided to pee in. I turned a corner and saw a moose and her calf. I froze like a tree and tried concentrating on a butte way off in the distance. I imagined myself as a snow rabbit trying to stay hidden in a snow bank from a hungry mountain cat. I heard Big One Eyed Jack whistling a song that he played on the harmonica as he filled the water canteens. He found me just a moment later and stopped. We both stared at the moose in fear. She had the calf behind her. Everybody knows that a mother moose is the most dangerous animal of all, for when she stands on her hind legs, she stands almost as tall as a teepee. One running on her hind legs can weigh down with hooves crushing a frail human. We waited out the standoff. The mother and calf carefully moved to our left at a comfortable distance for her. When they were far enough away, Jack hugged me. "I can only do so much to protect you," he said.

Many days later we traveled by the pretty lakes just before reaching Fort Benton. We camped beside Shonkin Lake. The next day I felt comfortable enough to bathe with Big One Eyed Jack. He was singing a cowboy ditty. His goofy voice transformed into a husky singing voice. I was really starting to like being with him. The smell of him was familiar, the scent of tobacco smoke in his hair, skin washed by pine soap. He didn't hear me coming from behind him as he bathed. He turned around and smiled. By him trying to be a gentleman, but floundering just a bit, I was slowly warming up so much that in time I naturally became hot.

I had the novel idea of lathering his body with the soap and he lathered mine. He said that all masters and their traded women bathe together. I cleaned his body gentle and slow. He told me to soap every part of his body. I wasn't accustomed to cleaning every corner of a man. I asked him to lather every part of my body. He lathered every part of me that made me blush a couple of times. In return, I lathered every intimate crevice of him, and he went "whoa!" I took a pail of very cold water and rinsed him off. We both stood naked waist deep. Our bodies instinctively pushed together. I shivered not from coldness but from the intensity of the moment. He moved his mouth forward but his mouth opened as if he was going to bite me. I frowned and moved my face away from him.

"Why are you acting like you want to bite me?" I asked.

"Oh, now I remember what I was told. I'll explain a Napikowann custom. We move our faces closer, slowly while staring into each other's eyes. We press our lips together for a little bit. Then we put our tongues into each other's mouths while gently rolling our tongues around. Then if you want, we move our tongues around faster to get all giddy," he explained.

"Why?" I felt so confused because my people didn't have a custom like that.

"Because we like each other."

He put his arms around my shoulders. He moved me toward him and gently pressed his body against mine. Our lips touched. His lips were softer than I ever imagined a man's lips to be. His tongue felt warm and wet. As we moved our tongues faster, he gently bit my tongue. Not hard but soft and quivering. It made me moan. He nuzzled his lips on mine a little rougher, and then he gently nudged the tips of his teeth on my bottom lip with a loving bite. Normally biting hurts, but he knew what to do with his mouth that made me finally respect him, and therefore the people of his heritage. I knew that I would never ask him to return from where he came from as I felt the grooves of his tongue rubbing against the grooves of my tongue. He moaned and I felt the subtle vibrations of his moaning while his mouth connected to mine as the perfect fit in this world. I was willing to please my Jack in any way he desired as we stood in the chilly waters of Shonkin Lake. The cold water balanced our heat in a combination of temperatures that made everything equal.

Chapter 14-Apikuni

I was ready for some company after being with Jack and nobody else for two long months. Fort Benton was called the center of the territory of Montana. I was excited to see it. Lodgings were made out of big thick tree trunks connected together as we finally got to the fort. My man said they were called cabins. We passed a stockade of logs and rode by a large wooden doorway. The smooth and soothing scent of dried wood was everywhere but blowing dust had me sneezing. Jack ordered me to secure animals at the adjoining corral. We walked inside the lodge and smiling behind a bureau was a white man.

"Apikuni, it's been so long since we last met," Jack said.

An older man with long scruffy hair like an Indian was filled with mirth and life. He was the great trader who everyone in my tribe spoke highly of.

"Why Jack, what happened to your eye?" Apikuni asked.

"Oh a long story, I have an Indian name just like you now. My name is Big One Eyed Jack. My woman gave me my name," Jack said as he pointed at me.

Apikuni looked at me with surprise. His eyes widened as his eyebrows shot up.

"I suppose your name sounds accurate enough, although I suppose she would be the one who knows," he said as both men laughed.

A native plains woman came in. I immediately knew she was Blackfeet. Not all tribes looked the same. She was tall for one thing. Blackfeet are some of the tallest plains people. In addition, she wore a beaded pin of the butterfly cross. She smiled and waved at Jack, took one look at me and smiled in recognition.

"My woman's name is Dawn Red Sky. I traded this darling woman for ten rifles from the Apsaalooke," he bragged, "She was adopted by those Apsaalooke but I got a great deal. She's Blackfeet just like your wife."

"Fourteen rifles!" I corrected him.

"Oh yep, fourteen."

"Fine Shield Woman meet Dawn Red Sky. Have you two ever met before?" Apikuni asked us.

"Yes, during the sun dance a few times," Fine Shield Woman said. I immediately felt at home being in the presence of a pleasant and well-liked Blackfeet woman. We immediately began speaking in Blackfeet while the men caught up with their shoptalk.

"What happened to you?" she asked.

"Some horrible things," I sadly said. I felt pain by having to relate my events to her, but I continued, "There's this dark spirit by the name of Summer Fire."

Fine Shield Woman winced, "Oh I don't like him. He has this hateful sneer and he insulted some of the women in my band with rude remarks at the sun dance."

"I'm glad you told me that, so it won't be difficult for you to believe that we've hated each other since birth. He doesn't like me because I'm literally stronger than he is. I have beaten him in two physical fights."

We both laughed hysterically at that.

"Then I hugged another man while married. I don't love my husband Swift as Lightning. Summer Fire lied saying that he saw me making love to Scruffy Hunter, but you know me, I would never do that."

"No never!" she sarcastically said. She wasn't convinced.

I laughed a second, and then I gave her a serious look. "Summer Fire even got a child to lie to the elders on his behalf."

Fine Shield Woman shook her head in disgust.

"I sensed my husband wasn't quite sure about the accusation, but such an accusation hurt his pride. He should have just returned me to my parents demanding a return of goods, but he didn't. I escaped from being a cut-nose. I fought off a rattlesnake, defended myself from three plainsmen who wanted to hurt me. I ran into the Apsaalooke. They treated me well, but lies were spread to them from Summer Fire too. They didn't trust me around their men, so they traded me to Jack."

She gave an amusing look to Jack and then gave me a sympathetic look.

"I'm sure he's treating you well. We know him well here. We've been trading with him for many years. He's an honest man. My father traded me to James, then James married me and our people respectfully named him Apikuni. Look how successful our life is by owning this trading post. I'm sure you and him will do well together too," she said while giving us a look of tenderness.

"Well, it would be a fabulous day for a feast," Apikuni announced.

Chapter 15-Western Bound

The next morning I ate oatmeal for the first time, which I didn't care too much for. The dirty white sludge had the charm and taste of cedar chips. Fine Shield Woman put some honey in it and stirred. The sweetness made the muck palatable because I ate three bowls. I found it more convenient to eat with a spoon rather than scooping it up with my fingers. We drank black soup for a time. I noticed the trading post to be lifeless. Jack told me earlier that there might be many people at the trading post with a buzz of activity. I knew Fort Benton was an important trading post for the Blackfeet. I was hoping to maybe see some people from my tribe. Fine Shield Woman was the only Blackfeet woman and the only Indian I saw there. Apikuni mentioned that business was getting slower since the peak was when the Blackfeet had many buffalo hides to trade.

We were ordered to help unload Jack's stuff. Once the very heavy loads were taken off the donkeys, Apikuni counted eighteen sawed-off rifles. My man traded all those guns for a bigger tent covered wagon. He got two more barrels of whiskey, now the total was eight barrels. He also got more provisions of sugar, dried meat, coffee, tobacco, cartridges, dried beans, and canned preserves of fruit. Fine Shield Woman explained to me that the guns were going into the hands of Blackfeet. They gave many animal hides to trade for guns. Apikuni said that the Blackfeet were attempting to get a stockade of guns. He related that treaties are always signed between two nations as allies, but the Americans acted like traitors and that was why the Blackfeet were getting militant. He shipped the hides back east where animal hides were difficult to find. Fine Shield Woman explained that the big game escaped west like many of the eastern tribes.

I gave Fine Shield Woman a hug hoping to see her again. She gave me a happy wave goodbye as I climbed into the wagon. Jack tied two of his donkeys side by side in front of the bigger tent covered wagon. He placed his horse and other donkey in back. He said that the terrain would become more difficult. Each donkey would take turns pulling the bigger wagon so that they each have to pull and to tag a long alternately and not get overworked. His palomino was his prized possession. He treated that horse by the name of Sage like a child. I turned around; the black square shapes of Fort Benton slowly became one with the landscape.

I enjoyed riding in the tent covered wagon. The wagon afforded me relaxation and privacy, and perhaps a false sense of safety and security since I didn't see outside. Nevertheless, it also felt like I was in a bumpy teepee that moved. I did ride in front from time to time sitting beside Jack as we talked while soothing breezes swept through our hair.

We were following a white man trail named Mullen Road.

"This road goes all the way from the plains beyond the foothills and deep into the mountains. Once we get off the road, we'll be hitting some difficult land until we make it to a town called Helena. I need to dicker the whiskey to a saloon there. A man will give me lots of money for the barrels. Little girl, your mind is going to be swept away because I know you ain't seen a town. Helena is downright an ace-high town."

I heard descriptions. My curious mind imagined manmade cliffs with white people in their foreign attire walking between square dwellings. Wagons driving over mud everywhere. I was getting excited about it.

"The white chiefs over yonder. They want to send your children to a Napikowann school. That ain't right to kidnap children. Ten years ago in 1867, the white chiefs said it was okay to steal your Indian children like your men steal horses," Jack suddenly said.

"They want to take our children? How horrible! How horrible!"

"Well, sort of, they want to teach your children American customs."

"Why? We have our own customs already. Why force your customs on us? I've seen some of your customs, they're not better than Blackfeet customs. Your customs are different but not better, sometimes worse."

"I agree wholeheartedly," Jack said, "but," he hesitated, "Your culture has some seriously bad issues with your warriors' love of war and violence with other tribes, intertribal warfare."

"And the Americans don't love war! We aren't ignorant as much as you would like to think we are. We know from traders that there was a big war back east between a southern tribe and a northern tribe. Thousands of men were lying dead on the ground there, so tell me about my people's love of war again."

"I can't understand why we can't all just speak to one another, but we're still half vicious animals I guess. Too many men are downright cheats and belong handcuffed in the darn calaboose," he said in a voice that shone some light in me.

"I don't want a man who fights. I want a husband to live a long life so he can make love a long time," I said.

"You're my type of woman," he said as he placed his palm on the back of my neck rubbing it for a short time.

"Yaw!" he whipped the donkeys. We moved swiftly westward.

Chapter 16-Last Chance for Love

Jack was getting angry because we ran out of Gayetty Therapeutic Paper that he bought in Fort Benton.

"Ah shoot! Where's a darn Sears Roebuck catalogue when you need one?" he asked the sky miserably.

"Just go in the streams and rinse afterward," I suggested in amusement.

"What do I do when we aren't near water?" he snapped.

"Then use this," I said. I started to collect the velvety soft Mullen leaf and he didn't complain after that. I told him to use snow when it got cold. Jack also ran out of tobacco. I got some kakasiin, known as bear berry leaves, drying them for him to smoke. I felt love for the plants remarking that they were not only good for a smoke, but I couldn't wait for the bearberries to ripen so we could eat them. Rattling Butterfly showed me how to prepare kakasiin as a tea to help us if we became constipated, because we always ate so much dried buffalo. I also missed the bull berries that grew along the Missouri River. Bull berries were sweeter than bearberries. All around us were riches. Jack had no idea what riches were around when needed. He was lucky he had me traveling with him.

My tribe never went beyond the first few mountains of the Teepee Liner Mountains that the Americans called the Rocky Mountains. I had no idea that the mountains went on forever and how beautiful the scenery. It seemed the deeper we got into the mountains, the prettier the landscape became. Pine scent permeated the air and our clothes. Small streams and waterfalls passed us by. Water seemed the chatter to the trees as it trickled. I discovered a new paradise. I smelled sweet grass sacred to many tribes for smudging ceremonies and basketry. The valley bottoms had golden meadows of grass like in the prairies. Pine trees covered the mountains until meeting the blue snow at the peaks of the mountains.

"Do these mountains go to the grand water far west that some have spoken of?" I asked.

"Nah, we thought so at one time. We looked for a rumored northwest passage through the mountains, but explorers Lewis and Clark let us know it ain't true."

We were getting bored traveling so much. We really didn't speak that much being entranced by the scenery. After two weeks, the scenery was getting boring. Jack started to get goofy and sometimes crossed his eyes at me or made squinty faces. Finally, he asked me to tell him a Blackfeet story. I began to ramble on about my life: "I always tried to be a virtuous woman. Most people strive to be virtuous, man or woman, but there is a very strong reason for a woman to be pure. We see the most moral woman at the sun dance. That's when the Blackfoot Confederacy comes to camp in one place when the days are longest. We gather when the serviceberries are ripe. We call it the all tribal gathering. We all sing, pray, dance, trade, and invite friends from other bands to eat. Within the all tribal gathering is the sacred sun dance. The Great Spirit shines the longest that day. His name is Natosi. Each solstice we are renewed and that comes about in social ways. To be social balances all the times a person goes within to pray and sing to Ihtsi-pai-tapi-yopa, translated it means the essence of the creator. A person can't just have only isolation to learn about life."

"What?" he asked.

"A person must balance being alone and being around people," I said.

"Oh," he nodded.

"I learned healing from a medicine woman named Rattling Butterfly. She told me about the wisdom of spirit beings. Most spirits are beautiful, but some are tricksters and like to try to joke. Some are like your ghosts, lost and confused. They were mean in life because they were lost while living too. Every smart girl wants to grow up to be a holy woman. We do so by making a public vow after we grow up, but it's up to the others to petition the elders during the all tribal gathering. Only one wise and virtuous woman is allowed in the middle of the sun dance. My grandmother was a medicine woman and I wanted to be one just like her. She was lucky enough to be chosen to be in the center of the sun dance. Among hundreds of teepees and dancing people, my grandma had her teepee located right in the middle of the big camp that was in a circle. My grandparents made an offering to the Great Spirit of one hundred buffalo tongues. My grandparents fasted for four days to purify body and soul. When the fast ended, an arbor was erected. Right in the middle stood a center pole. People put offerings of cloth on the pole. Natosi sees those offerings and hears the prayers too which always gave us a good year. Our sun dance is the dance to Natosi. It lightens all our days."

"That's real neat," he said.

He looked at me with a smirk, head cocked sideways. "You speak a pretty language, too bad I only speak cowboy." He placed his hand on the back of my hand rubbing it before grabbing the reigns.

"Did you know the sun is married to the moon and their child is the morning star?" I asked.

"No, but have you heard that the Great Spirit had a son by the name of Jesus. This Jesus feller had sacrificed himself on the crucifix to cleanse the sins of mankind?" he asked.

"Ho! White man's superstitions, you people are so imaginative," I said in laughter.

"It ain't superstition, it really happened," Jack angrily said.

"I'm sorry, but my mentor Thorn in Moccasin is a half-breed who was invited to go to boarding school so he knows. He told me that when he went away, you people always saw your religion as right, right, right, but that dangerous attitude leads to killing, killing, killing," I said repeating the meaningless of such arrogance.

"Maybe the word of Jesus is supposed to be the law of this land and all people, including all the Indian tribes, the entire world should be guided by him," he said.

"Believe what you want, but I won't murder you or disrespect your people because you think differently. I'm not a warrior of your soul. I was just joking about your Jesus god. Perhaps the Great Spirit did bring forth a son for all people to worship." I knew that would shut him up for some time.

We remained quiet and contemplative after that tense moment. I realized that even though Big One Eyed Jack was handsome, he was too different from me in both mind and spirit. The warmth I had for him faded a little. Perhaps our passion wasn't able to grow into a fond love. I wasn't feeling sad about that. He was taking me to a place called the Last Chance Gulch or Helena. There was to be many like him when we got there. I had to grow fond of him despite his different religion. I wanted to see their sacred lodges with paintings of the medicine man named Jesus. I was going to tell that to Jack, but when I glanced over as he drove the wagon, he looked ornery. Thorn in Moccasin said white men act strange and mean when you start questioning their religion and debating facts about Jesus. I didn't want to push him further away.

"You might like the Catholic Saints. There are pictures and statues of them in churches. They're like medicine people that you can pray to, like Saint Mary, the mama of papoose Jesus," he said breaking the silence.

"I'd like to see such a medicine lodge called the church," I said.

"Then we actually might have something in common," he said in a bold manner.

He stopped the horses and we kissed, a kiss was the holy blessing that was needed, why any other? Cleansed we traveled to Helena.

Chapter 17-The Cosmopolitan West

Jack told me even though we were in an official territory. Some people referred to the land beneath us as Montana Territory, or just plain 'ol Montana. Others called it America or both. He said some people wanted it as a separate country and others wanted it as another state in America. I had a hard time calling this land America, because it meant it wasn't Indian country no more. Even though I taught myself to say America as Jack and I spoke while traveling, in my heart this land will always the Blackfoot confederation called Nitawahsi. Nobody could ever take that away from us.

It took twenty-six days to get from the foothills to Helena. Squares and more squares were everywhere! The white man town had so many of them in the distance. More horses and curved tent buggies. People were walking on a dusty road that entered Helena. The sounds of people talking and piano music from the beer halls welcomed us. The rank odor of horseshit was everywhere. The gentle hearted sweetness of the mountains was slowly left behind.

"Shoot! I was getting all balled up back there. It ain't right for two people to be alone all the time. This town sure looks grand!" Jack said in joy.

The town was placed on the side of a steep hill. Hillside camps didn't make sense to me. A camp that did not pack up and move should be on flat land. The houses were big and were painted different colors, green, pink, but mostly white. Many of the houses had signs with symbols on them by the entranceways. Some buildings were very close to each other. Some had only narrow spaces for one or two people. Other buildings connected.

I compared what I saw to my Blackfeet camp. The teepees at home were well spaced throughout. We did so for privacy because even quiet voices were heard clearly through bison skins. A few Helena houses were made of square stones but most were made out of split timber. That was probably why they were so close together, because it wasn't easy to hear through such materials. Everything in the white world seemed to be square. Square carved rocks, square entrances, square windows, and square signs. I heard children laughing through some of the openings in their dwellings.

Jack glanced over at me from time to time checking out my reaction to the new environment. The buildings were not as tall as a buffalo jump that Thorn in Moccasin told me about. I gasped at the strangeness of the five-tiered building. I couldn't believe people lived on top of each other like that. Ho! There were white birds on the ledges of their homes. "This is so different," I told Jack. Ladies held fans and parasols. They were dressed in material from neck to feet. We Blackfeet had fans made out of eagle feathers. Many of the women wore black dresses. A few had brightly colored dresses. A couple of their hats looked like they were decorated with real flowers. New flowers that I never saw before. Jack stopped the wagon on the side of the road and tied his donkeys and Sage to poles. There was a metal tub of water where the animals drank.

Two Helena women passed us by. Their shoes mad a clump-clump on the wooden boards that were on the side of the dried muddy street. They glanced at me and nodded but continued to rush, in fact, everybody was walking fast. A woman hurried with her children. I saw four black men as Jack led me somewhere. I only saw two black men in my life when they passed through camp to trade. Jack said they were descendents of escaped African slaves. I found them to be quite lovely like the shimmering night sky. The twinkling sweat on their foreheads was like stars shining. I heard strange tongues. I knew immediately that English wasn't being spoken.

One. Two. Three. I counted three languages as we walked the wooden plank walkways that lined the streets. Dried mud was everywhere in crumbling bits and pieces.

"Are there many tribes here?" I asked Jack.

"Yes, about half of the people in Helena are from distant lands from way across the big water. So far, I heard German. Even though it sounds like they're speaking a different language, I heard a couple of Scotsmen. Those two with long beards over there are speaking Yiddish." He held my hand as we walked. He told me to wait outside an entranceway below one of the manmade cliffs. He went inside. He came out moments later with a pronounced frown.

"Damn. The hotels are all full," he said.

I didn't ask Jack why a man wore a tall round hat with a flat top. Several men were wearing glasses. I made a mental note to bring glasses back to Scruffy Hunter if I ever returned home, and if I became his wife, I would make sure he never stomped on them. I was saddened at remembering his face. Jack left me again at an entranceway to somebody's home. I stared at the unfamiliar white birds as I waited. He came back and happily said, "We gotta room at this fine hotel."

He led me into a fancy big room. "Sit on this sofa while I get the wagon and the animals. I need them to hanker down in a secured corral. A thief might steal my whiskey and horse if I'm away for too long. Honey, I won't be gone very long. I'll drop half the liquor off at the saloon. I'll sell the rest throughout the week. When I return I'll take you upstairs."

I sat on the sofa of the fancy room. I didn't care that I had to wait. So many fabulous things were in that large room. Jack went to where a man stood behind a bureau. He spoke to the man who was dressed in black and white with a red butterfly looking decoration underneath his neck. Jack pointed at me. The man nodded his head once he saw me. Jack went outside.

I studied every little detail of this strange new world. A campfire was lit beneath a high wall of river rocks placed on top of each other. Fresh and fragrant varieties of flowers were in colorful and beautiful glass tubes that looked like upside down teepees. A few fine ladies chatted quietly in the corner while smiling. My eyes stopped at a white haired man who was sitting on a sofa staring at me. He winked. I smiled and nodded at him. He opened his mouth and his tongue waved at me. I looked away not knowing if I should wave my tongue back at him. I was going to ask Jack about that custom. I stared at lights with glittery jewels and golden horns hanging from the ceiling. The ladies passed me by smelling quite flowery. I noticed the white haired man was limping into another room while using a stick with a curve at the top for balance.

The smell of cooking food came from somewhere. More men and women came into the lodge speaking to the man behind the wood bureau about "rooms." A big thick rug on the floor, the biggest I ever saw, was placed under tables and sofas. It had fancy swirly patterns. I wondered what the fancy shapes meant. I was a newborn seeing the world for the first time. I recognized a sharp looking chap in a familiar cowboy hat and buckskin jacket. Jack gave green papers to the man who talked to everybody. He gave me our packs and we both went up some fascinating wooden planks up a passageway. The planks were like the level ones outside that many people walked on, but each plank was higher above than the one before.

"What are you stopping for? Oh. These are stairs, they get us higher in the building," he told me. We went into a long room that seemed to go on forever, it was skinny, and on each side had many doors. We got to a third entrance where he opened a door with a key. He told me that keys were the ultimate symbol of being in a world of too much. We went inside a smaller room with a bed.

"This room is great," Jack said.

The bed was covered with a fuzzy blanket that was colored a bluish white, like the color of snow in a winter night. I ran my fingers over it, it felt so soft, a new sensation."

"Well I'll be darn, look here," Jack said. He led me by the hand to a big bucket.

"No more bathing in streams. This here is a wash bucket. I'll have a maid come in fill 'er up with some pails of hot water!"

"Wow, this is like a home for the Great Spirit," I said.

"Holy shit we got a chamber pot in the commode as well!"

I stood in the corner for a while, while a maid came inside and dumped several buckets of steaming hot water in the wash bucket. She was sweating and looked sad. "I'll help you," I said.

She looked confused.

"No ma'am. Me and another one empty your dirty water with them buckets tomorrow, now you be all fine standing in the corner. Don't get near me now," she said.

"This is how the rich white people bathe. You should be good for another month after this. An Indian like you is mighty lucky to be with me," he told me.

A month? I knew that I was going to be looking for a stream before the month was over because it was stinking summer.

He asked me to get undressed. I took off all of my clothes. I submerged my body into the pleasant water and relaxed. The smell of steam was light and subtle. I got out of the bucket and stared into the chamber pot. I liked it better than the outhouse shitter that Fine Shield Woman taught me to use because the chamber pot had pretty roses painted inside of it.

There wasn't any sewage deep in a hole either, just clean and clear water. It was made out of some sort of shell material.

"Jack, where does the poop and pee go?" I asked.

He laughed which confused me. "The maid empties it outside."

"We're lucky we got this here mansion turned hotel. Seems the owner went bankrupt before the mansion was finished. Only fancy places have such luxury, otherwise you'd be running outside pissing in the moonlight again."

I returned to lounge in the bucket again. I smiled as the steam was rising which clouded the looking glass, or what Jack said was a mirror. Later after I dried off, I went into the other room and Jack was already undressed. He went into the bucket and bathed in my dirty water.

"Don't get dressed. We'll sleep in the bed together without clothes," he said.

I was confused, what about the red pajamas? I assumed that he only wore pajamas while sleeping outside and wore nothing while sleeping inside.

The bed was super soft and the pillows were thick. It was more comfortable than the creaky and lumpy bed at Fort Benton. A painting of a cowboy hung on one wall. The walls had fancy swirly designs the colors of deep blue and huckleberry. A glass oil lantern was on a small wooden table beside the bed. A fancy chair was in a corner made from the same fuzzy material as the blanket. A decorative vase, explained to me from Jack as with everything else, was in the corner. Jack came out of the smaller room dripping wet. He gently pressed himself on top of me and started to kiss me.

He asked me if I wanted to try a different way of making love. I said "yes," why not everything was new. He put a pillow in the middle of the bed. He had me lay on my stomach. He put his strong hands on my hips and hoisted my hips up a little. Normally he put Vaseline on his dry lips but he rubbed it inside of me instead. As he entered me differently, he told me, "This is the way we don't make a papoose." I jolted from intense pain. He kept on telling me to relax for a long time and patiently kept at it. I was absolutely relaxed by the hot bath that eventually it felt beautiful and different just like everything else around me. Perhaps it was even more pleasurable since he seemed even more concerned about being gentle and slow than ever before.

Chapter 18-A Woman Changed

Jack went downstairs early the next morning and came back later rubbing his tummy. "I'm so hungry," he hollered. "Darling, don't do any cleaning, the maid will do it for us," Jack said.

"Then what am I good for?"

Jack didn't answer me but just leered with a smirk. I sang a Blackfeet song while I attempted to make the bed very neat like the way it was before, but it didn't look the same. I had trouble adjusting some of the unsightly ruffles. Some moments later, a man knocked on the door. Jack answered and the man rolled in a small cart covered with a beautiful white blanket. Two silver bowls were upside down on top of two plates. A red rose was in a cylinder. Jack gave the man a silver dollar and thanked him. We rolled the little table near the hanging blankets that were lit from outside. I stared at the long vegetable that was on the plate. Jack poured a bowl with steep sides into two small cups made out of shell-like material, and to my eagerness, it was black soup. I looked around at all the strangeness, nothing was real. Nothing was natural anymore.

"What's this?" I inquired as I picked up the deeply hued vegetable.

"It's a plum," he said. He took a big bite of the vegetable and smiled as the juice ran down his closely cropped beard. I took a bite. The taste was sweet, but not too much; it was very pleasant like wild berries. Then I realized it was a fruit.

We finished breakfast. I noticed a second painting on the wall. This one was of a woman in a white gown lying in a field of daisies. She was staring at puffy clouds. I didn't like the painting unlike the cowboy painting hanging on the other wall.

"Why is the painting messier than the other one?" I asked him.

"Don't know. I wouldn't be surprised a fancy hotel like this has a residential artist sent straight outta France. That cowboy right there is a velvet oil painting, American cowpoke art, yes sir," he was used to explaining everything to me by then.

Jack told me he was going to buy me some clothes. We headed down the tiered stair planks out of the hotel. We walked along the street while Jack seemed skittish as white men and women passed us by. I noticed two Salish men and a Salish woman passing us by. They were dressed in their traditional clothes. I turned around and they were lost in the crowd of white people. I passed by another Indian. I think he might have been Nez Perce because I had never seen that sort of tribal clothing before. Jack said the name of the store we were on our way to was called Last Chance Dry Goods.

We went inside seeing if there were many items to trade. The room looked similar to the trading room at Ft. Benton. Only the dry goods trading post was much larger and with more clothing. The scent of new clothing was of clean crisp cotton. The new clothing had a faint odor of something natural, like pussy willows in a marsh during an autumn breeze. Fresh and light. The shop was void of dust. There was nothing natural and dirty about the shop. Jack told me to wait near the front entrance. He walked up to a very fancy lady who wore a lavender colored dress which had me missing the early summer fields of lavender within the Blackfeet nation. She wore a necklace that hung around her neck of big round white beads reminding me of smooth large hail. Jack was quietly speaking to her while she glanced at me while nodding. She came over to me gently leading me by my waist to stand beside a wooden chair near big mirrors.

"We're going to measure your size, and then we'll have you pick out a dress to your liking. I'll have my seamstress making you look like a refined lady, if that's possible," she said. I didn't like the tone of her voice.

She took out a strip with markings. She put it around my body in several places, and then she put it sideways from my feet to my neck. She took out a pencil and wrote something on the paper.

"What's your name?" she asked me.

"Victoria," Jack said for me.

"Oh how marvelous, that's such a classy name," the lady said as she smiled at Jack. She didn't seem to see me at all.

"Now look at some of these dresses and pick the one you like best," she told me. She pointed to dozens of dresses hanging on a sideways wood pole beside the big mirrors. Some of the dresses had flowery designs, others had fancy swirly designs, and some had simple patterns. Most were one color. I pointed to the one I liked best after touching and inspecting several of the garments.

"You like colors. So many women who live in Helena like black or grey, good for you. Let the Indian princess have the periwinkle dress with chartreuse trimming," she said to a weasel looking man who was hurrying around the store.

"You'll look even more beautiful than before, you'll be an envy little girl when I'm through with you today," Jack said.

I pondered my white name for a moment. Vic-tor-ya, I repeated it to myself in my thoughts. I considered it an honor to have a white name, probably in the same way Willard Schultz liked his name Apikuni. Victoria sounded pretty.

"Come back this afternoon and she can try the dress on, and if she wants to, she can wear it out of the store," the woman said. Jack went over to the weasel looking man and traded money with him.

Afterward Jack took me back to the hotel. He said that I should wait for him while he went to a saloon to gamble.

"Don't go anywhere," he warned me as he pointed a finger at me lifting his eyebrows under serious eyes.

"What shall I do alone in this room?" I protested because I yearned to explore more.

"Talk to your spirits or sing. Rest my darling. Learn to be relaxed, it's all right good to be lazy once in awhile."

"We Blackfeet women are never lazy, we don't like lazy people."

"Then stare out the window and count clouds for Christ's sake."

"Window?" I asked.

"Yes window! Any 'ol white lady would be fine and dandy in an ace-high hotel like this. You don't know how lucky you are." He seemed amused at having to show me to do things for the first time, especially the night before in bed. He pushed apart two blankets that covered a wall. That is where the glass on the sides of the buildings was!

He tipped his silver flask upside down and swigged whiskey. "You can watch people walk down the street. There're so many types of people from distant lands," he waved his hands making a sign for water. "You might find Napikowann interesting when they don't know you're watching them. Shoot! There are a few fellers who are odd sticks standing around on that street corner over there, so don't answer the door when a stranger knocks unless she's the cleaning lady. It's hotter than a whorehouse on nickel night now since I restock whiskey town. Look at that bandito right there loaded on the whiskey since it's Friday. Dang it, every frickin' day is Friday when we have warm weather in Montana! I might be loaded as tick on liquor so don't stay up late waiting for me 'lil girl."

I peered out the window. I was high above people all right, but all I saw were hats and swinging arms, not interesting to me at all. I wanted to go to the saloon too. I saw two cowboys arguing with each other, they entranced me. I didn't hear Jack leave the hotel room.

He came back as Natosi was shining his brightest; he was stinking of whiskey coming from his breath.

"I plumb forgot. We need to pick up your dress," he said.

We hurried like all of Helena. The trading post lady was busy showing dresses to two women when we arrived again. She told a younger woman to get the dress.

"You can put the dress on in the dressing room," she said.

"Go into the tiny room and put on the dress," Jack said pointing to the littlest room I ever seen. Another woman went into the room with me to help.

"Be patient, we know you're new to wearing clothing like this," the woman said. She was very nice as she slowly told me the names of the clothing. "These are stockings." She put the stockings on me. "The garters keep your stockings from falling down to your ankles," she put straps on my upper legs. "First the underskirt, now a bustle," she tied a frilly half-skirt with no front strapped around my waist. She put on a top on me that she called a chemise. Finally, I was completed with a skirt that draped me from the waist down to the ground. I stared at my tight sleeves that had loose lacy cuffs. I turned around seeing lacy ruffles behind me. "This is a corset, repeat after me, core-set," she said. I repeated, "Corset." She put it on me standing behind me tightening it.

"This isn't comfortable, why are you making it so tight?" I asked.

"I'm tightlacing it. Nobody likes wearing this but they make us look womanly." The woman took out a strip of material and put it around my waist, "Good. Nineteen inches is almost adequate."

Just when I felt like I couldn't breathe, she tightened the corset even tighter. I began taking shorter breaths.

"Annette, are you almost done dressing her? I have two other customers who need to try something on," the trading post lady yelled.

"Almost," Annette yelled back.

"One piece princess dresses are coming into style. You might want to buy one because this fancy dress might be too much for you. You need to get your husband out there to buy you an evening dress," she said inspecting me from head to toe. I looked down at ruffles decorating me just below my neck.

I walked into the big room. The older trading lady was standing by the weasel looking man as he held a hat. The weasel man smiled for the first time, "Your gentleman friend helped me pick this fabulous one out for you. This accessory should go with the dress because it's cream, a neutral color," he lisped. He put the hat on me. "Das senorita manifique!" he gleefully said placing his hands on his hips with a little swish.

"Nice try Elmo, you ain't sounding international yet," the lady barked at him. When she smiled the paints on her face cracked, as she looked me over. He gave her a bitchy look and then proclaimed as he gestured to me for Jack, "Such a classy woman now more than ever before. She's as frilly and fluffy as a wedding cake! This one is so pretty. She'll be betrothed in no time flat, even though she's an Indian. Look at yourself in the mirror," the weasel looking man said happily in a fake and slightly nasal tone of voice. I felt like I was a doll and the trading post people were enjoying dressing me up. I gasped as I stared at a woman in the mirror. Nothing seemed natural anymore. My braids stuck out below the hat and my tan skin contrasted with such clothing. I didn't know what to think or say.

"You really should get rid of those braids," the younger woman said.

"We're going to get her some shoes and her hair done," Jack said.

"Well good luck, she's off to a good start," the older lady said.

We went back outside. Jack rushed me to another trading post. He said the shop was called Rosemary's Mercantile. We went inside and I saw little packages and brushes. It smelled quite musty like an old teepee that was abandoned with moss growing on the insides. Jack spoke quietly to another lady. The lady looked at me with a very surprised look. The shop was very tranquil. A little girl was playing a beautiful tune on a piano in the corner.

"Of course I will do her face. Honey, we're gonna paint you up like an English rose. You'll be as sweet as the Queen Mother," she said. I was asked to sit on a stool in front of a round mirror. The lady took out little boxes. She began applying paints to my face. She explained that the lipstick went on the lips. The eye shadow shouldn't be brushed too heavily above the eyes. She took a pencil drawing a small line around my eyes. I looked at myself in the mirror. I was startled at the changes.

"She's a little too tan. I'll get some powder." She took out a puffy feather like cloth. She dipped it in white powder and she put it carefully on my face.

"There, now you're even more beautiful than before. Last but not least, let's pin your braids up inside your hat. Don't look into the mirror just yet," she said as she fussed with my hair. She finally asked me to turn toward the mirror. The transformation was complete. I didn't know if I really liked the person who stared back at me. I didn't recognize her. I put my palms up to my cheeks to see if it really was me.

"She doesn't seem to really like it," the lady said to Jack.

"She might just be in shock. All this might be too much for her in one day," he said.

"Honey are you okay?" she asked me.

"Yes, I think so," I said. Jack traded some money with the lady. She put the boxes of powders and paints into a bag.

"They're all yours. You're so lucky with that guy, he's rather cute. What's his name?"

"Big One Eyed Jack," I said.

"Oh my," the lady said softly as she looked him up and down. He smiled, he was proud of his real authentic red Injun name. The lady's face flushed crimson. We passed a saloon while back on the busy street when Jack said, "Hold on" and went inside. He came back out moments later smelling like whiskey. "We're going to get you some shoes." A white man with an Indian woman almost passed us by, but he yelled back to us.

"Jack you wild boar!" the man said. Jack stopped, turned around and smiled.

"Howdy, it's been a long time," Jack flatly said.

The Indian stared at me, she did not look away. She was Salish from her clothing. I felt ashamed of my appearance and looked down at the wooden planks.

The man put his hands on the Indian woman's shoulders. "She's my wife. She's a Salish maiden. Don't laugh at this; she's sensitive when I introduce her. Her name translates as Dirty Bunny," he said.

"This is Victoria Redsky, she was a Blackfeet woman," he introduced me.

"Oh she's Indian? I couldn't tell," the man said.

"Yes, I picked one fresh off the prairie." They chuckled at that.

"What happened to your eye?" the man asked referring to Jack's patch covered eye.

"I got in a fight doing some business back east," Jack said, twitching slightly.

"Oh I see," the man said in suspicious tones.

"Well, we're getting set up to go to the Bitterroot Valley eventually. We're camping just outside of Helena right now. I'll probably see you in one of the saloons tonight," the man said.

"Will do," Jack said seeming rather uncomfortable.

We began walking away toward the shoe trading room when I asked, "Old partner of yours?"

"Not really, we used to do crazy things together when we were younger. I thought a posse would have hanged him by now. A cutthroat that can't ever be taken seriously; his name is Bobby 'Guns' O'Riley." My eyebrows rose. I felt angry the way the Salish woman stared at me as if I was a monster who emerged out of water. I looked away from Jack and refused to go any farther.

"What's the matter?" Jack asked.

"You're ashamed of me. You don't want anybody thinking you're with a Blackfeet woman. You're trying to make me look white," I said very angrily.

"No, I'm just trying to civilize you."

That statement made me feel even angrier.

"I'm not your wife. I don't care how much you said you traded me for. I'm leaving town, and I don't care if I die out there. I survived once and I can do it again," I began walking away from him. I knew that even though I couldn't see the edge of the Napikowaan town. If I continued walking in one direction, the wilderness appeared. Jack followed behind me trying to get my attention to stop.

"I bought you a dress, bought you some makeup, and this is how you thank me? What about the Cherokees that took a white captive and forced her to dress like a Cherokee? When in another culture, do like them. It's only good manners. I felt like you might respect and understand America if you dressed like one. Those clothes are so beautiful, I felt they were a gift worthy of a beauty such is you."

That last statement stopped me. I turned around and started to smile, but I felt like crying inside. Jack's face was one of genuine concern. His one dewy eye looked like a lost puppy.

"Thank you," I said.

We went into a shoe shop. The man inside was surprised that under the hemline of my dress revealed two moccasins. The shopkeeper looked at my face and upon closer inspection realized, I was an Indian. The slight twitch in his eye told me.

I walked out of the store wearing brand new white women shoes. They were comfortable but felt more constricting than moccasins. I heard the familiar hard clump-clump on the plank boards outside.

I loathed any return to the stuffy hotel room again. There was nothing to do but stare out the window while Jack went outside to do his business. I thought about how I felt when I was in the Apsaalooke nation. How my masters made me sit in the teepee all day unless asked to do a duty. I sighed as I breathed in the stale dry air of the room. American dwellings did not have enough fresh air, and the corset was smothering the life out of me. If I sat by the window for too long, I felt like fainting. I reclined comfortably on the bed. Lying down was the only position that felt comfortable. I soon fell asleep.

It was nighttime when Jack came back into the room. He had three wrapped presents held in his arms.

"Missy wake up. I got you some gifts," he slurred. He was drunk.

I sat up clumsily due to the awkward clothing on my body. He sat on the side of the bed. The sharp smell like whiskey was below a stronger tobacco stench emitted from his clothes. “Gosh it’s stuffy in here,” he moaned. He opened the window letting in fresh cool air. The daytime sounds of horses clopping down the street and people speaking to each other gave way to crickets. He kissed my neck briefly as he placed the packages between us. Three packages were wrapped in brown paper. I tore open the largest package. Inside was a black article of clothing made out of the some fuzzy soft material. It was soothing like the blanket that covered the bed. “That’s velvet to be worn. It’s used in those curtains, on that oil painting, on the bedspread. Mighty fine material for a fine looking lady. Now I won this dandy thing here in poker. I guess it was meant to be. A fancy lady at the saloon told me it's a pendant," he eagerly said.

He put the necklace dangling the pendant on me then quickly rubbed his whiskers into my neck. They tickled. I pushed him away and stared at the glittering diamonds in the mirror. I felt grateful for such beauty to be worn. I looked powerful and full of dignity, just like the painting of the lady on the wall. Jack handed me a second package that I tore open. A fancy bottle was inside.

"Perfume, press the button at the top of the bottle. It's lavender water to keep you smelling like the springtime."

I pressed the button on the top. Water sprayed the scent of lavender onto my breasts. I breathed in and closed my eyes. The scent was as if I was standing in the middle of lavender fields just below the glacial mountains. I opened the smallest box and inside was a diamond ring.

"This ring means that I'd like you to be my wife," he knelt down on one knee.

"Will you please marry me?"

He had a puppy dog look on his face. I couldn't resist him.

"If I can be your only wife, then yes, you can be my husband," I said.

He smiled, "White men can only take one wife. Some down in Utah have more than one wife though. Hell one man and one woman together, that's normal for us. We prefer it that way."

He put the ring on me and to my surprise it fit well. Then I remembered that the lady at Rosemary's Mercantile put a couple of rings on my fingers, but Jack didn't buy anything there. He must of went back and picked one out. Jack threw me against him, but not too hard, just enough to surprise me. We kissed the longest ever; in fact, we kissed the entire night without making love. On and off we kissed and only stopped when Natosi was rising outside the glass. Jack went over to close the curtains to block the sunshine. Goodbye, Natosi. I was shivering from the chilly springtime morning air that wafted over the bed from outside. He held me as we slept all morning keeping me warm. We forgot about breakfast and lunch. One never thinks about food when busy making love off and on all day.

Chapter 19-A New Friend

I woke up alone the next morning. I lounged around before dressing again in white woman clothes. I didn't look good in the dress without having to wear that damn corset. I wished I didn't leave my ordinary clothes behind in the trading post the day prior.

I fumbled with the corset realizing a second person had tied the back of it. I took the soft velvet blanket that was on the bed wrapping myself in it. I sat by the window waiting for him to strut up the street.

"Hello. Misses breakfast is served," came a husky voice from the other side of the door.

I felt suddenly shy wearing nothing but the blanket around me. I ran into the tiny room with the commode beside the wash bucket both emptied earlier that morning.

"Enter the room," I said to the servant.

The familiar rattle of the plates entered. I heard his breathing as he stood in the room for a moment. The door shut. I came back into the room. I lifted a silvery dome cover on top of the plate. I saw round cakes and a little glass container on the table. The glass was filled with something that looked like dirty tree sap. I dipped my fingers in the goo. I remembered that Jack and Apikuni poured the sap over flapjacks. The coffee tasted good between the bites of mushy sweetness.

Jack finally returned smelling like cigar smoke. He started eating breakfast looking at me with his bloodshot morning whiskey eyes. I decided that if I was going to have to live as a white woman did, Jack had to help me understand a foreigner's culture. Therefore, I began with, "What is that flat thing beside the wash bucket?"

"It's a chaise, where ladies like to lounge naked waiting for their husbands to come home."

The day was stimulating as we talked about white culture. I learned many new phrases, concepts, and how to correctly say words in the manner of a woman of finery. Jack told me that a local church gave lessons on how to read. He looked at me sheepishly and said, "I don't know how to read." He looked ashamed. "We'll learn how to read together," I said. He seemed to feel better after I told him that.

"The professions I worked in, well I just didn't need to know how to read. I only had to do some math and use a lot of muscle."

Jack reminded me that there were many new speakers of English in town. He explained that if they were not embarrassed to ask the meaning of a phrase or word, then I shouldn't be. He said that some people were offish, that they were stumped about having good 'ol fashioned manners. "If they're rude when they answer your questions, it's just petty American snobbery. It reflects ill of their upbringing and heritage. Even if they are soaked in money most Americans came through Alice Island dirt poor so they got nothing to be all uppity about."

Most of the concepts I understood easily, but some I had difficulty. Since I couldn't understand everything completely, I knew that I had to experience much myself. Jack seemed tired at explaining such a complex tribe as the Americans and said, "I told you just about everything I know, but then I'm just ignorant about many things myself."

It was just past dark as we ended our discussion on American life and living, when Jack said he desired for us to eat at a fine restaurant. He was just as confused as I was about how I should get dressed in complicated white women's clothing. He was quite frustrated as he helped to dress me through trial and error. "Jeez, it's easier to get ladies undressed then dressed," he complained.

Once outside I felt like I could breathe again in the open air. I felt nearly invisible when dressed in Blackfeet clothing, but everybody stared at me dressed in American clothing. They were staring at me with admiration. Jack was proud that he was with a beautiful woman. Not only was I more beautiful than most Indian women were, but also most white women. I was told only once how to apply makeup. I practiced the prior evening and found it quite easy to put such paint on my face. I wanted to look poised and confident, a woman Jack deserved. I was off to a good start being a fiancé to a rich man.

The restaurant had rather charming flowers and candles illuminated everywhere. There was an inside campfire, Jack corrected me saying it was a fireplace. There were framed paintings of landscapes hanging on the walls. I stood motionless as I marveled at one of the paintings. Then I realized what Thorn in Moccasin meant when he said, "white man's teepees grow together like a web of rocks." The painting of the majestic city at the edge of water intimidated me. Jack noticed me staring intently at the painting. "New York City," he explained. I thought the town of Helena wasn't very big. Thorn in Moccasin once told me that he heard from traders that many towns grew as fast as mold on the bottom of an old wild turnip. I was concerned that cities that huge covering an entire island with squares would overtake Indian country.

Velvet lined the booths, in between the booths were translucent white curtains. I held my posture proudly as we were ushered to our seating places. There was one problem. Both of us didn't know how to read. We decided to point out the selections on the menu.

The waiter came to us and said, "Hello my name is Bruno and I will be your waiter for tonight. Our two international specials are Beef Bourguignon served with a baguette. Chicken Cordon Bleu with rosemary potatoes, and for dessert La Gateau Crème de Parisienne. For the domestic special we have prime Montanan Angus steak, buttered corn, and mashed potatoes with freshly baked buttermilk rolls, ending with Indian pudding for dessert."

"I'll have that Frenchie grub," my man said. The waiter blinked in confusion staring at him. "You know, that fancy beefy chow for me and the chicken for my lady. I can shoot any 'ol cow and sizzle a steak so forget the American stuff. Hey, is it real Indian pudding from a tribe?" Jack asked.

"No sir, I think it's just a name. Would you like anything to drink?" the waiter asked as he took our menus away from us.

"Any type of wine you got! Any wine is good wine," Jack said letting out a hefty laugh.

The waiter looked surprised. He didn't seem to know what to say. "I'll let you try some Merlot," he said cordially.

Jack looked at me sheepishly, "Well the menu is probably half in French. So we both wouldn't understand it if we knew how to read anyway."

The restaurant was full by the time the food arrived. Most people sat at the tables that were near the fireplace or the windows. I enjoyed the booth we sat in, it felt more private. People were staring at me. A couple of women giggled.

"Please eat with utensils," Jack said.

"No, the fork scares me, it might cut my tongue. You never cared if I used a fork until now," I said suddenly becoming insecure as a man pointed at me.

"It's unsanitary to eat with your fingers," Jack said in a whisper.

"I've never been sick when I ate Buffalo with fingers," I said.

"You know and I know that the white world has brought new illnesses to your people. Think, anybody, even here at such a pretty restaurant might have a sickness," he warned.

"Oh, I see. Very well." I tersely repeated what I heard a refined lady say earlier. Indeed, I tried to be quite restrained at my first attempt at being proper, mimicking a trading room lady's tone of voice and subtle elegant gestures. I clumsily picked up the fork skewering a potato cutlet while trying to take a dainty nibble.

Threat of disease did for me. I used cutlery ever since that day. We went back home and Jack derived pleasure at helping me undress the complicated layers of clothing. We then fell asleep exhausted in each other's arms.

The next day I awoke to an empty bed again. I expected Jack to come back from the saloon where he mentioned he sold the barrels of whiskey. The day began well with breakfast delivered again. Then the day dragged on until evening without him returning around noon like before. I stared out the window looking for a familiar cowboy hat. There was no sign of him at all. I began worrying. I decided that even though I was dressed in only bloomers covered by a blanket. I decided to go downstairs to the front desk to ask the wise man who answered all questions. He who operated the front desk seemed to be one of intelligence. He gave me the weirdest look as I walked up to the front desk.

"Ma'am, did you accidentally lock yourself out of your room?"

"No, we don't lock it. Have you happened to see Jack anywhere?" I asked.

"Mr. Jack Scheel in room 241, no."

"He never told you where he went?"

"No, is everything all right?" he asked showing me concern behind wire-rimmed glasses. He was enunciating his words to me. He asked me to repeat myself because I think my thick accent confused some people at first.

"He usually comes back around noon," I said showing him my worry.

"I'm sorry. All I know is he does some business, maybe he got busy. I'm sure he'll be back. Listen. News goes around quickly here in Helena. If something bad happened to him, we would've heard about it by now. Did I already tell you that you speak very good English? How long have you been speaking it?" he asked.

"All my life," I said. I frowned out of concern for Jack unable to accept his compliment. I began missing my prior mentor Thorn in Moccasin who taught me so much in ways of communication and languages. I felt closer to him knowing he spent so much confusing time with white folks just like me. He told me that I would never fit in with white folks. I believed him wholeheartedly that moment.

I went back to my room feeling uneasy. I barely slept that night. I kept on dozing off feeling around the bed for him. I began to think that a horrible accident happened and nobody knew about it. I visualized him being run over by a horse carriage. He was bucked off a horse landing roughly and breaking his neck. Jack told me about the unlucky men who were kidnapped in saloons and sent as slaves on pirate ships over the big sea to the Orient.

The sun was shining brightly the next morning and said, "Jack," he still wasn't there. The breakfast man knocked on the door. "Come inside," I said. I didn't get out of bed. I was curled up facing away from him. He told me, "Mr. Jack Scheel didn't order any food this morning, so all I'm bringing you is the complementary continental breakfast."

I said "okay," Jack told me just to say okay when I didn't know what to say. He said people usually responded nicely to that word.

That morning lasted forever. I wanted him in the room and on the bed absolutely at that moment and not a second longer. Each breath away from him felt like my breath lasted forever. I began thinking in delirious terms. Jack will come into this room after fourteen breaths. I took fourteen long deeply hopeful breaths. Jack didn't come. I took a silver dollar that was on top of a small table. I saw what Jack had done before with a coin that resulted in small prophesies of sorts, if the coin lands on the face side, then Jack was safe. I flipped the coin and it landed on the wrong side. I tenderly wept as gently as a feeble wind. I sensed an elusive pain, not merely a worry, but a dark haunch of misfortune.

A knock came at the door. "Come inside," I yelled. "Jack?"

"Hello?" an older lady's smoke hazy voice came from the other side.

"Come inside," I said.

A gray haired woman came into the room. She had very kind eyes with a compassionate smile on her face. She smelled like roses, probably rosewater I thought. The scent of flowers contrasted with my aching heart. She went to the window opening the curtains. She turned around and gently smiled at me standing beside the bed. She sighed as she gave me a glance up and down.

"Honey, I bet you're sick with worry. Let me clear up any misgivings you may be having about Jack."

"Jack, do you know where he's at?"

"Yes darling, let's just say he's in a safe place at the moment. We better get you dressed so I can take you to him," she said with a frown shaking her head slowly from side to side.

"Please hurry," I told her as she helped me dress.

"Not so fast, he ain't going anywhere soon," she said as she laced up the back of my corset.

"Don't leave any valuables in this hotel room because this is the last you'll see it."

I walked around the room taking one last glance around where I felt so trapped. Just as we left, she said, "Oh, by the way, I don't mean to be rude," she put her hand out for a handshake. I just stared at her hand not knowing what she was doing. I thought only men shook hands."My name is Gerta

Gundersunn. Consider me a new friend." I hesitantly shook her hand.

We went outside. I felt that white women spent too much time inside their dwellings. Maybe that was why they were so pale. I felt better when I smelled fresher air. The warm sun was shining brightly on my face. We hurried down the street toward where Jack was.

Chapter 20-A Fork in the Road

We went into a building where some men looked like the soldiers who traversed the plains keeping an eye on us Indians. My particular band avoided them at all costs. Two men were standing near a desk wearing identical boots and clothing. I noticed they both were wearing silver stars on their shirts. I suspected the stuffy building was the place where the bad people were put in cages, but not my Jack, he did not seem like a criminal! He seemed like a very honest man. There was nothing cutthroat about him.

"What could I do for you?" one of the men asked.

"Officers, we're here to visit a Mr. Jack Scheel," Gerta said.

The interior of the room was simple and sparse, very different from the hotel and mercantile. The color was a drab green with just a desk and a long wooden chair.

"Yes, ma'am, he's been expecting you," the officer said.

He led us beyond a thick metal door into a dimly lit passageway. We stood in a booth. A caged wall separated us from the other side of the room. An officer led Jack from an entranceway past the booths. Jack had his wrists connected together by two metal bracelets held together by a chain. That chain reminded me of how my hands were connected when I was a captive, although my wrists were tied with rope. He spotted me right away giving me a look of remorse.

He sat down on a wooden stool on the other side of the caged wall. I didn't like the black iron bars. He said, "I'm very sorry Victoria. I'm in here because I robbed a bank in Chicago before coming back to Montana. I figured I wouldn't be found it being so remote here, but I was wrong. Lots of army has come here to make law and order, not only in the towns but also especially for the Indians. I had it planned out so well. You see

Victoria, I lost my eye from a gunshot fired from a policeman. The bullet just nicked my eye but it still became infected and a frontier doc had to get rid of it. I got away with a grand sum of money. I used the money to buy barrels of whiskey at a trading post and sold it to saloons. I'm mighty sorry to tell you this, but where whiskey goes, I flow. That is how they found me, drunk as a skunk."

"Whiskey gold. Miles City has a population of two thousand people and sixty saloons, the entire dang town singing well into the night," Gerta added.

"Somebody must have ratted me out," Jack said to Gerta.

"You told me the only person who knew you were back in Helena was Bobby 'guns' O'Riley," She said.

"He'll do almost anything for a buck. I hope he enjoys the reward. That four-flusher fucker is the one who got me here in this dreaded Calaboose," he said.

He looked at me for a very long time. Tears welled up in his eyes.

"Victoria, I'm going to be in a cage for a long time. You can go back to your people, or you can leave with Gerta. She's a nice woman who will look after you."

"But of course," she softly smiled.

I felt like a black thundercloud was above my head and miniature lightning was burning points into my skin. I knew that I couldn't go back to my people risking the wrath of Summer Fire and his dad. I felt like I had no choice but to go with her.

"I will leave with Gerta. Is she my master now?" I asked.

She looked at Jack, lifted her eyebrows, and laughed heartily at the ceiling. Her mouth opened as she was at a loss for words.

"You're free, but Victoria, freedom isn't free. It requires a lot of responsibility. I have a job for you, but it ain't in Helena. I'm just visiting Helena to finish some business here before the heat of deep summer. I can't get down here again until fall," she said.

"I don't know what white women do. You will need to teach me?"

Gerta glanced at Jack. She said in a serious tone, "Living like a white lady is easy if you don't pass the buck on housecleaning. I live with three little pigs. Three women who expect to live like princesses at home in Missoula. My poor maid Cindy will die of a broken back with all the work of taking care of us all. I need a second maid, but I can't afford to pay you. I have an extra bed because one of my ladies recently died. You can take her bed. I can pay you with hearty food and lodging," Gerta said.

I looked at Jack with an unsure look.

"Don't ask me. I ain't in a position to make decisions for you no longer," Jack said as he stared at the ground.

"I suppose that will do," I said.

"So we leave tomorrow," she said.

I didn't want to leave Jack helpless in that dreary place. He looked too lonely. I felt it wasn't healthy for a man to be kept away from sunshine and fresh air. I was sure from the way he acted that he was already getting sick. I wanted him to look at me in the eyes, but he refused to look up.

"Jack, I don't want to leave you," I said feeling helpless.

"We don't got much choice Victoria," he muttered.

I held my tears. I felt that if I cried, I would make him feel worse. Gerta grabbed my hand. We got only one step forward when Jack finally looked at me eye to eyes. I felt his anguish. I knew that we both felt our souls touch each other's and our emotions were one. He felt what I was feeling, I was feeling abandoned and in shock. I felt what he was feeling; he was feeling trapped and angry. The desolation of my soul was as lonely as a tree on a barren and windswept hill.

"Victoria, you've made me see the world in a different way. Thank you. I'll never forget you," he said as he began weeping.

I couldn't say anything. I stared into his eye for several long moments. He finally took off his eye patch that he diligently wore through every type of weather and every situation, even while sleeping. His eye was gone with just a slit there. I wasn't repulsed at seeing the flaps of skin around his wound, both our hearts were wounded. He was the most handsome man in the world at that moment. Gerta gently grabbed my hips with her hands and led me away from him. I turned around one last time. He continued his somber gaze as the metal door shut with a lifeless thud.

My legs were shaky as I was led out of the dim and poorly ventilated jail. My heart was frozen. I wish that I had died before meeting him. I knew as my tears flowed that I'd never forget him. I hoped deep inside my heart to see him again. If I lived to be a gray haired old woman, senile and frail, I promised myself to never forget clumsy and tender Big One Eyed Jack. The way his eye looked innocent and warm. I may forget my grandchildren's names, but never, ever would I forget Jack's face. How I felt as he caressed my back as we stood hugging in the wilderness. How can any woman forget his deeply reverberating voice and the way he said 'lil girl?

Chapter 21-Lost not Found

I don't know why people always came into my life and gave me happiness for a short time. They went away to be lost and never found again. I was beginning to grow cold to the spirits who claimed to help me. The essence of the creator wasn't felt by me in those split wooden dwellings. I tried hard to hear the voice of the Great Spirit, but there wasn't even a whisper. I didn't even hear voices muffling. I felt like I was in a bad dream as Gerta led me away from the jail to a two storey white house. I loathed going into another stuffy dwelling without much fresh air wafting through it. Cold drafts invaded our bodies like bad luck follows the good and innocent. I had to just get used to it. I wasn't going back to a teepee anytime soon. I yearned to tear my clothes off and run as far as my legs would let me into the wild, into dangerous true freedom, not constricted freedom.

Gerta led me past the porch through a doorway. Several women were sitting around a table sipping tea. I smelled the odor of boiling vegetable stew. I was so upset that I almost vomited. I was introduced to the women but I didn't say anything. I was too heartbroken to speak and too heartbroken to breathe. My heart had a steady beat within reminding me of my grief. I wished my heart not to beat anymore, but like my life's path, I had no choice. It just happened. I was so tired. I didn't know the exact date I was born, but I knew sometime in the first moon of the forthcoming fall I was going to be nineteen winters. I already felt like a sullen widow despite my agility. Gerta led me into a bedroom and I collapsed on a bed.

My thoughts drifted from Jack to Scruffy Hunter. I felt colder when I thought about how I missed Scruffy Hunter and his awkward smile. I missed my mother and father. I missed my son most of all. My parents probably stared at other daughters about my age in our tribe. Such resemblance probably had them wishing that I never had to escape meanness and cruelty. I missed my adopted Apsaalooke sister Bear Woman. The way we understood each other despite the limitations of knowing each other's languages. I was finally alone in the world. Gerta said she was my friend. My heart didn't want to accept new friends only to lose them again. I just wanted all my old friends back.

I knew that dying of heartache was a very real illness. My tribe had known women who died from heartaches as their warrior husbands never returned from battle. There was a grandmother in my band whose daughter died from scarlet fever. The grandma didn't cough or catch any sort of physical illness. She caught heartache illness and died while crying in front of her husband.

I slept for a while because it was getting dark outside. Clammy sweat covered the bed. I stared around the dim room. There wasn't a kerosene lamp anywhere like there was in the hotel. A few unlit white candles were placed throughout the room. I did not have any matches so I just stayed in the dark, too sad to move. The wallpaper had fancy flowers, but such artificial beauty did not make me feel any better. The room felt terribly hot being that it was June. I knew I was getting ill. It felt as though the walls were closing in on me. If I were back at home, I would have walked out of the teepee and stood on a boulder. The fresh cool wind would have blown from the west. Wind always cleared my mind.

"Victoria," a knock came from the other side of the door. Gerta opened the door. "Oh my, it's dark in here." She lit a candle with matches grabbed from out of her white apron pocket. She stood over my bedside giving me a look of concern.

"You don't look well." She put her palm to my forehead. "You're burning up hot as hell. I'm going to get you some medicine." She went downstairs returning with a dark brown bottle.

"I got you some good old cough syrup. This medicine has lots of morphine in it. I'll make you feel better in a jiffy."

She poured the bottle. Out came syrup similar to what was poured on flapjacks. Brown liquid flowed onto the spoon. I expected the syrup to be as pleasant and sweet. Once in my mouth, I almost spit the medicine out. I managed to swallow the cough syrup without gagging too much. In my stomach, it felt warm. I knew there was some alcohol in the medicine, which I didn't like.

"Now Victoria, you need to eat to keep up your strength. Those women downstairs boiled a nice roast on my late aunt's old cannon stove. We got some preserved green beans and some jarred peaches for you too."

"Please, I hate food right now."

"Well, all right then. We're going to make you some vegetable soup tomorrow. Just let the medicine help you sleep," she blew out the candle. "Goodnight," she said like a mother.

I thought that I was on my deathbed. Traditional medicine wasn't available. I felt vulnerable without a sacred medicine bundle near my bedside. There wasn't a medicine woman to give me a tonic of herbs, roots, and twigs. There wasn't a bundle of sage burning smoke to purify the unbalanced essence around me, but I was ready to die. I had nobody left in my life close to me who loved me anymore. They were all too far away. I owned nothing. I tried to sing a medicine prayer, but my voice just cracked. I didn't have any strength. Just when I felt like I couldn't take the pain anymore, the painful joints in my body began to disappear. I began to feel the heavy pain sweeten as the room felt purified even without a sage bundle. I felt myself fall gently into waves of seductive sleep. My last thought before sleep was that the medicine of Napikowann worked fast. Ho! That morphine made me feel just better.

Chapter 22-A Taste of Sweetness

If only the medicine had kept me sleeping. Damn the women were loud in that house! The shrill laughter as they passed in the hallway just outside my door had me seething. Gerta mentioned that five women lived in that house, but I heard males speaking. I woke up six or eight times that night because of them. The first time I woke was leaving my room to try to find where Gerta put that medicine at. I went into the hallway seeing a woman done up in heavy face paint wearing a ruby red dress. She giggled in the hallway while holding the hand of an older man who was dressed in a suit.

"Hi, that's Victoria. She's new and not feeling very well, poor darling," the fancy lady said. He smirked as he was led by her into a room.

I suddenly felt shy and plain. I bent over trying to hold my vomit. Another lady came dressed in a dress as pink as a wild rose and had kinky hair, her smile turned to concern. She was staring at me from on top of the stairs. A man was standing on the stairs right behind her.

"I was told you be all sick. We get that corset off you and into a nighty. I got too many clothes anyhow. Mr. James, please wait just on the top of the stairs, honey, 'cuz I be gettin' back to you real soon now," she gave him a peck on the cheek. "Sugar, hell I'll do anything for you." He stood at the top of the stairs with the same sort of smirk that the other man had.

"Now the men here know me as Sugar, but my real name is Stella," she said as she led me up to a third story in the house. I gasped at the beauty of her large room. She had a small statue of a winged baby. She had a fancy desk with a big round mirror outlined with pretty white etchings of leafy vines. Many perfumes were on the desk. The room itself smelled like sweet gardenia. Fresh white roses were in a vase surrounded by glowing white candles. She had a frilly structure above her bed.

"What's that?" I pointed.

"Oh, you mean my canopy bed? Yeah, a mister bought it for me," she chuckled.

Stella went into a very large walk-in closet. She returned holding a white cotton nightgown. "Now don't get sick while I undress you, if you do, let me know and I'll get you a bowl." I got a better look at her as the candles illuminated her face. I could tell that she was a half-breed black woman. "Them dresses are mighty loose you be wearing honey. You better eat some more. I got a second dress for you also. I hate that white woman fancy dress but work is work. I got seven dresses and one is for your beginner's wardrobe," she went to her closet returning with a yellow dress. "Wear it when you be all better. Yella' don't look good on me. Makes me feel like a canary. It be a simple one-piece dress," she said. Her accent was charming and relaxing to me. I realized that her African accent made her speak differently just like I didn't correctly pronounce my R's. Jack sometimes laughed at how I said certain words, which made me mad. I didn't dare laugh at Stella, for she came from a people who were forced to learn English. Jack told me that slaves were whipped like horses if they spoke in African languages around their masters. That made me feel bad for them because we don't even treat dogs that way.

I thanked Stella before walking back to bed. I felt airy and light in her nightgown. I woke again to laughter from outside. I got out of bed and looked out the window. Three young men about my age got out of a carriage and eagerly went into the house.

"Sleep you people," I said weakly as I cuddled my pillow in bed. I finally fell asleep again despite the sounds of two inconsiderate loud women. Moans of delight came from bedrooms on both sides of mine.

"You're becoming a big ordeal," Gerta said crossly when I opened my eyes the next morning. "I was supposed to be leaving for Missoula today, but I can't take a sick woman on Mullen Road there. If you died along the way, I'd never look Jack straight in the eyes ever again. Old favors!" She took out a spoon of morphine cough syrup. I dreaded the taste but anticipated the pleasant effects. "Here, one more," she said. She forced the second spoonful into my mouth. "Really, I'm not so wretched every morning before my coffee. A day wasted for me is a missing wad of cash from my women back in Missoula. I'm missing out on some of their tips from customers right now as we speak. We'll attempt to leave tomorrow. Just try to get some shut eye and rest." She poured me some water out of a picture and had me drink some out of a glass. She left the water on the small table beside the bed. "You're getting dehydrated. You better drink more water today." Her boots clumped on the hardwood floor across the bedroom. She slammed the door shut. "Shit," she said as I heard her clump downstairs. She came in later that day with some vegetable soup. I didn't touch the soup only to leave it cold on the bedside table. I was grateful that the daytime was quiet at least.

A doctor came into the room the next morning to look at me. He checked my body heat with a glass stick. He put a peculiar tube up to my chest that led to his ears, telling me to breathe deeply a few times. A strange wooden stick was put into my mouth. “Stick out your tongue like this,” Gerta ordered. She stuck out her tongue like a lizard. He told me to say "Aaah." I wondered if "Aahhh" was a sacred healing word. I thought that some medicine people of my tribe had strange rituals until I met that doctor!

"She's just getting over a small bout of flu. She's in good enough shape to travel today," the doctor said.

"Oh, very good. Well thank you doctor. Stella is downstairs. She'll see you to the door," Gerta said.

"I'll help you get dressed honey. We're taking you to a new home." She straightened out my clothes. "I wonder how much that doctor is going to cost me," she said. "Well no time to worry, we need to go. I'll dress you."

I felt dizzy as she dressed me in a yellow velvet princess style dress. I was very confused, because she said that the new style given to me from Stella had the corset worn under not outside the bodice. She left but quickly returned with a ruffled thing and put it under my exposed neckline.

"I hate these new styles showing so much of a woman. This is called a chemisette to keep you from catching pneumonia by covering your bare skin." At least the hem of the dress didn't drag. I was led by a sneering blonde haired woman introduced as Fannie to a horse covered wagon. They fixed me a bed in the back. Fannie sat by my side as Gerta sat up in front. The bumpy rocking of the horses and smell of horse dung on the road made me feel like vomiting. I leaned over the back of the wagon and the only thing that came out of me was water.

"Why do I have to be back here with Victoria? She's going to get me sick just looking at her. If you vomit on my new dress, missy, you'll have to pay for it. I can tell you're an Injun. You'll never be able to pay for a fine dress so highly expensive. A politician bought it for me as a tip. You hear me? You're either deaf or just stupid."

I just closed my eyes preparing to endure a trip with such a pleasant mannered lady that could freeze hot springs. Later we hit a rocky patch of road.

"Jesus Christ, Richie! I can drive this wagon better than you. You son of a gun!" she yelled at the driver.

Later on Fannie had to use the bathroom. She hid behind some bushes. She stopped for a moment when she returned. She look around at the grandeur of nature and said, "Piss on this wilderness!"

"Will you just shut up you big baby!" Gerta yelled from the passenger side of the wagon.

I looked at Fannie. She was a fully-grown woman with unusually sized breasts. She wasn't a baby at all, but I found babies to be more pleasant than her. She was dressed fancy at all times. She looked bored while she fanned herself during the midday heat. She had her curly blond hair in a bonnet. She always put on makeup with layers upon layers added in bits, wavy smears, and flowing smudges to her pretty face throughout the days we traveled. She sneered and glared at me a few times when she did recognize my presence. She often held a hand mirror even when she wasn't staring at herself. She occasionally put on water lily perfume. Once she commented, "It stinks in here and I know it isn't me." She took out a wine bottle and began sipping it.

"Are you thirsty Victoria?" she asked me.

"Yes," I said.

"Don't drink too much of this, it's coca wine. It's got cocaine in it, which is a wonderful health tonic. A doctor said it gives you nerves of steel. That's what I need, because I'm not my best when I travel." I declined her offer. I hated wine, why anybody wanted to drink rotten juice is beyond me. "No thank you."

"For Pete's sake! You act more prissy than Queen Victoria and the Pope who both drink this. Oh well, more for me," she said. She drank from a bottle of Vin Mariani. The more Fannie drank wine, the more she attempted to talk to me. I was in no shape to socialize at all. I still felt sick despite what the doctor in Helena said as I rested in the makeshift bed. The bumpy ride in the covered wagon didn't help either. Fannie giggled to herself occasionally.

"Good I feel way better," she said in a singsong voice.

We camped in a desolate mountain valley. Fannie insisted on sleeping inside the covered wagon. She didn't want to be on the ground because of bugs and wild beasts. Richie, who was the hired wagon driver, Gerta and I all slept outside that cool June evening. Richie made a great campfire that warmed us. Nobody was in the mood for food, which was canned beans again.

"I curse myself for ever volunteering to bring that baby with us to Missoula," she said to him.

"Gee, why's that?" he said peering into the fire.

"The other four couldn't stand living with her at my aunt's Helena household, so she gets her own room in one of my boarding houses in Missoula. That's if she doesn't like the man who gave me money to set him up with a blonde beauty. She has to pay more money for rent if she does stay in town. She might stay at my home with the others. I'll help manage her feisty ways. She never had a good ma. She minds me though, because I know how women tick better than any man does. She's still young and got some time to change into a better woman," Gerta said.

A scream came from inside the wagon.

"What is it now?" Richie demanded in an irritated manner.

"Bed bugs! There was a bed bug on me! I know it came from her, dirty woman," she pointed a finger at me. I was very irritated and tired, especially after several bumpy days on the journey into hell. I went over to Fannie and slapped her across the face as hard as a man could slap a woman. Blonde hair flew across her face. She looked at me with shock. She held her cheek.

"Every time you open your mouth to speak for the rest of this trip, you get slapped across the face," I growled.

Fannie looked at Gerta, then at Richie, then back at me with wide eyes.

"Gerta," she said.

"You best be quiet then. I'll be right behind her with my hand," Gerta said.

"Please, I won't complain anymore, so don't hit me. Richie, please find the bed bugs," she said in a gentle but quivering voice.

"I guess," he said without enthusiasm.

He lit a kerosene lamp and brought it into the wagon. I loved how the covered wagon glowed when lit from inside. It was as pretty as the glowing teepees back at home. Richie returned to us shaking his head in disgust. He went over to Gerta and showed her the bug. "Here's the damn bed bug, just an innocent summer beetle looking for a place to hide."

"Good," she said. She climbed into the wagon and shut her mouth for the rest of the night.

Fannie was quiet for a while, until we reached Mullen Road that was along the Clark Fork River. Every morning I insisted on bathing in the ice-cold river. Gerta preached that doing so would cause my sickness to return. I didn't heed her advice; in fact, I traveled only in my nightgown that Stella gave me back in Helena. I wore that nightgown so I didn't have the inconvenience of somebody helping me tie and untie my corset every day. Fannie inquired why I wore sleepwear all dang day. She was smart enough to understand that I hated corsets, at least. She dug into a chest of clothing and took out a bodice.

"This feels better. Although I consider it peasant woman wear. Some man got it for me, but I never wear it. Do you want it?" she asked me.

"No," I said.

"Too bad, there it goes," she said throwing the bodice out the back of the wagon. She gave me a petulant look. She often remained quiet all day waving a lacy fan in front her face. She took off her bonnet on and off several times a day while staring into the mirror. As the traveling continued, she started acting like a baby again.

"When the hell are we going to get there? Go faster! It's so damn hot. I don't want to be near Victoria." She said several times separately and sometimes in quick succession. I slapped her across the face again. She cried a little, but shut up once more.

I was getting drinking water from the river when Gerta came up to me.

"I bet you're getting tired of riding with Fannie in back. You know why she shuts up after you slap her? She was with a husband who used to beat her all the time. She only knows how to respond to ill treatment. The other women in Helena hit her too. Getting hit is normal for that stupid thing. Her stories about her husband will make your skin crawl. Now he was a sick prick! I'm setting her up with a high-ranking government official who wants me to get him a pretty blonde. He has money, she'll marry him. His money will keep her in line. Luxury often shuts up loud-mouthed women," Gerta said sipping a bottle of gin.

"I've never dealt with a woman who is so difficult. I feel bad about hitting her," I admitted.

"The other women felt guilty too. I also don't think brutality is appropriate to teach people good manners. I hope that the governor will be gentle as a rabbit with her. Fanny told me her ex-husband was so cruel; she had to escape his bullshit in the middle of the night. She crawled out of her kitchen window and ran away from the town of Pony, Montana. Shit! Coldhearted bastards have a habit of making women feeling guilty. The senator from the state of, oh goodness gracious, I forget where he's from, but he'll be good for her because our public servants are trustworthy. If she doesn't accept him, then god be damned, she might have to stay with us. I should honor my self-imposed mandate about helping women. That's why I own a female boarding house in Missoula. Nobody else is helping those poor things." Gerta always opened up more after sipping gin in the evenings after traveling all day.

"Are we going to sit here all day? For Pete's sake, we're all lazing around like fat cows," Fannie crossly yelled from inside the wagon.

"Ride in front tomorrow, a break from her will do you good," Gerta whispered into my ear.

Chapter 23-Welcome to Hell's Gate

"Damn times are changing fast. Like this river, everybody still knows it as the Missoula River, but now we have to be all fancy and call it the Clark Fork River. They say they named the river in honor of one of those three explorers known as Lewis, Sacajawea, and Clark. Don't get me started on the names of towns. I was fine and dandy with just Missoula Mills, but no, the town fathers Cap Higgins and Frank Worden now just call it plain Missoula. They said just their gristmill should be called Missoula Mills. Ha, ha, ha, not very much of a difference," Gerta explained to me.

Richie added, "One hint for you Victoria, don't call Frank Worden by his real name which is Francis, he thinks it sounds too sissy."

"Yes, we respect the town's founders. They scared off some red Injuns who sometimes tried to steal fruit and vegetables from the gardens. The townsfolk are hoping this Mullen Road here will bring in more people. This dusty road is our only vein to civilization," Gerta said as I sat between her and Richie leaving Fannie by herself in back.

"What happens Victoria when towns on the frontier don't get enough settlers?" Richie asked me.

"They stay small?" I asked.

Both Richie and Gerta laughed.

"They just plumb die and turn into ghost towns," Richie said.

"You are fooling me. Towns can't die and turn into ghosts," I laughed.

"No honey. Ghost town is just a saying. It means the town becomes empty and the buildings get in shoddy shape. The men in the town are really scared that their enterprise might flounder," Gerta explained.

Mullen road ebbed and curved like a water snake. The Clark Fork River beside the road was a great convenience. Many trails across Montana didn't parallel water. When Jack and I traveled from Ft. Benton, water was scarce. I guess Jack cared more about his whiskey barrels more than a barrel of water.

At least a barrel of water was brought with us while I traveled with my new friends. When we ran out, we had the river. I always wondered why Blackfeet people didn't live in the splendor of the mountains, choosing to live in the barren, windy, and overly dry foothills and rolling plains. I knew it was Bison that we followed, but I wished Bison were plentiful in the valleys of the Rockies. Those who have always called such majestic mountains their home are blessed. *I thought that earlier on in the trip*, but after three weeks of traveling on twisting roads high on the sides of cliffs from sometimes scary heights, I was convinced that the Salish were probably foolish. They liked living among the difficult terrain of these giant mountains. The travel was treacherous. Dangerous cliffs seemed to be around every curve. Our poor horses worked so hard at steep grades.

Richie explained to me one evening that many white pioneers went through the plains as they headed for gold and fertile land in a place by the big sea called the Pacific Ocean. Many got stuck and died in the Mountains because travel was difficult. He said that mountains of beauty could also be mountains of death. I told him many things beautiful are also deadly. He seemed to like that statement because he stared at me and said, "I wish I wasn't married no more."

I forced myself to eat disgusting trout that Richie had caught. We Blackfeet didn't like fish, and trout was full of needle-like bones. It was either trout, beans, some fruit preserves or nothing at all. I was spoiled from eating Bison and hotel cuisine. I found myself not really wanting to eat much of anything on the trip. I was losing weight fast.

We went through a steep canyon that Richie told me French fur trappers called Port de L'enfer or translated into English, Hell's Gate.

"There you go Victoria. Over there is Hellgate town," Gerta pointed.

I looked over and saw some ramshackle cabins in the distance one with a broken window. A screen door was hanging off a doorway. Weeds were growing in what looked like what once were roads. Smoke was everywhere in the valley.

"What the hell? I bet a forest fire is blazing way off yonder," Richie said.

In a way, it looked like we were in a place called hell. I was aware of white man's religion told by one of the storytellers at my camp. Hell is a place where the white people go who have done malicious acts called sin. A horned man, who has a spiky tail and skin red as a wild strawberry, has demons with giant eating forks torturing the evil white people forever and ever. The campfires of hell singed their skin as punishment because jail wasn't good enough when alive. I was scared as we passed into the wretched valley despite all the beauty. I was hoping no such creatures were hiding behind any boulders or trees. I wearily looked to my left and right as I sat in the front of the wagon snuggling up to Richie knowing he would protect us.

"I don't think hell is real, but what if it is? I'm frightened," I said to Richie.

Richie scowled in confusion explaining, "No, this isn't really leading us into hell, if that's what you were thinking. Your Blackfeet ancestors attacked the Salish so many times in this canyon. Skulls and skeletons littered this place. Some piles of bones were two feet high. The wind was so cold in the valley, the French fur trappers were convinced they reached the gateway to hell."

"Oh, that must have happened a long time ago. My people signed a peace treaty with the Salish. They promised not to come to our land to hunt buffalo, and we promised not to ambush them in the mountains. That peace treaty was made in front of The Great Spirit as a witness."

"Now how can your god be a witness to a meeting?" Gerta inquired.

"The chiefs smoke from a sacred peace pipe," I said.

"Darling, you are so sweet. Do you want to tell me some more about your people while we are alone sometime," Richie said as he rubbed my back.

"Watch it loverboy," Gerta cautioned, "You got two kids at home."

"Yes ma'am, that's true. That is true," Richie said in a hopeless manner.

I found Richie to be charming, but I was more interested in why my Blackfeet warriors ambushed the Salish. I was saddened that so much terror occurred in the canyon. How did so much pain happen in such a beautiful valley? The mountains were steep making escape from ambushes difficult. Rocky cliffs dived into a cascading river canyon. I felt ashamed that my tribe massacred so many. I planned to return to the fields to light sage. There were no more bones from what I saw. They probably were collected and buried by a missionary.

While at the gates of hell, I told Gerta that we Blackfeet know that there is no such thing as hell, there is only heaven. Our medicine people communicated freely with spirits. No spirits ever mentioned such a horned beast as Satan who transformed into a serpent that liked apples. Many of my people traveled into the spirit world in dreams and vision quests and no such land of fire appeared, and if it did, they were probably seeing only a forest fire or a grass fire caused by lightning. If forest fires existed in the other world…Gerta finally stopped me.

“Darling, what I’m getting is that you are taking my religion too literally. The tree of knowledge and the serpent are just metaphors. Apples are a perfect poetic metaphor. Hell is just a state of mind,” she explained.

“You sure sound smart!” Richie added.

Another American town slowly came into view in a spacious arid valley. "Missoula," Richie yelled to us. Richie said Mullen Road went right into the center of the town. Missoula looked just like Helena. Although Helena was built on a slope of a mountain where Missoula was level at the bottom of a valley. People hurried their way as we slowed to a halt in front of a building. Fannie got out of the wagon looking haggard. She frowned as she looked around the town. "I want a man and a whiskey," she bluntly said.

"Not so fast. You’re too unclean after such a long journey. You aren’t some common shack town wench. We need to get you settled in your hotel room. Remember about the charming rich man I told you about? He should be checked in eagerly waiting for you in that hotel. Get yourself cleaned up. The hotel staff know what to do," Gerta breathlessly and tiredly said. She tried to sound excited as she spoke.

Fannie finally smiled as she spoke to us. "I’m so sorry to you three. I hate to travel. Gerta thank you so much for arranging for me to seize an opportunity. I know that I was such a headache to everyone." She looked at me in the eyes for the first time; her eyes were sparkling with life.

"Victoria, thank you for keeping me in line," she sweetly said.

"Fannie, you shouldn’t have to correct your bad behavior only after another person hits you. I’m sorry," I felt my face turn red after saying that.

“I’m half loco. I’m working on becoming a better person and not such a prima donna. It’s easy to do in this profession.

Oh, I'm sorry Gerta, I slipped. I know I wasn't supposed to say anything to Victoria."

I gave a questioning glance at Gerta. "Never mind," Gerta said with a wince and a dismissive wave of the hand. Richie unloaded Fannie's luggage. She had a heavy chest and an empty brass birdcage. His impressive muscles brought it all up to her hotel room.

I was waiting outside beside the wagon when a rainstorm happened. The realization that I was going to spend my first summer in an American town hit me. I was ready for a new life. I was tingling with joy as I lifted my face skyward and felt heavy raindrops falling onto my skin. I noticed a drunken man staggering down the wooden planks. He stopped and stared at me as I twirled in happiness in the rain. I've always loved the scent of rain as clean as windswept cotton. He walked over to me and said, "Lovely miss, would you like some company?"

"No, I already have Richie and Gerta," I said.

He stumbled back and then leaned forward a little too close. The stink of beer came from out of his mouth. "Wow, manage à trois," he said with a thumbs up signal.

"Get away from her you hound dog! Go take a hike up the river to an abandoned shack. Go to the old Hellgate town over yonder to sober up," Gerta said as she came over to protect me.

She shooed him away like she was shooing a dog away.

"Sorry young miss, and sorry Madam Gerta, I was mistaken. Thanks as always for scaring me sober," he said to us. He tipped his hat to us and stumbled away. I had no luggage except a plain white cotton bag filled with my fancy dresses from Sugar and Jack, and the small gifts given from him too.

"You!" she pointed at me with a stern look.

"Standing in the street dressed only in your nightgown acting like a little girl. The entire world can see your naked skin through that thin wet cotton," she suddenly stopped. "Gee, I am thirsty for a Coca Cola. It strikes me I haven't had one since Helena. Damn it, I'll just hurry and get one despite your immodesty."

She led me two blocks down the street to fetch a Coca Cola for a quick perk. She seemed proud as the men gawked at me. I followed behind her with my head lowered suddenly feeling ashamed of wearing my nightgown during daytime. I noticed the drunk man stumbling in the distance. "Where is he going?" I asked. She told me that a few drunks who didn't have any more money stayed in a couple of buildings in Hellgate that we passed. She told me that the pitiful area of scruffy buildings was the original settlement not more than just a few years before. "Hellgate is the sort of place that has had some problems with some outlaws. Shit! There was even a saloon shooting and some hangings there of the notorious Henry Plummer gang. What happens when a sheriff goes loco? Many innocent people dead. Poor Higgins and Worden were even robbed there too. Most of the men had moved four miles over here to Missoula where the jobs are at. That fellow with the filthy mind belongs there," she explained between gulps of Coca Cola returning to the wagon.

We traveled just a little to the outskirts of town while passing gardens. The outskirts were just some split timber houses and other log houses separated by fields. Gerta pointed to her home in the distance, "We live in a half decent house. I ain't living in a log cabin like a mountain mama." Across many beautiful flowers was a two-story house and three smaller houses behind it. "I make good money from my women and selling the flowers in those fields beside my house. That's why I have such a nice home. I wish it was made out of stone, but only the rich can afford it. They have the darndest luck."

I loved the valley we were in. There were gardens all along Mullen road for quite a distance abundant with strange varieties of fruit and vegetables. The flowers were what really impressed me. We went up the porch stairway. She got out a brass ring with dozens of keys. We entered a room that looked as fancy as the hotel room back in Helena.

"This is your new home. We shall get you dressed so you can meet the other ladies of the house." Richie put her possessions into a room. She led me through the house and out the backdoor. I saw a woman peering outside the window of one of the smaller houses through the curtains. There were three little houses in the back all painted white. A tiny house had a moon crescent carved in the doorway that I recognized as the outhouse.

"Do you know what a bunkhouse is?" Gerta asked me.

I stared in silence not knowing what one was.

"You sleep in bunkhouses," she said.

She unlocked the door with a key. We walked inside a musty smelling room. I sneezed. I never wanted to sleep in a stuffy American dwelling again. I wondered if they allowed Blackfeet to pitch teepees in the fields beside their houses. There was a small woodstove and two beds inside. A desk, a kerosene lamp made the room a little more interesting, but that was just about it. There were no paintings or fancy wallpaper, just plain white walls. I did see a crucifix hanging above one of the beds. Gerta helped me change out of my nightgown into my regular clothes. She continued talking as she helped me dress.

"Your bed belonged to a woman who worked for me but she died. Syphilis. She wasn't careful."

We walked into the main house after Richie put my bag on the bunkhouse bed. She led me down a hallway that reminded me of a hotel. We went into the kitchen where a young blonde woman named Cindy was cooking. I was told that the kitchen was shared with the others. All the women in the household pooled their earnings to pay the young woman to cook them breakfast and lunch.

"They ain't paying you. We're doing you a favor. Cindy will teach you how to cook and clean the common rooms. Let's see who's in the sitting room so we can get you acquainted. They like to spend their days there."

We went into a larger room. The room wasn't as extravagantly decorated as the hotel room, but was still quite lovely. There was a simple table, some shelves of books, and a piano. A few simple paintings hung on the beautiful pink walls.

I noticed a very pretty woman sitting on a sofa with fancy flower patterns covering the soft cushions. A sterling silver tea set was arranged with cookies on a wooden coffee table. "Ladies, this is Victoria Redsky, she'll be our second maid," she said as the ladies stood up and curtsied.

Gerta brightened as she began the introductions. "This lady sitting down is Mandy." Mandy was dressed in a pretty long white cotton tea dress. She smiled, and then sat back down continuing to read. She had long cascading red hair with well-balanced features, but she had peculiar dots on her face. Two other women were staring at me. One had brown hair tied in a bun under sharp angular features. She had a serious face. The other had wavy black hair that flowed down the back of her neck.

The longhaired one was dressed in a blue flowing tea dress. The one with the bun was dressed up in a fine black dress complete with the required frilly trimmings, as if she just came from walking the streets. They said, "Hello," then continued to play cards on a table. Silver dollars were in the middle of the small table. "The one with her hair down is Cascade. The other is Julia. Well now, let's get you situated. I'll have young Cindy show you around Missoula. She's your roommate. You know the one who is cooking."

She went over to kiss my cheek. "That's how women greet each other in town. They kiss each other on the cheeks and say 'Dahling! Hello dolly! Marvelous to see you. Cheers!' We all try to treat each other with deep respect, because we look out for each other." I didn't want to kiss Gerta back on the cheek.

"If you get bored, there are games and books in the sitting area. If you get hungry, there is always food in the pantry. There ain't much here yet. I noticed you swiped money from the hotel room back in Helena, some poor concierge's tip. There's the trading post called Worden and Company where you can buy something." She gave me a little wink and went her merry way up the stairs. I heard her heels clomping on the floorboards above our heads.

Chapter 24-The New Woman in Town

I sat in the bunkhouse staring at my dress wishing I still had my Blackfeet robes. I just wanted something familiar near me again. I was immediately bored with my surroundings. I wanted to be busy. I craved to sew buckskin, to tan hide, to do quillwork, or to make pemmican. I yearned to hear the laughter of children running throughout the teepees. I missed the cooking fires and distant conversations of the elders of my tribe. My new room was eerily silent, but at least I heard birds outside which calmed me. I felt frigid isolation because the thick wooden walls were separating me from others. I felt walled in from nature.

I thought about sitting in a chair in the middle of the garden of flowers. I opened a small window breathing in the cool summer air. Fresh air immediately cleared my head. Pretty views of mountains were in the distance.

Since I was alone, I closed my eyes trying to contact the spirit helpers. Somehow, it was harder to hear their voices. Perhaps I always heard them better outside. I sat outside on the dirt closing my eyes silently calling them in my mind. I tried calling them for a long time. After awhile I heard somebody in the breeze saying, *"lost one, we are here."*

"Dear spirits, please guide me in this new world that I can't fully comprehend. Help me learn to be a good and wise person in this new land. Should I return home?" I asked aloud in Blackfeet.

I looked around straining my eyes to see them, but I only heard silence. I heard the benevolent voice rise up again in the breeze, *"You must have patience with your new surroundings. We know that you won't survive next time if you depart alone. We could try to help you feel better, but there are many perils in your path. If you leave into those mountains, you will perish."*

I squinted my eyes attempting to see the spirit. I caught sight of spirits before, even when not praying. Occasionally they appeared for a few minutes with white light emitting from their bodies, but I only heard her sweet and distant voice. Her voice was distant and hollow, as if it was trapped in a wall. I gave up trying to contact her. She went away somewhere as her warm presence wafted away gently from me to the other side with the other ancestors.

I returned to the bunkhouse. I suddenly became distracted from an odor of something disgusting yet familiar. Such stink was covered somewhat by the scent of my strong lavender water. I sniffed around following the stink that came from underneath a bed. I saw a flowery white ceramic pot that had a top on it with a small knob. I pulled out the pot from under the bed. It resembled a cooking pot that Cindy was cooking on the stove. I opened the pot and realized it was filled with urine. I almost vomited.

A knock came at the door.

"I’m in here," I said.

Cindy came inside dressed in a brown dress with an apron. She seemed skittish and was wringing her hands.

"Hello, Gerta asked me to give you a quick tour of the town. If you aren’t busy or tired or anything," she said in a timid voice. She was looking down at the ground.

"I’d love to, but before we leave, we should empty this because we are the maids, right?"

“Does it really matter? This place is filthy no matter what we do.”

We left the building to walk along the gardens and houses until we arrived in town just a few minutes later. I saw some people hurrying this way and that way. None of them noticed our presence, which had me feeling more isolated.

Everybody knew everyone else back home. We all knew each other by rights of sharing a human experience. I told Cindy that we were invisible.

"The daytime crowd on Front Street refuses to see us ladies. You'll notice that when we walk far away from this street, some friendly fellers and a couple of dames will nod. Strangers do wave, just not at the single gals walking this street. Front Street has got a bad reputation already, and this town is still pretty new."

I noticed a long black wagon led by two horses, followed by a couple of other wagons. Cindy told me the black wagon in front was a hearse leading a procession to a burial field.

"So sad. There's a small outbreak of syphilis killing a few of the ladies, like the gal who recently died in your room. It takes them a long time to die of that disease. Jesus Christ, she was going mad. We knew she was nearing the end, because she acted so offbeat and erratic," Cindy explained.

A couple of men walking down the street stopped. They took off their hats placing them on their chests. A very fancy lady was dressed in a sleeveless ruffled dress all in black. The dress had a neckline showing the top of her chest, which shocked me. She was wearing lots of perfume. Her lips were painted as red as a cherry. Men stared at her as she walked from an entranceway of a building. She stopped and did a strange gesture with her hands. I noticed Cindy did the same gesture as the fancy lady. Both had their heads bowed with palms pushed together. The funeral procession passed us, followed by several young ladies looking very morose.

"Make the sign of the cross. Oh, I forget, you're Indian and not Christian, at least not yet," Cindy said.

My braids were exposed from the bottom of my hat past my shoulders. They were on show purposely so the world could see I was Blackfeet. The fancy lady in black passed us and said to me, “I love your braids.” Her genuine smile made my day feel brighter, despite seeing a funeral.

Cindy introduced me to a butcher, a baker, and a dairy farmer. I was shown a marketplace that was the only stone structure downtown and the only place to get beer and a cola. It was called the brick block. We walked beside gorgeous gardens that lined the Clark Fork River. Cindy said she loved walking beside them as we held hands giggling. She looked into my eyes and said, “I consider this valley to be a spiritual place. Sometimes it feels like we are in the Garden of Eden during warm weather.” She told me that they were the Hughes Gardens. An array of colors hugged peacefulness in my heart keeping me in gratitude. Cindy gave me a quick education on the plants. The orange flowers were called California Poppies. There were blooming watermelons. Corn was growing taller than a child! I thought that corn only grew southward. Little strawberries were sprouting out of green. She commented how temperate the day’s weather was due to an early summer.

We walked across a bridge over a cascading smaller river. “This area is known by the Salish Tribe as Nl-ay. There’s great bullhead trout fishing here. We now call it the Rattlesnake River, how pretty. This is a great place to meet a gentleman who’s into fishing by the way.” She giggled.

The Missoula Valley was like an enchanted fertile land, so gentle and peaceful, but the loud gristmill down the river disrupted the tranquility somewhat. I noticed smoke rising from a metal structure. I couldn’t believe this was the place of outlaw hangings, civilian vigilantes, and Indian massacres of other Indians.

"What’s that?" I asked Cindy.

"That’s an incinerator that burns up everything that isn’t used for logging. That’s what Missoula is, lumberjacks and prostitutes.”

"What?" I asked completely confused.

"Lumberjacks cut down trees. Prostitutes keep the men going." She laughed uneasily at having to explain that point.

We sat down catching some sunshine by the riverbank. The Rattlesnake River was chattering below our feet. I noticed that we strayed very far; we were near the mouth of the dreaded Hellgate Canyon. I was glad we turned around toward the center of town again.

When we returned to the main intersection, Cindy entered Worden and Company buying a bottle of medicine from a wall. I marveled at the multiple brown bottles that were placed on shelves. We began walking over a wooden bridge over the Clark Fork River. The wind was roaring, I tried to hold onto my hat but it blew off my head into the water. I leaned over the railing raging with anger. As the hat floated down the cold rapids, it felt like a part of Jack was being taken away from me.

"You'll have to get used to going over this bridge. It's rather new. There isn't much on the other side, except somebody who teaches people how to dance properly."

Back at home, three women were complaining about being hungry because lunch was missed. They accused Cindy of making them run late for work. She hurried into the kitchen and began boiling sausages. I returned to the bunkhouse. A gorgeous green dress was placed on my bed. I went into the kitchen. Cindy read a paper that was pinned on it. The message read: "Thank you Victoria for telling me that it isn't normal for a woman to be hit by anyone, with peace, I give you this dress. From Fannie." I quickly showed Cindy. She forgot about cooking, and ran with me excitedly to the bunkhouse. She helped me change into the dress that fit perfectly.

"You can't be wearing such a pretty dress while doing housework. I have a few old dresses that you might fit you," she instructed.

That night, I didn't sleep well. I thought I'd never get used to American beds, so high off the ground and creaky. I took the mattress and placed it on the floor. There I slept like a hibernating bear. Cindy warned me that garden spiders would bite me and box elder bugs would crawl into my ears.

The next day I went into the sitting room where Cascade and Julia taught me how to play games. The game of poker confused me so I gave up. “Just because something is hard, you’re gonna give up so easily now,” Cascade said in a cross way. Mandy was reading a book as always. I sat beside her on the sofa. She told me that the book was called The Adventures of Tom Sawyer. She explained that she was also was reading other books on and off. There was a book by Charles Darwin. She showed me a very old book written earlier in the century called Frankenstein by an English rose named Mary Shelley. “This old book is an antique heirloom in my family. My great, great grandmother passed it down through the generations. She brought it all the way from England through Alice Island. My mother told me that great granny was scared on the boat reading Frankenstein,” she said.

Cindy told me that she was keen on books too. She offered to teach me how to read. “You don’t need much help with your speaking. Except how to pronounce certain words,” she said. She suggested that I should practice my writing in a diary. She warned me that it might be harder for me to learn how to write than to read.

"I used to teach schoolchildren to read in a little schoolhouse in Stevensville, but my husband died from gangrene after being kicked by a horse,” Cindy put her hand in front of her mouth. “I can’t talk about it much. Luckily Jesus led me to the mercy of Ms. Gerta Gundersunn." Cindy looked sad as she sat at the sitting room table.

“Reading usually is a healthy distraction from daily sorrows,” she said as she went over to a shelf. She took out a big thick book. “I like to glue newspaper clippings into this clipbook. This might be a good way to teach you how to read.”

She had multiple newspaper clippings. There was a photograph of a chief wearing a war bonnet. “Who’s he?” I asked her.

“Ah, I see you are a curious one. Curiosity is the first step to becoming educated. He is Chief Charlo, the leader of the Bitterroot Salish tribe. Once you learn how to read, you will know what he had to say in his letter to the American leaders.” I looked at the symbols on the paper knowing that there was a new world being offered to me.

Chapter 25-Meek Mandy on All Fours

It took me a long time to realize that I was doing the same hard work that I was forced to do when I was captured by the Apsaalooke tribe. I didn't complain at first. I wanted to be liked by them all. Months went by as I trudged along. Cindy spent a few hours every night showing me how to speak, read and write. I was grateful that I was getting a good education from a former schoolhouse teacher. There I was a captive a second time. Living with those women wasn't easy, but I had nowhere else to go. I wasn't familiar with the mountains even if I tried to leave.

I was instructed how to scrub the floors properly, wash the dishes in a basin, and clean the tub after the ladies shaved their legs. I fetched items in town for them and fetched pails of water from the well across the fields. I heated water to a boil over the coal fired stove, which took forever. I washed their bloody underskirts sometimes. I did all of that so I could be free.

By day, they dressed like typical fluffy ladies in public, but at home, they often wore flowing tea gowns. At night, they dressed in red or black sleeveless French evening gowns, with shoulders exposed and cleavage showing. They giggled as satin gloves covered their mouths looking pretty wearing neck ribbons. I couldn't wear my nice clothes given to me. I wore a raggedy white cotton scullery maid dress.

Cindy sewed her own clothes, always wearing black dresses with puffy sleeves covered with an apron. I kept my hair in braids, while Cindy tied hers in a bun. The ladies were usually cordial and sometimes helped out with the chores, but one of them tried acting like a first wife. Holy cow she liked ordering me around like a second wife. She was Mandy.

White women lived such a soft lifestyle compared to plainswomen. They played cards, sang and dance, read out loud the newspaper, and lived like princesses while Cindy and I worked all day, every day. The problem was that Cindy was paid with money and I wasn't. They also talked to Cindy like she was an equal, but they spoke down to me, especially Mandy.

They hardly ever called me by my white people name. All three called me something else instead. "Indian girl, go and fetch me a glass of water. Indian girl, I better not see any stains on my dresses. Wash them like a Spanish maid does. Indian girl, stop acting so damn lazy like your people are."

I was scrubbing the outdoor privy when Mandy came in dressed up in a fancy dress. "Go fetch me some sweets at the trading shop," she said with a sneer on her face.

I obliged, because I thought that was what I had to put up with in the white world. I caught Mandy staring at me with blatant disdain as I scrubbed the floors. She also sneered at me while I polished the wooden chairs. One day I was about to explode and slap her across the face like I did to Fannie. I threw a washrag into the dirty lifeless water inside the grey bucket. I grabbed Mandy's hair and pulled her over to the bucket of water.

"You keep on ordering me around like I'm a slave. You just hang around the house complaining and saying you're bored. If you're so bored then scrub the floors. Come on woman, scrub the floors!" I said forcefully under gritted teeth. I looked over at the other women. Cascade was staring at me in complete fear. Julia started to scream and cry. Gerta was laughing while slapping her knee. I got myself under control and let Mandy's hair go. Gerta stopped laughing and then looked at me crossly.

Julia complained through her tears, "See Gerta, I told you she would become violent. I never trusted her! Do something!"

Gerta's face grew dour and said, "If you're ever insubordinate again Victoria. We will banish you to the wilderness."

The thought of me alone with the wolves scared me, but I refused to show any fear.

"I can survive out there alone. My medicine is strong. I have the spirit of a lone wolf," I said as I felt fire burning inside my soul.

"I told you not to let an Indian woman live with us. See how mean she is. She's acting like a wild animal and is talking crazy," Julia said between tears.

"I didn't really say anything before when you hit Fannie. Now I'm saying something. We can't have such vulgarity in my presence between my women. Victoria, if you can survive out in the wilderness alone, then why don't you just leave right now?" Gerta asked with such finality in her voice that it scared me. I walked over to the window and stared at the snow covered by the autumn snow.

I wondered to myself if I should go against the spirit's advice and just leave, and perhaps, find a friendly tribe before the snows. Such perilous mountains, I knew I'd freeze to death trying to cross them. I looked down at Cindy as she meekly scrubbed the floors despite the ruckus. I stood at the window looking outside with silent tears running down my cheeks. An image of my father smiling filled my soul. I missed him too much. The women quieted down and continued to play a card game they called bridge. I looked sadly into Gerta's eyes as she pointed to the floor. I got back down on my hands and knees and scrubbed the floor beside Cindy. I couldn't understand why Mandy treated Cindy with respect, but talked to me like a child.

I didn't want the women always mistrusting me. For a long time they refused to speak to me after I lost my temper. I wasn't unhappy about that. I wasn't one of them, nor did I want to be. I knew what work they did to live like luxurious prima donnas.

I never acted so violently while being a captive of the Apsaalooke. The Apsaalooke had a blatant tone of derision expressed toward me, and sneers on their faces like the white women sometimes did, especially Mandy. Although those Indian women thought that I was a Blackfeet whore who ran away all because of Summer Fire. I was wishing him dead. I saw myself slitting his throat. Two wrongs often don't make a right, but two wrongs sometimes makes a point. I breathed deeply and scrubbed feeling guilty at having violent thoughts directed at him.

At least The Apsaalooke women thought they had a valid reason to treat me without respect unlike Mandy. She treated me like a lowly servant by rights of an imagined reign of a queen. Plainswomen were tough and always on-the-go traveling from camp to camp by putting up and down teepees. My Apsaalooke masters were an equal fight if I reacted violently to any unkind treatment. The ladies living in Gerta's house were soft and skinny and very weak, they were no match for an Indian woman. They didn't scare me. That's why I think I acted up like I did.

Despite the ruckus, Mandy and I eventually became friends. She even taught me how to sew white women clothing out of a tool called a sewing machine. I had trouble learning how to operate it while pumping my foot on a treadle. I started to dress nicely when they allowed me and Cindy to eat with them more often at the table. I was slowly becoming one of them, but I knew that I looked somewhat different. I preferred to wear light pastels of my newly made dresses, but there was one fine black dress that I decorated Indian style. It had shiny black beads on the sleeves. I sewed some ribbons on the front. The ladies adored that dress. I wore it on Thanksgiving with my beaded headband decorated with an eagle feather. They asked me to wear it on the anniversary date of Columbus discovering America, but I declined.

A few dozen men worked at the Missoula Mills. Most of them didn't have wives. When Cindy showed me around town earlier that year, I hardly saw any women at all. The sheer abundance of men made me feel intoxicated thinking that one might marry me. He'd take me away from being a maid who emptied bunkhouse bedpans. The majority of the Missoula Mills workers visited our house from time to time. There was an upstairs room usually meant for the sexual escapades. Who wants to bring a drunken flour mill worker back to a measly bunkhouse, but Julia often did.

The ladies always stayed up late, while Cindy and I went to bed early so we could get started with the morning duties. Julia in the next bunkhouse often kept us awake with her high-pitched moaning. I was envious and disgusted at the same time. That night I couldn't sleep, so I peeked through the window out of curiosity. Julia was on the clock. He was covered with white flour from the mill. He pushed his hips back and forth, as she moaned very loudly. I never saw two people making love before. I felt a mixture of shame and fascination. I loved seeing the two mounds of his naked bottom moving vigorously on top of her. She licked her lips and kept on calling out to god. He stood up and was covered with muscles from head to toe. It was like the exciting passages of a banned novel that Cindy kept under her mattress.

He stopped moving on top of her and stood beside the bed. His wet penis was glistening beside the kerosene lamp. Julia was on the bed rubbing her soft and syrupy privates. Her breasts and stomach were covered with splotches of white flour. She looked like the nude Venus painting in one of the picture books inside the house. The men seemed to like Julia's long flowing brown hair. She had flowing curves like gentle hillsides. I was very jealous seeing her with him. She often tied her hair sternly in a bun when she wasn't working. All that hair was loose and flowing across her pillow. I lifted my nightgown and compared my black pubic hair to her brown pubic hair. She stopped moaning, so I looked up again. He walked away from the bed. I saw him totally naked from his messy hair to his big feet. He took a big swig from a bottle of beer that was on a desk in the corner. He went back over to her after taking his short beer break from being inside her. His moving buttocks were covered with a light layer of hair as gorgeous as light brown velvet. The hair of his privates matched the color of his goatee. She took her fingertips and caressed the soft patch of hair on his chest between his nipples. His little nipples were hard. He was bouncing on top of her. I never saw a male anus before as it occasionally peeked out between his buttocks while thrusting. His anus seemed fragile like his lips. Julia wouldn't have a nose if she lived in my Blackfeet camp.

The next day, I scrubbed and cursed, cried in bed, and swept the floor. At least I wasn't the only one having to work that hard. I felt better knowing that I had a partner maid who kept house with me. Cindy must have felt so lonely before my arrival. She was less than plain and more than ordinary. I understood why she wasn't a whore like the others. She had a brain to offer men, but somehow many don't like stuff like that. She taught me much knowledge late at night as we lingered in front of the desk. She taught me math, and told me about the great scientists of the day. She even told me about creatures called satyrs, Irish myths, saints and sinners. I was told some scary ghost stories at night, like the headless horseman in sleepy hallow. I told her some scary Blackfeet ghost stories at night, like the lady who lost her little papoose to a deadly sickness. She wanders the two-medicine hills screaming at night searching for her papoose.

Chapter 26-Pop Goes the Cowboys

Gerta, Mandy, Cascade, and Julia all complained at one time or another that the newly arriving frontier wives of the area were uptight and sometimes downright rude to them.

"They refuse to see my presence while they stop in town for provisions. I'm not a threat to their marriages. I never ask our visiting guys if they're married or not, how rude of me if did. I don't know what's wrong with those ladies," Julia whined.

"Maybe we should go to church. Then they wouldn't be so damn high and mighty," Gerta said.

"Like they will accept working women to pray right beside them," Julia said.

"At least the Indians are nice to us when they stop at Worden's," Cascade added.

The Salish Tribe kept a peaceful and close presence. They often camped just outside our town. I took a walk and it dawned on me how different my people and the white people were. The five conical teepees of the Salish contrasted sharply with the right angles of all the buildings in town.

I loved reading the Missoula and Cedar Creek Pioneer. I sometimes read it out loud after breakfast to the women with the aid of Cindy. I wasn't very good at reading at first. Cindy sometimes finished reading out loud my articles after correcting me. Mandy, Cascade, and Julia often corrected my pronunciation of words. Cindy, missing being a countryside teacher, was proud that I was making great progress learning perfect grammar. She said that people might think of Indians with higher regard if I spoke well. I told her that new languages were a natural talent for me. I spoke many of the regional dialects and some French showing off for them. They were truly impressed.

In the newspaper, I saw a photograph of a Sioux warrior wearing a war bonnet by the name of Sitting Bull. There was a photograph of a man by the name of Custer. Cindy explained that Custer was a civil war hero, powerful in the eyes of Americans, yet he was massacred two years before by the Sioux tribe. She read to me an editorial stating that the Indian Menace was an impediment to growth of the plains territories. The pioneers didn't feel safe. Rumor was that Chief Sitting Bull was believed to be gathering Indian tribes in Canada to return to defend his Sioux lands.

I remember reading a newspaper article about the Nez Pearce War. I marveled at the photograph of Chief Joseph how he looked like my father. I returned to stare at the newspaper photograph later that same day. "Those Chiefs look like they could scalp good white men," I said out loud when I didn't think anybody was in the room. "How horrible!" Cascade remarked hearing what I said. I didn't apologize to her as I secretly thought *hurrah for the Indians*. Ki yo! It seems every time a picture of a chief was in the newspaper, a journalist ran off his big mouth about how savage my people were. I kept track of the clashes between the cowboys and Indians when we read the newspaper together. I always silently cheered for the Indians to get rid of the white menace once and for all, but where would I go if that happened?

So many new people came through town that nobody got to know each other properly. They often cherished their privacy to the point of seclusion. I felt more isolation surrounded by dozens of people in town than when I was traveling alone with my dog Smoke Jumper. I wondered if the travelers going through town felt tension when seeing my tan skin. I was far from the action of cowboy chiefs killing Indian chiefs and vice versa. At first, I was treated well by most of the townsfolk, then quickly over time, some newcomers in town found out I was Indian. They acted rude and obnoxious in the quietest way possible. That gentle aggression was something so-called civilized people turned into high art.

The Salish were not seen as a threat like they once were seen years before. They not only had their camp of teepees just outside town to trade with the locals, but also most of them converted to Christianity. Cindy said that if the Nez Pearce or Sioux converted to Christianity, they'd become enlightened too.

Although there was a peace treaty signed decades before between the Salish and the Blackfeet, the Salish Indians ignored me and I ignored them. Who was I fooling? They knew I was Indian dressed in white women's dresses. Perhaps they weren't sure what tribe I came from unless some big mouth gossip told them. I knew there would be continuing resentment about my people ambushing their tribe, even thought it was a long time ago.

I stopped wishing for the white people to go back from where they came from one afternoon. I invited Cindy to have tea and cookies in the sitting room. Cindy told me about how her parents came to New York City in 1856. The Irish tribe was being starved to death because of the English tribe's occupation on their lands. The lords of the manors ate cake while the Irish peasants starved during a potato famine. The Irish had nowhere to go but to America where they had a chance at survival. Some didn't want to go to Canada because too many Canucks idolized the queen. At least in America the Irish could join the rest of immigrants and make fun of the English behind their backs. I realized that some white tribes were more aggressive than others. The Irish really didn't have a choice but to leave their own land.

It sounded to me that the way the English were treating the Irish was similar to the way the Americans were treating the Indian Tribes. The French were good to us by just trading women and beaver furs. They helped to create The Metis tribe of half-French and half-Indian blood. The English people, however, sounded more bloodthirsty than the American people, but then I realized my Jack was American. Dealing with Americans meant tricky business.

Everyone around me wanted to be American. They wanted Montana to be a state rather than a territorial backwater. I hoped we remained a territory with more dialogue between the native tribes and the newcomers. If we remained a territory and became the sovereign country of Montana, perhaps the reservation system the white chiefs back east thought up wouldn't happen anymore.

None of the ladies had any interest in learning about my people except Cindy. I told her the story about First Man and First Woman arguing if people should die or not. First Man threw a buffalo chip into the water. If the buffalo chip floats, then people only die for four days and come back to life again. If it sinks, we die forever. "We can blame our deaths on shit," I said to Cindy.

She laughed and laughed and said, "Oh shit!" Then she told me the story about Mary being a virgin but still having a baby.

I laughed and laughed and said, "A virgin mother!" Why she didn't laugh with me, I don't know.

By 1883 at age twenty-four, I spoke so well that I was considered a proper lady and regained some respect despite the Indian Menace. I was invited to a Christmas party at the banker's house. I was asked to go by a gentleman named Gregory who worked at Worden and Company. I was out shopping when he said that I picked out the best eggs. I smiled and he quickly invited me to the party with him. Just like that! He had a tan, blue eyes, and brown hair. He was pretty for a man and younger than most settlers. At the party, the townsfolk engaged me as one of their own for the first time. I was so nervous that I just stood in the corner smiling.

It was beautiful with a fancy Christmas tree, crystal, and silver decorations. People drank eggnog beside the plants of holly. A man played Christmas tunes on a violin. I knew almost everybody. They all knew I was a maid for the ladies of Madam Gerta's house." Founders of the town chiefs Cap Higgins and Frank Worden were there. They stood looking powerful yet gentle in front of the fireplace talking with residents.

I never talked to Cap or Frank much because they were always busy running the mill and working on town projects. Cap came over and asked me if his workers often came to visit the ladies. I said "yes." He said, "I don't know how I feel about that." He was interrupted by the butcher. I wanted to talk to him more.

Gregory took me by the hand and led me outside to the back porch. Nobody was outside in such frigid snow and wind. I looked up and saw mistletoe hanging from above. He kissed me on the cheek. We both were tipsy on eggnog. He held my hand all the way home on the slippery road. On the porch, he looked into my eyes and we kissed for what seemed like days. I gladly lost time. Once I was inside, Mandy, Cascade, and Julia were mad that they never were invited to such a party by the townsfolk. I felt sad for Cindy who asked me many questions about the party and how it felt to be with Gregory. She sat in front of the stove while petting our housecat sadly staring at nothing.

Gregory winked at me when I went shopping again. We talked on the street and he asked questions about the ladies of the house. He wanted to know what they did during the night. Who visited them? What did they wear at night! Were they nice? I was wrong about him seeming like an honorable young man. He was only twenty-one years old, just a few years younger than me. He wasn't ready for love, and my heart sank knowing that.

One evening I was staring at the moon praying to her. I turned around hoping my housemates wouldn't see me praying.

It was dark and I realized that two dark silhouettes were standing in front of the doorway of the bunkhouse. Mandy was holding Gregory in a tight embrace almost violently kissing him. He moaned a deep throaty growl. He breathed in a quivering sigh. Hearing him made me want to scream at both of them. He waved goodbye to her. She stood in the moonlight looking like a woman of ill morals in her bloomers with no top. It was chilly and I remember hoping she would catch pneumonia. Mandy yelled out toward where I hid, "This isn't a fairytale." I stood still hoping that I remained an inanimate shadow to her. She went into her bunkhouse and slammed the door.

Gregory tried speaking to me when I went shopping for coffee and flour, but I ignored him. He followed behind me trying to get my attention. I saw him standing in front of the store staring after me out of the corner of my eye. I bumped into an angry-looking woman who quietly muttered, "Clumsy fucking Indian squaw." I was stunned.

"Hey, that isn't nice," Gregory said to her as she went outside.

Meeting such a foul woman was my first encounter with a business rival of Gerta's. Her name was Mary, and she was no virgin.

Throughout the years, some people were friendly. Others sneered at me with disdain. Some didn't even speak to me when I spoke to them. It depended on what a person read in the newspapers and what a person believed about Indians.

Front Street and Main Streets were growing crowded. Many of the buildings were touching each other. Some had second stories; a few even had third stories. They were made out of wood being that the town was too poor for bricks. The town once seemed like family with just Frank Worden, Cap Higgins, the Missoula Mills workers, and the prostitutes. More loggers began moving in with their wives. Many more pioneers settled in the area. Too many newcomers arrived that the town didn't seem to belong to us anymore.

Gerta didn't think that a simple farm house was decent enough for ladies of finery. The mill workers were not coming out as often to visit the humble whorehouse, to be blunt. There were plenty of prostitutes on Front Street that were closer to them. Some of them were just up the stairs above the card rooms and saloons. She decided that her three working ladies should move to Front Street closer to the customers. I was wringing water from clothing when I heard Gerta and Richie discussing quietly what they should do with me.

"She's pretty though. I think the men would want to dance with her just out of curiosity. I don't think any of them are ready for a relationship with anybody who isn't white," Gerta said.

"What if the men don't want to pay a dime to dance with her at the hall?" Richie asked.

"You see how the men stare at her in town? Christ, I see you staring at her when you think somebody isn't looking. Ah, somebody's blushing now. She'll get plenty of men who'll want to dance with her. I ain't worried about that," Gerta said.

"Why don't you ask her to become a working woman?" Richie asked.

"She's a fucking injun squaw. Who would want to screw her? I hinted about that vocation. She doesn't seem interested in doing that. I'm not going to force her to do it. Why? Are you thinking about being her first customer?" Gerta asked him with big hearty German woman laughter.

"You say the darndest things lady," Richie said.

I stared at the dirty laundry water in the metal tub before me. I thought about the naked man thrusting his hips on top of Julia. Then I felt fear.

Gerta worked quickly with setting up everything for the move. A few months later, she walked with all us to Front Street so we could view our future home. We were all relieved that the newly built building was closer to everything. It was one block from the main intersection. Each of us got our own rooms. The two story boarding house was right over a cafe. Gerta got some mill workers to work on a house that she planned to live in on other side of the river. She was one of the first people who decided to build a house over there. She said that she was finally able to build a beautiful three story Victorian brick house. “My girls know how to work hard for me.” Cindy and I looked at each other in anger.

Gerta stared at me and said, “Victoria, you can still be my maid at my new home when it gets finished. It’ll be easier helping just little ‘ol me with the housework instead of cleaning up after these three here. Now that you’re fairly accustomed to living like an American does! You can either rent an empty room having some privacy, or you can be my maid.”

“I don’t like being a maid,” I quickly said hoping for an option.

“Good. I have an opportunity for you. There’s this little dime-a-dance hall that a lady friend of mine runs. You can pay for rent that way. Did I tell you all that you’ll be paying me rent. I bought this building,” she said with glee. We all cheered in excitement because we knew that we would never be kicked out to the streets with her as our landlord.

Gerta added, “We are a street of liberated women free from the tyranny of male domination. They don’t like free women here in Missoula. As you all know, this street has women just like us. Unmarried women who choose purposely not to have husbands. If anybody gives you any problems, you come to me. I’ll soon be living in my swanky digs. Cindy will show you where I live. She’s still going to clean up after all of you, poor thing. Rent is only .75 cents a week. I’m keeping the rents cheap because I want my women to flourish not flounder. Tips given to me will be great too, if you like to keep your rent low." She took out a set of keys and handed me a key with room number 12 etched on it.

We all giggled in happiness that our lives were quickly progressing. We gave each other hugs and went into the five apartments. We all needed to share the kitchen and the bathroom, but at least it was better than the bunkhouses. Cindy brought with her a jug of homemade dandelion wine. We met again and stood around the parlor room with smiles.

Cindy usually didn't drink at all. She sat down on the floor and said, "Nobody ever wants to love me. Nobody thinks I'm interesting. Nobody wants to pay any attention to me." Tears were springing out of her eyes. Gerta sat down beside her and said, "One day you will find a man to love you." She gave her a hug.

"A man will never find me lovable, not with my wrists slit," she wailed.

The night grew into somberness. We had no idea that she felt so alone.

"You have a lot to offer a man."

Cindy stood up with her eyes looking wild. She began screaming absurdities at us. "Yes I do. I have tons of good qualities. Nevertheless, the men here don't dare touch me because I work for you. You fucking bitches! You fucking sows! You syphilis brained damsels not even going to purgatory but straight to hell. They think I'm the ugly one who gets fucked at the cheapest price! I'll do anything because I can't get a man. I don't want them thinking that I would screw a five year old boy, or a dead horse, because I'm the homely one who gets used the most," Cindy screamed.

We all stared at her as she wailed. She seemed to have caught what she said, while in a shaky voice said, "I'm sorry. I have no other place to go. You women are all that I have." We all were crying by then. We were all that we had.

"That's okay Cindy. You finally got it out. You yell at us, so you don't harm yourself," Gerta said like my mother. Nobody had any hankies to wipe our tears. Gerta became my mother and as I saw her holding Cindy, I felt such an anguish that it can't be described, only felt to be understood. My mother Fawn in Rain was gone out of my life forever. It was almost worse than death, because in death, they never come back, but when away, I was tortured not knowing what happened to her. The fact that she was on the same soil as me, but I couldn't see her was too horrible.

"Gerta, some of the guys are saying such bad things about you all. That we bring in kids to corrupt, that unspeakable perversities are happening on Front Street. They told me in detail because they know that I pray. What I revealed to you isn't as bad as a couple of other things that I heard. I can't believe words can hurt as much as getting hit. Sometimes I'm afraid of even passing by the mill workers because I'm afraid one might harm me by saying horrible things about you all. It hurts me because I know it isn't true," she cried.

After Cindy calmed down, we all drank. Later we all walked quietly back home. The night was long. Everybody was drunk on wine, including me and Cindy. Even though I woke up with a headache, the next day Cindy led me across the river to a dance instructor.

"Gerta will be living that way on this side of the river. The woman who runs the dime-a-dance hall lives on this side too. South of the Clark Fork River is becoming known as the place where all the wealthy people want to move," she said as we crossed the bridge. I noticed how lofty and majestic the Victorian houses were in the newer neighborhood. Once we got on the other side the wind seemed to calm down. We headed to a frilly sky blue house on a corner.

I was introduced to a crabby lady by the name of Shirley. Shirley told me she was a dancer all of her life, but that she was old, she had nothing but cramps. She was dressed all in black and waved a cane around. She barked orders to a shrugging piano man. I was led into an empty room with shiny hardwood floors and a piano.

"Gerta told me that we are teaching you how to dance. There will be none of that primitive hopping around here," she said to me in a cracking voice.

"George, play the little ditty called Springtime Robert," she barked.

The piano man began playing a bouncy melody. She faced me and told me to follow her footsteps. I followed her instructions slowly for some time, but she quickly grew impatient. "No! Be more flowing! You aren't going to get anybody to dance if you jerk around like that. Smile some, if you don't look like you're enjoying yourself, then how are the poor men going to enjoy themselves?" She gritted her teeth like she wanted to be anywhere but there in the empty room. "One, two, three, four….well you're a fast learner! There is one thing you need to do. You need to tie those braids up under a hat or get somebody to cut 'em off. It's a requirement. If you refuse, you won't be working for me."

I wanted to tell her that my hair is the seat of my soul. Did she understand that my hair is as sacred as the sun? We danced so long that my feet hurt. Cindy came into the room and told me it was time to return home. I was glad to leave crabby ass Shirley. She didn't know that Indian women cut off their braids only when in mourning. I hoped not to cut my braids off for Cindy. She was growing more faint with each day.

My first day of work dancing with lonely bachelors was exactly like my thousandth day of work. The job wasn't very exciting and quite boring most of the time. Sometimes a handsome and charming man chatted me up nicely. The hall itself was simple and elegant. The wooden floors were as shiny as Shirley's floors. The ceiling had fancy crown moldings. What was most vivid were the scents of pomade and aftershave intermixed with sweet perfumes imported from France. In front of brick walls stood big black iron candelabras almost as tall as the women. Men stood on one side of the room staring at us until they approached for a waltz and gave us a dime. Shirley sat in a wooden chair in the corner writing into a book keeping track of how many dances each woman received. We were to give her 30 percent of our earnings. It was an easy life. One I chose to live for a few years.

It was fairly evident in the community that all of the women who lived in the boarding houses on Front Street were soiled doves, not some, or a few, or a lot, but all! Except me and Cindy, it seemed like. They put on heavy makeup and their finest low-cut dresses smelling of sweet flowers showing enough bosoms to attract money. The men showed up like flies to a bucket of milk. They followed the ladies like lost puppies in the hallways all while the exotic ladies giggled and acted excited. My boarding house mates were good actresses. They had to pretend well because although many of the men were handsome, many more were very undesirable in grooming. The stink of whiskey and beer was atrocious on many. I didn't approve of what they were doing, but they were my friends. I couldn't ignore that I loved them. I just didn't want to hear about what they did in private....okay I was curious about what they did in private. I just didn't want to admit it like many others for fear of catching the mind disease I heard about called perversity.

I was getting older and wiser to the hidden tricks of the mind. In the fall of 1883, I had just turned twenty-four years old. It was a special year in the area. Missoula officially became a city. We elected the first mayor by the name of Frank Woody. There was a celebration and picnic. Everyone was there including all of us Front Street gals. Cascade bragged that she was going to the festivities to make better business connections to get a different sort of customer. Better ones that didn't frequent the saloons but had families, like the men who were stationed at the new Ft. Missoula. Our town was growing quickly since the Great Northern railroad went through town. Even more customers, traveling men, conveniently visited them. Not surprisingly, the railroad brought even more people that are interesting into our hazy town. Some men brought a new exotic facet that arrived with them.

One day I was walking with Cindy with dry goods from Worden and Company when I saw a woman who had slanted eyes and shiny decorative clothing of white flower patterns. I was dumbfounded by her refined beauty as she strolled peacefully by. She was exquisitely delicate.

"What tribe does she come from?" I asked Cindy.

"She's an Oriental. Men are paying higher prices for the exotic. You probably could make loads of money if you wanted."

I was finally fed up with working at that wretched dime-a-dance because commodity prices were getting higher. I was considering becoming a soiled dove just like my neighbors, but I hesitated because I still felt apprehensive toward sex. Almost being a cut-nose made me that way. At home, I found a bawdy poem written in ink hidden under a vase one day that made me blush. The title of the poem caught my attention called Lil the Whore.

In a town of Louieville
There lives a well known whore named Lil,
Now it was known for miles around,
that no two men could hold her down,
then over the hill came a bare ass Greek,
Who said his name was Piss Pot Pete,
He laid his cock across the bar,
It was seventeen inches long and twice as hard.

Lil knew then that she had met her fate,
but to back out then was too late,
So they chose a spot up on the hill,
In back of the shit house behind the mill,
He mounted her like a Belgium Stud,
And threw her ass into the mud,
and they fucked and fucked for hours and hours,
Until they killed all the trees and flowers,
Lil tried some stuff, some super stunts,
Unknown to other common cunts,
Finally a sigh and a cough,
Lil gave up and Pete jacked off.
Now Lil is no longer a well known whore.
And Pete is the father of four or more,
They no longer do it behind the mill,
For now they do it on the window sill.
Pete better teach his kids right from wrong,
Or they will go about singing this song,
Garter Fixer,
Darling let me fix your garter,
Just an inch above your knee,
And my hand slipped up farther,
And she shot all over me.

I blushed wondering if Cindy or Mandy brought the dirty poem into our home for they were the only two who liked to read. The poem said it was written by Shakespeare, but I had my doubts. I was conditioned to be a good woman in a grim way. Although sometimes at night I fantasized I was with some of the better looking men. I was told every western town and city had whores, but ours were classier. The ones in the rowdy city of Butte were said to advertise themselves in the windows.

Chapter 27-Lonesome Crises

I made it through the next few years relatively unscathed. Cindy had a couple of attempts on her own life. She took half a bottle of morphine and we almost lost her. We kept a keen eye on her letting her know that she was well loved. I told her that if she were in my place, constantly being judged on whether she looked savory or not to dance with, that she would feel worse. I was by far the oldest woman at the dances by the age of twenty-nine in the year 1888. All the dancers were an average age of eighteen to twenty years old and it was made worse because I got the nickname of "ma" by my co-workers. Front Street had grown fancier with some three and four story buildings with fancy decorative cornices on the rooftops. There were a couple of small cafes and many more saloons.

Everybody knew that many towns throughout the frontier west were growing just as fast as our own. Cindy, Mandy, Cascade, and Julia eventually all moved out of the building. I was left behind with new boarding house mates. All four of my original friends went forward with their lives. Cascade married one of her customers and moved to Seattle. Mandy owned her own home based business baking cookies and delivering them around town. Julia married a wealthy man who was rich from prospecting gold. Cindy got a job teaching children. She finally met a man. She never came around to visit me and Gerta after that. She never truly needed us, just a man.

Prices were continuing to get higher. I asked Shirley to raise the prices of the dances. She said that she would once she stopped leasing the hall at the hotel and got her own fancy joint, along with cheap alcohol. "So the men really would want to pay higher prices and tip better," she said. She told me that Big One

Eyed Jack kept her in business for many years with cheap whiskey before the law caught up with him. She had to keep the prices just a dime because she was in competition with another dime-a-dance hall that the men frequented that was in a hotel. If she raised dances to .15 or .20 cents, she would lose customers.

Most of the dancers moonlighted with secondary employment as working ladies. They used the dances as opportunities to slip their room number into the pockets of their partners as they danced. Shirley encouraged that in the dancers while looking the other way.

Shirley and Gerta were best friends. They bought a couple of other rundown boarding houses together. Nobody was coerced into the profession. I wasn't ready to do it yet. I had a few regular men who I danced with who knew I didn't do everything with men. They kept on coming back kidding that they should be my first customer if I expanded my job skills. A couple of the more classy gentlemen didn't have anything to do with the working ladies and dancing provided them with comfortable intimacy. One of my regular customers who waltzed with me said, "All the regulars want you because they've been dancing with you for years now and they know you're still tight."

My feet always hurt after dancing for hours that I took more and more morphine medicine. My favorite was the Indian Herbal Cure. I knew that no Blackfeet would ever let white people know about their sacred herbal cures. I often wondered what tribe gave away their herbal secrets. Nonetheless the drink made me feel light and airy. Another morphine magic potion was a medicine called Turkish Cough Syrup. Morphine was a miracle drug and it was in toothpaste. I often read *Sherlock Holmes* while feeling the floating effects of the angelic substance. I learned that morphine was first given to some wives as a cure for hysteria to save their marriages.

The Sears Roebuck catalogue had the most popular hysteria cure, a long rod, which to me looked like male anatomy. They were to insert the rod into their womanhood and that calmed the symptoms. I preferred morphine instead. One thing that was never a good idea was morphine wine. We heard morphine wine knocked people out, so it was at the drugstore and in the saloons for only about two months.

My favorite of favorite places to go was the drugstore at the Missoula Mercantile, where everything was under one roof which was just dandy. It was even better than Worden and Company that used to be the only store in town. I often went there and shopped in a very cheerful mood after getting all giddy on cocaine. At home some women got to feeling peppy while sipping on Pemberton's French Wine Coca that had cocaine in it too. Cocaine was loved by just about almost everyone. It was advertised in the Saturday Evening Post. Mr. Pemberton was also responsible for concocting Coca Cola that was all the rage.

We ladies liked to sit at the bar of the drugstore to chat. The soda jerk served us Coca Cola with glee. The men usually called the soda fountain the "hop joint," because they got a lift from the arousing leaf. For women it was the only acceptable alternative because we weren't allowed to drink in saloons. The drugstore soda fountain often mimicked the saloons. I spent many afternoons chatting and laughing with my neighbors.

We often bought Pep Pills that also contained the healthy herbal cure of wonderful cocaine. It made the world seem shiny, clear, and sleek. No matter how dusty the town became, it felt like we were in an oasis in the midst of a drought wasteland giddy on a third glass. Mostly we enjoyed the thirst quenching effect as we took a break from our lives. That medicinal leaf seemed holy to me being in my medicine cabinet for when I got sick. Not surprisingly, I heard through the grapevine that a Corsican monk invented the popular Vin Mariani, which was a competitive brand of Pemberton's wine.

Some people drank too much of coca-wine and were just plain over-talkative drunks.

Speaking of drunks, when Missoula celebrates, I swear that I almost heard the mountains echo the giddy laughter of rowdy crowds. Especially on November 8, 1889, the day Montana became a state in America. We celebrated with fireworks, balloons, clowns, grilled hamburgers in the gardens along the river. The mood was one of hope, but I felt left behind and disappointed that I just turned thirty years old and I was still working as a dancer. A new horse drawn streetcar drove across the newest Higgins Bridge as more people moved away from the crowded downtown to the other side of the river. Officially our little mill town became a city very quickly over just several years. Visitors said that it wasn't big as San Francisco or Seattle, but it had a certain charm.

I couldn't even see the Salish teepees anymore just outside of town. Just as Cindy predicted years before, the south side became the neighborhood where the wealthy lived. Marvelous Queen Anne style houses were constructed here and there. Business wasn't good at the dime-a-dance hall for me. I really felt old around the newest dancers. They looked almost like kids to me. I felt like I really needed a friend to talk to.

I sent a bike messenger to Pine Street asking Mandy to meet me at the drugstore. I hoped that we could visit and get giddy on soda. Mandy showed up just after I dissolved two cocaine breath mints. I smiled at her as I felt perky which hid my true everyday feelings of futility. She sat on the soda barstool next to me and ordered a Coca Cola.

"I just don't know what I'm going to do with my life," I said to Mandy,

"You're doing well Victoria."

"No, I feel trapped. I'm not making any progress. I just feel stuck at that damn job. I'm getting too old to dance with twenty year old men. Hardly any man asks me to dance anymore. I don't have enough money to live the type of life that I want to live."

"You can always bring men back to your room," she plainly suggested.

"I don't think that I can do that at all," I said.

"Why not? Look at me. I've earned enough money to construct a house. I have a younger man who wants to stay living with me despite my desire not to marry him. What other options do you have?"

I remained quiet as we drank. I was so broke Mandy had to buy me a second and third drink. She got really talkative while we drank soda. I half listened to her while thinking about my life. There really weren't many opportunities given to women. We're expected to be wives and have babies, and be the embodiment of motherhood. Some got lucky and worked at their parents' businesses, or taught children at school. We weren't allowed to do many things the men got to do. We couldn't vote, drink in the saloons unless a man snuck us a shot in our sodas or under the table. Some women were lucky to be born with talent and became stage actresses or sang at the light opera. Sadly I didn't fit any of those categories.

I wanted to become a seamstress, but the tensions between Indians and whites grew even more apparent. I was blatantly ignored by one seamstress. The other said she would "get back to me" with an icy face as animated as petrified wood.

I felt more confident as the herbal kicked in and said, "I'll give entertaining men a try!"

"It isn't as bad as you think it is. There were only a few times I wanted to vomit," she said.

Mandy went about explaining the finer details about how Gerta kept her soiled doves in two saloons. I always thought that two men who visited my boarding house roommates were customers. I learned that Jonah and Max had the easiest job in the world. They kept an eye on the working women while sipping their beers making sure the women were all safe. Both men had expert memories. If a woman got hurt by a man, they searched for the culprit.

It was very, very rare that a woman got hurt. We heard about Jack the Ripper in London, but Missoula wasn't London. Jonah and Max made sure Gerta's ladies acted appropriately flirtatious, and were treated with respect. They didn't want us to drink too much while entertaining men in our rooms. Allocating alcohol was difficult for them to do, since some customers had small bottles in their pockets for the ladies. Gerta's working women were expected to remain poised and classy. I already knew what I was getting myself into from what the ladies described who lived with me. My heart was going to be made out of gold.

Chapter 28-The Look of Love

I felt that prostitution was a risky occupation. Men worked perilous occupations such as coal and gold mining or logging where deadly accidents happened. I was especially hesitant since a couple of Front Street women caught diphtheria after seeing men from Helena, around the time of the deadly outbreak. We were scared that the outbreak was spreading in Missoula from those two, but luckily it didn't spread. They remained here five years later after the outbreak. I couldn't have imagined myself as a spinster dancing with men half my age. I was already looking ridiculous. Being a prostitute was my only ticket forward. I had to despite such risks.

Gerta was filled with joy for me and for herself. I might finally pay back all of the loans she gave me. She knew I was disciplined to save enough money to grow old comfortably. I was required to give a silver dollar apiece to Jonah and Max. Of course to keep my rent low, I had to give generous tips to Gerta. She said I was an asset to her since I was exotic. The men were starting to develop specialties for the different. The competition was getting hot.

I did my face up with more makeup than ever before. I was given encouragement from a couple of younger women at home.

"It's just like fishing for men," one of my housemates said. She crouched her shoulders just a bit as she bowed her head just a little. She looked over her left shoulder with her eyelids lowered somewhat.

"Give them sleepy eyes, the look of love," she put her fan over her mouth and giggled.

I walked down Higgins Street to a saloon past a large sign that read: 'Homes for settlement in the Mission Valley.

Stake your claim today.' That instantly distracted me as I went to work my first evening. I knew the Mission Valley was right smack dab in the middle of the Salish and Kootenai tribes Flathead Reservation. I thought, "They can't do that! That's a sovereign nation. How can a foreign government sell the land of literally another country to Americans? That's totally illegal!" Then I remember reading in the newspaper about the Dawes Act.

The days of white people needing a special permit to go into a reservation were gone. I suddenly remembered that I had to sleep with white men to get ahead in life. I didn't know why I just didn't go back home to my people. I left before my tribe was sent to a reservation. I was too scared to see the changes that brought havoc to them that were reported in the newspaper. I reminded myself that I had to be a good actress to make love to the enemy. Perhaps that's why their cities have suffered wave after wave of illnesses, as divine payback from Grandmother Earth from being seen as just a whore to be used. At least I had something in common with Grandmother Earth.

I walked into the Oxford Saloon. I felt men staring at me right away. I looked like a white woman, the way I had made my face done up with makeup, but there was something different about me they couldn't pinpoint. Plus the regular patrons of the saloon were always interested in a fresh rose in full bloom. I sat at a table waiting for a gentleman to buy me a drink. I was craving a ginger ale. I tried to hide my nervousness. Coca Cola pepped me up to a heightened sense of awareness that made me too nervous when in new company. Jittery nerves were a known side effect of cocaine in our remedies and beverages. Even though doctors have said it was good for the mind, the women on Front Street were becoming aware of the dark side of not only cocaine, but also morphine.

Two clumsy looking men came into the saloon wearing ragged suits that were covered with dust. Their knee high boots were muddy up to their ankles. At least the scruffy two's moustaches and goatees were trimmed nice and neatly making them appear almost like gentlemen.

"Now behave Boomer. This here is a classy joint," the first man said.

"Ah shucks Jeremiah, I dint wanna stop playin' poker," Boomer complained.

They walked up to the bar. Jeremiah ordered a gin mixed with Coca Cola. A frisky combination of drinks I thought. Boomer ordered, "A plain 'ol beer, I like my drinks like I like my women, not too fancy, and heavy on the quenching effects, 'er," Boomer stopped at a loss of words.

They were dressed up in some of their finest clothing. That Jeremiah was the more handsome of the two. He wore a wild rag necktie with a shiny bronze pendant, and a derby style hat. His canvas cotton vest made him look ready. That Boomer fellow was somewhat goofy with a slouch hat and a silky neckerchief. I noticed his pinstripe pants were also all crusted with mud like he tripped outside. I could tell they were laborers since they both were covered with dust. I figured they were hard working men and deserved a little rest and relaxation. I was ready to provide it for a sum.

"Shut that damn whine Boomer," Jeremiah said.

Several minutes passed by. I heard several improper conversations over a fiddle. Jeremiah spotted me. He smiled while I looked down at my ring given to me from Big One Eyed Jack. I slowly but hungrily looked back at him. Ah, the look of love does open up doors as he came over to my table. "Darling would you like a drink?"

"Yes, I never thought you'd ask. A ginger ale please."

"I reckon I'd buy a sassy lookin' gal like you just about anything."

"I don't care about gifts. I care about how well a man makes love to a lady," I teased and then giggled. I was very nervous inside. My every action was designed to hide my nervousness.

When Jeremiah went to the bar, I noticed many more ladies entering. A bunch of ordinary women were dressed in white. They looked around sadly at us. A couple of them nodded and smiled at a few of the gamblers playing in the corner. I made eye contact with one and she gave me a blank look. I realized that the women were high profile women of the community. One was the wife of a businessman, and a couple of the others were the banker's daughters. Both sisters looked prim and clean. There were six of them staring at us for a short time all looking nervous.

Over the piano they sang a chorus. "Our father is the dove to the heart. Jesus is the maker thou is his art," they sang a song with great vigor in merriment. They clapped their hands to the corny tune. The piano player rolled his eyes and dabbed the sweat of his brow with his hanky. "Repent ye sinners!" a woman yelled. Four soiled doves stared at the spectacle completely bored. They finished their song and all was quiet for a sec. Everybody suddenly busted out in laughter at them, which disturbed them. They stared in somber silence. A couple of them glared at everybody with hands on their hips. Nobody approached them at all. After awhile they just left.

"Women's Christian Temperance Union, stay away from them like the plague," a fellow working lady said to me with a sneer as she fluttered her fan.

I noticed Jeremiah at the bar ordering a shot of tequila. He turned around, lifted his eyebrows at me, and winked. He got quickly distracted by a friend who was tapping him on the shoulder. I waited patiently for him to return when another man, a man I recognized as a policeman from the Missoula County Sheriff Department, was off duty and ready for some tension release.

He winked at me as his elbows rested on the bar. He was wearing a black frock coat, shiny rounded toe boots, and a cowboy hat. His face was shiny and his eyes were bloodshot above his nicely curved handlebar moustache. I admired his fancy black and dark gray double breasted vest that had a flowing pattern. His vest was expensive reminding me of the wallpaper in the Helena hotel. He had fine taste that probably included his fine taste in tasting women. We flamboyant ladies were like cheap wine in the disguise of vintage just for frivolous tasting. Shouldn't I be savored instead? He came swaggering over to me with a cocky arrogance.

"I've seen you around here," he said with a cheeky grin as he pointed at me.

"Gee. I would have remembered your handsome face if I ever saw you before," I said what I practiced in front of a mirror.

He was drunk. Many drunk people have a tendency of grandiose fantasies, because when he told me he was a senator from Washington D.C., I just played into his fantasy. I wasn't really a person to him anyway. I was just a fantasy to all those men. All of the women on Front Street were fantasy women acting and performing. I didn't say I wasn't enjoying my job, because I was having fun being on stage.

"Senator, I'll have to do some extra effort tonight. Well, I better go back to my pretty room."

"Would you like me to accompany you?" he asked.

"Please, I'll show you my room, it's sweet as peaches and cream," I said with a high-pitched lilt.

We went back to my room holding hands as I kept a smile at all times. He looked at me with intense desire while we stood on a street corner. We began climbing the stairs to my room. I turned around and he was watching my ass as I was going up. I stopped on a stairway landing. I moved forward to kiss him. I closed my eyes and thought of myself kissing Scruffy Hunter.

We hurried back to my room. My dress landed on the floor. I wore a bustier that was easily unzipped. He slowly moved on top of me. We both moved our hips quickly back and forth in a dual sprint. I imagined Jack, and by doing so, I acted like I was enjoying the moment.

The policeman acted strangely afterward. He refused to say anything or even look at me. He seemed ashamed about what he just did. He put four silver dollars on the bedside table. I felt glad of actually having some spending money. I had the energy to make more money. I went out fishing again.

I noticed Boomer was nowhere to be seen upon returning to the Oxford Saloon. I walked past Jeremiah and said, "Where's my ginger ale? I'm thirsty." He stopped talking to the men at the bar and followed me to a table in the corner. "I'll be back, sorry ma'am I plumb forgot your drink. I'm just having a hog-killin' time shooting the shit with the fellows." He returned with my drink. I drank the ginger ale out of a straw like a lady. I noticed lipstick smeared on the straw. "You're so beautiful," he said.

"Oh, I never heard anybody describe me like that before."

"Yeah right," he sarcastically said. He stared at me saying nothing as he watched me slowly sip the soda. When I finished he asked me, "Would you like some company?"

"Of course," I smiled. We held hands back to my room.

The next day I went to a very nice restaurant by myself. I don't mean to brag, but I ordered sirloin steak a la jardinière for .50 cents, a pint of California zinfandel wine for .40 cents, and a .10 cent apple pie. It was years since I ate out. I never was able to afford it before. I felt like a princess tipsy on wine. I acquired a taste for red wine after so many years living in Missoula.

I loved the second floor of the rugged wooden two story boarding house. Flowers were placed in marvelous vases made out of crystal. Little statues of the busts of man and woman were on a piano. Impressionist style paintings hung on the walls. Gold colored crown moldings were on the ceiling. My only complaint was that the sitting room was small and crowded. All of us women were content but I ruined it all.

Chapter 29-Shivering Dignity

Everybody was talking about it. They said that the Bitterroot Salish tribe planned to travel through town. I knew that some of the Salish already moved from their traditional land called the Bitterroot Valley. The government was forcibly relocating the rest northward. Nobody knew why they were being moved, especially since the Salish were not a threat.

"That's because they can," Gerta explained with distaste.

"They like to play the poor Indians like a game of checkers. To make a tribe move somewhere else for no good reason is just a play for power. 'Look how powerful we are, we can make you do this.' White fuckers!" Richie added with a scowl. My eyes darted to his blonde hair.

The townsfolk could see the mouth of the valley just south of town. The tribe traditionally used to camp near the Clark Fork river, but our little city displaced them. I knew that their leader named Chief Charlo felt betrayed by the white chiefs back east.

We were ordered not to get close to the tribe at all. My curiosity overcame me like a blast of cool air overtaking a scorching summer afternoon. I couldn't resist the storm of witnessing bitterness crossing cold waters. Cindy read to me from a journal what Chief Charlo wrote to the newspapers when the government wanted to tax the Indians. I couldn't believe the dimness of thought. Stupidity weakly was shining through gray clouds of those who thought to tax the starving. The tribes had no money at all. How could such avarice become consensus to strangle the hungry?

Since Cindy taught me how to read and write. We discussed Chief's Charlo's response about taxes. I felt a yearning coldness reading the Chief's words of anger. Dull aching covered me like the near constant gray skies. “He, the cause of our ruin, is his own snake,” Cindy read out loud. I heard that some of the Salish elders didn’t want anything to do with the white man’s god. What can they do when the young ones were promised so many blessings after death? The hungry grow weaker in their bodies, not allowed to go anywhere off the reservations to hunt. It takes a lot of wild game to feed hundreds of people. Men not allowed to hunt off tiny parcels of land couldn’t hunt for a proper amount of game. Cap Higgins and his buddies got to go anywhere in the mountains to hunt. Moose heads and the like decorated their homes.

I defied official orders from the men at Ft. Missoula. They were not my keepers. I felt rebelliousness. A disrespectful government is easy to ignore. I headed out to walk along the muddy banks of the river. I sat on a mound so I could get a good look at them. The sky was gray and drizzly. It was October and when I shivered, I felt more alone than anybody should be allowed to feel. Was there a god anymore? Coldness inside my soul and outside my body swept over me. The dampness outside the cozy houses seemed stiffening. I remember when I was younger it never felt so cold outside. Indoor living did that to me.

I saw hundreds of people in the distance moving very slowly. They were crossing the Higgins Street bridge on their horses. Skinny warriors can’t fight very well. They were purposely not fed, as I saw emaciated people of all ages slowly and hopelessly go across that wretched bridge. Over a hundred people looked at nobody but at the ground as they were passing through.

A sight made me so homesick that I loudly wept. The women were trying to keep warm in their blankets. I saw the chief. He was walking proudly overcoming the cold waters of humiliation from the land of broken promises. I wanted to run up to all of the Indians and tell them to take me away with them. They were made so destitute even their horses were skinny. I knew that I would only suffer more if I left with them. Their kids seemed mesmerized at crossing a bridge for the first time. They had no idea where they were being led to. They just knew they were going to a place called the Jocko Valley.

How strong those men once were, yet how weak they became. The Chief words, his poetic protest that Cindy and I studied, played in my mind as I saw an entire nation move from one side of the river to the other side. “His laws never gave us a blade nor a tree, nor a duck, nor a grouse, nor a trout. No; like the wolverine that steals your cache, how often does he come? You know he comes as long as he lives, and takes more and more, and dirties what he leaves." I looked around at houses and the mill in the distance. All these years I felt friendship with the white people, but I yearned to be with Indians not just in spirit but in body.

Seeing the defeated warriors proud that they did no wrong to their people. Their families showed me all that I could have been, should have been, not by myself but with a family. I vowed somehow I will meet an Indian man to be with forever and faraway from the sicknesses of society. I didn’t know how, but I wanted to find one passing through town. He would take me away from my dirty life. I would be forever silent about what I had to do to survive in the city. He, my warrior in eagle feathers could save me from being trapped.

I went back home and appreciated the warmth of the stove. I stared out the window as it began to rain harder. I wondered if the Salish knew that an Indian woman was staring at them as a witness to their relocation. I sat on the side of a bed that had too many visitors, and wept all afternoon. I cried myself to sleep. When I awoke it was time for me to start work.

I wept on and off while putting on my makeup. Perhaps my bloodshot eyes wouldn’t bring anybody home that night. I became worried. I didn’t want to take out a loan from Gerta. I walked down the street with my chin up and stiffened my emotions. I got to the saloon and began acting.

Several bachelors stared at me with sad eyes. In fact everybody in the saloon was somber. A man won some money playing poker and he just sort of shrugged. Within all of those walls of riches, there was a deeper sense that there was something being lost, not just for the Salish, but for everybody. I went home alone that night.

I was just about completely asleep when I heard a tapping on my door. I was angry thinking it was one of the neighbors. I yelled through the door at whoever to not bother me after sunset. I was about to yell at them to go away when I felt that the door needed to be answered. I opened the door and there was a stranger standing at my doorway. There's a first time for everything was my first thought. If that's how it's going to be, with visitors coming to my doorstep instead of me having to go out to pose for them in the saloons, then so be it. He was a cowboy going on his way through town looking for quick riches like everybody else. He was dressed in a white button-up shirt, and wore tan buckskin chaps over his Levis. He tipped his cowboy hat at me. He was younger than me. I suppose he was about twenty-four. He was tipsy of course. I said in a flat tone, "Come in." His cowboy boots made a clunking sound behind me in the hallway.

He said something that caught me off guard. "I'm sorry," he said in a soft and gentle voice. I turned around and frowned, "What?"

"I'm sorry," he said all teary eyed.

I felt a maternal gentleness come from me in an unexpected way. "Oh honey," I said letting down my guard. "You didn't do anything to me."

"I disagree," he said. His voice was young and slightly grating. He said his words slowly and carefully while his cute face stared at the floor. He looked up at me like a lost child.

I was not in the mood to get into a debate with him. We sat beside each other on my bed for awhile. He leaned over wrapping his arms around me. He held me for a time. His face was clear and soft when I kissed his forehead. I ran my fingers over his face feeling such young smoothness. His light brown hair was messy after he took off his hat. A short slightly unkempt beard framed his boyish face. A man who looks like a kitten has an odd yet adorable way about him, but his eyes. There were burning secrets in his searching gray eyes.

"What's your name?" I asked him.

"Daniel," he said in a very quiet almost high-pitched lilt for a man.

After awhile we got comfortable in bed, but didn't get undressed. We cuddled all night that was refreshing. It felt so good just to be warm with a nice man for once.

We kissed for a long time as the red dawn warmed up the next morning. I didn't have to think of something to get my juices flowing when he entered me. I truly had a memorable experience. Most men were hastily passionate, and were impatient for the end. That young frontier bachelor, he glided very slowly like how the clouds take their time going from one side of the valley to the other side. He often stopped to tell me confessions of sorts. "I'm trying very hard to be a better person. I can't run away from who I truly should be." He kissed me after he spoke. He went on to say while slowly pushing his hips into me, "People like you are the reason why I'm trying to move forward with my life. I need to think correctly by not be so egotistical." His voice quivered in nervousness as he made love to me. I felt shivers down my spine as he spoke in near whispers. He even made eye contact with me while on top. Somebody must have taught him well with him being so expertly artistic in his motions.

"What's your name?" he asked me while dressing.

"Victoria," I said as I stretched out in bed.

"No, I mean your real name?" he repeated.

"Dawn Red Sky."

He gave me a serious look. "No. What do your people call you?"

That caught me off guard. I wondered if I could say my name in my language again. I don't know when I stopped thinking in my own language. The fact that I didn't know when I started thinking completely in English disarmed me.

"Waapinako Maohk-spomi is my real name," I said very softly.

He nodded with tears. He turned his back to me like he was ashamed of his tears. When he turned back around, he sheepishly smiled at me that lit the room. What an adorable smile he had.

I was glowing in bed as I watch Daniel finish getting dressed. I walked him to the door. I held my palm out while looking expectantly at him. He readily placed in my hand a large wad of cash of twenty dollar bills. I was thinking, how in the hell did he get so much money? "No, I can't." He gently clasped his hands over mine and said, "Yes, you can." He nodded at me and that was the only time I ever saw him. I counted the money after he quietly closed the door. My jaw dropped while counting a couple hundred dollars. I closed my eyes tightly and held my breath. *There will be no tears,* I repeated a few times. I was risking big disappointment to get attached to just any fly-by-nighter. There were too many charmers flying through. What's a girl to do, but become numb?

Chapter 30-A Hunk of Burning Love

On a scorching hot August day in 1892, something happened that is very hard to admit. There was this handsome half-French/half-Nez Pearce man by the name of Charles Francois La Grande with also the Indian name of Fire Spear. He had a hazy and smoky glow to his complexion. He worked as a dishwasher at Wong's Chinese Dumplings. A cuisine that took some time for me to grow accustomed to after it arrived west with the railroad workers. Charles looked like a full-blooded Nez Pearce bachelor from some angles, with stark contours and deeply contemplative eyes. He also looked like a full-fledged Frenchman. He had dark stubble on his face and a soft not too prominent nose.

I always felt lightheaded and out of breath when he paid to dance with me at the old dime-a-dance that closed. He danced with me once or twice a week after his shift at work. He waltzed only with me and not the others. He told me that he could not afford to dance with more than one woman, yet he always spent .30 cents to dance three dances with me. I was eating a roast beef sandwich and drinking soda at a café on West Front Street. His eyes lit up with excitement as he spotted me. He immediately entered the café and sat down on a chair at my table.

His face was reddened from the sun. He was clean shaven and had the subtle scent of earthy pumice and pine soap. His short black hair was shiny being slicked back with pomade. We quietly chatted and he had me laughing. He whispered to me that he knew what I did for a living. He heard through the grapevine that I went further with just about anybody. I was offended at what was being said about me. I had a lot of discretion about who my clients were.

I wasn't new to whoring anymore. Most of the white men were very good lovers, all had their different methods and intensities. I somehow knew that Charles was going to be the one who was going to take me to the next level. I thought of three reasons. Pardon my blunt vulgarity. I knew it was true when Charles asked me, "What do you get when you combine French blood with Nez Pearce Indian blood?"

"What?" I asked.

"A horny savage," he said quietly so the lady with the child who ate lunch at the next table didn't hear. I was intrigued if that was the case. He knew the right things to say to me that was reason number one. Reason number two was that he was at least half Indian, and I hadn't been with an Indian man since Swift as Lightning. I was keen on knowing more about their methods. Reason number three was he seemed romantic.

It was just my great luck, I suppose. He had the patience to romance me when he always paid me to dance with him and not the others. His attention was longstanding that he patiently raised my awareness regarding his loveliness over time. I suppose there was a fourth reason, I found out he was so poor being not a proper white man. He worked as a dishwasher for a pittance. He said he had to go home. I wasn't ready to make love in the shack town where he was living. I didn't feel right about the possibility of placing my hand inside his pocket to fondle for change. I desired to fondle for something else in his pocket.

He was waiting for me beside his horse outside the café after I agreed to take him home. I told him to keep his horse tied to the pole since I only lived three blocks away, but then recanted because I was going to invite him to stay with me for the entire evening. I didn't want just a quick visit. I thought that if he surpassed my expectations, I'd let him spend several nights with me eating breakfasts together. We rode on his nice black gelding the three blocks to my building anyway. He wasn't overly discreet like the others, he seemed proud that he had me on the horse behind him. We didn't even wait to get to the front door.

We kissed and embraced in front of my building on the sidewalk. We hurried up the stairs to the second floor. He laughed as he chased after me and lightly slapped my butt. I fumbled for the keys and he rubbed his bulge against my behind. I dropped my keys and gave his bulge a little squeeze. He then looked intently and gently into my eyes. I admired his faint sideburns as he squeezed me with his nice strong arms. Then he gave me a kiss. "You aren't paying me," I said. I finally managed to unlock the door simultaneously while kissing him. I'm glad my neighbors didn't see.

Once inside he undressed me to complete nakedness. He studied me, pursed his lips and went "wow" as he looked at me while on his knees. His perfect ivory teeth contrasted greatly with his dark half-breed tan. His sun-reddened prominent cheeks sculpted his face. He kissed my hips and my tummy. I lit one candle. He looked like a warrior in the dim golden light. He fondled my breasts and unzipped his pants. His dark penis flopped out of his pants. By then I was so ravished by his good looks, I bent over and he entered me from behind without undressing.

He was slow and gentle at first. He brought me a quick series of orgasms. Each subsequent orgasm was more intense than the prior. They were innocent and lovely ways to release my pent up energy. I was close to a fourth time of releasing the pleasurable waters. I asked him to pump harder. He began to pump so vigorously that I heard my butt cheeks flap against the front of his nude hips. I looked down and saw that his wool pants fell around his ankles. I noticed my long thick hair shaking below my face as I was bent forward in the dim candlelight. His pomade smelled sweeter as he perspired.

We weren't making love. Our frenzy was a passionate escape from the mundane for both of us. It was greater than making love. We experienced such a rare moment of intensity together. I lit a kerosene lamp as he continued his pumping motions. I yearned to see him better after thinking about completely undressing him, because he still wore his undershirt despite being without any pants. The next release I screamed and lost control. I fell forward knocking the kerosene lamp onto the ground. The oil spread rapidly all over the floor instantly with violent blue and golden flames. I screamed as my foot got singed. I ran in a complete panic looking for a pitcher of water.

"It's too late," he yelled.

We both ran nakedly down the main hallway. We didn't want to get caught for suspected arson. I frantically knocked on my boarding housemates' doors and yelled "fire!" We ran down the back stairs of the building and hid in the bushes. I was crying as I saw the building go up in the largest flames I ever saw. The fire spread to the other buildings close by. The shock of so many buildings going up in flames was replaced by the realization of our uneasy nakedness. That was probably how Adam and Eve felt when they discovered their own unnatural nakedness. Gerta was screaming and crying at the top of her lungs, "Stop!" She turned around and saw me and Charles hiding in the bushes. She came over with tears pouring down her cheeks.

I explained, "When somebody knocked on my door telling me there was a fire. Charles and I didn't have time to dress." Gerta whistled to her new maid.

The maid was ordered to go all the way to other side of the river to fetch me a dress and men's clothing for Charles. She had some of Richie's clothes at her house since he became Gerta's unofficial lover. The fire burned all night and into the next day. There was nothing we could have done. By the end of it all, twenty-one buildings were burned beyond repair. Charles and I kept mum. We let the authorities believe what they wanted about the cause of the fire.

Months later, the city decided to rebuild the entire two block stretch made out of bricks so if a fire happened ever again, it wouldn't expand to other buildings as quickly. We moved back into a brick building after staying in Gerta's wonderful house for several months. Nothing felt right again once we were inside the new building. All of our belongings and part of our identities burnt with those flames. Some things can never be replaced.

I tried to enjoy the simplicity in the new building. It was a shell of its prior incarnation. Gone were the paintings, the piano, and the red Victorian chairs. Replaced by plain wooden chairs, and a hastily built table with uneven wooden legs. We spilled coffee and tea all the time. I only owned a bed and a small table with a ceramic flower vase. I bought another kerosene lamp, which I kept a keen eye on while working with my customers. I hoped to see Charles again, but I think the fire scared him away from town.

Chapter 31-Women in Ruins

There was an angry three-hundred pound madam who invaded the area with some cronies some years back. She was the one who barked “fucking Indian squaw,” when I accidently bumped into her at Worden’s. She got rich, built and took over some buildings on Front Street. After the fire she had many of her burnt buildings rebuilt in a jiffy. She was part owner of a brickyard. People often whispered that she was the culprit of a clandestine plot. Rumor was that she hired somebody to torch the street, so she could make money rebuilding everything. She was hostile, rude, and if you were not one of her working women, watch out! She said vicious comments to us whispered out of the corner of her mouth. Her name was Mary Gleim.

I was glad I was working for Gerta and not Mary. I heard Mary slapped around some of her women to keep them in line. Fannie would have been perfect working for her. Fortunately Fannie left with a government official who brought her home with him back east. Mary was the direct result of the good time girl industry growing to such a point, that Missoula was getting known for its female boarding houses more than logging.

We tried to remain discreet and quiet, but there were so many female boarding houses that nobody could ignore what was going on anymore. I was living in a bona fide red light district called the “badlands.” Some said it was on par with many of the bigger cities back east and on the west coast. There were close to forty Saloons on Front Street. Many of the town Christians decided that the problem had grown to the extent that they’d force us to change.

Things were changing fast in 1895. Two groups wanted to pass some reform laws to shut Front Street down for good making prostitution illegal. The first was a group from New

York state called The Women's Christian Temperance Union. Two actions were declared public enemy by them, drinking alcohol and consensual sex. Although money was involved, the sex was consensual. Two big sins that have plagued their Christian society since the time of Christ has been prostitution and carousing. I didn't think that something that happened regularly for the past two thousand years or more was going away anytime soon. I was doubtful they'd have any influence. Some speakers from the union came to the city. I walked by seeing them speaking on a soap box through a bullhorn in the middle of the busiest intersection. They said that some horrible things were going to happen if the town didn't clean up for good, like the Apocalypse. That got some goody-goodies all riled up.

The second group called the Philanthropic Women of Missoula decided to go around and have people sign a petition to make my profession illegal. We were shocked, especially Gerta. Our boss used to be in the philanthropic organization when they still had bake sales for orphans, or cookie sales for public works such as repairing a victim's home from a fire. They used to sell homemade patch quilts to help destitute families, but those days were over. Now they were after our souls. Gerta was so busy managing her own business affairs that she was caught off guard.

We on Front Street had much in common with both women's groups. We all believed that since it was 1895, it was time for our society to make it easier for women to start their own small businesses. We all believed that we should be able to attend the recently opened University of Montana. Most of all we wanted to vote. We were confused that such organizations wanted to shut us down for good. Closing our businesses was fine with us. If other tangible options were given, we would've gladly of sought other opportunities. If there were no concrete offers for advancement, then where would have gone? The shack town by the river just north of Front Street wasn't a hospitable place for ladies who lived alone. It was rife with crime. Many of the shack town residents died too early from ill health or broken hearts. After living a sad life, most were buried in the pauper's graveyard deep in the Rattlesnake Valley. Everybody feared ending up there.

Gerta asked me to spy on the union. She bought me one of the most divine outfits I've ever seen. "You need to look respectable," she advised. The dress had white ruffled sleeves, with a button up lace turtleneck, and gold buttons. Real gold buttons! If they asked me, I was just a clueless business assistant to her. I was to tell them that I lived with her in her posh Victorian house. She told me not to mention that I lived on Front Street.

I set off to the women's meeting at the town hall on Ryman and Main. I was greeted cordially by all of them. They asked what I did for a living as a single adult woman. I said I was Gerta's personal assistant. One of the women asked me, "Do you know what type of business your boss is in?" I smiled and played stupid. "Of course, she owns female boarding houses for the poor and unfortunate ladies who can never seem to find a husband, poor things. We have an overabundance of men on the frontier. All those men think about is whiskey and gambling, not marriage like they should. People do whisper that some of those women are up to no good. I wouldn't know. I suffer from claustrophobia. I despise downtown. I have a hard time even being here, but good morality calls!" They all smiled sweetly at me.

The head of the organization was Mrs. John Monroe. I almost coughed in surprise since her husband was Officer John Monroe. He was one of my regulars. In fact, once I was introduced to all fourteen women, three of their husbands were my regulars. I was a lucky businesswoman. When younger, the women in the business usually had to see dozens hoping for regulars. If a lady was lucky, she got one wealthy customer and never had to get any more. I had four that I saw on a rotating basis. I still made them wear sheep intestine condoms. Some regulars thought that because they were my regulars, the reduction of men meant less risk of an infection. They didn't want any condoms worn.

Mrs. Monroe stood on the little stage and she began her speech: "This meeting is about trying to rid this city of vice. How can women progress and be taken seriously when we are either thought of as just wives or soiled doves? We have come to believe that those women who choose to live a life of such ill-repute have become complacent in their morals. This city has become demoralized. Though the women on Front Street may complain that they have nowhere else to go, there is a workforce out there. They have to create their own honest opportunities for themselves. They can't rely on others to do it for them. Many of them may say they do not have enough money to start their own businesses. If they work together and hard enough, nothing is impossible. They could pool their money and resources and work with a collective strength. These petitions that have been signed by so many will surely help pass decent morality into law. The goodly citizens of Missoula will force these women out of apathy toward a moral Christianized lifestyle. We are working with the lawmakers and authorities to actually enforce these possible city ordinances. If the ladies can't hack this city's change for the better, there are other cities out their where they can go. There is Butte, Virginia City, or even Wallace, Idaho." All the rich wives stood up. I was clapping loudly thinking that I wish that I had their opportunities, and then I could act high and mighty too. Their warm smiles contained cold judgment. I wished they had walked in my high heels. All I could think about was how their husbands performed in bed as I stared at their wives.

Officer John Monroe had the looks and charm to get a better looking woman. Mrs. Monroe looked like she was always eating something sour. Judge Gonse's wife looked smarmy and pompous as ever. University of Montana professor Dr. Strangemann's wife was as pretty and gracious as ever, but he told me while at home she was the ultimate nag who was vindictive in her attitude toward everyone behind their backs. Some women had said men stray because they're weaker in their sexual restraint, but at that meeting, I understood why men of such high standing searched for greener pastures. I never saw such a bunch of self-righteous and arrogant women. They dressed fancy and had lots of money given to them from their husbands, which was another form of prostitution. None of them lived on their own! Life dealt them a better hand. The richer never have truly represented poor people.

"There is an evangelical tent revival coming here. I propose we use our combined rhetoric with this revival to make consumption of alcohol and gambling illegal. We can drive interest and publicity to the women's rights movement of pure morality," Mrs. Arthur Lee Gonse said.

"We also got a Jesuit priest, a nice fellow by the name of Father Antonio who is giving sermons to his congregation to rally support to our cause," Mrs. Strangemann said.

I was seething with anger. I didn't think their husbands were of great integrity looking at who they married. I decided not to see their husbands anymore. Seeing their wives for the first time made me feel very uneasy. When actions are kept at a distance, like wars, they do not affect the emotions until seen firsthand. Infidelity is not a pretty sight seen up close. I had enough money to see just one regular anyway. I liked him the most and couldn't give him up. He was a bartender who told me he was a bachelor for life. He was more generous than those so-called men of high standing, he gave me all his bar tips.

Why is one person to love not enough for some people? My regulars told me many secrets that they never told anybody else. I was their confident and friend. Discretion was rule number for any prostitute. Some men snuck into through the back doors of the buildings, and never gave their real names to remain anonymous. Other johns saw working girls only when they traveled. The risk of seeing one of us in their hometowns was too much. I was many things to my guys. Making them feel relaxed and at home was my primary objective. Our intimate relations were always less important. Whether or not I knew they were married is moot. I did not pry.

Front Street gals were isolated within the city, not straying too far from our homes. Our business arrangements, so to speak, was an arranged relationship that I can't explain adequately to those who exalt monogamy as the only standard. I wasn't just a mistress, but perhaps I was closer to being concubine to my regulars. I always affectionately called them my sugar daddies.

I wanted to confide my feelings of resentment about everything to somebody after I left that meeting. I sent a bike messenger to Cindy. I didn't feel like visiting her ever after she moved out of my building. I told her that I wanted to meet her at the library after school. I said I was interested in meeting Father Antonio.

The slight damp smell of mildew permeated the library as I waited for Cindy. The silence of the room cured my headache. It was so quiet in the town library that I thought that I heard the clouds moving. My anger settled a bit. I took a deep breath of faith in, and an exhale of fear out. My friend finally came to me after our long departure away from each other. She wanted to know if I was still in the business on Front Street. She seemed disappointed that I still was, but she led me to the Catholic church anyway.

The church appeared to me as very distinguished from the other buildings in the area. It was fairly obvious that the church meant a lot to many people. I saw the spire looming in the distance in most areas downtown, but never had the urge to get close to the church. The other buildings next to it were not as ornate and made out of wood. I stood on the top step before the big doors. The spire pointed to the sky like an arm reaching toward the Great Spirit. It's quaint majesty made the other buildings near the church look slightly shabby. We walked past double doors to where Cindy placed her fingertips into a ceramic bowl on a table in the foyer. She did the same hand motions that I saw a nun do years ago as she walked down Front Street. She urged me to do so.

"This is the sign of the cross. The action represents our affinity with the teachings of Christ," she explained. She made the sign slower so I could mimic the gesture. We walked down the middle aisle of the church. I felt impressed with the powerful beauty surrounding us. Wind rattled the stained glass windows. There was a crucifix hanging above the altar. I stared at the man who sacrificed himself for our sins. Somehow, the statue seemed like it was alive. The statue was made from carved wood and painted white. I half expected Christ's body to start moving and speaking to us. "This statue seems alive," I remarked.

"He *is* alive, it's filled with the Holy Spirit, the loving energy from Christ our Lord," she said.

The soft light in the church was quite luminous. I stood entranced by the geometric design of the colorful stained glass windows. Another statue of a blanket clad woman holding a papoose touched me as precious.

"The Virgin Mary," Cindy said. Cindy put her hands together and prayed. I was used to praying to the sun, to pray to a statue was too new to me. Cindy seemed to glow from lightness. Staring at her, I felt like I finally understood Christianity as a religion of sacred wisdom. A man clad almost entirely in black with a white strip below his neck came from behind us. I recognized him as the "black robe" that the Salish were said to be so fond of.

"Father Antonio," Cindy said.

"Hello my child," he said, I noticed he had a thick accent.

"Father, meet Victoria from the Blackfeet tribe."

I curtsied.

"What brings you to such a faraway place? I've never met a Blackfeet woman face to face before. I've met Salish and Crow, they being open-minded to the Lord's message. Perhaps your tribe is finally waking up to the gentle sweetness of the heart."

"I don't know why I'm here," I admitted.

"We don't know many things, but with the Lord, we begin to grow very wise. What a long road you must have had to be sent to this place."

"What tribe are you from? You speak slightly different than the others?" I asked him.

"Italy, it's farther away than the Blackfeet reservation, way over the Atlantic Ocean."

"This is a very pretty church. I like the cross at the top of this roof," I said wondering what type of sacred ceremonies happened inside.

"I carved it with my own hands," he said.

"Victoria lives on Front Street," Cindy said.

Father Antonio looked at me with concern. He appeared quite physically strong, even though he was getting up there in years. He had no hair on top of his head, but he had black hair leading to wispy grayness, gently curly toward the ears. He had very thin lips and a prominent crooked nose that curved at the bottom toward his left.

"Victoria. Please be very careful on that street. Meanwhile you might want to come to Sunday services with Cindy," he gently said with an evocative voice.

"Thank you father," I said. I was touched by his sense of peace.

We went outside into the brightness of the afternoon hurting my eyes.

Cindy explained to me as we walked away, "That Father Antonio, he's so revered by the area's peoples. He's very good in medicine. He'd probably been a doctor if he hadn't chosen a vocation with the Lord. He's a carpenter too. He carved some of the wooden statues inside the cathedral."

"He has good medicine," I said. Cindy walked me back home. She looked uneasy and out of place in the badlands. She asked me if there was any way she could help me. If my work got too much for me to handle, I was always welcomed in her home. She was a good friend who I felt that I neglected for awhile. I saw her around here and there. We always made small chat. I felt a deep love for her when we worked together as Gerta's maids. That love grew because she became a sister to me. Cindy was a big part of my initial intellectual curiosity. I hugged her goodbye and thanked her.

I was walking back to Front Street when a poster of an Indian Chief caught my eye. It was an advertisement: 'Indian Land for sale! Get a home. Perfect title! Find land in the west.' I wondered if it was former land that belonged to the bigger reservations, before the American chiefs shrank the sizes of the already tiny reservations to even smaller prison camps. Evil disguises itself in many legitimate ways, I thought as I carried on.

I went into the stinking saloon that evening wanting to save up for my retirement. I wondered how many pricks I had to suck on to get to be as comfortable as Gerta and some others. I was not a cheap whore like the others, if men wanted a tan-assed goddess like myself, they would have to pay more. Everybody knew that. Some white women where quite jealous of me. A few blonde women were the most expensive, and I was almost as expensive as them. Many fellows preferred an ugly and sulking blonde than to sleep with a dirty Indian, even if I kept it cleaner down there than them. I started feeling very bitter. All my thoughts starting becoming angry and vulgar.

I looked over at an aging gambler on his way through town. He walked up to me stinking of stale cigars. It was as if he smoked twelve dozen of cigars while his grey woolen suit filtered every bit of the smoke, and what was worse was the underlying rankness of his body odor. I was numb. We spoke a bit, and I was smiling my fake smiles while my eyes told a different story.

"You aren't enjoying yourself tonight. I can tell," the old man said.

"I'm just a bit tired," I admitted.

"Well I guess I'll just find some other girl. Too bad. Your kind is hard to find. One would have to be brave to go onto a reservation to find the likes of somebody like you. You Indian gals are the most beautiful women in the world."

"Gee thanks," I said with artificial enthusiasm.

All men were looking the same to me, said the same things, and their cocks were all the same, all boring.

"I think just a bit of food will give me some energy, then I can go all night," I said.

"I got something to feed you," he said while grabbing his crotch under the gambling table.

"You'll have to pay more to feed me," I said. I then stuck out my tongue at him. That was it, and we were on our way back to my place.

He undressed and his big beer white beer belly was sticking out looking like a hump back but on the opposite side of the body. His saggy ass cheeks reminded me of smoothly white cheddar cheese. The hair around his cock was trimmed neatly. He was well groomed despite his odor. He looked down at my pussy and literally was drooling.

"Your pussy will taste better than Eden, by god I found paradise," he said. I had to laugh. I really did. He stuck his tongue inside me, and was massaging my breasts, and tickling my clit with the tip of his tongue. It was so routine that I started to daydream. A distant memory came back to me as he was eating me out; I was thinking about my childhood.

I remember when a grandma sat in front of the central campfire and told us a tale about man's creator of Napi.

"Napi found a beautiful bluish silvery stone. That stone was as shiny and radiant as fool's gold. That jewel was accidentally dropped from Kikomi-kisomm, the moon. Always her blue silver rays of light illuminate us. She is very powerful when she's a full circle. Napi went to pick up the shiny stone.

Kikomi-kisomm said, 'Please do not touch the stone. It is one of my prized gifts given to me by my son Ipiso-waahsa, the morning star. For he feels great respect at my majestic rays of light that wake him and his father Natosi every morning. That stone is sacred because it is a celestial gift. Humans are forbidden to touch it, especially you Napi because you are clumsy and you will fall and break it.'

'But the stone is pretty and radiant, I must touch it,' Napi argued with the moon.

'Only Spirit Beings and Above Beings In The Sky are fit to touch such a gift. One of them will retrieve my gift back to me. Since I'm Kikomi-kisomm, I must always stay in the sky and keep enough light so the animals can see at night. Otherwise I would retrieve it back myself.'

'I can jump so high I can probably touch you. Please let me touch the shiny stone. Let me jump up and throw it up to you. Surely the stone will reach you,' Napi pleaded.

'If you touch my stone gift, you will turn into ice as frozen as the Two-Medicine River in winter. The next day you shall be melted completely by my husband Natosi's hot rays of heat. You will think summer is cool when his fires turn you into steam.'

Napi ignored her warning anyway. 'What the hell does she know? She's just the stupid moon who does nothing but floats in sky,' he said. He bent over to grab the stone but instantly turned into ice. The next day Natosi was shining very hot. It was the hottest day of summer and by noon; Napi was only a puddle of mud."

The disgusting white man was fucking me and I wasn't feeling a thing for him. I sometimes stared at a painting when a particular customer wasn't stimulating me. I closed my eyes as he was grunting and plowing away at my body. I remembered how the old grandma continued her story to us children.

"Some say she is First Woman, but others call her Old Woman. Even others call her Earth Woman. Whatever name she goes by, she sure seems smarter than old man Napi. One day First Woman was walking to a stream to pick serviceberries. She was startled when she heard Napi calling her name. She looked all around. He was nowhere to be seen. 'Where is he at?' she complained. 'He must be in trouble like always,' she said. Finally she looked into a dirty little puddle where a skunk was taking a crap. She was shocked because she didn't see her own face reflecting back in the puddle. She saw Napi's face in the dirty water instead. 'Now what did you do!?' First Woman yelled.

'Ask that crazy woman floating in the sky to turn me back into an old man again. I made you. You can pay me back by at least doing that,' Napi said.

That night First Woman pleaded to Kikomi-kisomm, 'Napi has finished making everything on Grandmother Earth, but he keeps getting into trouble. What should we do with him?'

'It is lonely in the sky. My husband Natosi doesn't talk to me and his heat is going to burn out for good. Men have a way of doing that to their wives, ain't it always so? His spirit left his body becoming a human. You call him Napi because he is very old. He is even older than Grandmother Earth. I shall send my husband to inhabit his body once again. You see his body rise in the sky every day. It is this burning ball of light that is the sun. Together we shall keep guardian over all of creation. You will feel our presence in this word of 'ihtsi-pai-tapi-yopa.' Such a long word means the essence-of-the-creator or Great Spirit. She hummed a magical note making Napi rise up head first out of the puddle. He looked all around, then up at the sky really scared. He told everybody he would be back one day and ran into the mountains. He ran to the top of the highest mountain. Kikomi-kisomm hummed another magical note making Napi float all the way up to the sun. We call the sun Natosi. Natosi means Holiness. Together the moon and the sun hover majestically in the sky. Both honorably named Kikomi-kisomm the moon who is our mysterious night guide and Natosi the sun who is our superpower. That is why we pray to Natosi and to Kikomi-kisomm. First Woman was relieved that she didn't have to watch out for accidents caused by Napi anymore." All the children laughed at grandma's story. Napi was really an idiot! How an idiot caused so much goofy happenings in this world explains everything.

That idiot created some men who liked to fuck anything they can pay for. The old guy put his cock in front of my face and I got a few extra dollars. I almost felt like vomiting but kept it down. I wished that I were as pure as the moon. The wedding between the earth and the sun must have been the most beautiful event ever. If I was the moon, I could shine beside my man, my brightly shining lover always. The sun and moon's love for each other is everlasting. Me, I lost hope, love is an eternally elusive fraud.

Chapter 32-Blue Laws

I felt an empty void inside from being homesick after all these long years. Being away from my people meant being away from the spiritual life I was accustomed to. I never replaced what I lost with a more contemporary spiritual life. One that was more conducive to living in a city.

I felt disheartened after the Women's Christian Temperance Union meeting and the introduction to Father Antonio. I was constantly questioning myself and my lifestyle. I didn't know if I believed that I was as helpless as I once thought. Perhaps I made the wrong choices. The moralists seemed to really believe in what they were doing, and that was to clean up downtown for good. I needed to talk to somebody about the void I suddenly felt inside. Mandy was a good friend, other than her, I felt like I had no true friends. Cindy was a good candidate, but though I loved her like a sister and she dropped what she was doing to help me, she was uninteresting to me.

Cindy was prissy and stayed within the confines of safe conversational topics like quilt making, education, and flower gardening. She shuddered when even a hint of sex was mentioned. She ignored my mentioning of bestselling books like The Woman's Bible written by a suffragist named Stanton. Cindy avoided ghost stories, or even attempting to discuss the popular contemporary reading, like Freud and his psychoanalysis. Freud's theories made Cindy's dirty novels hidden under her mattress look like nursery rhymes. I often found myself blushing reading Freud at the library.

There was a woman who I always found interesting in town. Her name was Yin Chow. I found myself wondering if she could become a friend. She always read books while on her breaks from work.

She was the daughter of the Chinese launderette below my room. The steam always was rising from the coal burning stoves that they boiled downstairs. It warped their ceiling, which was my wooden floor. It truly was a balmy and sticky nightmare in my room during the summer. I was living right above Missoula's dirty laundry. I ran into her about once a week when I needed my clothing cleaned. She seemed one of exotic innocence. I went downstairs seeing her stirring clothing with a stick. Steam was rising above a hot pot with white clothing inside. Her face was flushed red. I will never do degrading work like this; I thought when I saw her. Sweat dripped down from her bosom to her apron. The smell of steam smells clean like newly fallen snow. The plopping wet sounds of water boiling came from a metal tub behind her. I waved to her and she went to the desk thinking I had some dresses to get cleaned.

"Yin Chow, why do you always seem at ease?" I asked.

She seemed confused that I asked such a question.

"I really need somebody to talk to," I told her. She seemed surprised that somebody was interested in speaking with her. She said something in Chinese to her father who was pressing clothes with a flat heated iron. She motioned for me to walk around her sweaty parents out the back door. I thought my room was unbearable with humidity and heat from the launderette below. I felt like I was in a sweat lodge for a moment walking through the launderette. We sat on the backstairs. There was a perfect view of the gently flowing Clark Fork River and snow covered Lolo Peak in the distance. The cascading waters reflected off the sun. The chattering trickle of the river over rapids soothed me.

"I feel a void inside my heart," I said.

“I'm sorry to hear that,” she said giving me a sympathetic look. We both sat beside each other feeling uneasy because of the long silence between us. She finally added, “Thank you for thinking I’m a woman at ease, but sometimes I get angry. I deal with unhappiness by meditating on the bodhisattvas. They are many, like the Catholic Saints.”

I was intrigued.

"What do they look like?" I asked.

“Very different. Some have four arms, and some are on fire. I meditate on the Green Tara, a woman Buddha. She has beautiful green skin. She relaxes on a giant lotus flower. Green Tara answers my prayers no matter what. I also meditate on Maitreya. He’s the Buddha of love. I feel love when I meditate on him. He sits on a throne of jewels." Green skin? Now this is getting interesting I thought.

“I usually pray to the sun. Can you show me what the green, what’s her name?”

“Green Tara.”

“Do you have an image of her somewhere?” I asked.

"You visit me after work one day. I take you home to show. I cook some Chinese food for you. I’ll show you paintings I own. You feel better now. I have to go soon," she said in her thick accent.

I felt better by just being in Yin Chow’s presence. She seemed happy that somebody wanted to speak with her. I suspected that books were her only friend. I saw people often trying to intimidate her at her job. She spoke near perfect English, but her thick Asian accent irritated them. To me she was more well-spoken than those who spoke the frontier lingo. Many pioneers were illiterate anyway, at least she could read.

There was a gentle tugging sensation in my heart like I had in St. Xavier Church with Father Antonio earlier in the day. The essence of the creator visited me on such a nice day. I returned to my room excited at the possibility of learning another line of thinking with her.

Once upstairs I looked into a mirror. Did anybody who looked at me while I was dressed up all sultry for the night think I had no morality at all? Did they think that I had no yearning for any spiritual direction? If they thought I was empty inside, they were all fools.

The reformists had great influence over the actions of the police. Laws were swiftly enacted out according to their interpretations of good morality. Foremost the ladies of Front Street were not allowed to go out on the streets during daylight hours. We were always asked by the foot patrol to return to our rooms. Some of the women were actually arrested if they tried to leave while the sun was out. That certainly made daily chores difficult. We couldn't shop for food when the market was open. I lived one block away from the market, but I was threatened with arrest trying to go there.

A full-time policeman was hired to patrol our street to keep an eye on us during the daytime. It became obvious to us that we could only leave at night. We never got harassed by any patrolling policemen after six in the evening. The policemen were only doing their jobs. They seemed to halfheartedly ask us to return home when the sun was out. They only got threatening if some of the women sassed off. That didn't appease my neighbor Nora's anger.

"I'm gonna git some rat poison. Sprinkle an entire box into them policemen's horses' drinking water. They just want me to make headway over yonder. I ain't a going back to Appalachia. Too dang far," Nora complained.

Her friend looked at her and let out a chuckle, "That'll make 'em spiteful all the more. Nora, we just need to slip 'em a silver dollar to let us go get flour and coffee. Victoria, what do you think we all should do?"

I looked sadly at the floor. “Maybe they will be happy if we committed a mass suicide,” I said in utter defeat. The discussion was halted as we looked at each other sadly.

We had to pay errand runners to do daily business for us, which spiraled down to us having less money to save. Broke women couldn’t leave Front Street easily. The moralists perpetuated a problem they were trying to solve. I tried to leave the street for good a couple of times long before the blue laws were enacted out. Nobody wanted to sell me a plot of land because I was an American Indian. I wasn’t legally a citizen of the United States. I was stuck between a rock and a hard place.

There was more prodding from the good citizens to shut us down. The policemen, who were some of our best customers, began raiding more boarding houses. Gerta had to bail her employees out a few times, which meant money lost. Every woman was broke around me. I still had my bartender regular who gave me all his bar tips. The fact of having one regular customer made it easier for me to avoid incarceration. The new women without regulars were usually arrested by the undercover vice squad. We weren’t educated in an institution, so we were ignorant about laws. It was hard to tell what was true and what was rumor. Were the blue laws written in the law books at all?

By word of mouth, we heard that a peculiar law went into effect that may or may not have been in the law books too; men who dressed in the clothing of women were to be arrested. I knew of only one man who worked on Front Street who dressed in women’s clothing. He passed easily as a real woman. He was known as Miriam Love. He was from the Shoshone tribe who once worked as a prostitute in Wallace, Idaho for awhile, before setting up shop in Missoula.

He once drunkenly blurted out to everybody at a badlands shindig, "I like to think of my body as a surprise gift to my customers." I felt scared for his safety, but he said that his regulars knew what they were getting into. Any new customers were word of mouth. That law had me wondering, maybe there were more ladymen in the boarding houses. Quite possibly I passed some ladymen by and didn't even know it.

The authorities went straight into the heart of the badlands. They arrested Gerta Gundersunn on charges of running bawdy houses. Mary Gleim was already arrested several times, because she wasn't very discreet and notorious in the community. Her places were shut down because she was found guilty in a plot to blow up somebody's house. After Gerta was arrested, several other madams went to jail.

Max said that Gerta advised us to keep our rent money until she got released from jail. They refused her bail. She took the city to court on grounds of illegal arrest. It was a busy day when she was in court. Several of my neighbors and myself read a transcript of the court proceedings in the newspaper. The headline was *The People of Missoula vs. Gerta Gundersunn.*

We learned that the evidence was overwhelmingly guilty. The police confiscated her notebook of how many women paid her tips. The police confiscated Max's tally of how many women left the saloon with men. Now that we knew she was guilty, we knew that the female boarding houses would be shut down for good.

I read the long winded speech that was printed verbatim in the newspaper: "Good men and women, how can you throw those vulnerable women to the streets? They have nowhere else to go. Search inside your hearts. Sometimes good and evil walk a fine line. I worked with those ladies. I can say with a clear heart under God that those women aren't evil. Throwing good women out to the wolves is evil. So like I said a fine line. Some laws that initially seem right at first are actually made out of ignorance. We are supposed to be living in a country of freedom. Civil rights were violated. How dare you restrict another American from walking down the street only at certain times! How dare you regulate the sexual lives of strangers! You all disgust me with your prying noses sniffing between strangers' bed sheets! You're restricting the freedoms of perfectly valid and consensual acts between adult men and adult women. Your regressive laws did not help or liberate those women. They were already liberated. I see Mrs. Gonse, Mrs. Strangemann, and Mrs. Monroe giving me petulant looks and rolling their eyes. Is it out of jealousy that you have a vendetta against prostitutes? Are you angry at your husbands' lustful eyes? Let the record show to the world that your husbands were my best customers. Don't be shocked! The sheriffs were some of our best customers too. As well as a barber, a couple of bankers, businessmen and university professors, miners, farmers and students. I won't name any more names. You're a bunch of liars, especially the biased newspaper. This won't be printed for the public to see I'm for sure."

We were lucky to get the first limited edition of the newspaper, which was quickly retracted and disappeared before most people were out of bed. Our copy was secretly given to one of my neighbors from a john who worked as a printer at the newspaper. The second edition replacing the first omitted that speech.

A court order was placed on our doors. We were given twenty-eight days to get out on our own or face prosecution. I had nowhere else to go but down. We all felt panic. Some of my colleagues vowed to move to another city. I began drinking absinthe to escape the harshness of my lifeless days. Business was nil. The blue laws even scared my generous bartender away. I spent much of my days in a daze waiting for the day to pack my bags to live by the river. I had terrible nightmares at night and days of anxiety.

I dreamt that Scruffy Hunter was killed in a drunken fight. I had a nightmare that Summer Fire found out where I lived. He entered into my room in the middle of night to slit my throat in bed. I dreamt that Big One Eyed Jack's empty eye socket was enticing to a perverse fellow prison inmate. He was leering at my poor Jack waiting for the moment to accost him. Jack was screaming as the man was violently thrusting his hips. That nightmare jumped me awake to feelings of unworthiness.

I vowed to stop drinking absinthe if it was giving me bizarre nightmares. Others warned me they had horrible dreams after drinking too much of it. Why did I always have to learn the hard way? I started to cry in bed. I missed Jack too much. I tried not thinking about him anymore, but it felt more unnatural when I related that nightmare to Gerta over afternoon tea. Gerta looked like she was really bothered by something. Then she told me the truth. Jack was never released from jail, because apparently he omitted a very important detail when I saw him in that jail for the last time. The sheriff who damaged his eye was shot to death by him, which ensured that Jack received the death penalty. Seems like Gerta purposely failed to tell me that. I asked her why, and she said "My poor darling, Jack never wanted you to know. He said that you needed to go on with your life." I asked her if he ever mentioned me in letters to her from jail before he died. She said yes, but I never saw those letters. Saying goodbye was always a difficult thing in life, but never saying goodbye was even worse.

I was so distraught about the community throwing us women away. I thought about trying opium for the first time. I heard all sorrows drifted away with the smoke. The high came from the sweet innocence of flowers. The opium dens were in secret basements under various locales downtown. The police knew about them, but didn't do anything since the people who frequented those places hardly caused much harm to others. The opium dens were such an underground phenomenon. The people who frequented such places were very discreet. I don't think the reform groups even knew about them.

I was led to a backdoor in an alleyway that went down two steep flights of stairs. I smelled the basement mustiness combined with the earthen smoke of opium. I went into a lavishly decorated room. A bizarre looking lady who looked like she put on abstract face paint was playing a lavish harp. She looked like she was wearing a dyed potato sack synched with a rhinestone sash. Nobody was having any conversations. The place seemed all ambiance and no deepness. There were many foreign decorations, from East Indian carpets to Moroccan lamps, Chinese silk tapestries of lotus flowers designs and cherry blossoms. The furniture was upholstered with red velvet.

One look at those poor souls lazing their lives away on chaises didn't fit in with the extravagant surroundings. The lifeless stared into nothingness on couches, which made me too terrified to smoke anything. I was given an informal tour of the underground by a former bawdy house customer. He was pale with dark circles underneath his eyes. He showed me the doors to the 'cribs.' On the other side of the closed doors worked opium prostitutes. I peeked inside. It was close to hell. A half-dead Asian prostitute smoked opium from a pipe while waiting for a customer. She sat in her underclothes on a dirty mattress placed on a concrete floor. I hurried out of those connecting basements. A week later I read in the newspaper that an opium den was raided.

I was grateful that I never had to work in such deplorable conditions. My life was making a downturn, but I wasn't going there. Perhaps that's how the women's groups viewed all of us who worked on Front Street. I stared meekly out my window after I returned home. I heard a familiar male voice in the hallway along with a woman's giggle. I peeked out my door and that was when I saw Father Antonio standing in the hallway speaking in low tones. He was speaking with one of the new women in the building by the name of Ellie. His eyes widened with surprise when he saw me.

"Hello Victoria. I like to visit some women on this street to counsel them one on one about the Holy Spirit. Maybe one day I can visit you alone. We can study the Bible together."

"Thank you Father for the offer. We may be able to find similarities between Blackfeet spirituality and Christianity. I felt the Great Spirit in the church when I visited."

"You mean the Holy Spirit? Yes, you can feel holiness anywhere, on the Indian reservations or back in my home country of Italy."

"Come on father, let us pray," Ellie said as she opened her door. She let Father Antonio go in first. She slapped his butt when he passed her. She giggled then winked at me. That Father Antonio, he was very dedicated to the Lord. He went out of his way to help the wayward ladies toward salvation. He was such a good medicine man willing to work hard to make women feel the pleasures of God.

Chapter 33-She Who Speaks as Both

The first time I was acquainted with Miriam Love was when we both weren't working. I somehow managed to find an afternoon date at a restaurant with a gentleman who told me he liked to take it slow. I knew of his kind almost immediately after we first met. I spent such an amount of time being around men, whether in public at saloons, or in my room alone with them. I was an expert at reading signs, subtleties, and peculiar habits of the sort who frequented us. The fellow stood me up. I knew he would do it, but hoped he was an exception. Miriam was busy blending in appearing as the angular yet voluptuous femme in the day café. She attempted to overcompensate with exaggerated flowing movements. She used gentleness as a paintbrush softly painting her manly face.

The gentleman she spoke with appeared to be an easterner on his way through town. He was dressed formally in a top hat but with clothing of typical western flair. He was an odd one indeed with mismatched styles of clothing. Miriam noticed my look of disappointment as I stared at the check. I let out a sigh knowing that I needed to pay for my Irish coffee and hot cross buns myself. I took out an Indian head silver dollar thinking how ironic a chief in a war bonnet appeared on metal. How that dollar was a more potent symbol that Manifest Destiny was complete, more than churches lording in the center of reservations. From what I heard, a church was built on the Blackfoot reservation made from river rocks. My thoughts were interrupted when I felt a large light brown hand on top of my hand. I looked up. Miriam stood over me with a kind grin.

"He didn't show for lunch. I don't like when it happens," she said in a deep manly voice. Her accent was the thickest Indian accent that I heard in a long time. She spoke in broken

English, the way of speaking that had many immigrants thinking they were better than us, even when they spoke just as badly.

"Unfortunately some people aren't reliable," I told her. She boldly grabbed the dollar and placed it back in my coin purse.

"Do me an honor, I pay lunch now for you," she said.

That act of kindness made my heart feel lighter. I often felt lost in a sea of various shades of beige. Seeing somebody whose skin color matched mine was refreshing. I smiled and let her pay wondering what I could do to return the favor. If she was traditional, I wouldn't be expected to reciprocate the kindness, but I would anyway.

"Thank you ma'am," I said. I felt at home again seeing what the French fur trappers called berdaches, or what I called ladymen. The last one I saw was years before with the Apsaalooke. The Jesuit Missionaries called them sinners. *But* everybody is a sinner to the Jesuits. That just meant that berdache men and women were in good company. I never liked accepting gifts or charity from anyone. Some of my clients might have confused my working duties with falling in love if I accepted gifts. Miriam was such a beautiful stranger, she left with the man. I placed the money that Miriam gave me on the table as a tip for the waiter.

"Miss, you forgot some money," the waiter ran after me a few steps away from the restaurant. He smelled like aftershave and sweat that was in stark contrast to the musty scent of dust and horse manure always present outside.

"No sir, I believe in being generous when a lady can be," I said. He muttered a reluctant thanks as I continued.

Many Blackfeet warriors had faces that were pretty, but they were also distinctively manly. There were Blackfeet men who were quite stunning who seemed quite content dressed in female buckskin dresses. I wondered why white people never had men dressed up as women, and women dressed up as men, or appeared somewhere in between. To me that was one of the stranger aspects of white culture. There appeared to be only two sexes to them, men and women. Everything in the American world was black or white, evil or good, cold or hot. Such limited thinking had people jumpy and rigid. The only thing that relaxed most of them was alcohol. Having almost forty saloons up and down my street convinced me of that. My people relished the median between opposites, and ladymen and manly-hearted women were in the middle.

We called the men a'kiihka'si aawoowa'kii, and many were the pipe holders for sacred ceremonies. We called the women sakwo'mapi akikiwan, who often were better trappers than men. I felt disarmed and vulnerable feeling a sense of yearning for Miriam's androgynous beauty. That desire had me feeling nervous and came out of nowhere. I've never felt any attraction to women before. Women were pretty in many ways, but they lacked the scruffy beauty that I found in men. Later that evening thoughts of Miriam crept into my head when I was working. I tried to stop my thoughts and urges by distracting myself. Perhaps men were really beginning to bore me. Something that I never thought could ever occur.

I remember when my people tried to get Scruffy Hunter to be like the a'kiihka'si aawoowa'kii. He was in no way like them. No he couldn't hunt at all. No he couldn't be a lookout guarding our tribe. He was tragically clumsy with a bow and arrow, so warring was out of the question for men with bad eyesight. Those who couldn't do manly duties were usually inclined to become a ladyman, but his mannerisms were absolutely masculine unlike some of the a'kiihka'si aawoowa'kii. The spiritual sensitivities of those who were not like men or women were more in tune with the spirit world. Scruffy Hunter didn't have any spiritual powers to offer others. He didn't seem to fit in with anybody in my tribe, like me we both felt lonely at being different.

That evening I was walking home without getting a date. I noticed a woman with very big feet and broad shoulders in the shadows. She was stunningly beautiful. Something told me that there was something not quite typical about her appearance. From a distance she appeared to be a few years younger than me. How from certain angles this formidable person appeared to have Asian qualities. Her eyes were slanted giving her feline qualities. I liked that.

She spotted me and waved. Most people didn't give her a second look earlier that day in the cafe, but I knew what she had hidden underneath that frilly evening dress. The powder caked on her skin gave her away, not that she was a male to some people, but she was an Indian instead. She stood suddenly before me by a flickering gas lamp.

"You're having bad night!" she said.

"What do you mean?" I asked.

"Early on your date did not show for lunch, now nobody goes home with you."

"I know. I'm getting older. They've all seen me at the saloon too many times I suppose."

"You what tribe?" she asked.

"Blackfeet."

"I am Shoshone."

"Are you working?" I asked her.

"No, just bored."

"Bored!? You stand on the street corners at night because you're bored?"

"No, Miriam is hot because boarding house window not opens. I hate heat," she said.

"Who's Miriam?" I asked knowing full well her identity.

"Me. What is your name?"

"Victoria Red Sky."

We shook hands. Curious about how she got into such a predicament of being a working woman, I desperately wanted to get to know her better. I wanted to hear something familiar.

"Would you like to talk?" I asked.

"Yes. I thank you much. Nobody talk to me much," she said. What looked like the tenseness of hunched shoulders became looser. Her face warmed just a bit after she smiled.

She followed me up the steps to my room. It was god awful hot inside. She immediately began sweating. I smelled the aroma of underlying manliness under her sweet flowery perfume. What a strange paradox of a scent.

"It's too hot!" she said.

"I know. I can't help that because of the Chinese laundry downstairs, but at least my window opens up."

"Yes," she said as she started fanning herself with her frilly little fan.

"Would you like a drink Miriam?"

"A whiskey please."

I lit a kerosene lamp. The night began without my typical lonesome longing. She was telling me some funny stories about working. Miriam swigged her whiskey too fast. I drank too fast at first long ago, but I learned quickly what it did. I really didn't like drinking spirits, but it was an American custom to offer it to company. I didn't want to be rude. Some badlands women didn't deal with the stress and lifestyle of being working ladies too keenly. They slowly destroyed themselves with drinking. Men gave better tips while drunk so it was a necessary business decision to have some on me. Her flowing movements began getting clumsy. She spoke in a gruffer tone with every drink instead of soft and womanly. I began drinking quickly too, and before we knew it, it flowed like waterfalls down our throats.

"I don't mean to be rude, but I have not seen a'kiihka'si aawoowa'kii in a long time," I slurred.

"What the fuck you say? Jeez speaking Blackfoot," she said. She began crying for no good reason.

"A'kiihka'si aawoowa'kii is what we call men who are ladylike in my tribe," I explained.

"Oh, I see. You know. Nobody else can tell," she said.

"The white people call your types berdaches, but it's your kind that are special, helping us in many ways."

"Maybe that is why I cry myself silly. White people hate my kind. They say I am a bad person, but I am what I am," she said wiping her tears on a napkin, and then went on, "I am trying to stop feeling bad, it is so hard."

"I feel bad about giving you this drink. Our people have been hurt so much by firewater." I looked around my apartment that was blurry, "at least I got my own fucking bathroom now." We both laughed hysterically at that.

"Holy smoke you're fancy! Even with a Victorian water closet brought all the way here," she said.

I was surprised that Miriam's grammar was getting better even though she was slurring her words.

"My people are the Shoshone. They call my kind tainna wa'ippe. We advise all. I was respected by my people for a long time," she said. She began bawling again.

I was touched by her tears and felt an intense connection. Crying like that came from the seat of the soul. I knew she needed to let somebody know the root cause of her tears. I waited and ran my fingers over her hair like a mother, it made her cry harder.

"What happened honey? You can trust me," I said.

She looked at me and stopped crying. I looked into her bloodshot eyes, they were already swollen. The intense summer heat refused to subside deep into the night. The acrid smell of alcohol was already pouring out of our pores. We both were fidgeting. I was beginning to feel agitated.

"I was out trapping rabbits for some kids who have parents no more. They made me their mommy. They were like my own kids. I was getting the rabbit when two French fur trappers came to me. They were really handsome. They were speaking to me by sign language and I knew that they wanted directions. I tried my best to show them which way to go. Then one of them came up and kissed me, after we ate the rabbit, of course. We talked past sundown. I let him do anything he wanted to do to me. I feel bad about myself, because I should of went home and fed my poor kids. I cooked flapjacks the next morning anyhow. They knew right away what I was." She was looking down at her lap with regret.

"How could they tell?" I asked.

"Like anybody else in the tribes, they just somehow knew. One of them, the one who was nicer than the other one, he pointed to his thing. Then he pointed to my thing, and he nodded. I nodded too and dropped my robe. After eating flapjacks we finished with a breakfast whiskey. I made love to him again. I knew right away that I loved him. Nobody believes that a person can love right away, but it happened to me, and to him. I knew that my people wouldn't have accepted him. He was an enemy. So I left the kids behind."

"How did you get to Montana?" I asked.

"Jesus Christ, let me finish! I went far away with them. Then they got sick in the middle of a mountain valley. I tried every herb, every rite that was taught to me. We made it to an old white lady who lived alone in the woods. They said she was a witch. She told me she was a widow. That woman there let me take roots to make a brew for them. The men felt better enough to travel again, but they both died by a river. I cried and was going to fling myself into water. I put one foot in front of the other instead. I met the Kutenai tribe. They were nice to me. They have their men who are with men called Kupatke'tek, and their women who are with women are called Titqattek. Then one day I married a white man. We came down here to Missoula. Everything was good, but he disappeared."

"Where did he go?" I asked feeling pity for her.

"I don't know. He was good to me when with Indians, and good to me while we were alone out in the wilderness. Then he gets to Missoula and acts guilty," she said.

"Yes I know. White people have their awkward ways too, just like our people."

"So now I work here and don't know what else to do," she said.

"But this is home for us now, so we must accept it. This might be the last best place for white people, but for us it's the only place. It might not be paradise all the time, but at least we're still alive," I said trying to comfort her anyway I could.

"Darling I must go home, I'm getting too drunk."

I nodded. I led her to the front door and gave her a peck on the cheek. I looked out my window and noticed that she was staggering just a bit. She managed to regain her composure passing a lone man who stared at her like a hungry tiger. She was smiling at him while walking slower, but he continued onward. She got lost in the shadows. I hoped that she was okay walking alone at such an hour. She seemed a foolish one standing on the street at night because her apartment was too hot!

Chapter 34-Rescuing Innocence

I saw Miriam a few days later when I had the flu. I relished being alone and independent in the boarding house, being as free as the world allowed. With every sickness there was a thought of dying. Some ladies came to town working for a short while, and then disappeared from sickness. A sickness could be given to me anytime from any man, because I touched too many. I often wished for a man to love me and to pamper me. I convinced myself that I wasn't ready for a doctor yet. I heard shouting outside. I recognized a voice.

My head was pounding like an arrival of a steam train. I went to my window and yelled at them to shut up. The yelling continued for a time after I plopped back down on my bed. I just knew something wrong was happening outside, knowing that it wasn't typical drunks arguing. I almost vomited getting out of bed, but managed to get to the window again. Miriam was crying as two cowboys were pushing her back and forth. The cowboy in front of her pushed himself offensively into her. I frantically watched for a moment hoping a passerby would stop to help, but it was a weekday night when the streets usually remained quiet. The cowboy put his arm around her shoulders and grabbed Miriam's breast.

"These suckers are downright purdy even if they're fake, dumb cocksucker!" he yelled and then staggered backward. The cowboy reached down Miriam's cleavage and pulled out a rolled up hanky. He threw the hanky onto the ground. "You'll be sorry, you sorry excuse of a gal. You should be paying us you sissy. You hear me, you redskin cunt," he yelled. The look on his face as he yelled was one of perfect hatred. I was scared for her safety. I ran down the stairs as fast as I could. I shrieked as the cowboy in front of Miriam smacked her face.

"Leave her alone!" I screamed.

The two men redirected their stinking attention at me.

"Her? You tell me he's a she, but it's a thing," the man behind her said. He pushed Miriam who was sobbing onto the ground. She landed in mud. I felt like her mother seeing such a sorrowful sight. I gave the cowboys a fierce glare. I had my knife hidden behind my back. I killed men before, and they noticed it in my eyes. They didn't try out their luck with me. They staggered away. The faint odor of whiskey went away with them.

"Get up honey!" I said.

She was sobbing up a storm by then. Her pretty dress was sullied and surely was permanently stained; at least she wasn't hurt too much. She was limping with her arm around my shoulders. We slowly went up the stairs to my apartment. She sat on the side of my bed with her hands in front of her face.

"I'm ugly," she said.

She wiped the back of her hand against her nose to stop her sniffling. During my earlier days with my people, we used to hear crying through teepee walls. Wood and bricks hid the wails of misery efficiently. I remembered how shocked I was seeing her cry when we got drunk together. I never thought I'd get used to hearing another person cry again.

"You're beautiful," I reassured her.

"No, I was told I was ugly for many moons by some boys. I'm not like pretty women," she said.

"I know how it hurts to have others make fun of you. A couple of boys used to make fun of me when I was younger too, two mutts by the name of Beaver Teeth and Summer Fire." The voice coming though my mouth didn't sound like my own. I hadn't muttered their names for many winters. She cried a little more. She finally swept her hair back. She ran her fingers though several thick strands as black as the darkest colts. We looked into each other's eyes. Her eyes appeared like jet marbles to me. Two tiny pools of infinity like the night sky stared into my eyes. How can anybody think you're ugly? I thought. The masculinity of being born a boy showed in her always, but becoming a woman made her appear beyond lovely. I wished that all men were like her.

"You have hair prettier than any woman," I told her.

She looked at a strand of her hair thicker than a strand of black thread. She pulled several more strands of hair in front of her face. Her eyes crossed a bit while inspecting them.

"No, my hair is ugly."

"There don't be silly," I said as I began caressing her hair.

The lateness of the night always lowered my inhibitions. Perhaps the light of day made me think anything that was potentially a secret might be seen by all. I stared at her as she stared back at me. I never felt such an overt yearning for a woman before. A silly thought occurred in my mind that led me to ask, "Miriam, have you ever kissed another woman before?" Miriam seemed surprised; her eyes darted downward toward her lap. Her silence was unnerving to me. I wasn't sure what to do. I clearly knew what I wanted to do, but her silence told me only what I assumed. I was to be the one to decide what to do. My headache went away, but I wasn't quite sure if I wanted to proceed. I wasn't thinking straight.

I took it slowly just in case I was wrong. I moved forward until I felt my breasts touching hers. Her breasts did not have the warmth and suppleness of real breasts. Close to her face, I discovered an angularity not noticed from farther away. She swallowed hard as her Adam's apple retracted just a bit. I parted her hair moving forward and put my lips softly and gently on her lips. I was kissing neither a man nor a woman, but another soul. She stared at me after the kiss with a look of nothing. She didn't seem affected by what I did one way or another.

I didn't want to disappoint her. I tried even harder the second time. I imagined myself as one of her customers seeing her for the first time. A fist kiss imagined with a stranger was always the most passionately acted out. I acted what I imagined. I slowly pushed myself on top of her. I vigorously kissed her with selfish desire. She softly moaned. I acted unlike a gentleman, but I was a lady. I halted my aggression hugging her softly. We positioned ourselves on top of the bed holding each other for a long time. Our world became calm. I felt safe and entirely human while holding her.

Later that evening I awoke to the annoying snores of a gruff looking woman beside me. Images of Blackfeet women appeared in my dreams that night. My dreams were eclipsing each other until I couldn't tell which was which anymore. Was the kiss just a dream?

During winters the teepee got very cold as the night fires burned out toward early morning. I sometimes walked from my side of the tipi to my parent's side. I had no siblings to keep me warm. I slept between the warmth of my parents. My father's arms made me feel wholesome and safe, the way if felt when Miriam held me as I slept. She quickly got out of bed.

She checked herself in the mirror. I saw the reflection of her face looking ghostly and pale. She seemed entirely awestruck at seeing herself. "Why the hurry?" I asked. She turned around cocking her head sideways over her shoulder.

"I can't see you ever again," she said in his raspy voice resembling two voices at once.

She hurried out the door. I felt entirely empty. I realized that I knew very little about that woman, yet I wanted to know more about her. Somehow I felt that I've known her forever. When I felt her body move the night before, her facial expressions, the quality of her breathing. It was more than just a comfortable familiarity. Most importantly, we had similar heritages. Despite all that, I heard her footsteps clomping down the stairs toward the front door of the building.

My eyes filled with tears, because she felt like a piece of my lost homeland. She who was a reminder of all things in my memories that never changed. When she held me for that short time, she felt equal parts mother and father to me. She made me feel weaker than any man ever did.

Images of my father transfixed me. I miss you father so much, where are you? Are you alive or dead? A boulder was hanging by rusty chains around my neck. My body ached from heaviness. The orphaned heart of loneliness strayed too far from a home. Two cultures never fully adopted me. Nobody ever fell in love with me. While many went full circle when love went on a journey, my circle would never be completed. Fate didn't go all the way around for some. The medicine wheel was broken.

I didn't know which way to go with my life. I felt that my life was spinning totally unguided by any wisdom. What direction should I have gone, east or west? Four sacred directions meant nothing to me anymore. The spirits of my younger years were the result of overactive fantasies from ignorance. I walked over to the kitchen to make some English breakfast tea. I took some sage from a medicine bundle and smudged myself before relaxing to drink. I looked at my calendar hanging on the wall. No wonder I thought about my father. I scared Miriam away on father's day.

Chapter 35-A Spiritual Escape

There was nothing to do during the last week at home. I sat sipping tea while in near despondency, and at times contemplative. I admit that my lifestyle was difficult sometimes. I was merely a convenience at the very best and a fantasy to most, and to some, from the depths of their dark souls, I was disposable. I was somebody to be despised as they used my body to vent frustrations and inadequacies. They thought that they knew me. I was some Indian woman who only knew how to give pleasure and make some spending money, but I was more than that.

I was grateful that my career paid so well that it gave me plenty of time to read. The public library had a soft man who ran it who loved to sip with us ladies at the soda fountain. His real name was Grayson Davies. Our nickname for him was Mr. Muffin, because he loved to bake sweet nothings. There were countless times he brought in fresh baked muffins to our boarding house. Some of the girls fell for him, but he never seemed interested in them at all. We giggled behind his back. We were going to set him up with some gal's boyfriend who admitted he's *that* sort of adventurous buckaroo. Mr. Muffin quickly left town before he got any of our men, because he got fired for drinking on the job by the city. The city replaced him with a very dour Mrs. Stone. Whenever I smell the warm buttery flour of muffins, I always have sweet thoughts of him and books.

Mrs. Stone allowed me into the library at first, but once she heard from a whispering goody-goody that I lived in the badlands, she quietly asked me to leave for good. Somehow I contaminated the intellectual atmosphere. Gerta told me not to even think about complaining. I thought about what I learned from words written by Socrates, Freud, Shakespeare and Darwin. I never revealed to anybody the intellectual knowledge stored in my prostitute head. How dare a lowlife show off and attempt to be better than what I was supposed to be, just a dirty whore without brains.

I read *The Bible* from beginning to end and found it to be an epic worthy in the league of *Satyricon* by Petronius. Oscar Wilde would have made a glamorous friend. I read about his visit to America in the newspaper. I remember wishing he would visit Missoula instead of San Francisco. I imagined myself sharing a toast of absinthe with him before I quit drinking it.

Several times Yin Chow came upstairs to visit. A couple times she read from a Chinese book translating it into English the teachings of Buddha, which to me just sounded like old-fashioned common sense. Like Buddha my Blackfeet brothers and sisters sat in silence, many under cottonwood trees with their minds empty feeling sublime nature, gaining wisdom of the spirit. It was a spiritual similarity that I learned the last days of my Front Street residency. It had me regretting that I've never heard about nirvana before. When I told Yin Chow about my Blackfeet spirituality, she didn't see it in a negative light like some others.

I told a couple of Christian prostitutes who lived in the building next door about Blackfeet spirituality while we chatted at the drugstore bar. They said that if they saw me holding a medicine bundle, waving an eagle feather over rising sage smoke, they'd think I was practicing devil's work. They said they thought that my spirit helpers were demons. The spirits never harmed a living soul in my tribe. Some of the spirits were my ancestors. They helped me and guided my life, so those two women called my ancestors demons. I fondly remember telling those saintly whores that "devil's work never felt so damn good!" They avoided me after that. I then realized what I lost when I stopped talking to spirits.

However being in the white man's world gave me the chance to learn many new lines of thinking previously not available to my people. Much went through my mind as I sipped my tea: The women's group didn't directly call me a sinner, but they mentioned that "soiled doves" were sinful. To me living without sin was getting through the day trying to be a good person, being friendly, and helping people when you can. Don't treat others with meanness and cruelty from insults, or purposely intimidate and disrespect with actions. Despite not being perfect, being a good person was always my constant goal. One thing I knew I was perfect at, and that was easing men's fears. I was one of the best shoulders to cry on in Missoula. I had no guilt, not one once of shame. If people didn't like it, they were wasting their time.

While I had no shame, I had fear. An incessant swiftly paralyzing fear that was as dreary and bone chilling as the winds that roared from Hellgate Canyon. Was I going to be the next one to catch syphilis? Every customer was a potential loose cannon. I knew that Max and others kept tabs on me, but what if someone intoxicated on hate, choked me to death while Jonah and Max were down the street? Some women disappeared never to be seen again in such a transient town. My humble little apartment, the door to the right in the grim and narrow hallway of 221 West Front Street. Much fear and loathing was about the future. Each wrinkle was a markdown in the clearance aisle despite my expertise in all things erotic.

There were no regrets, but there was a hollow anger that made my days gray. I never predicted when that anger came, because why did other women find love? Why did other women find respect and adulation? What did I ever do to have a man sneer at me and throw a crumpled greenback at me? What did I do to have a man ask me if I was his "dirty little whore?" Why did some men purposely get rough with me during intercourse? I had my rifle under the bed if they got too rough. I wrote all my thoughts on paper, after writing them. I burnt the paper in the tub. The paper curled and charred. I went to rest on my favorite chair when a knock came at the door.

"Yin chow at the door," my friend announced.

I answered the door. She stood at the doorway with a little Buddha statue.

"A gift for my new friend."

"Thank You," I felt touched that she barely knew me, but she was willing to give me a gift so early in the friendship.

"You sit cross-legged, Indian style, and you say sacred prayer. You want me to show you how?"

"Why yes," I said.

She placed the Buddha on the table where I was sipping my tea, and she sat cross legged on the ground. She bowed to the little bronze statue. She began repeating something that I thought was in Chinese. She repeated the phrase repeatedly. She patted the ground and I took it as a cue to sit next to her. I began chanting the sacred prayer, fumbling the words with her for some time. I was saying it correctly after twenty minutes. I felt better after an hour. I felt lost before she visited. I was grateful that the right friend showed up at the right time.

"Kwan Yin, the female Buddha is called Mother Goddess by the Chinese. She's the Buddha of compassion. She soothes all suffering even for prostitutes."

I was touched at her openness. The judgments from others weighed heavily on my heart. To have another outsider show me such friendliness made my day.

"I thank you, is the statue from China?" I said while wiping my eyes with a tissue.

"Yes."

"She came a long way like you have," I said feeling truly honored.

"It is good that you give offerings of money, food or water, or you can give sage to Kwan Yin, but shhhhh! Cowboys say we are practicing idol worship, so be careful," she said very seriously for a moment, but she let out a little giggle afterward and placed a palm in front of her mouth.

I laughed at the ludicrous statement of what she just said. I did hear men complain in the saloons that the Chinamen loved to perform idol worship and smoke opium. That harsh view was stated by them to set them apart. They were just mad because Chinese men worked on the Great Northern railroad for cheaper money, and some non-Chinese men didn't get the jobs because they wanted higher pay. I knew without the Chinese in Missoula, there was no Peking Duck at Wong's Restaurant and no cheap launderettes. Yin chow bowed to me, which I liked, and then went downstairs to work.

Later on I saw Miriam on my way to work. She was just leaving a restaurant when she waved at me. I was wondering why she was suddenly being nice considering that she was giving me the cold shoulder.

"I should go home, but I don't have a home," she said.

"Have you been working at all?" I asked with disdain. I wondered how she could have been so careless as to get into a situation of being homeless.

"Don't be bitchy," she said. Her dress was permanently stained from falling the night that I rescued her. "Ouch," she said as she limped.

"Are you feeling all right?" I asked.

"Yes, I twisted my ankle when my high heel broke. Thank you for asking. I've been ignoring you and I'm very sorry about it," she said.

"That's okay. I feel worthy when I say hello, and you walk away," I said trying my best not to sound sarcastic.

She turned around and looked at me in the eyes.

"I thank you very much. You who seems as strong as a man." She winced a little after she said that. I smiled. "I mean you're a lady, but act like a man," she clarified as we walked up the steps to my room.

"Yes, and you ma'am look like a lady, but don't act like a man. You're stronger than both men and women," I laughed.

I made her some tea when we got up to my room. I felt heated excitement in her presence again. I took some water from a ceramic bowl. I tossed some water on myself and into my hair. I decided to pry; she was a puzzle to be solved.

"Why don't you have a home anymore?" I asked.

"Since the law has been cracking down, no more customers, hardly any," she said with a look of disappointment.

There was a hint of melancholy under her apologizing smile, like she was ashamed to tell me. A woman whose business was floundering too. I decided to dose her shame with words of reassurance. I moved just a little too close to her as we sat on my bed. If she moved away or stiffened up, then that told me everything. She seemed to relax as she leaned back on her arms. She asked me to undo her braids that were thick as black rope.

"To tell you the truth, I'm very happy that I have new regulars. Any new customers are being scared away by the police, but not mine. Once a lady becomes an expert, she can charm anybody into coming back for more. I don't know where to go if everything shuts down for good," I admitted.

Besides the Apsaalooke people and my people, Missoula was the only place that I truly knew. I was scared of whatever was out there. I heard there were some American cities that were worse than others. I heard that Phillipsburg was a good place for working women as travelling men between Helena and Missoula often stopped there for the night.

Miriam looked at me with a sultry charm that only a lady could ever give, and instead of me being the more dominate one with initiative, our faces moved together at the same pace. We kissed for a very long time.

I noticed that the moon was rising just above Mount Sentinel to the east as we lay nakedly on my bed. Later when I wanted to go further, the moon was almost directly south shining into my window. My hand moved down Miriam's belly where I noticed that she was as smooth as a woman. She must shave her abdomen and legs I thought. As my hand slowly moved over her pubic hair, she grabbed my wrists a little too hard.

"No," she said.

I didn't go any further. All night I couldn't sleep as I held her. It was as though Miriam was like the Russian eggs on my shelf. How each egg inside the other looked the same but different. Miriam appeared all woman while dressed in clothing, but when her makeup was off, she looked like a pretty Shoshone male warrior. When I was hugging and caressing her body, he felt all man.

The next day I served him the blackest coffee in the world. We chatted like lovers about our hopes and fears. He didn't dress like a woman that morning. He found some clothes one of my customers left behind and dressed in them. He spoke in his regular voice. He told me that he didn't want to be a man that morning, but he had no choice, that the police knew who he was. If they caught him during the day dressed in a frock, he'd be arrested, like before. They put him with some tough men in the county jail. He told me they all threatened him in the most crude ways.

We connected so much when he told me about his past. His eyes looked vulnerable as he told me about how his father fell off a horse, and how his father was paralyzed and left behind when the camp moved away. When they came back after hunting mountain sheep later that year, his father was dead. Miriam told me how he couldn't have children. That he used to dress like a man and do all the manly Shoshone duties, and when he married, he couldn't get the woman pregnant. She ran off with another warrior and they had a baby together. He was ignored by the other women and felt inclined to dress up in women's clothes at the age of eighteen winters. He was subjected to the affections of an older chief and was to be married to him just after he turned nineteen winters, but he foolishly fled with those two Frenchmen that led him astray. Those damn Frenchmen were charming.

"I can teach you how to be a man again," I said.

He looked pained when I told him that. "No, I'm Miriam. I have learned to like who I am. I'm blessed to be with the men who adore me, and you," he said. He gave me a kiss and walked away. I felt such a frustration that was unlike me. I wondered where he was going so early in the afternoon. I stared after him out my window. I noticed a cowboy was standing on the corner. They didn't shake hands with each other. The cowboy looked sheepishly around and gave Miriam a great big bear hug. As a stranger passed them by, the cowboy patted Miriam on the back.

An Indian in the white world had more difficulty making it. The people of Montana treated us with lower regard than the other immigrants. We were worse than the black men and the Chinamen. Miriam was getting by the best way she knew how. I loved her any which way she was. I never saw her again after that lovely morning. I cried for many weeks after she left town. I hope you did well Miriam. I never got to tell you how much I loved you. I will always regret that.

I thought about the story that I told Miriam the night before as she held me in bed. "There once was a woman who lived a long and treacherous life. Everybody who she thought loved her abandoned her. On her lonesome journey, she stood at the edge of a cliff. She said some prayers, but there was only silence. Through rain and shine, she kept hope that her wishes for peace would be fulfilled in all the angry and disappointed people around her.

While on her way back home she found a stray cat in a field. The stray cat was limping with a broken leg. She nursed the cat through the winter. When springtime came, she drew her last breath. Although the cat gave her love, the woman died from a lonely heart from lack of contact with other people. Even the doctors didn't know what was wrong with her before her demise. The cat left their home searching for her everywhere. No matter where the cat went, she could not find her master.

When in the twilight world, the woman looked up at a glowing light, and she cursed God. "Where were you when I needed you? You never appeared before me. You are an invisible God." The light answered back, "You were lit by me every day. The God you tried to find in the world of life shines in both worlds. I am the Sun, and I have given you life every day. I now shine love on you even after your death." She looked down in sadness. God knew that the she missed her cat in the afterworld.

The cat died from a disease due to lack of care again as a stray. "I never had much love when I was alive," the woman bitterly complained. "You had one of the purest loves of all," the man said. She felt peace and warmth when the cat came to her from the light. She somehow realized the cat saw her as an eternal parent, and it felt to the woman like her child came back from being lost. During the separation, it felt like she was not gone for long, but to the cat, it was months that she was searching for her human companion."

I hoped that one day I might be reunited with my family again. I always loved cats too much to own one as a pet. To lose one was too heartbreaking, because I already lost one cat forever. Scruffy Hunter's spirit animal was a cat. He looked like one too.

Chapter 36-The Preacher Man in Business

It was 1898, and everyone was getting upset, almost to the point of mass hysteria. People felt dread thinking about the year 1900. Most thought that 1900 would be the end of the world. A street preacher stood on the corner screaming about how the apocalypse was going to come. People believed it, except me because I wasn't superstitious. If my people were on this land for untold moons, then why would one day the world just end?

Many people anticipated a tent revival that was setting up just south of the city. I was curious to see what all the excitement was about. I dressed modestly in a simple white flower dress. I took the Higgins horse drawn streetcar to the end of the line. I thought about how Missoula was going from wild to mild. There were plans to build a river dam for hydroelectric power. The city wanted to get electrical street lamps. Concrete was going to replace the wooden plank sidewalks and muddy streets. There were plans for a sewer line so people didn't have to live near the river anymore. The clay pipes that were in our boarding houses that led to a dirty ditch in back toward the river were going to be replaced with metal ones. Missoula wanted an electric streetcar like the ones they had in larger cities like Seattle and Chicago. It was changing so fast, right down to people's attitudes. Austerity was part of their new daily regimes as the bars were closing right behind the female boarding houses.

That silly talk about the end was near made people so scared that they wanted to keep themselves from going down a wrong path of sin. Such fear led many to walk the fields in pilgrimage to a large white circus tent. I went out of curiosity since everyone was speaking about it. Once inside there was a frenzied electricity to the air. The dusty smell of outdoors was replaced by the sweet aroma after a downpour. Dozens of conversations were going about. Children were wailing, and mothers were gruffly hushing them up. Above it all, some noisy women were singing, "Jesus loves me, I should know, for the Bible tells me so." People were standing around with their eyes closed and some were fainting. The preacher man was walking around yelling things like "Jesus loves you! Feel the Holy Spirit in your blood." Women were crying with complete spiritual intensity. "The blood of Christ is flowing in rivers. His blood is flowing down your street. Say hallelujah!" The preacher man waved his arms in the air as if conducting a symphony. The entire crowd yelled, "Hallelujah!"

I recognized some repentant faces there. Mr. and Mrs. Gonse were there, as well as officer Monroe and his wife. Professor Strangemann and his wife were oddly absent. "Now we need to bring it down! Everyone be quiet to hear the Lord whisper," the preacher man said in quieter tones. Everyone became quiet for several minutes.

"Now everyone, we know my fellow children of God that the apocalypse is near. There are signs of it everywhere, the cities that burn, the floods and the droughts of the last few decades. The funny weather is God's warning to his children. The Lord is giving not-so-subtle signs, but he loves us so much that he's giving us a chance to change our sinful and lustful nature. Missoula was a city of vice, it was once known as Hell's Gate, but now it is the Gate to Paradise!!! Sweet Lord almighty thank you. Thank you for giving us a chance to be born again!" the preacher man yelled in a hoarse voice. "Now this traveling ministry can't go on without some money. God's generous children will give, because that is in their nature. Please look into your hearts. Give me what you can give, so I can travel to spread the word to other towns on the frontier. It isn't easy travel, and it ain't cheap." He had three children going around the crowd with baskets. People were handing over their cash. The preacher man was going around touching the tops of heads of people saying, "In the name of Christ, you are born again!" Some of the people he touched fainted. Some went into what looked like seizures. The preacher man looked over at me and nodded. I started getting scared and left before he got to me.

On my way back home I saw two former Front Street ladies who were modestly dressed. They were walking in a field toward the evangelical revival. One of them spotted me and declared very sweetly, "Victoria, why are you leaving us. Don't you want to be saved?" I refused to look at them. I walked as far as Pattee Creek. I sat at the edge of the water as I sang a holy Blackfeet prayer. I didn't have a drum to beat as I sang, so I clapped my hands instead. I sang it repeatedly in a trance wanting to dance. I looked to the east as the hazy sunset ignited the clouds.

AYO A' PIS-TO-TOO-KI
ISS-POM-MO-KIN-NAAN
NAH-KAY-ISS-TSI-TSI-SIN-NAAN
NAH-KAI-KIM-MO-TSI-SIN-NAAN
NAH-KAY-II-KA'-KI-MAA-SIN-NAAN
NAH-KOH-KO-KA-MO'-TOH-SIN-NAAN
NAH-KA-WA-TO-YII-TAK-SIN-NAAN
OOH-TO-KIN-NAAN, A'PIS-TO-TOO-KI
KIM-MIS KO-KO-SIKSI
II-KSI-KIM-MA-TAP-SI-YA
KAA-MO-TAA-NI
NII-STA-WA-TSI-MAANI
NAA-PIIO' SINI

I looked around feeling peace. I sang the prayer in English:

Our Galaxy, The Wolf Trail

Creator
Help Us
To Listen
To Be Kind To One Another
To Try Hard
To Be Honest
To Be Spiritual
Hear Us, Creator
Have Pity On Your Children
They Are In Need
Grant Us Safety
Help Us To Raise Our Families
So That They May Live Long Lives

Only men went out alone in the wilderness when I was a little girl. Women who went out alone were considered improper. My parents always knew I was like a boy, so I often escaped to pray alone. I never strived to be proper. I've seen too many people hurt others trying to be proper in the eyes of others. I closed my eyes and breathed in the scent of Pattee Creek hearing a wise thought. One knows the inner-goodness of the self without permission from other people in choosing to live where the heart shines.

Chapter 37-Crib of Treachery

The rent was cheap at the shack town by the river. Such a move wasn't as bad as I expected. I was accustomed to the finer material things in life, but the shack afforded me a simplicity I never thought I'd like again. My shack had a wood burning stove, a bed, and a small table for eating. I took baths in a small metal tub after boiling river water. I used the tub to wash my clothes with a simple washboard. I didn't see any rats, but I saw some stray dogs around. There were stray humans, a drunkard here and there. There were some drunken dramas with my neighbors on the weekends. It wasn't any worse than downtown. The shack town had a bad reputation that was undeserved.

I wasn't able to find work. I spent my extra time getting reacquainted with the spirit helpers, walking in solitude by the Clark Fork River. I went into Hellgate Canyon and blessed the many Salish that were slaughtered. I never had any visitors except Yin Chow. Cindy said she was going to visit, but I think she was too scared to enter my neighborhood. Mandy decided she was too good for me after she stopped drinking Coca Cola. She barely muttered a "hi" when she saw me downtown. She was boring without cocaine in her anyway.

I had enough money hidden in a coffee canister to last me for awhile, if I lived simply. I was surprised myself that I lived past forty. I still couldn't put money in a bank, because I wasn't considered an American. Perhaps the banker was only used to banking with males when he said "no" because he didn't know what else to say.

Yin Chow's parents grew fond of me as they began to trust me. I finally received "honest" employment at the launderette. Since the Blackfeet had some subtle oriental features, some of the customers mistook me as Chinese. My American Indian accent came out which surprised some. I worked for meager funds, but I was glad to get out of my little shack.

Yin Chow was beginning to change in alarming ways. At first she became quieter than typical. We became concerned when she lost a lot of weight. The absences began. Her mother and father were concerned enough about their daughter's sickness that they sent her to a doctor. The doctor didn't find anything wrong with her. He only said that she was overworked, and to give her a couple days of rest. She came back to work after a couple days off. She looked even worse and barely spoke in full sentences.

Yin Chow didn't arrive for work three days in a row. She wasn't home. We searched all over the city asking around for her. The police seemed slightly unconcerned about a missing Chinese woman. Her mother was in tears several times as we performed the hard labor of cleaning Missoula's dirty laundry.

I had my suspicion about the whereabouts of Yin Chow. She was my only friend in a world of distance. I was willing to look everywhere for her, even if that meant risking going down into the unsavory opium dens again. The newspaper reported that the police raided a drug den, but I suspected that all the dens didn't get closed down for good. It was nine o'clock in the evening. It was nearly dusk being a hot July. The sun was a glowing red from forest fires clear off in the distance. A thick haze covered the city that resembled a gray rainy day. The mountains normally clear and blue, were shadows in the haze. The dusk was other worldly as I went from place to place. I knocked on a door of a business, nobody answered. I went to the backroom of a saloon but it was locked. I was beginning to think that all the dens closed down. I thought about one last place.

I went into the alley through the back door of a restaurant. I remembered when I first visited; I went into the opium den by walking through a kitchen and down the alley that led to a steep stairway. When I was led out, it was out the back of a hotel lobby one block away. I heard that there weren't many dens, but they all connected. There were five or sometimes six of them. Those who were arrested during the raid paid their fines and bail to the police. Only for them to eagerly return to the over-decorated basements days later.

I walked down a cobwebbed stairwell. I felt threatened as I walked through a basement that was dimly lit. I passed boxes and piled up pipes. I got to a non-descript door. I knocked on it. A once handsome man opened it pale as a vampire. He had dark circles underneath his glassy eyes. Behind him were four addicts who were lounging in the candlelight. A woman was dressed up in the finest satin. Her partner held her hand dressed in a top hat and tuxedo. They were both all dressed up with no place to go. Japanese lanterns glowed over Persian rugs. I walked past a bright orange curtain, down a very narrow passageway lined with bricks.

I took a turn to the left. It was a very spooky place with candles placed along the floor. The passageway led to a large octagon room that had three doors. I opened a door. A group of men was in line waiting to get with a prostitute who was squirming on a tattered mattress. I recognized the woman as my lost friend. Her skin was glistening in the dim light of a kerosene lamp. One man just got done with her as he buttoned up his jeans. She was covered with sweat and lecherous liquid. I turned around with a glare. The men who were waiting in line were absolutely disgusting. There must have been a dozen of them, and they seemed very impatient, but enjoying the show at the same time.

"Come on Yin, I'm taking you to my home to clean up," I told her.

"No! no, no, no," she kept on saying.

"What are you doing? I've been waiting to be with her for an hour," her customer complained.

"She's my friend. She doesn't belong here. I'm taking her back to her family."

Some men laughed at me, which really bothered me. I helped Yin get dressed. I waved the men away. They just went into other doors to other opium addicted prostitutes.

"My money is under the mattress," she said in a weak voice.

Only four silver dollars were underneath the mattress. It took all my will to keep from crying.

"I'm glad you came to get me, but I don't want to go. No, no, no, I need more money," she said.

We got out that horrible place. We walked several blocks to my little shack. Yin tossed and turned, grinded her teeth, vomited and moaned. There were a few times that I thought she might die. I took some rope and tied her wrists to my bed. She wailed on, but I didn't let up. She started to feel better after a few days. She begged me several times not to tell her parents where I found her. I felt bad for her parents when I told them that I felt too sick to work two days in a roll, so I could secretly take care of their daughter. They were both elderly and getting frail. They had to do all that laundry all by themselves. I worried that they'd get too far behind and lose some regular customers. I told her parents where I found her. It was the noble thing to do. They kept a keen eye on her everyday making sure she never went back there again.

Yin never opened up to me again after that night. I had nobody else visiting me at my home, so I became crafty. I wanted to make a traditional Blackfeet robe just to see if I ever forgot. I got some cow hide from a tanner. I never forgot how to make a buckskin jacket. I sewed a black velvet dress in a cut of a Blackfeet robe. I wore my dress and jacket proudly around the city. I was happy to receive a lot of attention from folks. There were a few dirty looks of course. Several people asked where I was from. I said I was visiting civilization from the reservation for the first time. They wanted me to speak some Blackfeet for them and I did. They seemed amazed at hearing my language.

There weren't very many American Indians in the city to begin with, and the Salish weren't allowed off the reservation without a permit. We became virtually non-existent, so seeing me was a novelty. Some people who've seen me regularly around town thought I was Asian, until I dressed traditionally Blackfeet. I wondered how different reservation life was after being away from my people for so many years. Were all my people thinking the end of days was coming too? It was getting close to the apocalypse for so many.

It was December 31 1899. The clock was counting down until the end of the world. Apparently nobody wanted clean clothes to die in, because business was very slow at Chow's Laundry. I was sent home early by Mrs. Chow. The saloons were very full that evening. Apparently some wanted their lives to end with a party. I walked past the mayhem of drunks and some scared looking sober people. Seeing the crowds raised a doubt in my mind. How can so many people be wrong? If I was to go, I wanted to die in my Blackfeet dress.

I went home and put on my dress drinking tea alone all evening. When the clock struck midnight, I looked around. I waited in silence. A dog barked in the distance. Then distant cheers in the saloons hailed a new round of drinks. The next day I went down to the river and thanked the Great Spirit not only for another day, but also for a new century. I prayed for a century full of new potential. I felt a peace inside reassured that the next one hundred years were going to be the most peaceful century mankind would ever see. Humanity was becoming more civilized. Rumor was we were going to be getting some flush toilets soon.

I spent the next three months after the apocalypse getting used to the fact that I had the rest of my life to live. Springtime arrived and all my days were slow and peaceful. Chow's Laundry went out of business and the family moved to San Francisco. Every morning I went to the river to collect ice to melt for water at home. I went outside into the crisp dark morning. I returned back home and I felt like something was terribly wrong. I tried to concentrate on what was possibly wrong. I looked into my tin coffee canister. My cash was stolen. All three thousand dollars were gone. My money was all tied neatly in a wad with a rubber band. I dumped all the coffee grounds onto the floor, but nothing was revealed. I frantically looked all over my home thinking somehow I misplaced the cash. Perhaps I put it in a different hiding spot. I sat on the floor dejected. I just knew somebody took it in such a near vagrant neighborhood. I truly had nothing then. Nothing was going to stop me from drowning myself in the cold river.

I walked toward the river silently yelling at the red clouds illuminated by dawn. Somehow I garnered enough inner strength to do something else. The river calmed me when nothing else did. I smelled the various layers of nature. Above musty dirt was a scent of freshly sprouting grass through patchy snow, and above those scents was the deep mysterious smell of river water. I heard the water gently wafting against some willows. I was tired of going around in circles going nowhere. I had to return to my people.

Chapter 38-The End of the Road

I was still agile although older. In town I couldn't afford a horse or a buggy. Women were harassed if they were seen driving a buggy alone. They only accepted women riding side saddle, preferably with a man. So even if I had the money, nobody would have sold me a horse as a single gal anyway. I was glad I was forced to walk everywhere. It kept my legs strong towards middle age.

I packed a bag of goods to help me survive the long journey. I secured my sawed-off rifle in my backpack. My rifle was hidden in my chest of bloomers. Luckily the thief didn't take anything from there. I wondered if my hunting skills deteriorated. I took what I needed, and left everything behind.

I felt better while in the outskirts of the city on the big golden hills north of downtown. The last thing I saw was the sad toot of a steam train. The clouds of steam were rising out of the locomotive into the air. The farther I got away from the city, the better I felt. I found a road that went north. The terrain wasn't as difficult as I had anticipated. Wagons and buggies traveled past me.

A friendly store owner let me get water from his establishment in the small town of Evaro. A teenage boy filled my water container in the town of Arlee. The good sisters of St. Ignatius Mission fed me potatoes and gave me encouragement to move on. I knew that their prayers and angels were guiding and protecting me. I slept in fields near the road.

I knew I was making progress when I reached the town of Pablo. I saw many Salish living in rundown houses. They all seemed at peace as I walked through their town, but how they stared at me! I continued to the wondrous Flathead Lake and envied the Salish and Kootenai tribes for having such beautiful terrain within their reservation. The beauty of the Mission Mountains kept me feeling alive. Wonderful snow covered bluish peaks towered over the gigantic lake. The bright stars at night revealed a faint milky fog of our galaxy, the celestial wolf pack. They call it The Milky Way, but to us it is The Wolf Trail.

I awoke one day seeing a lone fawn staring at me. She had cute white spots on her back. She wasn't scared when I stood up. She followed me a little. I realized she might be an orphan and hoped I was her mother.

My skin seemed about four shades darker after spending several days traveling in the sun. I put face paint on my lower cheeks. The red paint I mixed two days before I left Missoula was just to see if I could still mix it old fashioned style. I never wore face paint walking the streets of Missoula. Only clowns wear face paint there.

The dark red paint felt soothing on my skin. The threat of sunburn was gone. I had a small glass jar of some clear lard to moisturize the lines around my face. Natosi, I almost forgot about him being away for so long. He warmed up my aching joints making my mission back home easier.

I got to the highway and a buggy stopped. A friendly man came out and he shook my hand. He said that he was a photographer, and asked if he could take a picture of me. I obliged. He set his camera on a stand. I posed kneeling in the grass. His smile had me peer to my right. The fawn had followed me. She was so adorable standing beside me. I reached out my arm to the baby. She felt soft and warm, as I felt her quick breathing motions. The man took the photograph. The flash scared the fawn away. We both watched in amazement. She hopped away into the recesses of the field. The photographer thanked me and headed southward.

For days I headed northbound from Flathead Lake. I was scared to the core. I didn't have a compass. I hoped that I hadn't gone too far north. I prayed for guidance. When it felt right, I began traveling eastward. I recognized the mountains as the glacier mountains that I had to pass through to get back home. I had much difficulty with my heavy backpack. I had canned sardines and salt cured pork for an emergency, and I hunted. I ate only once a day at the most. The memories of the spirits telling me that I would not survive if I ever traveled alone again played constantly in my mind.

I almost died several times in the cold. I tried to stay at the lowest elevations while following as much water as possible. The frigid spring temperatures did not subside very much, even when I covered myself with dried brush keeping my wool blanket from blowing away. It was a miracle that I survived. I traveled without eating a meal for a week. When it snowed, I survived eating only snow for days. One night a storm happened. There wasn't any snow during the storm, but the winds from the north blew violently. Freezing rain pelted everything turning all slopes into slides. The winds were so frigid, that I knew I was going to die from hypothermia. I killed two snow rabbits. I gutted them and wore their bloody carcasses as my snow boots. The next day I ate rabbit for breakfast. Nothing was going to kill me. Nothing at all.

I recognized a familiar lake my tribe camped at. I sat on the shore of the lake remembering the last summer I spent with my people. I was thin as a rail staring at Lake St. Mary on the other side of the glacier covered mountains. I stood up waving my arms in glee despite my exhaustion. I finally felt like my true self again after so many years. Victoria was gone forever.

To breathe deeply is to be at home in the world. Home has a certain tranquility found nowhere else. Rolling foothills went on and on before me. I kept a slow pace toward the town of Browning. I stopped and smelled the spring clovers while on my way there. I was filled with both apprehension and anticipation. I wondered who was still alive after the removal. I wonder who died after the national controversy of the starvation winter.

The majestic flat golden landscape spread wide as far as my eyes could see. Oh, how I missed the big sky not blocked by towering pine covered mountains. I breathed deeply and spread my arms wide in the longest golden field called the plains. I stared at the fluffy white clouds as I arched my back. Natosi was kissing my face. I forgot about the blisters, and my bloody moccasins of my overworked feet. I felt my spirit soar in thankfulness.

I will always need to be surrounded by plants and lushness. Greenery or yellow hills, dirt and grime, clean air, bugs, critters and fish will always be my guides on how to live properly. All people need Natosi on their skin and the moon in their eyes. Moonlit nocturnal animals glowing eyes like campfire lit amber, all who gaze at Kikomi-kisomm. I almost forgot about you stars and our galaxy The Wolf Trail. I'm grateful at seeing many red dawns I could cry. Nature can be ferocious. Snow has frozen limbs and forest fires has singed skin. Better to have smelled pine, felt the sandbars beside rivers under bare feet, and roll in the mud like swine, to have splashes in a clear stream taking a naked bath American Indian style than to have not lived at all. Anything that is beautiful is also deadly all duality not one without the other. Oh why, Great Spirit, am I so addicted to dangerous and peaceful nature?

Gone were the days of crying on empty beds missing my family. My dark emotions were replaced with the wind. The wind was my breath. I took one long breath. I closed my eyes and prayed to Ihtsi-pai-tapi-yopa face to face feeling its warmth and love as I moved forward to my homeland. "Dear Natosi, I promise to find at least one bison if there are any left at all. I will give you an offering of a bison tongue if you allow me to return home alive." I focused on moving my sore legs forward. I was near collapse and total starvation. I felt an inner knowingness that I may die before finding one person in my tribe.

There were only Blackfeet who were walking around the wonderful village of Browning. It looked very similar to a Napikowann town, but it had a different flavor, a different energy. I went into the Browning Mercantile. A man who worked there kindly smiled. I spoke to him in Blackfeet. I asked him if he knew of people by the name of Fawn in Rain and Bearsnarl. He gave me a sad look. "They didn't make it through the starvation winter of '83-'84," he said. I stared into oblivion in shock thinking about how my parents died.

The man who worked at the mercantile was a young man. I wasn't used to Blackfeet men with short hair. He seemed odd and out of place to me. He noticed me staring at him. "You must be Dawn Red Sky," he said in astonishment. He said my true name. I was nearly blown over with emotion. I didn't hear my name for so long in my language.

I asked him if he knew of a man named Scruffy Hunter. He said he did know him, and that Scruffy Hunter lived in the Two-Medicine River valley. "I've been away for 23 years," I said. I sat on a wooden chair too exhausted to do any more walking. I felt haggard and dusty.

"You survived out on your own! My auntie knew you, her name was Rattling Butterfly," he said.

"A very nice woman," I remarked.

He looked at the wall in pain. "She's gone too. She died of measles."

"I'm so sorry to hear about that."

"You want to know something? Scruffy Hunter never married. He always mentioned to anybody who'd listen, 'that Dawn Red Sky, she was the nicest woman ever. I wish that I had left with her when she ran away.' He used to say that all the time."

My heart began fluttering with lightness. I sat up and walked toward the door.

"Where are you going?" he asked.

"I'm going to the Two-Medicine Valley," I said.

"Just wait. I have a wagon. I'll take you to him. Two-Medicine is too far away to walk," he advised. I rolled my eyes. If he knew how long it took me to walk from western Montana. He locked the mercantile door and we got into the wagon.

"What's your name?" I asked the nice man.

"Bobcat Guardipee. You probably don't know what road I'm talking about. Scruffy Hunter lives at the end of the road on the west side of the river."

I felt like weeping all the way to the Two-Medicine Valley. Every bump in the road felt like forever. I spotted a small white house with smoke rising out of the chimney. I knew it was Scruffy Hunter's house. "Stop the wagon," I said. I quickly climbed out of the wagon. I ran as fast as my tired legs let me. The front door was left open. The screen door slammed shut behind me by the wind. I quietly entered into his home. Sitting alone at the small kitchen table was Scruffy Hunter.

"Nephew is that you?" he asked.

I walked up to him with tears rolling down my checks. He looked almost the same the day that I left him, but with salt and pepper hair parted by two long braids. Just a few light wrinkles decorated his forehead. He looked straight at me, but his eyes were a grayish blue. "Dawn Red Sky is that you? Is it really you?"

"Yes," I said with a shaky voice.

I realized he was blinded by eye cataracts and couldn't see me. His lifelong bad eyesight that kept him from being a true warrior and hunter finally got him. I only saw him cry two times; once when his father died. He bowed his head as his shoulders shook. He cried as he hugged me.

"I knew you would come back to see me, even when others told me that you probably passed away."

We held the longest hug never wanting to let go again. The feeling I had for him at that moment felt like the most sacred bond ever. We kissed each other. He slowly caressed my face with his open palm. I closed my eyes feeling the warmth of his hand.

"Please never leave again," he muttered into my ear.

I turned around and Mr. Guardipee was staring at us from the front doorway with teary eyes. No matter what happened in my life, good or bad, the path led me full circle back to the arms of Scruffy Hunter. We tried but failed to keep our love a secret from everyone long ago. I knew his fingers caressed the face of the young seventeen year old woman, the married one he made love to by the river years ago. Spying eyes were prying what should have always remained a secret. I was never a convincing liar. I planned to tell him about his possible son adopted by the Apsaalooke tribe when the time was right.

"You're home," he whispered.

Our love is all that matters. Very few things are completely pure in this life. The absolute purity of loving embraces and the other is our galaxy The Wolf Trail. All the wolves on the ground howl at night in euphoric splendor at the stars that represent them in the sky.

Author Biography

Theo Cecil DeCelles, or his Pikuni name is Chief Mountain (Ninastako in the Blackfoot language) lives in Montana. He is an enrolled member of the Blackfeet Nation and is also Little Shell Chippewa, Gros Ventre, and French. When not writing, he spends his extra time stargazing at The Wolf Trail of the big sky night.

www.ingramcontent.com/pod-product-compliance
Lightning Source LLC
Chambersburg PA
CBHW030818310726
48980CB00006B/544/J